Also by Linda Davies

NEST OF VIPERS

WILDERNESS OF MIRRORS

LINDA DAVIES

A DELL BOOK

Published by
Dell Publishing
a division of
Bantam Doubleday Dell Publishing Group, Inc.
1540 Broadway
New York, New York 10036

ISBN: 0-440-22295-8

Reprinted by arrangement with Doubleday

Printed in the United States of America

Published simultaneously in Canada

November 1996

10 9 8 7 6 5 4 3 2 1

OPM

TO MY HUSBAND, RUPERT,
FOR EVERYTHING.

ACKNOWLEDGMENTS

I owe thanks to many people, some of whom I may not acknowledge publicly, so I say "Thank you" here to the anonymous ones.

My husband, Rupert, taught me many useful things that have found their way into this book. My parents, Glyn and Grethe, have been wonderfully supportive and enthusiastic, as always. Andrew Lamont and Andrew Bone of De Beers provided me with valuable information on diamonds, as did Thomas Helsby and Ed Epstein. Richard Garnet and Professor Peter Nixon, of Leeds University, provided me with technical data about how diamonds are found and mined. Amber Rudd and Andrew Hyslop told me how diamond ventures are financed, and provided particularly useful information on the Vancouver Stock Exchange.

Rupert Allason, and Andrew Hyslop in another incarnation, were customarily helpful on the intelligence front. Mark Broadley very kindly allowed me to stay with him in Hong Kong while I did research there, and to use his flat as a base from which I could explore Vietnam. My wonderful agents, Toby Eady and David Black, were kind and assiduous as ever.

Huge thanks go to everyone at Doubleday, particularly to Steve Rubin, David Gernert, Ellen Archer, Amy Williams, Jackie Everly, and Jayne Schorn for enthusiasm, support, and brilliance.

And thank you to the intangibles.

PROLOGUE

APRIL 1991

She had never realized how easy it was, that one wrong step—the wrong time, the wrong place, a hand on the shoulder, death. The simple, inescapable conclusion. It was a sunny afternoon. Hot as always.

She knew, really, that this was not her first wrong step, but the end of a long journey that had started years before. Still, it felt as though things would have been different if they had passed by ten minutes earlier, or later. Getting caught that afternoon did not feel like the consequence of four years but more like a random act, as if they were victims of a horrible accident.

They had known the risk. It wasn't even as if they had played the odds, thinking that they stood a nine-in-ten chance of getting away with it. They had thought they would never get caught, that the odds didn't apply to them, that they were somehow protected. That was almost the worst thing—the realization that it could happen to you, that the god or fate or luck you thought always protected you had abandoned you, that you had constructed your whole life on an error, and now you would pay. With your life.

There were two of them, the Englishwoman and the Thai, flying into Changi airport in Singapore with their consignment of heroin. And they were caught. It was a tip-off, a setup. The man behind the operation, Robie Frazer, had heard that one of the top couriers in his organization was an undercover intelligence agent. He wanted to test his hypothesis. If she was caught and set free, then she was an agent. If she was caught and hanged, then she was not. A simple test. But the mechanics went wrong. Unknown to Frazer, the suspect, Sun Yi Sim, shared the run with her best friend, Eva Cunningham. They were both taken in.

Waiting at the luggage carousel, Eva read the sign hanging from the ceiling: DRUG TRAFFICKING CARRIES THE DEATH PENALTY. She looked away. She collected her luggage and walked slowly through the airport, pushing her cart, smiling, talking calmly to Sun Yi, masking her fear with laughter.

It was cold inside the terminal building. The air conditioning was biting, and goose pimples covered her arms as she rounded the bend into the customs channel and began the long walk past the lines of agents, who stood, eyes sharp, well trained, looking for signals. Only it wasn't like that. Eva knew from the beginning it was a setup. As always, she and Sun Yi were composed, sheathed in fake innocence, but today it didn't protect them.

As soon as they came into view, two men and two women approached them—the hand on the shoulder, the grave eyes, the windowless room, the search. An almost paralyzing shock set in straightaway. Eva felt a strange detachment, as if she were watching it happen to someone else.

She watched Sun Yi being led away. She watched the small, thin woman go, saw her back for the last time, knew it, as she too was led away. The image stayed in her head as she submitted to the body search, absenting her mind from her body, rising somewhere above it. But she couldn't banish the image of a woman walking to her execution.

She was allowed one telephone call. She dialed from memory, the emergency number.

"It's Eva. I'm at Changi. I've been picked up."

She sat alone for four hours in a locked room. No one was allowed to see her. She was allowed to see no one. That was a good sign, she supposed; they were protecting her, they were on their way. But if they didn't come? A life sentence, twenty-five years? The Singaporeans rarely hanged Westerners, but it did happen, could still happen to her. Sun Yi would be hanged. There was no one to protect her, no noble cause behind her. The noble cause would rescue Eva, take her away somewhere safe.

She wondered whether she ought to wish for the same fate, to hang with Sun Yi. Every part of her screamed against it. Not for a second did she wish to die. The guilt of surviving would corrode her. It had started already, when she saw the fear, the anticipation of death in her friend's eyes. But as she sat in her windowless room, sweat running with the tears that had started flowing when the first merciful, deadening shock had subsided, the sensation she felt, stronger than anything she had ever experienced, was an overwhelming desire to live.

To watch yourself walk toward avoidable death is the most poisoning, sickening thing. You could retch your heart out. She wouldn't die. The Secret Intelligence Service, MI6, had never promised her a safety net, but she refused to believe there was none. She was a freelance agent, deniable. There had been no contract, no pledge that they would come to her aid. Still she felt, with the certainty born of desperation, that they would get her out of this. In her own mind, she knew in advance that whatever the price, she would pay.

Andrew Stormont, her controller, arrived at dusk. He had flown in on a Hercules C-130 from Hong Kong. Customs met him at the runway and took him to Eva.

He walked in, heard the door close and lock behind him. He stood looking down at her. Were it not for her eyes, the intensity and the life still shining in them, he would not have recognized her. Her clothes hung from what was left of her body. She was thin, her face gaunt, the strong features harsh. Her skin was sallow, her blond hair long and limp. She bore the stamp of heroin addiction.

He walked toward her. She got up from the floor. They said nothing. He took her arm and tapped on the door. Customs let them out, led them to a side door, through a series of corridors, and back onto the runway to the Hercules, which stood ready, engines running. The customs officers turned their backs. Eva and Stormont went inside. The plane took off.

Eva watched Stormont hand her luggage to a plain-clothes officer who sat quietly at the back of the aircraft. He would destroy it, everything inside it, and with it her life of the past four years.

"Where are we going?"

"Back to England. To a clinic." Stormont ran his hands over Eva's skeletal arms.

For four years she had worked for SIS as a deep-cover narcotics agent in Southeast Asia. Stormont spoke to her regularly on the telephone, but no one from SIS ever saw her. She had played her part so well, no one had ever suspected that she had become an addict.

"Why didn't you tell us?"

"What difference would it have made? I had no choice. There came a point where I had to take it. I knew if I started I wouldn't be able to stop. But it was that or discovery. They had their suspicions about me right from the start. This was the only way to prove myself."

"They must have begun to suspect again."

"It was a setup. No question. But I wasn't the target. I wasn't supposed to be there. It was pure coincidence. I had to do a run sooner or later, decided to do it this week. I found out Sun Yi was doing it today, so I teamed up with her, last-minute. Customs went straight for her. They took me in because I was with her. But they didn't want me. If I'd been alone, I would have got through. For weeks now there's been a rumor that Frazer thought one of his top couriers was undercover. Right suspicion, wrong suspect. Now I'm here, and she's dead."

Stormont started to say something, but Eva cut him off. "She's as good as dead. I'd rather die now than wait six months to be hanged."

She sat beside him, her face emaciated, the skin drawn in grooves over the cheekbones. No beauty left, only a shell.

"How long have you been on the stuff?"

"Almost from the beginning."

"Eva!"

A trace of junkie's pride showed through. "I'm strong."

She sat rigid, withdrawn. Stormont wondered how long it had been since she had had her last fix, when the anxiety and the trembling and the screaming would set in. Already she was beginning to sweat. He looked at her and asked himself whether it was worth it. Intellectually he knew it was, but as she sat beside him, a casualty of his battle, emotions were more powerful than reason. He wondered how she justified it to herself.

As if reading his mind, she said, "I'm having trouble trying to pick my way out of this. I go home, get cleaned up. Then what?"

"What do you want to do?"

"Beyond my next fix, I couldn't care."

"Well, you'd better find something to care about, because there won't be a next fix." His words were planed of all emotion, sharp-edged. "If you don't think of something, then I might as well have left you to die with your friend."

"All right, then." Her words came out like a rasping cough. "You want a statement, a promise. I'll give you one. A promise for a promise. The reason I'm here is Robie Frazer. Robie Frazer and his guns and his drugs."

Stormont raised a hand, anticipating her. "Forget Frazer. He nearly destroyed you. Your cover's as good as blown. You can make a fresh start somewhere else."

"No. Frazer hasn't destroyed me. My cover is being a junkie. I won't be a junkie anymore. I'll get better, and I'll wait. I don't care how long it takes—three, four, ten years. I'll come back for Frazer then. That's all I ask."

She leaned toward him, straining against her seatbelt. "Give me a target. I need something. Frazer won't go away. And you won't get him. You'll always want him." She paused, and the light of irony came into her eyes. "You know these drug clinics—apparently they give you a special word, like a mantra that you're supposed to repeat to keep you going. Mine can be Frazer."

Stormont was silent for a long time. Reasoned arguments about the difficulty of making and keeping promises wouldn't save her.

"All right, Eva. Quid pro quo. You get better, and you get Frazer."

She sat back and closed her eyes.

Sixteen hours later, the Hercules landed at RAF Brize Norton. By that stage Eva was hunched in her canvas-backed seat, sweat pouring from her trembling body, mixing with the tears that flowed uncontrollably. Medical assistants met the plane. Stormont watched as she was carried off on a stretcher. He wondered if he would ever see her again.

In a rehabilitation clinic in the far west of Scotland, six months later, Eva read about the hanging of Sun Yi Sim.

ONE

MARCH 1995

For four years Andrew Stormont had tried to forget about Eva Cunningham and his ransom promise. He had changed jobs within the SIS, or the Firm, as it was known to insiders. He had moved from narcotics and was now the director of counter-proliferation, charged with monitoring the spread of military technology and weaponry worldwide.

Many countries, including those that had signed the Nuclear Non-Proliferation Treaty, dealt clandestinely in nuclear components and expertise. The unregulated sale of plutonium accelerated following the breakup of the former Soviet Union, spreading nuclear power to a whole new range of countries. Expanding chemical and biological programs posed another threat.

New responsibilities, new targets, new personnel. Yet Eva stayed in Stormont's mind, surprised him by appearing suddenly in a flash of memory, as she had been when he had recruited her: twenty-two, straight from Oxford, glowing with beauty, energy, curiosity. But even then she had had a touch of the tarnish that came with years in the Firm—a watchfulness, a readiness for the unpleasant.

She appeared too, more disconcertingly, in his dreams. Unbidden, unconnected to any logical stimulus, she merely appeared, as if to keep herself in his mind, to remind him of his promise. After many such appearances he began to think that perhaps it was at the bidding of logic that she came, for he found himself thinking once again of Robie Frazer.

Eva had been right when she had said, almost as a curse, that he would never let go of Frazer. It was Frazer, an indistinct, moving target, who had brought him now to Hong Kong. He suspected, but could not yet prove, that Robie Frazer was involved in the arms trade. He had pieced together intelligence and supplemented it with intuition. His calculation was that arms trading, with its huge profits, would appeal to Frazer's avarice, and its gleam of the *haut* criminal to his twisted morality. But even if Stormont was wrong and Frazer didn't buy and sell arms directly, he was certainly close to those who did.

After years of intricate dealings with the Chinese, Frazer was supremely well connected to the Chinese high command. China was an active agent of proliferation, having long been a supplier of nuclear technologies to Third World countries. The man masterminding much of this illicit trade was a high-ranking politician, Ha Chin. It was reasonable to suppose that Frazer knew Ha Chin. Now Stormont sought to link the two. But, whether Frazer knew Ha Chin or not, he could be a valuable source of intelligence.

Stormont stood, in the soft heat of March, three quarters of the way up Magazine Gap Road, on the Peak. The Peak was the smartest residential area of Hong Kong, where the old money, and increasingly the new, lived. Most of the taipans of the old trading families of Hong

Kong lived here. Robie Frazer, a new taipan, also lived here.

Stormont looked across the road and over the curving mountaintop at Frazer's house, a quarter of a mile away. It was a big white house, brilliant against the greenery. It seemed to cling to the hillside, rising out of the precipitous dense green foliage, anchored by some superior act of engineering. It was worth twenty-six million pounds, or so they said, and the house itself seemed to know the fact. It gazed out smugly, shining in the afternoon sun, as dazzling as the riot of pink, red, and yellow flowers that grew richly on the paths that cut across the hillside. To observers, the house was a symbol; it spoke of money, power, position, as was appropriate to its owner.

Robie Frazer was forty years old, slim, brown-haired, blue-eyed, a golden boy grown older, the gilt deepened into lines of experience, of living, which, like everything else, he wore lightly. He was liked and admired by men and women, although inevitably he attracted jealousy from both, which he enjoyed discreetly.

What he did, how he made his money, nobody was quite sure. But the sheer weight of his wealth, combined with an unimpeachable English background, put him beyond reproach and gave him a patina of respectability. He might have been a man of integrity. As far as the public was concerned, there was no cause to suppose he was not.

Stormont stared across at the big house as if looking for clues in the gleaming edifice. He knew that Frazer was corrupt—not mildly so, not made so by his riches, but fundamentally rotten. The streak of it ran through him as rampantly as the fungi that grew and seethed in the jungle, just as prevalent and, to those who inhabited the rarefied levels, just as invisible. But Stormont saw it, smelled it, as Eva Cunningham had many years ago. All he had to do was uncover it.

Stormont watched the big house for a long while before turning and walking away, oblivious to the heat.

After walking for fifteen minutes, he arrived back in Central, where he was to have drinks with an old university friend, Douglas Bairns. Bairns was a casual but excellent source of intelligence. He worked in the diamond trade. He was responsible for all the Asian activities of his company.

Bairns was waiting at the Foreign Correspondents' Club, on Lower Albert Road. Stormont stepped out of the heat into a blast of air conditioning. He found Bairns at the bar. The two old friends shook hands, sat down, ordered drinks, and talked genially of Stormont's flight, his health, the weather. Their conversation, like their surroundings, was low-key, elegantly casual. They might have been discussing cricket scores, or women, so light and easy was their tone.

After the pleasantries, Bairns moved on. "I have a bit of a problem in Vietnam." He smiled at the faint tiresomeness of it all. "It looks like there might be a big new diamond find, could be significant. It's largely uncharted territory." He spread his hands, palms upward. "Who knows? It could yield tens of thousands of carats per annum."

"Sounds promising. So what's the problem?"

"Character called Granger McAdam has staked the site. His company owns the site. It's listed on the Vancouver Stock Exchange. McAdam's chairman of the company, owns twenty-five percent, effectively controls it. He's American, and an uncooperative bastard. It's not our favorite scenario—new and possibly significant sources of diamonds in unfriendly hands."

"No indeed." Stormont knew the next question in advance. Bairns knew that he knew, and Stormont knew that too, but made no effort to make things easier for his friend. He wanted him to ask outright, so that the favor lay on the table, his to give and have recorded, a bargaining chip for times to come.

"I needn't tell you," said Bairns, "it would be helpful to us if McAdam were replaced by a rather more friendly party. Problem is, if we tried to take over the company, if anyone tried in the normal way, McAdam would fight tooth and nail. It's his baby. He'd never sell up voluntarily. Anyone who did manage to get hold of much of the company would have to contend with him. And he'd make life intolerable."

"Yes, I can see that he would. I'll have a think. There might be something. I've nothing in mind for the moment, you understand," lied Stormont, "but I'll file it away. Anyway, since you're here, you might as well tell me about McAdam. What's his story?"

Bairns spoke for fifteen minutes: Stormont stretched, as if bored. He glanced at his watch.

"I have to go, Douglas. Good luck and all that."

Stormont walked from the club, summoned a passing taxi, and returned to the safe house he was staying in on the Mid-Levels, halfway up the Peak. He went to the drawing room and poured himself a whiskey. He sat on a deep sofa, elbows resting on knees, staring out the window at the skyline, jagged with skyscrapers. Beyond that was the calm blue of the South China Sea.

He made his decision quickly, instinctively. Mechanically, for duty's sake, he went through the motions of rational analysis, which, molded as much by perception as fact, would still provide him with the same answer. Striving for cold rationality was a waste of time. Better just to take time to locate the bias, anticipate its kinks.

Stormont picked up the telephone and rang his deputy, Giles Aden, in London.

"Get hold of Eva. Get her out here now. I'll wait till she comes."

There was a long silence before Aden's voice clipped down the line. "What makes you think she'll come?"

"I know her."

"Are you sure this is wise?"

"We'll see, won't we."

TWO

It took fifteen hours to locate Eva. After leaving the rehabilitation clinic in Scotland, where she spent six months, she had effectively disappeared. As far as the Firm was concerned, she was inoperative. She went to Vietnam, lived her own life of freedom. She moved around the country, staying in villages, teaching English to the local children. She charged nothing for her work. She had some of her own money, and living cost little. She worked for the joy of it, and to recover. But recovery was incomplete in her eyes until she received that call, until Stormont kept his promise. She had waited four years.

Aden spoke to her on the telephone at 10 A.M. Vietnamese time. She had just come back from a swim in the sea at Halong Bay, in north Vietnam. Aden gave no greeting or explanation. He said merely, "Stormont wants you in Hong Kong, immediately."

Eva felt a wave of sickness, pain, and excitement. It washed through her, awakening her. She had wondered about this moment for so long. She looked around, taking bearings to record, trying to lengthen the memory in the making.

"Where do I go?"

Aden gave the address.

"I'm on my way."

She packed everything she needed into a small canvas bag and left her sloping, creaking wooden house with its view over a sea cut by giant tors of rock—her beloved landscape. She left the door unlocked, with the key on the table in the sitting room, as if laid out for the next occupant.

She took a bus to Hanoi and a plane to Hong Kong. Mile by mile, she took up her severed past. She felt her strength growing as gentleness waned. She closed up one part of herself to open another.

Her plane swooped over densely packed skyscrapers to land at Kowloon. She disembarked and walked swiftly through the airport, a feral beauty with a graceful walk and watchful eyes. Men and women turned to look. Her face was strong, full-featured, with deep blue eyes and rich lips; her skin was smooth and tanned. Her hair was shoulder length, drawn back into a ponytail. It was bleached gold by the sun. She was five-foot-six, with the slim, lithe build of an athlete. She radiated energy and confidence, but quietly, effortlessly, as if she had much to spare. Her clothes, torn jeans and a faded denim shirt, and the old canvas bag were those of the perpetual traveler, but there was no languid curiosity in her eyes. Her gaze and stride were purposeful, as if she were returning home.

She walked out to the taxi rank. The light was fading, the sky deep gray. Dark clouds loomed, almost sparking with electric energy. Eva hailed a taxi and headed for the safe house. As the taxi emerged from the tunnel that connects Kowloon and the mainland to Hong Kong Island, the clouds exploded. Lightning cut a sky turned liquid. Eva leaned against the window, looking out, thrilling to the storm.

The thunder still raged half an hour later, when she arrived at the safe house on the Peak. She knocked twice. Andrew Stormont opened the door and Eva walked in. They stood a few feet apart, studying each other, saying nothing. He moved toward her and took her hands in his.

"You look wonderful."

She looked at him standing before her, checking the man against her memory of him. He was five-foot-nine, slim but powerfully built. His hair was a gunmetal gray. His eyes were dark blue, watchful, veiled, usually cold. They revealed little of the strength of emotion that lay behind. He was a passionate man, self-controlled by necessity, but occasionally the edges of passion showed in his eyes, in the way he moved and touched things, in his sensuality.

Eva knew his house, his cars, his paintings, saw in them what was hidden in him—a voluptuousness. She knew too how he loved to roam the mountains, sleeping in the open or under canvas in the snow, how he reveled equally in luxury and austerity. As she looked at him now, she was, as always, surprised by his face. Her memory was good, but she never managed to carry a perfect mental image of his face. This was, she swore, because it seemed to change, even the contours—fractionally, but enough to alter the whole. Sometimes he seemed to have fine, elongated features; at other times they seemed harder, broader.

Today there was emotion in his face, in his smile, in his eyes, which watched her closely, appraisingly, with the admiration that had never been dented, even at Changi.

Then she had seen pain and sympathy in his face, but not the contempt she feared.

She dropped her bag on the floor. "Before I do anything else, I've got to take a shower. Lend me a pair of jeans and a T-shirt, would you?"

She walked across the room, unbuttoning her shirt on the way. She stopped outside the bathroom, in full view, and took off all her clothes, dropping them in a heap. Stormont watched her, taking in the smooth, tanned skin, the muscles and curves, a strong, womanly sexuality. The heroin-riddled girl was nowhere visible. Eva had recovered, was still clean. She had made her point beautifully.

Stormont opened up his suitcase and took out a pair of jeans and a shirt. He laid them on the floor outside the bathroom, then went to the kitchen, took a bottle of vintage Veuve Clicquot from the fridge, opened it, and poured out two glasses. He walked to the window and stood gazing out.

Eva reappeared minutes later, toweling her hair. Stormont turned to watch her. His jeans hung over her hips, exposing her navel and an expanse of taut, well-muscled stomach. She had knotted his shirt at the waist and done up only a few buttons, revealing a tanned throat still beaded with water. She walked toward him. He gripped his glass hard, sipping his champagne, raising his eyes over the edge of the glass to look at her. She wore nothing beneath his clothes. Her eyes were watchful but guileless. In any other woman he might have suspected a sexual motive, but not in Eva. Sex with her, however much he might want it, was impossible. He was her controller. There were rules governing their relationship. Neither of them was by nature predisposed to follow rules, but for reasons of their own, in this case they abided by them—

perhaps because the attraction felt by both was too deep, too threatening.

Eva took the glass he offered her and sat down on the sofa. He sat in an armchair opposite.

"So, how's Vietnam? I hear you're teaching English in remote villages."

"It's wonderful, hectic, exciting, tranquil—everything. I moved around a lot, but I have a house now, in Halong Bay. I teach in a local school."

"You've built a good life there."

"It's simple, happy. Something good to do in the meantime."

"You know why I called you back?"

"Your promise."

"You don't have to take it up. It's your choice. You can go back to Vietnam, forget we ever met, forget everything."

She took a sip of champagne, then put down her glass, carefully and silently, on a marble side table.

"Forget? I don't think so. Whatever you have in mind, I'll do it. The answer has been yes for four years. It always will be."

He looked at her, unspeaking, a last gentleness in his eyes. Then the shutters came down.

"I've changed areas. Counter-proliferation. I'm particularly worried about the Chinese. We think they're selling plutonium, technical capabilities, and finished weapons to all sorts of undesirables. On their side, the trade is being run by high-ranking politicians and a few well-connected businessmen. Private enterprise is growing. A number of real Mr. Bigs are emerging. On the surface, they're legal businessmen. Underneath, they touch anything—drugs, arms, nuclear weapons. I want to know what they're selling, and to whom. They're selling large quantities of arms to the Saudis. I want to track it. We have agents in place, but I want more. I need someone with top-level access and a good cover. A businessman, for example. Someone who deals with the Mr. Bigs and with the politicians.''

"Robie Frazer." Eva's voice was dispassionate.

Stormont nodded. "No one has better contacts with the Chinese than Frazer. They like him, they trust him. He and they understand each other. He's almost an honorary Chinese.''

"That's because they've never met a *guelin* who comes even close to loving money as much as they do. Frazer makes them look like ascetics.'' She took another sip of champagne. "I can see the logic. Frazer would be perfect. But why would he do it? It seems to me he'd have a lot to lose and nothing to gain. If he's discovered, he blows the most lucrative part of all his operations. He'd never be trusted in the East again. And he feeds off that, off trust and public recognition.'' She silenced herself as she was about to add, *Not to mention they'd probably kill him for betraying them*.

"How do we normally get people?" asked Stormont. "Money, loyalty, or blackmail. Money would appeal to Frazer, but he's a millionaire hundreds of times over. What we could afford to pay he would see as an insult. Queen and country don't translate into any currency for him. So we're left with blackmail. You said yourself how important his public standing is to him. He loves to play the rich patrician Englishman, loves the slight raffishness his money and his Eastern dealings give him. But all the time he revels in his respectability, sees it as a joke on the world. He screws people twice over, once in making his money, again in convincing everyone that he's a paragon.''

"Not everyone."

"No. But you've seen more than most."

"You don't have to see what I saw to suspect he's corrupt. No one makes that much money that quickly without taking shortcuts. You'd think anyone would see that."

"They don't want to. He's a hero, the patron saint of ambition."

"So how do you blackmail him?" asked Eva.

"We blackmail him. It's a long story, nicely circuitous, a perfect ambush."

"So tell me your story, tell me my part."

Stormont concealed a smile. This stage, the laying out of plans, the agent's consent, always felt to him like a seduction, the beginning of a chain of seductions, all justified by his purpose.

"You're to go straight back. To Hanoi. Hook up with a character called Granger McAdam. He owns a twenty-five percent stake in a diamond site in north Vietnam. It might be convenient if he were liberated of some of that stake."

"What exactly is our interest in McAdam and diamonds?" asked Eva with an elegantly raised eyebrow. "Spare me the bullshit answer. I know you won't give me the whole story, but at least give me something to go on with."

He looked at her with a strange fondness. He wanted to say, "Oh, Eva," and stroke her face. Instead, he gave her the formal response she sought.

"It's nothing personal with McAdam. He's simply the wrong man in the wrong place. He happens to control what could be a significant new source of diamonds. That makes him undesirable on two counts. First, he's an uncooperative bastard, by all accounts. Second, he's American."

He spoke over her as she started to interrupt. "Let me give you some background. This is all about the diamond cartel and the control of the supply of diamonds. The cartel controls, by public estimates, around eighty percent of the world's diamond production. This eighty percent is sold through its Central Selling Organization. In reality, the figure is considerably lower. But it still amounts to a form of hegemony over world supply and prices. What the cartel does not want is new sources of diamond supply owned by companies or individuals unwilling to trade through cartel channels." He paused to watch her, leaning forward now, sharp-eyed. "Americans pose particular problems for the cartel because the Sherman Act makes the monopolistic cartel illegal in the United States. This isn't insurmountable—the cartel has various means of getting around the Sherman Act—but it does curtail its freedom of operation. And there's a lot at stake. New sources of supply that don't go through CSO channels tend to depress world diamond prices. And there are lots of interested parties who don't want lower prices."

"Anyone who owns a diamond engagement ring, or any diamond jewelry," suggested Eva.

"Exactly. Diamonds are forever. Apart from their romantic connotations, they're supposed to be an investment for life, the value of which might rise but will never fall. Banks that finance diamond mines want to be sure that their loans will be repaid. Jewelers with large stocks want to ensure they hold their value. Everyone who owns diamonds would suffer, and there are plenty of hidden hoarders of diamonds, from the cartel to anyone who wants to have a secret and mobile source of wealth and security. The hoard of secret diamonds is vast, worth billions of dollars. A fall in the value of diamonds would be catastrophic."

"And McAdam represents a real threat because he's American and won't cooperate with the cartel and he might be in a position to control a significant new find?"

"Exactly. Nobody is sure how big a threat he is, because it's too soon to estimate the value of the diamonds on his site. There might not even be any. But as you know, it's easier to neutralize a small threat than a large one. The cartel could simply ignore him. It could try to neutralize new sources of supply outside its control by raising prices in that part of the world diamond trade it does control, but that's a contingency measure—expensive, and very much a second-best solution. Or it could try to take over his company, which owns the site. It's publicly listed, on the Vancouver exchange. But he'd fight any takeover, probably would never sell his stake voluntarily. If the cartel did buy into his company, with him being such a large shareholder, it'd be severely restricted in what it could do. Not to mention it would have a hostile shareholder in its midst."

"So the best solution is to ensure that the new sources of diamonds come either directly or indirectly under the control of the cartel," said Eva, "by getting rid of McAdam and replacing him with a friend of the cartel's. That much I understand. But what does this have to do with Robie Frazer, and what do we care about the cartel and its problems?"

Stormont drained his glass, peering at Eva as he drank. "This is a favor, and something that we can use. A perfect trap."

He got up to pour himself another drink. He waved

the bottle before her. She shook her head. He sat down, drank some more, then put down his glass.

"The diamond site is bait to lure Frazer into our orbit. He'd replace McAdam. I think diamonds might appeal to him, especially in Vietnam. It gives him an opening into the country. I'm sure he'd find a way to turn that to his advantage."

"How does it work?" asked Eva quickly.

"The diamond site is in early days at the moment. The company has done some preliminary tests, and the results look good. Now they need to raise more money to do some bulk sampling. You're going to help McAdam do that."

"Why should he need my help, and what the hell do I know about financing diamond mines?"

"We'll teach you more than you need to know. And McAdam will need your help. Get close to him. That's stage one. Then you have to get access to Frazer, present the deal to him. That's stage two. I'll work out the details of that, but the plan is to bring him in as chief investor, chairman of the diamond project, whatever. He'll have his eyes on the diamonds and what they can do for him." Stormont slowed his words, speaking very deliberately. "If you're clever, he'll never see what you're up to. It's a chance to get close to him, Eva, to find out every last thing about him. Things we can use directly, and to blackmail him into reporting on his Chinese cronies." He watched her carefully. "But you'll have to get very close."

His words were hard, uncompromising, deliberately stripped of softness.

Eva sat very still. The only indication of the inner turmoil Stormont knew she must be feeling was the slight bunching of muscles around her cheekbones. After a while nothing but a quiet readiness showed on her face.

"You have to be sure you can do that," said Stormont. "You know the risk if you give yourself away at the wrong time, without our protection. Frazer killed Sun Yi on a hunch. Just as easily he'd kill you."

"I haven't forgotten Sun Yi. And yes, I can do it. I can play a role as well as anybody, and I have all the incentive in the world."

"Maybe too much."

"So why pick me?"

"I made my promise, and you're the best person for the job. But there are difficulties. You've worked in the Far East, you know it, but under your old cover, you're known there. Similarly, you worked for Frazer's organization, you know a bit about him and his methods, but other people in that organization also know you, or knew you. Your strengths are weaknesses too. Double-edged sword as far as the Firm's concerned."

"Who knows about this, in the Firm?" Eva asked sharply.

"The chief, me, and my deputy, Giles Aden."

"I met Aden once. I didn't get the feeling that he liked me very much." She spoke lightly, with deliberate understatement.

"It's not that he doesn't like you. He's a natural cynic, pessimist—a touch of misanthropy. Doesn't like anyone very much."

"But you trust him?"

"Yes."

Eva thought about that, filed it away, moved on. "So my strengths, my weaknesses—the Firm . . . ?"

"Finds them acceptable. In your favor. As you say, you can act, you have all the training, all the necessary experience. You know Vietnam, you're comfortable there, and you've established a new cover, teaching English. The risk is that someone from Frazer's organization will recognize you from before. You looked different then, operated under a different name. And in your debriefing then you told us that Frazer had never met you. You should be all right. But are you absolutely sure no one in Frazer's operation, high up, ever saw you? It's the people who come into contact with both you and Frazer we need to worry about."

"You know how they run operations like that. The higher-ups never meet those way down the chain, as I was. Each link is insulated. I haven't met anyone close to Frazer. No one who knew me also knew him firsthand." Even as Eva lied, she thought of the one person close to Frazer she had met—Le Mai, who ran Frazer's black operations. But she had met him only once, when she was thirty pounds lighter and ravaged by heroin. He would never again recognize her.

"Fine. You go in clean."

She picked a hair from her shirtsleeve, then looked up to study him. "Do I, though? There is one thing that bothers me. That day at Changi, when Sun Yi and I were picked up, Frazer's people thought she was the agent, set her up. When she was hanged, they had their proof that she couldn't have been an agent. If she had been, she'd have been spirited away. But I was picked up, and I *was* spirited away. What if Frazer learns about that?"

"We dealt with that at the time, to protect you then, but it'll protect you now as well. We put out a cover story. Sun Yi was picked up, and a friend who traveled with her. But the friend wasn't carrying anything. She was released. End of story. We've made it stand up. You helped us. You were thorough, as always. We checked the list of passengers. You'd covered your tracks well. You hadn't even booked your ticket under the operational name Frazer's people knew you by. You'd used another name, another passport. So Frazer would never find you on that flight, never link you with Sun Yi's arrest. Only two customs officers knew what happened to you that night, knew that you were carrying heroin, and that you were spirited away. But they don't know who you were. And they won't talk about the woman they saw that night. Carrot and stick. They'll keep quiet."

"But there's still a risk they could talk."

"Always is. But who's to link the girl they picked up with you? Would someone who only saw you once, as a junkie, recognize you now?"

He always asked *the* question, Eva thought. Did he know the answer this time? "What do you think?"

"Unlikely."

"What about my sudden disappearance from Frazer's courier network? How did you handle that?"

"You made that quite simple, inadvertently. Everyone who knew you then knew you were a junkie. We put out a story that you overdosed and died. We had a body, in Thailand. A junkie. It became you. You died then. There were small stories in a few local papers. Frazer's people would have seen them. As far as they know, you, or rather, the woman you were, is dead."

"So who am I now, when I go to meet Frazer?"

"This time the cover is you, your real identity. It's the best cover. It works. You're a spoiled little rich girl who came to Vietnam to do good, to teach English to the local children. You just happened to run into a diamond prospector. If you succeed and you do get close to Frazer, you'll have to be ready to travel all over the world with him, quite possibly to London, where you're known. You'll have to operate under your own identity."

Whatever the hell that might be, thought Eva.

"And that, my dear Eva, is why you can't afford to get this wrong, to go too far. You won't be able to run away, shake off your cover, run back to yourself this time. Everything you do, you'll have to live with."

Eva glanced away, hiding her eyes. She turned back slowly. "Fine. I know the risks."

"You know the rules too. This is about getting Frazer to work for us. Your role is to use the story we discussed to get close to him. Then you get something on him, something irrefutable, that you know will make him bend. Then you give it, and him, to us, and your role is over. You will not harm Frazer directly. Is that understood?" There could be no room for misunderstandings, willful or innocent. Stormont watched her, ready to gauge her reaction, to search for a lie in her voice, in her posture, in the face he knew so well.

She faced him in silence, letting him see the emotions in her eyes.

"I did want to kill Frazer, for a while. In the clinic, when I was going through withdrawal. Then when I was getting better, I read about Sun Yi's death, and I wanted it to be Frazer who was hanged. But I had four years to myself in Vietnam. Four years of freedom, of living as I chose. I had to forget Frazer. It would have poisoned me. I couldn't live on revenge."

"So why take the assignment now?"

"A promise. I made one too. When I was in withdrawal, going half mad, the prospect of going after Frazer, making him suffer, was the only thing that kept me sane. I know it's schizophrenic. It had to be. I had to be. I had to want to kill Frazer and then not want to. Both healed me."

"And now?"

Eva spoke slowly, choosing her words with infinite

care, conscious of how much hung on her answer. "I will go after Frazer. I'll keep the promise, but for other reasons. For your reasons. I'll do what you want, hand Frazer over to you. I don't want any more violence. If someone puts his hands around my neck, I'll respond. But only then."

Stormont watched her in silence.

"I had to hear it from you." He stood up. She had shown the necessary reserve, asked all the right questions, seen all the risks. She was not messianic in her desire to go after Frazer, as some, such as Aden, feared she might be. She was measured, balanced. He could trust her, and he could use her. "All right, Eva. You know what to do. Stage two is Frazer, stage one McAdam. Concentrate on McAdam for now. Hook up with him, get close to him, find out everything you can about him, be ready to help him if he gets into trouble."

Eva stood, picked up her bag and clothes, and began to walk toward the door. Suddenly she turned.

"About this trouble?"

"Don't worry about that," replied Stormont. "You look after McAdam, I'll look after the trouble."

She gave him a last long look. "I'll bet you will."

The door slammed behind her like the crack of a whip.

THREE

Eva returned to Hanoi and set about finding Granger McAdam. It wasn't difficult. He was a noisy drunk who spent every evening in one, or very often all three, of his favorite bars. It was so easy just to sit down alone at a large table with unoccupied seats, to catch his eye, to smile and wait. And he came like Pavlov's dog.

It became a regular thing over the coming weeks. They both liked to drink and to talk. He was good company, but that made things harder.

Eva liked him. He was a clumsy, difficult, kind man who loved diamonds and alcohol beyond reason. And now she was going to add to his miseries: a small evil committed in an attempt, probably futile, to destroy a great evil. She at least could take some comfort from her impulse toward good. But for McAdam there would be no such realization. No one would tell him that he was a means to a noble end, that his sacrifice was all worthwhile. Why should he pay the price? Eva dealt with him as gently as she could without making her job impossible.

Tonight she sat in her car, waiting, listening to the

streets of Hanoi, which rang with the sound of a thousand horns—bicycle, car, cyclo, all weaving their elaborate dance like flocks of birds traveling in opposite directions. It was the perfect staging. She felt sick. She had made her weekly telephone call to Stormont twenty-four hours ago. This one was different. This time he gave her specific instructions.

She sat low in the driver's seat, veiled by a neighboring palm. Across the street she saw the small Vietnamese man crouched in the shadows between two cars. She turned her head and waited for McAdam to emerge from the Metropole Hotel, five yards back on her side of the street.

Forty minutes later he appeared. She saw him exit the hotel, weave toward his car, and fumble with his keys. He climbed in, started up the engine, and began to move erratically down the street. As the car picked up speed, Eva saw the Vietnamese run into its path. He took the impact in his ribs and bounced off, screaming, rolling on the ground, transforming pain into agony. Then, more terrifyingly, he fell silent.

McAdam lurched out of his car toward the Vietnamese, shouting to the crowd that materialized as if by magic that it wasn't his fault, that the man just ran out, that he didn't have a chance to avoid him. Eva watched two uniformed policemen and two soldiers appear from the darkness of a side street. All four carried holstered guns. The soldiers grabbed the American while the policemen stared at the Vietnamese immobile on the ground.

An ambulance appeared. The inert man was put in. McAdam was bundled into the back of a green military jeep. Even from a distance, Eva could see the fear in his contorted body, in his jerky, awkward movements. She remembered the sickening sensation of capture, could almost feel the arresting hand on her shoulder even now.

She watched the jeep drive off. When it had disappeared from view she drove to the Piano Bar on Hang Vai Street, where she was supposed to have been meeting McAdam.

The jeep accelerated through the humid night. McAdam sat hunched in the back seat, compressed by fear. Sweat poured from him. He had no idea where the silent soldiers were taking him. One drove; one sat next to him, pointing his gun at him.

After half an hour the jeep turned into a compound ringed by high walls and barbed wire. McAdam was taken inside to a cell. The two soldiers followed, nudging him along. Inside the cell, they got to work. He was a big man, but, drunk and terrified, he offered no resistance. Finally they left him.

He lay on the reeking floor, bleeding, wondering through the haze of pain what would happen next.

After a long time—he had no idea how long, although it was only two hours—Eva appeared. He shouted her name.

"Eva, God, thank God you're here! You've got to get me out of here. It wasn't my fault. I couldn't help it, there was nothing . . ." His voice trailed off. The guards appeared at Eva's shoulder. They unlocked the door and let her into the cell. She stood calmly before him, her eyes holding his. He found himself crying. No comfort, no soft words; instead she just stood there, dispassionate.

"I was waiting for you at the Piano Bar. When you didn't turn up, I tried the Metropole. They told me what happened. The man you hit is dead. He left a wife and six children. You're a foreigner, an American. You were drunk. They say you have only two choices. Pay his family fifty thousand dollars, which will be shared by them and various authorities, or spend the next twenty years in jail."

She watched him cry, watched his mind move ever downward. Then she gently touched his bloody face. He grabbed hold of her.

"You've got to help me. You must get me out of here."

"How much money do you have?"

"Nothing." His voice cracked. "I'm cleaned out. You know that. The site, the exploration took it all."

She watched, calm and patient. Logic was difficult, but he would get there, and she waited.

Finally he spoke. "I can't sell my stake in the site."

"What are you going to do, then?"

He didn't answer.

"I could try the British embassy," suggested Eva. "They might be able to do something."

He clutched at his broken ribs, gasping for breath. "What good would that do? I'm not exactly flavor of the month over there. Drunk, running someone over, not even British—they wouldn't put themselves out for me. They'd say it was inevitable, my own fault."

He paused and looked slyly at her. "What about you? You must have some money, your family. With your smart education and everything. How could you afford to live out here doing nothing but teaching English to the natives if you didn't have money?"

"I do have money, but my family keeps me on a strict allowance. You don't think they'd cough up fifty grand for me because a drunk American killed a local, do you?"

"Can't you tell them something? Say it's an emergency."

"Can't you, Granger? Don't you have family?"

She watched his head sink. She knew the answer to her question, knew the response it would provoke. McAdam had no family. Parents dead, brother estranged, no one else. She hadn't wanted to ask the question. She waited.

"I suppose I could try my family. They might give me fifty grand if they saw it as worth their while. But they're not the most charitable people, I'm afraid."

"Worth their while? What would it take? What would convince them?"

He saw the answer in her face. "My stake."

"A bit of your stake," she replied. "I'd never let them have it all. But if I present them with a good cold business proposal—ten percent of a good prospect for fifty thousand dollars—there's a chance they might wire me over some money."

"Ten percent? Have you got any idea how much that could be worth?"

"It's not worth much yet, is it? You haven't found any diamonds."

"But we will." His voice was hard. "You know we will."

"Granger, I'm only trying to help. But it's not up to me. It's up to my family." She shrugged, turning her face from his until she was sure her mask was once more in place.

Finally he asked, "How long would it take?"

She studied her nails. "If I telephoned them this evening, they could wire the money now—the banks are still open in London. It would be confirmed here tomorrow. I could get you out then."

He thought for a long while, looking around his cell

and out to the guards beyond, who sat at a table playing cards.

"Do it."

Eva rested her hands gently on his shoulders. "Don't worry, Granger. I'll get you out." Then she turned and gestured to the guards, who came to release her.

Granger McAdam watched her go, staring into space long after she had gone.

Eva drove back to the Metropole and headed for the telephone in the foyer. She inserted her credit card, rang Stormont, and spoke two words into the telephone.

"It's done."

Stormont smiled and hung up.

Eva went to the rooms she rented in the back streets of Hanoi. She poured herself a vodka, then drank nearly half the bottle before she could switch out the lamp and confront the night.

Eva and Stormont met again two weeks later, in Hong Kong, in the safe house. Eva sat down and took the wine he offered her.

"Everything's in place," she said. "Your 'trouble' was brutal but effective." She was dispassionate now, knowing he would be searching for weaknesses. "It got McAdam on the hook good and proper. I own ten percent of the company, of the site. All nicely documented."

"Good."

She shrugged. "So what now?"

"Frazer." Stormont got up to refill her glass, taking the time to watch her closely. "How would you like to proceed?"

Eva lit a cigarette and took a few drags. "I'd rather do it in London. Frazer's easier to get to there, less of the taipan crap, and besides, I have someone in the City whom I think he might work with well. A bit of bait."

"I thought you were the bait. You and the diamonds."

"Oh, we are. But the richer the lure . . ."

"I should have thought you were quite rich enough on your own."

"Let's stick to operational matters, shall we, Stormont?"

He shrugged lightly. "Tell me about your bait."

"Cassandra Stewart. Everyone calls her Cassie. She's a banker, with Case Reed. Quite high up. Beautiful, intelligent, trusting. Used to be my best friend at Oxford."

Stormont smiled. "God help her."

FOUR

The telephone rang just as Cassie Stewart was getting out of the shower.

"Oh, get that, would you, David?" she yelled at her housemate, who she knew was lounging somewhere in the vicinity of the sitting room, telephone at hand.

"Get it yourself," he replied goodnaturedly, immobile.

Dripping water, Cassie picked up the receiver in her bedroom. "Hello."

"Cassie?"

"Yes."

"It's Eva."

"Eva!" Cassie's voice rose an octave. "My God, what a surprise. Where are you? I heard you'd gone to the Far East, disappeared off the face of the earth."

Eva's laugh rang back down the telephone. She sounded delighted.

"I was in the Far East—I've been all over, for the past eight years, ever since Oxford. On the hippie trail, more or less. Anyway, the good news is I'm back. I'm in London."

"That's fantastic. Where are you?"

"Langton Street."

"That's ten minutes from here. What are you doing now?"

Eva sounded surprised. "Nothing, other than talking to you."

"Well, get into a cab. Come round. I have to go out in an hour, but now you're here I have to see you. Got a lot of catching up to do."

"Certainly have. What's your address?"

"Markham Street." She gave the number and then paused. "By the way, what's the bad news?"

Eva paused for a second, puzzled. "Oh yeah, that. Age and responsibility. I've come back to get a job."

"It's not the end of the world, you know. It's not that painful."

Don't be too sure, thought Eva, saying goodbye.

Cassie walked into the sitting room with a puzzled and excited face.

"Who was it?" asked David.

"Eva Cunningham. She and I were at Oxford together. Haven't seen her since then. We were really close, but then she disappeared off to the Far East. Just vanished."

"Sounds like a druggie."

"Hmm?" murmured Cassie, deep in recollection. "Druggie? Not her. That's the funny thing. She was the last person I'd expect to go on the hippie trail."

"Why?"

"Find out for yourself. She's coming round in five minutes. Unless, of course, she's changed. But I doubt it."

"Why shouldn't she? People do."

Not her, thought Cassie. *She's too strongly made.*

* * *

Eva walked slowly down the street, glancing around. A few new buildings had gone up, the legacy of the building boom of the eighties. The people looked as glossy or as rough as ever. London looked more or less the same, but it felt as alien to her as the streets of an unknown city. It was no longer home. She could not identify with the normality of the place, the rhythm, the people going to and from work and the pub as they always had, always would. She had changed, could no longer see things with the easy perspective of the twenty-two-year-old she had been when she left. Her life in the Far East as an undercover agent had exposed her to things that she would carry with her always—the suspicion and lies, the watchfulness, the closeness of death, the fear, and the courage. She was a stranger here, using familiar landmarks as props for her acting. She would play the part of the local she once had been. She walked down the street blending in, part of the neighborhood, a woman walking purposefully to a known destination. The disorientation she felt was something she had been trained to overcome, but still it ate at her, made part of her wish she was back in Vietnam, free of MI6, free of Stormont. She pushed it from her mind and concentrated on her first encounter with Cassie Stewart in eight years.

After ten minutes she stopped in front of Cassie's house. It was narrow, four stories high, in one of the side streets off the King's Road in Chelsea. It was a pretty house, in a pretty street where all the houses were painted pale pastel colors: pink, blue, pale green, blue-gray. It could have looked garish but didn't. It looked different, interesting, delicate and pretty, like its owner. *Pretty,* thought Eva. *Pretty is an insult.*

Cassie stood before her in the doorway. Eva's eyes

lingered on her face. She's horribly beautiful, she thought, like an orchid: pale, delicate, with veined, translucent skin. And those green eyes, curving up at the corners as she smiled—almost orientally exotic. And thin, so thin, thinner than ever.

"Cassie."

"Eva." They held each other at arm's length for just a second before embracing.

"Come in," said Cassie. "God, you look fantastic."

Eva followed her into the house, through a hallway, into the sitting room. A black cocker spaniel leaped around Cassie's feet, running back and forth between her mistress and the visitor. A man was lounging on the sofa. He got up and extended a hand. He was tall, slim, rangy, with a pleasant smile. Eva felt a tinge of annoyance, and of surprise. A live-in boyfriend? She hadn't reckoned on that. And he seemed an unlikely candidate. His dissolute air did not seem a match for Cassie's smoothness.

"This is David Wilson, my housemate," said Cassie.

Eva took his hand and returned the firm handshake harder.

"Come into the bedroom," said Cassie. "I've got to dry my hair and put on some makeup. I've got a client dinner. What a bore."

Eva followed her into a pale room, taking it in: floorboards of bleached wood, heavy white curtains, delicate white armoire and wardrobes, a black fireplace set in relief, a large window overlooking a garden, a single drawing—charcoal on paper, a few strokes, a dancer, head thrown back, hand raised, palm up, as if to ward off evil.

"Interesting," said Eva, nodding toward the drawing. "What's it called?"

"*Darkness and Light*. She's Light, fighting off Darkness. My favorite drawing." She took up a hair dryer lying on the armoire and began to dry her hair, studying her reflection in a Venetian mirror which hung above. Eva watched her brushing out her long coppery hair, burnished even redder by the setting sun, which poured in through the window. After five minutes, Cassie put down the dryer and began to make up her face, carefully watching her friend, reflected in the mirror.

Eva sat behind her on the bed. Her pose was casual, but she seemed, as she always had, coiled with energy. She looked bigger than she had at university, stronger. Not that she was particularly big or strong; she just seemed that way. Eva, at five-foot-six, was shorter than Cassie by some three inches. But while Cassie was fine-boned and skinny, Eva had sleek, muscled curves and the physical bearing of an athlete. Her long brown hair of university days had been blonded by the Far Eastern sun and cut to shoulder length. The effect was to emphasize the beauty of her features: the full lips, the gentle curve of cheekbones, the strong jaw, the large, deep blue eyes.

The light in her eyes was as powerful as ever. The sublime self-confidence that made her so attractive was undimmed. Had she had no shocks in all these years, nothing to challenge her, nothing to pierce her invulnerability? Had she been lucky, or did she just steamroller through? *No, that's unfair,* Cassie thought, *she doesn't steamroller. It's more that nothing touches her. Everything glides off.* Still there was that measured look in her eyes, the slight reticence. It was self-control, not shyness. Even in her wildest days at Oxford, Eva had never been fully uninhibited, never blind. Always aware, always watching. Still.

Eva watched Cassie brushing her hair. Her warmth, her lightness and effortless charm seemed to have grown over the years. Her inappropriate beauty too. Hers was a face to fit a ruthless mind, angular, unyielding. It was a threatening beauty, which she diffused by charm, offset by kindness. A necessary balance. But there was something new in her beauty, in her exaggerated thinness. She looked like something from a magazine. There was an element of artifice, of self-consciousness about Cassie's looks that had not been there at university. The makeup seemed to Eva like a device that allowed Cassie to study her own face.

The two women smiled at each other in the mirror, caught in mutual contemplation.

Eva spoke first. "So what are you doing now? Still in the City?"

"Yes, but I changed jobs. No longer takeovers. I do venture capital now, for Case Reed." Cassie spoke fast, as always, her voice light, soprano in song. Eva's, she noted, had slowed and deepened over the years. It was rhythmic, mellifluous, almost Caribbean.

"Venture capital, huh. What sort of thing?"

"Oh, anything, anywhere. But pure venture capital, the risky stuff—eastern Europe, biotech, that sort of thing."

"Enjoy it?"

"Yes, I do. It's a very intelligent form of gambling. You have to be very patient and very cool. It can be quite hair-raising. The odds aren't good. More deals go wrong than right."

"So how d'you make money, then?"

"When the deals go right, they go very right. We've more than quadrupled our money on a number of occasions."

"So you're doing well?"

"Not too bad."

"It's strange," said Eva. "It's not the kind of job I imagined you in."

"No? Why not?"

"Well, you say yourself you need a cool head and patience. Those were never your strongest qualities."

Cassie laughed. "No. You're quite right. That's one of the reasons I enjoy the job. It's a challenge. I'm teaching myself." Deftly she changed the focus. "But what about you? You've been in the Far East all this time—eight years, for God's sake. What did you do exactly?"

"Oh, where do I start? I didn't do much in the conventional sense. I moved around a lot. Thailand, Hong Kong, Vietnam, Cambodia, Laos. I taught English to local children. I just lived, really. That's challenge enough in some of those places, to live on your own, to be happy. You're thrown back on your own resources, with no friends—not to start off with, anyway—no support systems. You invent the life of your choice." She shrugged. "It was wonderful, but it doesn't fill a resumé."

"So what now?"

"I don't know. I'll look around, see what comes up."

Cassie glanced at her friend, who seemed, fleetingly, uncharacteristically muted. The moment passed.

Eva looked at her watch. "You'd better go, hadn't you? You'll be late for your dinner."

"God, yes." Cassie got to her feet. "What a bore."

"Nice client?" asked Eva casually.

"Don't know. Never met him before. My boss set up the dinner. One of his cronies sent the client along to us last week, thought we'd be a good fit. Client does a lot of venture capital in the Far East, apparently, and we're looking to expand there."

"What's his name?"

"Robie Frazer."

Eva smiled. "You'll be in for a good evening, then."

"Why? You know him?"

"Never met him, but I know all about him. Couldn't pick up a paper in Hong Kong without seeing his face or reading about his latest venture."

"And?"

"He's notorious with women. Good-looking, charming, fantastic lover. Real bastard, though."

"Is he now? And tell me, how do you know so much about him? Are you sure you've never met him?"

Eva laughed. "No. I haven't. But Hong Kong's an incestuous place. Gossip's a major pastime, and Frazer's well known. You don't have to meet someone to know about him."

"What else can you tell me?"

"That's all I know—his reputation with women, and that he's a very successful businessman, reputed to be worth several hundred million pounds, maybe even a billion. Any more than that you'll have to find out for yourself."

"I intend to."

Cassie saw Eva to the door and then went off to meet Robie Frazer. It was just another business dinner, one of many. This client was rather richer than usual, but as far as she was concerned, that was the only thing that marked him out. If she was at all on her guard, it was merely because of Eva's warning about his fondness for women.

Robie Frazer and Cassie's boss, John Richardson, awaited her at Rakes, in South Kensington. She walked downstairs into the restaurant, apparently oblivious to the gentle lull in conversation, to the sudden distractedness of the male diners and the alternately hostile and appraising glances of the women.

Frazer and Richardson stood as she approached. She smiled at Richardson and extended her hand to Frazer, letting her smile fade as she studied him. About forty; exceptionally good-looking, enough to spoil a man. Thick, dark hair, cut very short. A smooth forehead, but lined around the slightly slanting eyes, which seemed half closed under heavy lids. Amused, vaguely contemptuous mouth—an ageless, inscrutable oriental look, almost feminine in its sensuousness.

He was looking at her with unconcealed interest, not the diffident curiosity she provoked in most men but the scrutiny of a buyer in an auction house. That he could have her was to him a foregone conclusion. The only variable was his own inclination. He made no effort to hide the appetite or certainty in his eyes but seemed to revel in it. For all his trappings of urbanity, the custom-made suit and the rich, well-schooled voice, the impression Cassie got was of someone who did not remotely care for the conventions. There was nothing overt in his behavior, nothing with which anybody could confront him, but still the message of disregard was palpable.

Cassie, impassive as if she saw none of this, sat down. Frazer, still studying her, was struck as he greeted her by the likeness of her exposed wrist and hand to a swan's neck: thin, white, just as snappable. But wasn't there something about swans? Weren't they supposed to be able to break your arm with a flap of their wings?

Richardson poured Cassie a glass of champagne; then they scanned the menus and ordered. The first courses arrived.

"I'm surprised you're here," said Cassie to Frazer, "when you could be at the opera, or sailing a boat around the South Pacific, or sitting in a monastery in Ladakh."

"You mean why do I still bother with business?"

She nodded, her mouth full of sushi.

"It's a bloodless form of war, isn't it? Money represents the corpses of the opposition."

John Richardson quietly laid down his fork, covering his flash of revulsion with a laugh. Cassie merely gazed at Frazer.

"Good job we're on the same side, then." She found herself wondering what it would be like to have this man for an enemy.

When she returned home over four hours later, David Wilson was waiting up for her.

"Good dinner?" he asked.

"Mmm. Very."

"Why? I thought it was a boring client."

"Not all my clients are dull."

"What was he like, then?"

"Interesting."

"What, like your friend?"

"Which friend?"

"Eva."

"Yes, funnily enough. There is something similar about them, though I can't think what."

"I can tell you."

"Go on then."

"Unpleasant. Dangerous."

"Oh, don't be so melodramatic. And you've never even met Frazer."

"I don't need to. I've met Eva, and you say he's similar to her. And you had the same expression on your face when you'd been speaking to her on the telephone as you did when you came in a minute ago."

"And what was that?"

"A sort of intrigued curiosity—a welcoming look,

but slightly wary, combative almost. Like you'd found a new sparring partner."

"I suppose I have."

"I don't like her."

"Don't be ridiculous. You don't even know her. You were together in the same room for thirty seconds."

"That was enough."

"I don't know what's got into you. Eva and I shared a house together at Oxford. She's one of my oldest, closest friends. Everyone likes her, apart from a few jealous types, and I wouldn't have put you in that category."

"Well, I'm sorry, but I don't like her and that's that."

"Why so vehement and why don't you like her?"

"You're making me vehement, and I don't know. Yet. Intuition. It's not a female monopoly, you know."

"I'm going to bed. Perhaps you'll be in a better mood tomorrow."

"And I don't like this Frazer character either!" he shouted after her.

FIVE

Four miles away, in a safe house south of the river, Andrew Stormont and Eva Cunningham sat opposite each other in a darkened, dusty room.

"How did it go?" asked Stormont. He leaned back in an old leather armchair, body languid, lively eyes on her.

Eva looked thoughtful. "Cassie's toughened up since I last saw her, but that was eight years ago, so it's hardly surprising. She's a bit cooler, more rational. Watchful, funnily enough. She always used to be one of those people who gave everyone the benefit of the doubt. You know, neither spoke, saw, nor listened to evil. But something must have happened to her. She seems to have lost that. I caught her looking at me from time to time and I felt quite exposed. Don't worry, I didn't give anything away. It wasn't like that. It was just that she had this light of irony in her eyes occasionally, as if she could see right through you."

"She's a banker, for God's sake. What do you expect? It'd be surprising if she weren't downright cynical."

"She's not cynical. There's nothing world-weary or jaded about her. Just that she sees things, that's all."

"Better be careful, then."

Eva laughed. "She'd better be careful."

Cassie lay in her bed, dreaming vividly. Eva and Robie Frazer twisted through her dreams, sometimes separately, sometimes together. When she awoke the next morning, she tried to remember what they had done, but the dreams had gone.

She showered and dressed quickly. She put on a sand-colored cotton jacket and straight skirt, a white cotton blouse, and tan shoes. She applied face cream, lipstick, and scent. She brushed out her long hair, glanced in the mirror, and slipped quietly from the house, not wanting to wake David, who she knew would sleep until eleven.

His behavior had been strange the night before. Surprisingly vehement. It wasn't even as if he had been drinking. He hadn't had that air about him. Odd.

Pushing him from her mind, she turned into the King's Road and hailed a taxi. The taxi dropped her at the espresso bar on Clifford Street, in the West End. She bought a bacon roll and a large cappuccino, which she carried in a paper bag to her office across the street, at the intersection of Savile Row and Burlington Street.

Cassie had worked at Case Reed for four years. Before that she had worked for four years at a large City bank, with over one thousand employees in its London office. She had liked the nature of the work, funding highly leveraged transactions, takeovers, and management buyouts, but she had disliked the environment. She found it too aggressive, unthinking, impersonal. Although she had done very well, rising to the level of assistant director by the age of twenty-five, she had quit, taken a cut in salary, and moved to the smaller, more civilized environment of Case Reed. Here she specialized in raising finance for startup ventures, backing brilliant scientists or entrepreneurs who had exciting business ideas but insufficient capital. Case Reed looked at dozens of proposals a week, but it financed perhaps four deals a year. The venture capitalists' was a skill of perceptiveness, market knowledge, judgment of character, and patience. Sometimes it could take five years to realize a return on their investment, but if the deal went as planned, they could make huge returns.

On occasions Case Reed's investment increased in value tenfold over five years. One third of net profits was shared out among the twenty executives. The remaining two thirds were added to the firm's capital and made available for new investments. The firm's performance since its founding by John Richardson in the early eighties had made all of the four partners, and several of the employees just below them, millions of pounds over the years.

The atmosphere was hardworking but fair. Richardson did not tolerate the competitiveness, the internal conflict, the money mania common to many financial institutions. He was shrewd but kind. He and his firm made money, but they were not preoccupied by it. He was the main reason why Cassie had come to Case Reed. He gave her scope, allowed her to get on with the job unfettered.

Cassie arrived every morning at half past eight, just as the atmosphere in the office was beginning to quicken. Eight-thirty, quarter to nine was the cutoff time. Before that, everyone from partner down would sit quietly in his office or at her desk, eating croissants and drinking coffee, flicking through newspapers, composing himself or herself for the day ahead. Unwarranted conversations were kept to a minimum. A nod and a "Good morning" would suffice until after nine, when business began to intrude and distance and civility to retreat. Not that people were necessarily rude after nine; it was just that the demands of the business day invariably seemed to give rise to barked exchanges, marching into and out of offices uninvited or undismissed, and a general air of haste and impatience.

Cassie sat very still in her office as the bustle around her increased. Her secretary, Emma, arrived, telephones started to ring, and fax machines began to beep. Cassie sat reading her newspaper, half her mind preoccupied by Eva Cunningham, Robie Frazer, and David Wilson, who flitted between the other two. They had made powerful impressions, Robie and Eva, especially seen one after the other. She wondered what they would be like thrown together, if indeed they had ever met. There had been something unsatisfactory in Eva's answer to that question the night before. Cassie decided that she would like to engineer a meeting, to watch their reactions to each other. The prospect of it amused her, and she started when the voice of John Richardson boomed through her thoughts.

"Morning, Cassie." He was standing at her door, and when she looked up, he walked into her office and sat down across the desk from her. "What d'you think of Frazer, then?"

"He knows how to be good company—charming, amusing, intelligent." She spoke carefully, trying not to prejudice. "What do you think?"

He waved as if trying to clear the air. "Oh yes, good company. Apart from all that corpses stuff. Gave me the creeps. Felt like telling him we're venture capitalists, not merchants of war. Sounded like a bloody arms trader."

"He's just a grown-up little boy who's put all his nasty instincts into making money."

"Several million pounds must make him pretty nasty."

"Just think how nasty he'd be without that outlet."

"It was almost as if you were goading him. Asking him why he was bothering to have dinner with us, going on about our being on the same side."

"That's preferable to the alternative, isn't it?"

"Yes," said Richardson thoughtfully. "Wouldn't really enjoy being on the wrong side."

"You know," mused Cassie, "I felt that some of the time he was trying to make himself palatable, toning something down, as if he thought he'd gone too far earlier."

"Could be. So tell me, is he the kind of person we can do business with?"

"Every banker in town's clamoring to work with him."

"That's not quite what I asked, is it?"

"No." Cassie gazed at a bronze sculpture of a horse's head that stood on her desk. She spoke slowly, thinking aloud. "I don't feel entirely comfortable with him."

"Neither did I. Perhaps it's his Eastern inscrutability. After all, you can't live in Hong Kong for as long as he has without something rubbing off. But I'd still like to work with him, wouldn't you?"

"Yes, oddly enough, I would."

At one o'clock sharp, Robie Frazer walked up the steps to Brooks's, his club in St. James's, and into the bar. In a dark swath of suits he stood out. He was around six feet tall, one hundred and eighty pounds, slim and fit. There was no unsightly paunch extruding from his waistband, no heavy jowls. His face, though relaxed, bore none of the easy complacency that characterized so many of his fellows. It was watchful, aware of the possibility of surprise.

He greeted a few acquaintances, his manner casual and friendly, but still he stood apart. Had they been familiar with the concept, the patrons of Brooks's might have said it was his aura. Instead, if pushed as to why they felt an instinctive reservation about him, they would have said it was his money. He had made too much, too easily and too visibly, and among the casualties of Lloyds, that jarred. But he and his money could not be dismissed as *arriviste*. Even if much of his money was new, his family was old, and it was this combination that so many of his peers found discomfiting. Frazer, if he were conscious of their feelings, showed no sign of it. He was, whenever the surfaces of their lives touched, consistently affable.

Across the bar he spied his lunch partner, Angus Fawley, whom he had known for almost all of his forty years.

"Good to see you, Frazer."

"And you. How are you? Looking well."

"Not quite so well as you, I'm afraid. Old hair going south. Still. Drink, or shall we go through? I'm starving."

Frazer stepped back. "After you."

Ensconced at a long club table, they tucked into shepherd's pie.

"Will you stay in London long?" asked Fawley.

"Possibly. I'm fed up with Hong Kong. Too incestuous, claustrophobic. Need a change. I'll be here for a few months, at least."

"What you mean is you've run out of fresh women in Hong Kong. There are too many discarded ones running around. Even you are beginning to feel uncomfortable."

Frazer laughed. "You bastard. You're probably right. But I do have legitimate business reasons. I'm trying to diversify. I've got too much tied up in Hong Kong. China too. If I stay there, I'll see new opportunities all the time, so the only way to stop myself getting in deeper is to absent myself."

"You could always say no." The men exchanged an ironic glance. "By the way," Fawley asked casually, "did you follow up my tip, talk to that venture-capital house, Case Reed? When you rang and said you were coming to London, I thought they might be the people for you. They're a bit more adventurous than some of the established houses here. With all that you're saying about diversifying, they might be quite useful."

"As a matter of fact, I did follow your tip. I rang, set up a meeting. We had dinner last night."

Fawley looked up from his shepherd's pie with interest. "That was fast."

"No point in wasting time."

"So how were they?"

"Not bad. The chap who runs it, John Richardson—well, he's the usual sort, good at his job, reasonably sharp, plays the part. Not terribly exciting, but his firm does have a good record, lots of successful deals, so I'll give him the benefit of the doubt."

Fawley watched Frazer closely. His eyes were lively with an interest that contradicted the languor of his words. "And?"

"You know me too well."

"Let me guess. A woman?"

"Quite a woman."

"Tell me more."

"Her name's Cassie Stewart. Rather unusual." Frazer spoke with the controlled relish of someone who had a lot of time, who could enjoy a foregone conclusion anytime he chose.

"Attractive?" asked Fawley.

"Oh, yes. Definitely. In a rarefied way. Not to everyone's taste. She's cool, pale, and thin, with angular features. Fragile but strong, if you see what I mean."

"I do. Never went for that type myself, but then, they never went for me, always wanted someone more interesting, a bit more complicated. She sounds perfect."

Frazer took a sip of wine. "Not really. After all, we might end up doing business together."

"What, don't shit where you eat and all that? Why this sudden fastidiousness?"

"There's something about her. I just think it's wiser to steer clear."

"Oh well, I shouldn't worry. Dare say there'll be another one along sooner or later. Always is, isn't there?"

At three-thirty, the two men parted. Fawley returned to his office in the City. Before going in, he stopped at a pay phone on Old Broad Street and telephoned Andrew Stormont.

"Had a good lunch with your man. He seems quite taken with Case Reed, particularly with Cassie Stewart. I don't think he's averse to the idea of doing some business with them."

"Good. Thanks, Angus. And for the introduction. Very nicely done."

"My pleasure. Happy to help out." He put down the telephone and headed for his office in Broadgate Circle, returning to his guise as a merchant banker.

★ ★ ★

Frazer arrived home from lunch at four o'clock, his humor tested by the poor food. His house was in Wilton Place, on the border of Knightsbridge with Belgravia. It was toward the end of a terrace of brick houses five stories high. Some of the less meticulously tended houses were a dark brick color. The facade of Frazer's house had been cleaned recently and was a golden sandy brown. Each house had wrought-iron balconies on the first floor. Pots of flowers filled the balconies, some trailing fronds down to the windows below. There were gardens to the rear. Some were paved over, others carefully tended. Frazer's garden was the finest. There was a small patch of perfectly trimmed grass skirted by azalea and lilac bushes. Roses and wisteria climbed the brick walls, their scent filling the garden and trailing through into the quiet street. At both the front and the back of the house were two security cameras, angled downward from the fourth floor.

Inside, the house was rich, luxuriant, all dark woods, fine fabrics, and brooding oils. The sounds of the street were filtered out by storm windows. Light was excluded by heavy, half-drawn curtains. Peace and semidarkness. But not tranquility; more an oppressive quiet, broken intermittently by the striking of a grandfather clock, a sound that should have soaked into rich furnishings but echoed instead as if the house were empty.

Frazer walked briskly along the stone path through his front garden, let himself in, and headed for his study, which overlooked the garden at the back. The window was framed with climbing roses in full bloom, but he took no notice other than to register subconsciously that everything was as it should be, that the gardener had been doing his job. He sat down at his desk, leaned forward, resting his forearms on the polished wood, and smiled, as if facing a supplicant. Then he picked up the telephone and dialed.

It rang half a mile away, in the home of Xu Nan. Nan was young, intelligent, good-looking, and full of maturing promise. From a desperately poor Hong Kong Chinese family, he had been sponsored from the age of nine by Robie Frazer, who paid for his education. At thirteen, Frazer sent him to boarding school in England. From there he went to Loughborough University, where he took a first-class degree in computer studies. After that he joined a large British defense contractor, where he worked on developing computerized weapons guidance systems. He quickly made a name for himself within the organization as a man with exceptional talent and creativity. By twenty-seven, he had been promoted four times, enjoyed considerable responsibility, and earned a fair salary. This was topped up by money from Frazer, given as a tribute to his degree and his subsequent success. Nan hadn't liked to take this money, as Frazer had already given him so much over the years, but his patron had been insistent, and, not wanting to appear ungrateful, Nan had accepted.

His family was inordinately proud of him, because he had achieved such success. So much good luck. And now, inevitably, came the bad, for balance's sake. Only it wasn't a case of bad luck. There was nothing accidental about what had happened over the past six months.

It had all started with one of Robie Frazer's infrequent visits. Over the years, Nan had grown used to these encounters. Frazer came and went in a glow of charm and interested questions. Nan could never quite believe the interest shown in him by the Tai Pan, as everyone in Hong Kong called Frazer. Charity was the only explanation—the desire of the man who had everything to give back something. Only on this occasion, six months ago, Frazer had come to take. Sixteen years of charity were explained in one request.

Nan was to tell Frazer all about his work, provide as many details as he could about the weapons guidance technology. Frazer, of course, had made it sound like a gentle request, perfectly reasonable. He had asked casually, said the information was needed by a friend of his, that he was doing a favor and couldn't Nan perhaps do the same—an exchange of favors, nothing more. Nan had listened to the mellifluous voice, seen the look in Frazer's eyes: implacable, it brooked no resistance. It seemed to meet his potential objections and crush them. He knew then the futility of resistance. Frazer controlled him utterly, had by stealth and money sealed off all his exit routes.

Nan was caught in a vise of sixteen years' making. And he could see no way out. So he agreed to Frazer's request, told him everything he knew, copied and handed over documents when he could.

He had removed documents twice so far, had hoped never to do it again, but it was becoming clear that Frazer wanted a stream of information, that as long as there was information to steal and he was in a position to steal it, Frazer would have him do it. Each day, Frazer's unrelenting pressure unnerved him more.

He jumped when the telephone rang. It interrupted him as he was maniacally watering his plants. He had one hundred, counted to the last, lined up on the windowsills and balconies of his top-floor flat on Sloane Avenue in Chelsea. This watering was a cherished routine. The interruption caused him a disproportionate irritation. He put down his watering can and snatched up the telephone. His body stiffened when he heard Frazer's voice.

"Ah, Nan. I thought I might find you here. Off sick again?"

"Yes. But I was about to go in to work now. I'm just leaving, in fact."

Frazer laughed. "Would you rather I called you at your office?"

"No. No, that's not necessary. I'll call you back when I get some time."

"Time. Hmm." Frazer was thoughtful. "I'm glad you brought that up. It's been rather a long time since I've heard from you. By the way, how's your new flat?"

"Oh, it's fine. Fine, thank you. Very nice. I've filled it with plants already."

"Good. I'm glad you're enjoying it. Just don't forget where it comes from, will you, Nan."

"I haven't forgotten." He spoke with the petulance of fear, of hate, of futile rebellion.

"No. You've never let us down in the past." Frazer spoke slowly, as if pondering a change in the status quo.

Nan snapped back, "Did it ever occur to you that perhaps I've had enough of this, that perhaps I don't want to carry on?"

"No. And I'm surprised it occurred to you. That's not really an option now, Nan, is it? Things have gone too far. It's easier to keep going. It's like an arrow traveling through flesh. You can't pull it out, the barbs catch." Frazer listened to the silence. "Don't keep us waiting, Nan." He put down the telephone and stared out at the roses, at their bloody redness.

Xu Nan put down the receiver, picked up his keys, and walked out of his flat, leaving half his plants unwatered. He got into his car and, hands trembling, drove away.

Robie Frazer dialed another number, this time in

China. It was past midnight there, but the man he called was an insomniac and slept little, never until after 2 A.M. He answered on the third ring. Frazer spoke briefly.

"Ha Chin. Things are taking a little time, but it shouldn't be long."

There was a pause before an impassive, measured voice answered, "You said that two weeks ago. What's the problem?"

"There's no problem," answered Frazer evenly. "You'll just have to be a bit patient."

"You think maybe he's outlived his usefulness?"

"Oh, no. There's still some life in him. He's still hungry. And pliable. He's just getting a little windy, that's all."

"Windy?"

"Nerves."

"A little push, perhaps?"

"Oh, I'll push him all right. Don't worry about that."

"I won't. I have complete confidence in you, Frazer. After all, you've never let us down in the past."

Frazer laughed as his own words came back to him. Impudent Chinese bastard. He let his laughter run, neutralizing the threat.

"Goodnight, Ha Chin. Sleep well."

SIX

Cassie left the office at six. During the week she normally worked until around seven or eight, but on Friday evenings she always left earlier. She didn't mind the long hours. She enjoyed her work. It was exciting, challenging, distracting. It occupied her mind, paid her well, and gave her direction and purpose.

She walked out of Case Reed onto Savile Row. It was late April, the promise of heat had crept into the sun over the past week, and it washed over her now, lighting her face, making her smile. She turned into Clifford Street, on into Bond Street and Bruton Street, heading toward Park Lane and Hyde Park. She walked slowly, reflectively, as if taking a stroll in a garden. A slim, tawny man in his early forties caught her eye, provoking a smile: mutual attraction, mutual acknowledgment. That was all. They never did anything about it, men in this country. In America, Scandinavia, France, or Italy, they would stop to talk, sometimes gently, just for the moment, sometimes forcefully, to ply for dates. Here they just looked, smiled, felt vaguely awkward, and walked on, charming but passive.

She was used to this reaction now. Men and women almost always glanced at her as they passed, but it hadn't always been like this. At school she had been thought a freak, with excessively long, thin limbs and a small head. Her intellectual brilliance also set her apart, so she grew up with the impression that she was an oddity, and that had never quite left her. Her beauty still felt like a novelty to her, although she had learned how to enjoy it. Her lightness charmed people, brought out the best in them. She had never had to look below the surface, never really questioned the easy beneficence of life.

But in recent months she had felt a slight distancing, a growing objectivity, and whether she wanted to or not, she had begun to look deeper, to form judgments. Sitting in meetings, she would analyze her colleagues, glancing around the board table, imagining secret lives for the impassive businessmen who sat before her. Perhaps it was boredom, an overfamiliarity with her work. She was surprised by how easily such analysis came, and when she checked to see how closely her fantasies tallied with reality, she found that she was alarmingly accurate.

She was disconcerted by her newly found talent, unsure whether she liked it or not. She had grown fond of the state of innocence, even if it was preserved in part by a willful desire not to see. Knowledge brought responsibility, necessitated a specific reaction, limited her choices.

She walked on. The strength of the sun weakened, and goose pimples rose on her bare arms. She rubbed them briskly, walked faster, sprinted across the traffic on Park Lane, and entered Hyde Park. She walked amid the cherry blossoms, admiring their petals. The light breeze carried them through the air, and they rained down on her. She caught some in her hand, and her smile returned.

Half an hour later she arrived at her house. It was

west-facing, bathed in the lowering sun. Geraniums lined the windowsills in long narrow boxes, alternating with violets. Wisteria climbed over the walls, its thick gnarled branches rising to the upper floors. The flowers were just beginning to come out, and their scent hung in the air. Cassie paused to breathe it in, filling her lungs. Then she went in.

David Wilson jumped to his feet as she walked into the sitting room. "How are you, sweetie? You look happy. Had a good day?"

She sat down on the sofa and kicked off her shoes. "Mm, not bad. Had a lovely walk home, through the park. All the blossoms were out, and a rather interesting man caught my eye."

David laughed. "Interesting? That's what we say about ugly women we are forced to comment on. Interesting. Or nice."

"You are so politically incorrect it's unreal. It's a good thing you don't work in an office. You'd probably have a sexual harassment suit slapped on you."

"Think of the fun." He retrieved a whiskey bottle from the floor. "What's on tonight?"

Cassie glanced at him and then away. "Eva's coming around for dinner."

He took a swift swallow of whiskey and got to his feet. "Good. Well, I'll see you, then. I'm off to the pub." He picked up a creased jacket lying on the back of a chair, grabbed his keys from a table in the hall, and went out.

Cassie shook her head and lay back on the sofa. She closed her eyes and thought of Eva.

They had met eleven years ago at Oxford, at Magdalen. Cassie had been half sitting, half lying on the grass in front of the Fellows Buildings, head thrown back, enjoying the late-afternoon sun. Dazzled by the light, she saw a woman walking toward her, radiant like a Man Ray photograph. The woman paused to talk to a passing couple, then continued walking. As she drew near, Cassie could see her in more detail: a brown girl with long brown hair, not especially tall, graceful in body and movement, feline. She walked fast, confidently, with a long stride. She seemed to be concentrating on something. There was about her a wonderful independence, an immunity to the world around. She could have been anywhere.

As Cassie came into her line of focus, her eyes seemed to switch on suddenly. She approached, pausing on the grass before Cassie.

"You're new around here. A fresher."

Cassie nodded. Eva sat down on the grass beside her. "I'm Eva."

Cassie shook her outstretched hand. "Cassie."

"Ah. Cassandra. Daughter of the king of Troy, spurner of Apollo. The great prophesier, who is never believed." She smiled. "I read Greats," she offered. "Second year."

"So who would you be then, in the legends?"

"A siren. What else?" She paused, head on one side, scrutinizing Cassie. "You'd probably make a better one, though. You're one of the most sickeningly beautiful girls I have ever seen."

Cassie laughed, delighted. Eva's tone was one of pure appraisal, utterly disarming.

"I doubt that very much. But thank you. Anyway, I could say the same about you."

Eva shrugged.

"I don't know who I could lure onto the rocks," said Cassie. "I'll bet you have a hell of a lot more men chasing you than I do."

"Possibly. Your looks probably frighten them off. I look more human—they think I'm nice."

"And are you?"

Eva just smiled.

By the end of that week, the two girls had become friends. Cassie was drawn to Eva's strength and energy. There was a resilience to her. Cassie felt that nothing she could ever say or do would shock Eva, that she could be herself, be understood without fear of censure. At the same time, she knew—everyone knew—that you couldn't mess around with Eva. If you did, she would simply and quietly pass you by. It wasn't through coolness that she managed this, or insensitivity. She always seemed to Cassie deeply warm and compassionate. But she was difficult to know, to understand. What Cassie perceived most in Eva was a sense of self-preservation, stronger than in anyone else she had ever met.

Eva saw in Cassie a lightness of being. She was fun, and so extravagantly intelligent and beautiful that she never felt threatened by Eva, who seemed to many people to have an overabundance of gifts.

As the terms passed, Cassie would infrequently but regularly receive whispered warnings about Eva, suggesting that she might be a bit careful of her, that Eva did nothing without a reason, even make friends. Cassie always laughed. She had the openness, suppleness, and resilience of a falling cat. On impact she was relaxed, while the others, tense and prepared, shattered. Whether, like a cat, she was unharmed or not, she couldn't say. She didn't think she had been harmed, certainly not by Eva. That Eva had the capacity to harm was beyond doubt. Eva betrayed many lovers during their time together at Oxford. That, Cassie knew, Eva never saw as a crime. To her it was more an inevitability, an effect of the law of supply and demand: there was simply not enough of her to go around.

Cassie remembered again the university warnings and the comments of David Wilson, all urging her to be wary —as misplaced then, she thought, as now.

Two hours later, Eva arrived. Cassie opened the door, the two women kissed each other, and Cassie led Eva into the sitting room.

Eva followed slowly, taking in the details around her. She noted the feeling of warmth in the house. It was alive, glowing quietly. Paintings covered the walls: landscapes, portraits, dark drawings of faces, studies of horses, birds in flight, nudes, sculptures. There were many, but there was order in their variety, a quiet hand. The decoration was secondary to the paintings. It was warm, comfortable, naturally elegant, in tones of amber, yellow, and blue in the various rooms. There was none of the fashionable fuss or minimalism that characterized so many of her contemporaries' homes. In each of the rooms were beautiful rugs, old, Persian, silk and wool, in fine rich colors. Movement was everywhere, in eyes drawn from picture to picture, in the black cocker spaniel, Nesta, who ran after her mistress, in the lazy flick of two cats' tails as they lay in a patch of sunlight on the arm of the sofa. It felt like a home, not a craven sanctuary, but a place of strength.

Eva watched Cassie moving about, getting drinks, washing a salad, pausing, sitting down with a smile, and felt, to her surprise and discomfort, a pang of wistfulness for something she couldn't name. She took her drink— chilled white wine—and drank it away.

The two women sat opposite each other.

"Where's your housemate?" asked Eva.

"Pub. His favorite place."

"What else does he do, apart from go to the pub?"

"Scriptwriter." Cassie entwined her legs and leaned back.

"Done anything?"

"He's written plenty. If you mean has he had anything produced, the answer is not yet. It's a long haul, takes years. He's very good, though."

"How does he afford your rent?"

"He doesn't. He's a friend. It's nice having him here."

"Never were very good at living on your own, were you?"

"Unlike you, you mean. In the Far East. No, I never was. But why should I be? I prefer to live with someone, so I do."

"Lover?"

"Who, David?"

"Mm."

"No. What makes you ask that?"

"Nothing. Just thought he might have been once. He seemed jealous."

"Of you?"

"Well, yes. I did feel something."

"You're imagining it."

"You're just being polite. I don't think he liked me very much."

"Everybody likes you, Eva, you know that. And David likes everybody. He's too laid back to actively dislike anyone."

"Sounds a bit insubstantial."

"That's a mistake many people make."

Cassie got up to fiddle with the main course, pasta with lobster. Eva followed her into the kitchen, sat down on a high stool, and watched her.

"By the way, how was your dinner the other night with Robie Frazer?"

Cassie put down a spoon she was using to mix mayonnaise, turned around, and gave Eva a meaningful smile. "He's an interesting one, as you said—quite charming. Very bright, very sexy. Definitely someone to spend an afternoon in bed with."

Eva let out a shriek. "What? You haven't, have you?"

"No." Cassie burst out laughing. "No, I haven't. It's just an expression I've picked up. Men fall into two categories, those you could and those you could not spend an afternoon in bed with. It's quite amusing, dividing them up. Cuts across all other boundaries. The sad thing is, hardly any men in our set qualify. Oh, they all have some good quality or other. But how many of them are sexy? We might grow to find them attractive, if we fall in love with them, if they become dear to us, but how many of them are out-and-out sexy? It's a problem with British men of a certain class. They look bad, they're overweight, they dress like their grandfathers, but worse than that, they have no idea about sex. They've got absolutely no glint in their eye, no clue that they might actually enjoy it, let alone be good at it."

Cassie licked the mayonnaise spoon. "Mmm. Delicious. Try some." She spooned some into the astonished Eva's mouth.

Eva swallowed it happily, her eyes widening, nodding. "Good. Very good. But look. What on earth's got into you? You used to be so tolerant at Oxford, so accepting, thought British men were sweet." She grinned. "Who's been educating you?"

"I have. Anyway, do you disagree?"

"Good God, no. The men in 'our set,' as you put it, are totally unsexy. I'd forgotten quite how soporifically, paralytically unsexy they were until I came back here. There are one or two wonderful exceptions, of course . . . but as a rule."

"Mm. And Robie Frazer definitely breaks that rule."

"So, any plans?"

"No. He's a client." Cassie paused and took another spoonful of mayonnaise. "He might be all right for you, though."

"From what I hear of him, he's just a bit too smooth for my tastes."

"You should meet him. He's not smooth at all, under the surface. He tries to be, but jagged bits come through. Very easy to cut yourself on that one."

Eva gave a distant smile and fingered some more mayonnaise into her mouth. Cassie ladled the pasta onto plates.

"Come on. It's ready." They walked into the dining room, set the plates on the table, and began to eat hungrily. Eva told Cassie amazing stories about her travels around the Far East, the things she had seen, the people she had met. She always could spellbind with her stories. Her eyes and voice conveyed so much.

When they had finished, she put down her fork and glanced around. "I give you credit, Cassie. Wonderful food, beautiful house, garden, furniture, paintings, rugs. Everything."

Cassie shrugged. "The product of eight years in the City and a helpful housemate."

"It's a bit of a shock, coming back after eight years, finding a whole new London and seeing how everyone has moved on."

Cassie found it hard to imagine Eva shocked by anything.

"We haven't really moved that far. Just drifted with

the tide. It's easy. Lazy, almost. Not like what you've done."

Eva paused. "What I did was wonderful, but it didn't pay the bills."

"Any ideas?" asked Cassie lightly.

"Well, yes." Eva hesitated. "Rather outlandish. I've been carrying something around in my head for weeks now, didn't want to mention it to you. But if you're not the person to speak to, I don't know who is."

"Sounds intriguing," said Cassie.

"What would you say if I told you I'd found a diamond prospect in Vietnam?"

SEVEN

Cassie arrived at work on Monday morning in a state of excitement. Forgoing her quiet half-hour with her newspapers, she walked straight into John Richardson's office. He looked up in surprise.

"To what do I owe this early pleasure?"

"I think I might have something for Frazer, and for us."

"Tell me more."

"A diamond prospect in Vietnam."

Richardson laughed. "Don't do things by halves, do you?"

"Well, it makes sense. Vietnam is opening up. The Americans are pouring money in. There are good reserves of minerals and gemstones. The economy is growing fast, the whole region is booming. Frazer wants to diversify. I think diamonds would appeal to him. After all, they're sexy, aren't they? I can't imagine him getting very worked up over a widget manufacturer."

"Can't say I'd actually imagined him in the act of getting worked up about anything, but I concede your point. So where does it come from, this diamond project?"

"From a friend. And before you say anything, for that very reason I would like you to run this deal. I don't want a direct involvement. I realize I'm too close for that."

"What would you like me to do?"

"Meet her. Her name's Eva Cunningham. Then arrange to meet Frazer straight after. If you like what you hear, you can ask her to stay on. If not, she can go, and we can have a more general chat with Frazer."

"Glad to see you're not being sentimental. If she's good, she stays. Crap, she goes."

"And you decide."

"No. You decide. It's your deal, friend or not. We all do deals with friends. It's hardly novel in the City. And you know full well you're always a far harsher judge than I've ever been, especially lately. Which reminds me. What happened last week with the Tugwell deal? I heard you took one look at him and threw him and his business plan out. Everyone thought it looked so promising."

"It looked promising. He didn't. He was all hot air, nothing more, and a lot less, I suspect. I wouldn't want to bet what a private eye would get on him."

"What you mean is you would like to bet, and you'd be damn sure to get it right. I know all about your latest sport. That MacDonald character we saw three weeks ago —you reckoned he was a borderline alcoholic, had tried a little fraud in the past, and had a mistress who was bleeding him dry. And you were dead right. You've completely freaked out three of our investigators. The one who investigated MacDonald came to see me, thought you'd set up a rival service, were trying to intimidate him by showing yours was better. He refused to believe that it was a game, that you liked to sit in board meetings and imagine people's hidden peculiarities, and no matter what I said, he would not have it that just by imagining you could get it right. We pay him a bloody fortune, and you do it from sheer whimsy." Richardson jutted out his chin to make the point. "Perhaps for the sake of his professional ego, you might let him hand in his reports before you sit him down and tell him all his findings, before he's even had a chance to open his mouth. That other one, Owen Quaid —I know the two of you are as thick as thieves, but his ego's the size of the Nat West tower. He can take it, finds it a huge joke, no doubt tries to recruit you . . ."

Cassie choked off a laugh. Richardson watching her, puzzled. A distinct change had come over her in the last six months, a growing mischievousness. It showed in the twinkle of her eye, in the odd word, in a slightly more flamboyant style of dress, in the occasional unexplained absence from the office, and, most alarmingly and impressively, in this newly revealed perceptiveness. He was glad. With the mischievousness was a growing robustness. He had always feared that Cassie was as vulnerable emotionally as she appeared to be physically, with her fine, elongated frame, so lightly constructed, so fragile. But now there were signs of something struggling to the surface, a kind of cockiness long suppressed, now gloried in, almost.

"You know that if we do proceed, we'll have to get an investigator onto your friend Eva. Quaid, probably."

Cassie nodded but said nothing.

"So what would you predict for her, then?"

Cassie leaned back and stared up at the whiteness of the ceiling before answering. "I'm not sure. I get the feeling there's a very carefully constructed wall there. And it's tricky with her being a friend. You drop your critical faculties. Oddities become familiar, warning signs appear to be harmless idiosyncrasies. I'll pretend tomorrow that it's the first time we've met. The boardroom's always a good place, nice and quiet, nothing to distract me. Perhaps I'll pick up something new. After all, I don't want to disappoint Owen."

Richardson gazed at her in exasperation as she walked from his office. Nice and quiet, nothing to distract her in the boardroom . . . No. Nothing other than a few multimillion-pound investments.

He shouted at her disappearing back, "Call your friend and have her come in at ten tomorrow. I'll get Frazer in for eleven-thirty."

Cassie raised her hand in assent, walked to her office, and picked up the telephone. Eva answered after three rings.

"Eva, Cassie. Can you come in tomorrow, at ten? Good. Leave the whole morning free." She gave Case Reed's address and hung up before Eva could ask her any questions. She wasn't going to brief her. If anyone could look after herself, it was Eva.

Eva put down the telephone with a frown and the feeling that she had been dismissed. She shrugged. She'd call Cassie at home later and find out about the meeting. She rang Stormont.

"Cassie just rang. She set up a meeting for tomorrow. I'll need a clothes allowance. I'd better look the part."

"Fine. I'll arrange it. I'll give it to you later. There are a couple of things I want to go over. Shop in the meantime. Just don't go too mad, or it'll be on my head."

"Mm. That just makes it all the more fun."

"Come to the safe house around nine," said Stormont. There was no need to see her. He could have the money couriered to her. But he wanted to see her. It was, he told himself, to watch her, to check.

Eva rang Cassie at half past eight that evening. "Cassie, it's Eva."

"Eva, sweetie, how are you?"

"Fine. I was just calling to—"

"Oh, Eva, the doorbell's just gone. Look, I'm really sorry, I can't talk. We'll catch up tomorrow, at the meeting. See you then."

"Fucking hell." Eva slammed down the telephone, half angry, half amused. If she hadn't known Cassie better, she would have thought her friend was stalling her deliberately, but the image of harebrainedness, of Cassie running madly from live telephone to impatient doorstep, kept any suspicion of disingenuousness at bay.

Eva thought about her impending meeting with Stormont. She lit up a cigarette and smoked it down to the butt, got up, brushed her hair, put on lipstick, dabbed scent on her wrists. Just as she was leaving, the telephone rang. It was Stormont.

"Eva, I have a bit of a problem. Something's come up. I can't get to the safe house by nine."

Eva paused, shutting off a quick disappointment before it came within range of acknowledgment.

"I could always come to you."

Stormont paused. "Here? To my house?"

"Look, it's only once. I know it breaks the rules, agents and controllers meeting at home, but I'll be quick, and nobody'll be following me."

"Oh, fuck it. Come on round." In his keenness to see her, he carelessly broke the rule.

EIGHT

Cassie sat watching television, distracted, then abruptly jumped to her feet.

"Where are you off to?" asked David.

"See Eva. I was a bit unkind. She wanted some advice on this meeting tomorrow, and I cut her off." She shrugged. "Misplaced sense of professional rigor—you know, not supposed to help her, give her an unfair advantage. Anyway, claptrap." She reached for her jacket.

"If anyone can look after herself, that girl can. I wouldn't be in too much of a hurry to go and help her out."

Cassie ignored him and walked into the hall, followed by Nesta. She smiled down at the dog and ruffled her glossy black hair. "Out? Do you want to go *out?*" Nesta jumped and yowled at the magic word, dancing around impatiently as Cassie put on shoes and stuffed some money in her pocket. She picked up her keys from the hall table and walked out with Nesta scampering around her heels.

It was a quarter to nine; the light had faded, the birds were huffing and muttering and settling down for the night. People were on their way to and from the pub or home for dinner, walking the dog, having a quiet cigarette outside in the evening warmth. There was an air of gentle purpose. Cassie walked quickly. She smiled at a few people who caught her eye as she walked up the King's Road. After she had gone about a quarter of a mile, she stopped abruptly. She had seen Eva, or someone who looked very like her, turning off the King's Road onto the north side of Old Church Street.

Unsure that it was Eva, as distance and passersby obscured her vision, Cassie walked fast, trying to catch up. She turned into Old Church Street just in time to see the woman stop in front of a tall white house. It was Eva, Cassie was sure of it. She approached and shouted her name just as the door swung open and Eva prepared to step inside. Eva paused and turned. A man looked around the door frame. Eva appeared to frown for just a split second and say something under her breath to the man before she turned back to Cassie and smiled.

"Cassie. What on earth are you doing here? I thought you were entertaining."

Cassie walked up to the house. "No. It was one of David's friends who called. I came looking for you, actually. I was going to tell you about the meeting tomorrow." She turned to the man, who stood silently watching her.

He reached forward to shake Cassie's hand. "I'm Andrew Stormont."

"Cassie Stewart."

Eva leaned against the door frame, languidly, as if bored. Stormont released Cassie's hand, keeping his eyes on hers. She looked back directly, then turned to Eva, waiting for her to say something. Eva stood impassively watching Stormont. Stormont looked down at Nesta, who was sitting obediently at Cassie's heels.

"Nice dog." He ruffled Nesta's hair and she gazed up at him.

"That was an easy conquest," said Cassie.

Stormont's eyes, appraising, switched to her. "Eva was just coming round for a drink. Perhaps you'd like one too. Then you can tell her about this meeting, whatever it is."

"I really don't want to disturb you," said Cassie.

"You're not remotely," said Stormont. He gestured to her to come in. She walked into the hall. Eva followed and closed the door behind her.

"It sounds frightfully important, to come tearing out after someone," Stormont said.

"Yes, frightfully important." Cassie raised her chin and looked at him in open scrutiny. He looked back, saying nothing, before turning, moving on, leading them into his drawing room. He sat down in an old leather chair, gesturing to the two of them to take a seat. Eva sprawled on a sofa. Cassie sat upright in a cloth-covered tub chair. Nesta curled up at her feet.

"What would you like?" asked Stormont.

"Whiskey, no ice. I'll add my own water."

"Eva?"

"I'll have the same. With my usual quota of water."

Cassie resisted a smile. The easy familiarity, the "usual quota," both pointed self-consciously to a long history. And she had to admit, this Andrew Stormont was someone with whom you could spend the afternoon in bed. Very easily. He was good-looking, aware of his attractiveness, and had a quiet sexual confidence all the more powerful for its subtlety. His eyes were knowing, mocking, slightly challenging, as if he wished to be surprised, found the prospect unlikely, but might just give you a try anyway. And he would have, thought Cassie— tried too many women. He wore that sated look of faint self-disgust, cast outward, tinging everything on which it settled with a faint disdain. Only Nesta was absolved. Only when his eyes smiled down at her was there uncontaminated warmth in them. Oh yes, he would be wonderful at sex, just emotionally sterile.

She glanced at Eva, who was watching her with an odd expression in her eyes. They were perfectly matched, Stormont and Eva, thought Cassie, with their glamour, their hardness, their apparent languor, which covered an un-English zeal in Eva's case, what in Stormont's? Was there concealment, or was he just as he appeared to be— rich, spoiled, callous? She drank her whiskey and turned to Eva, who had decided to speak.

"The meeting. You were going to tell me about the meeting."

"It can keep. There's nothing much to say, really." She got to her feet. Nesta jumped up after her. "I'm sure you've got a lot to catch up on after all your years away." She began to walk toward the door.

Eva stood up. "There must have been something, to come all this way."

"Not really. It's not far. And it's good for Nesta. All I really had to say was to keep lunch free." She turned to Stormont. "Thanks for the whiskey." He nodded and got to his feet. Cassie and Eva kissed goodbye. "See you to-morrow, then," said Cassie, walking out.

Eva nodded and sat down again. Stormont followed Cassie to the door. She paused, allowing him to reach past her to open the door. His hand brushed her arm. She was conscious of the enclosed space. She looked up at him as she moved past and out the door. They shook hands, said goodbye. Cassie turned and walked away, feeling the imprint still of his fingers wrapped around hers.

"Fucking hell. How did that happen?"

Eva was on her feet, pouring another whiskey, when Stormont walked back into the room.

"Did you check for tails?"

"Of course I checked."

"Unsuccessfully. If I remember from our reports, Cassie Stewart's house is about a quarter of a mile down the King's Road from here. So naturally, if she were going to see you, she would have walked from her house up the King's Road, and she could easily have seen you turning off the King's Road to come here."

"I did a circuit—there was no one on me. Cassie must have just caught sight of me when I turned off into Old Church Street the second time. I didn't check again." She spoke with cold practicality. "What do we do?"

Stormont said nothing for a while.

"You have your cover. I have mine. Our families know each other. It wouldn't be unreasonable for us to know each other, to meet." Stormont paused as the outlines of an idea formed in his mind. He covered it up. "What we do is not meet again, not outside a safe house. And you take more care about being followed. Perhaps you're a bit rusty."

"I was complacent. I'll admit that much. I won't be again."

He took a sip of whiskey, saying nothing.

"Why did she come after me?" said Eva, breaking the silence. "It's a bit strange, to come looking for me, then to have nothing to say other than to keep lunch free."

"If she did have anything to say about your meeting, she'd hardly tell you in front of me—not if it were in the slightest way interesting, not if she's the professional she's supposed to be. And the atmosphere in here was like a snakepit. No wonder she chose to skedaddle as soon as she decently could."

"Oh, for goodness' sake, Stormont. I was rattled. She'd just cut me dead on the telephone for the second time today, then she turns up here. What do you expect?"

"Not petty jealousy."

"Don't flatter yourself. I've seen you look at a hundred girls that way. I'm bored with being a spectator at your seductions."

"I think it would take a bit more than a look across a room to seduce your friend."

"Don't go getting a madonna complex. She likes sex just as much as the rest of us."

Stormont got up and went over to the drinks table. He refilled his whiskey and walked slowly back to his chair.

"How did she get on with Frazer?"

"She said he was the kind of man she could spend the afternoon in bed with."

Stormont laughed. "And did she?"

"She says not. Says she has no plans to. He's a client. Off limits."

Stormont nearly added, "Just as well" but thought better of it, watching Eva, still coiled in her chair. No point in fueling any sense of competition she might already feel.

"So everything's on schedule?"

"Ahead, if anything, thanks to Cassie's and Frazer's meeting. You set that up very smoothly."

"A few words in a few ears. Couldn't have been easier."

"The old-boy network swings into action."

"It has its uses."

"Never said it didn't."

"But you disdain it, don't you?"

"I find it amusing."

"Your family members are as much beneficiaries as anybody else's."

"That's their business."

"You rise loftily above it."

"Well, in case you didn't notice, it doesn't quite exist for women."

"What about you and Cassie and her financing your deal, if she does so?"

"That will be done on commercial merit."

"Perhaps. But there's something else too, isn't there, between women in a position to help each other? A child's generosity on being let into the toy store."

"Don't bet on it."

"What is it with you and Cassie? You're supposed to be friends, but there's something between you. Some kind of edge."

"Wake up, Stormont. We're close. There's always something between close friends. Everything would be much smoother if we were just acquaintances."

"As long as it doesn't become a problem."

"It won't."

Stormont took an envelope out of his jacket pocket and gave it to Eva. "Your clothes allowance—two thousand pounds."

She got to her feet. He kissed her cheek.

"Knock 'em dead, Eva."

"Yeah, knock 'em dead. Like I always do."

Stormont paused, puzzled by the tone in her voice. "Anything up?"

"It would have been easier, wouldn't it, to have been an actress? And sometimes I think just as gratifying."

"Don't forget what this is all about."

"As if I could." She shrugged, breaking the tension. "I'm just not much good at delayed gratification, that's all."

"No one who lived in the Southeast Asian bush on her own for eight years is much of an instant-gratification nut."

"No. But it's different when I'm there."

"And you want to go back."

"Yes. I want to go back."

Stormont watched the face before him, so strong and defiant five minutes before, now open, yearning. He stroked her cheek. She jerked her head away.

"Cut it out, Andrew. However much you like to pretend, I haven't forgotten. You're my controller, not my comforter." She looked at him for a moment, head high, muscles stiff, then turned in silence and walked out.

Stormont stood motionless in the center of the room, where she had left him, looking into space, seeing her face still.

NINE

E va woke to the sound of her alarm clock at eight-thirty. She turned it off and lay back for a few moments. She glanced around her at the white walls, bare of paintings, then looked out the window into the sunshine. The glass was framed with fronds of ivy on tough stalks which blew sometimes in the night, tapping at her window like fingers pleading for entry. Now they just waved gently in the morning breeze.

She watched them swaying, letting her mind drift. In that slow, waking time her mind could wander, unguarded. It took her back to a crumbling house in Saigon where the sun poured in and at eight in the morning the bare tiles were already hot underfoot. The smell of dust baking in the sun reached her through the open windows, mingling with the rich tang of the first morning brew of strong French coffee. Outside, a quarter of a mile away, in the maze of long, dusty, tree-lined boulevards, the beeping, squawking, and hooting from the cavalcade of cyclos, bicycles, cars, and motorbikes had reached battle pitch. The notes reached her diminished, filtered by dust and distance, coming to her like echoes.

Here in London it was quiet, cool, almost antiseptic. Nothing from the streets touched or claimed her. It had been harder to reorient herself to the city than she had imagined. Her house in London held her like a complacent cocoon, unreal, falsely protective. Sometimes she felt it would be easy just to roll over when the alarm went, bury herself in the eiderdown, never move.

She got out of bed, forced herself awake, focused her mind to move into the groove of the day, of London outside, of work.

She pulled a long T-shirt over her naked body and walked downstairs into the sitting room. She switched on her CD player and put on a recording of Maria Callas singing *Tosca,* then turned the volume up high. She let the voice flow through her, gripping her throat, clenching her stomach. The strength, the ecstasy of lamentation in that voice. It captured her, transporting her. She listened motionless for a few minutes. Then she went to the kitchen, filled the espresso pot, and put it on the stove. Waiting for it to brew, she sat down at the kitchen table and lit up a full-strength Marlboro. She took a few puffs, then rested it on the ashtray. Slowly she rubbed her arms, tracing her palms over the brown skin, feeling the bones and muscles taut beneath. She ran her hands over her chest, down her stomach, onto her thighs. She glanced down at her skin, tracing faint indentations, fading scars.

The integrity of her body had been breached so many times, yet it was intact still, imperfect but strong. She stubbed out her cigarette, got to her feet, put the coffee on low, and returned to the living room. With the music filling her head, she performed thirty minutes of rigorous exercises. Sweating lightly, she returned to the kitchen, drank a glass of tap water, poured a cup of espresso, drank it back, and headed for the shower.

She dressed in one of her new outfits, bought on yesterday's shopping trip: a black pleated skirt cut just above the knee, a pale blue cotton shirt, and a fitted black jacket. She put on sheer stockings and black leather shoes with a strap across the ankle and medium high heels. Finally she took her mother's diamond earring studs from their hiding place in her bookcase. They lay twinkling in her palm for a moment before she put them in. They looked to her like the gleam in sparkling eyes. She paused before the mirror, looking at the diamonds, her mind cast back, seeing the studs in her mother's ears. She turned away.

A few minutes later she walked onto the King's Road, swinging her arms, enjoying the warmth of the sun on her face. She caught the number 22 bus, got off at Piccadilly, and walked up Regent Street, glancing at shop windows and passing faces, watching their urgency, their preoccupation as they hurried to work.

Nobody looked or noticed or really saw anything at that time in the morning. All the faces were closed up, all but their superficial vision turned inward. For Eva it was the reverse. She emptied her mind, focused outward, on everything around her. She wanted to carry no baggage into her meeting at Case Reed. She would be a blank, until by instinct and intuition she read what they were looking for, sensed what they would respond to. It was better that Cassie, for all her improbable mission of the night before, had not briefed her about the meeting. She wanted no preconceptions. Information was useful, but very often bore the prejudices of others.

Eva arrived at Case Reed at five to ten. She pressed the intercom and announced herself. A tinny voice instructed her to come in. The door buzzed; she pushed it open and walked into a small reception area hung with paintings and dotted with small abstract sculptures. She walked up to the receptionist.

"Eva Cunningham. I'm here to see Cassie Stewart."

"Please take a seat."

Eva sat on a low, squashy sofa, the kind that holds you prisoner. She perched on the edge, picked up a copy of the *Financial Times,* and flicked through it.

Upstairs, Cassie sat in her office with John Richardson. "Frazer's coming in at eleven-thirty?"

Richardson nodded. "He is. And he said something in passing about lunch. For a busy man, he seems to have a great deal of time for you."

"For Case Reed, you mean. And besides, he's not busy. He might have a lot of things going on, but he's the mastermind type, sits quietly in one of his no doubt beautiful houses, whiskey in hand, dreaming up brilliant schemes. He'll have minions to do the running, the dirty work. He won't be one of these blue-assed-fly types."

Richardson burst out laughing and shook his head. "Colorfully put. And yes, you're right, of course."

Emma, Cassie's secretary, appeared in the door. "Eva Cunningham's downstairs."

"I'll be down in a minute," said Cassie. She turned back to Richardson. "By the way, I saw her briefly last night. I invited her to lunch."

"That's a vote of confidence."

"Yes and no. I sort of had to, really. But anyway, I'm sure she'll have something interesting to say for herself. She always does."

"And? Lots of people talk well."

Cassie paused. "She's never had to deliver, professionally. She was bright at Oxford, very bright. Didn't study very hard, or at least appeared not to, but always did very well academically. Since then she hasn't really tried for anything. Not in the conventional, measurable sense. Living on your own in Vietnam, Laos, and Cambodia for eight years takes a hell of a lot of something, but this is the first time she's tried something professional, as far as I know. So I'm as curious as you are. This is a side to her I don't know. All I do know is that there is a power to her, a force of will. At Oxford she used to cover it up, play the party girl, but there was still such quiet determination, a sort of anger beneath the surface."

"Is that your professional opinion? Is Owen Quaid redundant?"

"God, no. On both counts. I don't begin to know where to start with Eva. I'd be surprised if even Owen came up with anything beyond the superficial. I doubt if anyone really knows what moves her, what goes on beneath the surface." She glanced at her watch. "I'd better go down."

She walked from her office, across the span of floor, and down the stairs. She almost faltered as she saw Eva stand to greet her. Eva was wearing tailored clothes, makeup, jewelry—the kind of things Cassie wore herself. She looked stylish, immaculate. Cassie had never seen her dressed like this, never known how easily she could slip from jeans and T-shirt into this sleek elegance, which she somehow regarded as her own. She thought of the night before, of Eva in jeans, casual. She recalled the intimacy she had sensed between Eva and Stormont and felt a quick flash of envy as she pictured Eva in his arms. Then she walked forward and kissed her friend on both cheeks.

"Eva, hi. You found us all right, then." She made no acknowledgment of Eva's transformation, as if she took it for granted.

Eva gave the shadow of a smile. "Mm, fine."

Cassie started walking toward the staircase at the back of the room, talking over her shoulder as she went. "You'll be meeting John Richardson. He's one of the founders of Case Reed. Some of the other partners may or may not join us."

Eva shrugged. "Whatever." Cassie was friendly but reserved, slightly detached, professional. Fine. That made it easier.

She followed Cassie across a small hallway on the second floor and into a bright, sunny conference room overlooking Savile Row. Cassie sat down at a long, gleaming board table, and Eva took a seat opposite her. Emma appeared at the door.

"Would you like coffee, tea, mineral water?"

"Coffee, please," said Eva.

Emma disappeared. A tall, well-built man in his early fifties, friendly but imposing, walked into the room. Cassie stood up.

"John Richardson, Eva Cunningham."

They shook hands. Cassie resumed her seat. Richardson sat next to her, facing Eva.

"You were at Oxford with Cassie."

"Yes. A year ahead. But I read Greats, so we overlapped for three years."

"Good choice, Greats," said Richardson emphatically. "Better than Russian. An odd choice—ideologically unsound." He smiled at Cassie, playing the much-repeated banter.

Eva said little, weighing him up: the amiable buffoon, well acted, quite convincing. Minimal ego for a banker. Many successful businessmen played the fool, to lull their opponents into a false sense of security. Most of them played it badly, because they could not resist producing what they thought of as odd flashes of brilliance or wit, could not accept that anyone might actually take them for the fool they tried to play. One or two of the very best could suspend ego, might even dismiss it altogether, but they were generally men in their sixties or seventies whose achievements belied their image. It was a ploy that rarely worked, and it didn't work now.

Eva was bored by the act, but it was useful in its predictability—Richardson was merely donning his usual business facade for her, which was exactly what she wanted. She would rather have dispensed with the small talk, which would ensue for five or ten minutes, and get straight down to business. That would be deemed laudable in an American institution, but with British financiers it would be seen as indecent haste, excessive ambition, an ignorance of how to play the game, so she smiled and chatted.

Richardson would be suspicious of flashy brilliance. It was obvious from the occasional glances that he cast Cassie's way, from the way he listened when she spoke, from his general stance, that he worshiped her and her radiant intellect.

"Eva, Cassie tells me that you have a most interesting idea. Perhaps you could tell me about it. I don't know how much Cassie knows, but assume I know nothing— about your proposal, about the business, the country, everything."

"Well, I'm sure you know rather more about Vietnam and diamonds than you're letting on, so forgive me if I go over what's obvious to you, but it helps me to go through it stage by stage." Eva spoke quietly, fluent and confident. He listened attentively, lapping it up.

"I've spent eight years in and around the Far East, not really doing very much—traveling, enjoying the countryside, teaching English—and I got to know quite a few different people. I've been living in Vietnam for the past two years, in Halong Bay and in Saigon and Hanoi. I go to the cities when I feel like a bit of urban noise and grime and company.

"Occasionally I go and have a drink or two in the Metropole Hotel in Hanoi. It's like an embassy compound—clean, spruced up, air-conditioned. It's a bit of a refuge, really, when you need some quiet and comfort and a well-mixed cocktail. Since the Americans lifted the embargo there has been something of a gold rush there, full of Europeans, Australians, and North Americans, almost all on business. Anyway, one evening I got chatting to an American geologist. He had worked for fifteen years around the world as a diamond prospector for one of the multinationals. Had a bit of a drinking problem—got abusive, I understand—and finally got himself fired. For a long time he was really down on his luck, but he was convinced there were diamonds in Vietnam, so he went looking for them.

"To give you some background, there are two sources of diamonds, alluvial and kimberlitic. Both were created by an explosive force which sent diamond-bearing kimberlite shooting up through the earth. This kimberlite rose to a level approximately one hundred and fifty to two hundred meters below the surface at the time of the original explosion, which happened hundreds of millions of years ago. Since then, several different things can have happened. The covering layer can be eroded by the elements, exposing the diamonds to air. Then the diamonds are carried by rain and streams, sometimes hundreds of miles from their original site, very often ending up at the coast. This is what happened in Namibia, for example. I've seen films of diamond miners with hand brushes, sweeping the earth for diamonds. They literally pick them off the ground. These are called alluvial diamonds.

"Then there are the kimberlites. Kimberlitic diamonds are mined from underground. The kimberlite that brought them to around two hundred meters below the surface at the time of the original explosion is uneroded. It might have been protected by the sea. Some of the uppermost geophysical layer will have eroded, but people still need to sink mines to get at the diamond-bearing kimberlite. This comes in what is known as a diamond pipe, a carrotlike structure, wider at the top. These mines can be hundreds of meters deep and as wide as half a mile across. Some of them are huge, some small. The best ones can produce hundreds of millions of pounds' worth of diamonds a year."

Eva smiled. "About eighty miles northeast of Hanoi, ten miles from the Chinese border, near a place called Lang-son, McAdam found what could well be a spectacular diamond pipe."

"How did he find it?" asked Richardson, leaning forward.

"It helps if you know what to look for. Granger went looking for indicator minerals. Their presence on the surface can indicate that diamonds might be present below. At Lang-son, McAdam found indicators: red kimberlitic garnets and green crystals of chrome diopside. So he went to the Vietnamese government, did a deal, and staked the land. Then he used all the money he had to have some independent tests done in a laboratory in Australia. The results were promising—the rocks showed a high concentration of indicator minerals, strongly suggesting the presence of diamonds. Granger needed a lot more money then, to do some core sampling. That involves drilling at a forty-five-degree angle hundreds of feet below the surface. So he formed a company, injected the land he had staked into it, and floated it on the Vancouver Stock Exchange. He raised a few million Canadian dollars, put together a basic drilling station, and did some core tests. They too came back positive. That's where we are now. The next stage is bulk sampling to determine whether diamonds are there in sufficient quantity and grade to make sinking a mine economically viable. We need to raise money so that we can take out one, and possibly two, five-thousand-ton samples of earth and rock to find out just how many diamonds there are."

Eva paused, her eyes distant as she lost herself in her story. Still she noted every nuance of expression in Cassie and Richardson. They had started with polite, formal, bankerly interest, deepened just slightly because she was a woman, beautiful, and connected to their world. Now they were openly fascinated. She continued.

"That was a month ago. Granger was all ready to go back to Vancouver and raise all the money he needed for the bulk sampling. I was going to help him." Eva shrugged. "There was something about him and his story —an earnestness, a sort of pure faith. Perhaps they're all like this, prospectors. I don't know. But I believed him. And I was intrigued by his story. There's a certain romance to diamonds, a fascination they have for people. Even rough diamonds, stones in the palm of your hand, uncut, are so incredibly beautiful. And their whole history and mystique—as talismans imparting good and evil, as the hardest substance known to man, hundreds of millions of years old, as the products of explosions—all that just fascinated me. So I arranged to meet Granger the next evening to talk about going to Vancouver with him. But he didn't show up."

Eva paused. Cassie and Richardson felt her sudden disquiet.

"I went looking for him at the Metropole. Someone there told me he'd been arrested. He was in jail. I went to see him. He'd been really badly beaten up. He was locked up in a filthy cell. He'd had a car accident, drunk driving. Knocked over a Vietnamese, killed him. He was really up shit creek, facing twenty years. The Vietnamese dish out hefty sentences, especially for foreigners, unless of course they have another way of atoning—money. Granger needed fifty thousand dollars. He had nothing, apart from a holding of twenty-five percent in the diamond project. I agreed to give him the money for a ten percent share in his project."

"That was a bargain," said Richardson.

"Bargain? I don't know about that. The tests look good, but we won't know until we've done the bulk sampling whether or not there are diamonds there in economically mineable amounts. Then we have to sink a mine. That could take years. It might turn out to be a bargain, but that isn't why I did it. Fifty thousand was all the money I had. It was a total punt on my part. That and a bit of sympathy too.

"I don't know if you've ever seen the inside of a jail, any jail, let alone a Vietnamese jail." Eva paused for a second, dredging up memories that had nothing to do with Granger McAdam. She let them burn into her. "It's pretty tough being in prison there, especially as a foreigner. Granger looked totally broken. I thought he was going to kill himself. He wasn't melodramatic or anything like that—just frightened, and all the life and hope seemed to have gone out of him. So I paid fifty thousand dollars to the victim's family and the police, and Granger was freed." Eva's voice became more businesslike. "Now we need to raise money. We can either do a rights issue in Vancouver or look for someone friendly to bid for the entire company and then pump some capital into it."

Richardson spoke first. "I must have heard thousands of business proposals in my life, but never have I heard anything like that."

Eva smiled. "I know it's odd. I couldn't decide what to do with it. It all sounds so outlandish . . . And I know you're not supposed to mix business with sentiment. This one has them all wrapped up together. And I have to confess, I don't feel coldly businesslike about all this. There is nothing in the world I would rather do than go back to Vietnam, build up this project, live there, and watch the diamonds come out." She allowed her mind to wander again. "It's so beautiful there—you have no idea. No crowds, just lush jungles, mountains, red earth, and the sea, birds and snakes and rivers and the fishermen and a few little villages dotted around. Oxen, carts, the odd motorbike. No newspapers, no outside world. You feel so alive. You can't do anything but live for the day, enjoy it and your own resources, because apart from nature and a few people, there's nothing there in the way of entertainment, no theaters, shops, or books. Not in the countryside. In Saigon and Hanoi, yes, but when you're in the country they feel a million miles away. It's hard to imagine they even exist. So yes, I have a great interest in doing this deal, in raising financing, for my own sake, for Granger—it's his lifetime dream—and for the excitement of it. I think it will work, and it's also time for me to do something with myself, something tangible." She paused. "I know this isn't very professional, presenting it all like this. I'm sorry. But I don't know any other way, and it's better that I don't try to kid you that I do."

"Quite all right. Understandable. Amazing story,"

said Richardson. "But listen, I have to ask you a few boring questions. This company is listed on the Vancouver exchange, correct?"

"Correct," said Eva with a sharp look of acknowledgment. "I know Vancouver has all sorts of dodgy companies on the exchange—cowboys, fly-by-nights—but Granger is not a cowboy. He looks like one, but he isn't."

"Granger gave you ten percent of the company to bail him out?"

"Yes."

"Was that straightforward, a transfer of ownership like that?"

"Not entirely. We didn't notify the exchange in a timely fashion. When what they deem a 'material change' in the company's affairs takes place, you generally have to notify them in advance. We didn't. But when we explained the circumstances, they understood, let it go through."

"What's the company called?" asked Cassie.

"Genius," said Eva, with a hint of embarrassment.

Cassie laughed. "And if McAdam is such a genius, why do you need us? Why not just raise the money on the Vancouver exchange?"

"Let's get this straight. McAdam is brilliant. He found a diamond prospect in a largely uncharted country, where until recently no diamonds have been found. His record as a prospector with De Beers was first-rate. I believe in him. I gave him all my money. Granger's problem"—she eyed the others, as if daring them to plead immunity from problems of their own—"is alcohol. What happened in Vietnam, killing the pedestrian, being beaten up and held in prison, really took a toll. The Vancouver exchange is a bit dubious now about his continuing as chairman, and I'm not even sure he can. He's lost

his nerve. He desperately needs someone else to take over
the reins. I'm a director, we have a good company secretary and accountant, but it's not enough. That's why I
came to you. The best thing for Genius, for Granger and
me, is for someone to take over the company, take it
private, spend the money, invest some energy, and do the
bulk sampling. If that goes well we can sell out, or take on
a joint-venture partner, sink a mine, and reap the pro-
ceeds. That's what I'm offering you. And no, it's not nice
and clean and straightforward. It's high risk. But the diamond business is also very high return. If it works out, we
could all make a fortune."

There was a silence as Richardson and Cassie, on one
side of the table, contemplated Eva, on the other.

"What's the stock price now?" asked Cassie. "What's
the trend?"

"It hasn't done a great deal. It started off at one dollar, went to five, back to three, then to four. But if we do
find diamonds when we start drilling, it could go to ten
dollars, twenty, thirty, who knows."

"That's what Granger thinks, is it?" asked Richardson.

"He and I think it, and some of the brokers in Vancouver."

Richardson looked amused. "I don't put a great deal
of faith in what Vancouver brokers say. They play the
most ingenious games with their stocks. It's an Olympic
sport over there."

"So I hear," replied Eva evenly. She spread her
hands, palms up in the air. "Like I say, it's a risky deal."

A brief look passed between Cassie and Richardson.
Time to lay off, for now.

"It's quite a project," said Richardson. "Could be

promising." He glanced again at Cassie, who gave an almost imperceptible nod.

"Eva, we have someone coming in shortly. I'd like you to meet him. He could be very interested in your project. His name is Robie Frazer."

Eva covered her excitement. "Robie Frazer." She glanced at Cassie. "The great Tai Pan."

"The very same," said Richardson. "He's looking to finance just this kind of thing. Can you bear to explain this all over again?"

"Of course. I could talk about this forever."

Richardson got to his feet. "I'll leave you for a few minutes."

Cassie got up and sat down on the table next to Eva. "That was one of the most incredible stories I've ever heard. I've never come across such an exciting deal in my life."

"Neither have I."

Cassie lapsed into silence, remembering late nights at the house in North Oxford, sitting with Eva and a bottle of whiskey, Eva holding the room spellbound with her stories. No one ever knew whether they were true or not, but it never mattered. Stories of weakness and compassion, told with fire, they touched everyone. And now this new one. But the geologists' reports, the cold, hard facts, would speak too. As for the rest of it, deals lived or died on passion, faith, and commitment. Those qualities were as valuable as any geological survey. There would be a million and one hurdles to the financing of a diamond mine in the Socialist Republic of Vietnam, and sheer, unrelenting force of will would be required to surmount them. And there was nothing for a share price like commitment and belief. Those few who could communicate their vision and passion, when backed up by a semblance of hard facts, were invaluable. Whether Eva knew it or not, she herself was a gold mine. With the sober backing of Case Reed and the entrepreneurial flair of Robie Frazer, she would be unassailable.

TEN

Robie Frazer walked from his house in Knights-bridge to his meeting at Case Reed. It was a sunny day, but cool, palatable, gentle and civilized. In Hong Kong, in the raging heat of summer, you never walked anywhere. Frazer loved the unyielding heat, the ferocity. It summed up Hong Kong to him, as the temperate weather did London. Things were easy here, the elements friendly. He expected no big surprises, no onslaught. As he walked through the leafy quiet of Green Park, his face was relaxed in comfortable complacency.

He thought of Case Reed and Cassie Stewart. An interesting woman. He didn't really expect her to have anything much for him. The British banks and venture-capital houses were too tame, too well mannered. His business appetites had been fed for many years on the richer fare of mainland China. But to his surprise, a line told to him years earlier by one of the most senior bankers in the City came back to him: "If they did on Brighton racetrack what they do every day in the City, they'd rip your face off."

Frazer turned into Savile Row and rang the bell at

Case Reed. John Richardson, friendly, urbane, polished, met him and took him to the meeting room. On the way they talked of the weather, of Green Park, of their well-being—a smooth performance, a perfected ritual. How many times had Frazer, the entrepreneur, the risk-taker, the money-generator, been paraded softly through marble banking halls? That's what they were looking for, a modern-day Midas. They would lay the options before him; he would choose—a takeover, a new venture, whatever it was—and enrich them all. That was the reality. They needed him; the balance of power lay with him. But as he walked pinstripe to pinstripe with John Richardson, they appeared to be equals, and Frazer was content to play the game. Unmasked talent, ambition, superiority, all worn with glee in China, were repugnant here. It bored him slightly, this bland facade, but here in England, in the company of well-fed and understretched bankers, dispensing with it would be foolhardy, so he smiled pleasantly, on autopilot. And then he walked into the meeting.

The first thing he saw was a woman standing with her back to him. She was still, staring out the window. She stood like an athlete, poised to run but perfectly relaxed, contained within herself yet confident of flight. She turned slowly, unselfconsciously, all the while aware of the scrutiny she had deliberately provoked. She looked at him for a second without expression, and he had the sensation of being expertly weighed up. Then she smiled, almost with satisfaction, as if her expectations had been proved correct.

Frazer rarely made a conscious effort to analyze those around him, so familiar and bored was he with the bulk of humanity. So he was surprised now at the chain of thoughts running through his mind. Scrutiny was his preserve, yet here she was, this woman, cool and bold, re-

garding him with a faintly amused, contemptuous eye.
When she finally came forward to be introduced to him,
there was none of the glow that most women bestowed
on him, none of the warmth, none of the professional
recognition, the subliminal rolling over, the recognition
of his superior status. And when she sat down and began
to speak, she was so levelly professional, her voice and
words were so well modulated and chosen, that he almost
forgot how overwhelmingly attractive she was. It was as if
she had allowed him one glimpse of herself, right at the
beginning of the meeting, only to shut off her appeal very
deliberately with facts, figures, projections, and summa-
ries. What she said was simple and irresistible.

She sat across the table from him. She spoke with the
cool rationality of a banker.

Cassie watched her. She had forgotten Eva's beauty.
At Oxford she had seen it, a fierce natural beauty. It had
dimmed slightly since, and its rawness fitted less well in
Cassie's world of aerobics, tailored suits, and make up.
Eva's lack of artifice seemed almost undeserved amid this
purchased beauty. But dressed up here, it competed on
equal terms. Cassie had seen the way Eva looked at Frazer, had seen how she lit up her beauty, how she used it.
Then, just as suddenly, she had switched it off. She was
now utterly self-contained, projecting merely her words.

Cassie glanced discreetly from Eva to Frazer. There
was a tension between the two of them. As Eva spoke, he
leaned toward her, eyes never leaving her, while she sat
back, chin in, making her body compact, as if in resistance.

Richardson and Cassie sat quietly, almost invisible by
design, as Eva recounted her story once again.

"There is a company listed on the Vancouver Stock
Exchange. I own ten percent; an American geologist

called Granger McAdam owns another fifteen. The rest is widely held. The company, Genius, owns a site staked over acreage in north Vietnam. Tests suggest the presence of a diamond-bearing kimberlitic pipe. There are about twenty-five hundred kimberlitic pipes in the world, and they are extremely difficult to find. Only one in ten contains diamonds, and only one in a hundred has enough diamonds to make mining economical. The odds have meant that only about thirty pipes in the world have been mined, and only around eight are now in operation. To reach the point of production we need an investment of around three hundred million pounds, but that's when the payoff comes. A single economical diamond pipe, even at the average yield of about fifty carats—that's eight grams—of diamond for every hundred tons of rock and earth extracted, will be worth two billion pounds over fifteen to twenty years. And pipes never occur singly. They come in clusters where the geological basement is weak or shattered. If you find one, you have a good chance of finding several. We think we've found one. We need to raise money to do bulk sampling, with a view to sinking a mine if the results come back positive. We need about fifteen to twenty million pounds to do the bulk sampling. If that works, we'll need another two hundred fifty million plus to build a full-fledged diamond mine."

Eva stopped and sat back, her eyes on Frazer. No one spoke. Frazer watched Eva with a quizzical look in his eyes. Most people would have found the scrutiny uncomfortable, but Eva looked back, seemingly perfectly at ease.

"And what makes you so sure that the diamonds are there?" asked Frazer.

"The tests look good."

"Tests can be open to interpretation."

"And this—can this be open to interpretation?" Eva

reached into the pocket of her jacket and withdrew something, which she held tightly in the palm of her hand. She then extended her palm across the board table toward Frazer, who watched her, transfixed. She opened her palm and offered up to him a diamond, raw, uncut, unpolished, about four carats. It was an object of unbelievable beauty and mystery. The symbolism invested in diamonds gave it part of its luster, but there seemed to be a power and beauty intrinsic to the stone. Frazer took it and handled it slowly, turning it around, running his fingers over it.

Cassie and John Richardson straightened in their chairs, eyes fixed on the stone.

"You found that on your site?" asked Richardson.

"We did," answered Eva levelly. "There's every reason to believe we'll find more just like it."

"Who knows about it?" asked Richardson quickly.

"Hardly anyone."

"Does the Vancouver Stock Exchange know?" asked Frazer.

"No," answered Eva, fully aware of the implications.

"And if it did, the stock price would shoot up?"

"You said it."

"Aren't you supposed to notify the exchange of finds like this?" asked Richardson.

"*In a timely fashion*—that's what the rules say," replied Eva. "I'll do it soon."

"And in the meantime we're all sitting on some rather valuable inside information," said Cassie softly.

No one replied. They sat lost in their own thoughts. Cassie glanced around. Frazer sat poised, all immobile concentration. Richardson fiddled with his tie. Eva sat quietly, apparently impassive, secretly raking her eyes over the assembled company, like Cassie looking for clues.

Their eyes met. The two women smiled, caught once again in mutual contemplation.

Frazer still held the diamond in his hand. Reluctantly, he handed it back to Eva.

"It's beautiful," he said.

Eva pocketed the diamond. Then she looked up and said slowly, "There are many more where that came from. I'm sure of that."

"And that this stock is seriously undervalued," said Richardson.

"That too," said Eva.

"We have a problem here," continued Richardson. "We're all insiders now. Neither Case Reed nor Robie has signed a confidentiality agreement. We need to do that straightaway. I'll get my secretary to type one up immediately."

Robie Frazer stifled a yawn and thought of China and Hong Kong, where there would have been a mass exodus from the room, everyone scurrying to the phone to place an order with his broker. He was in no hurry. He wasn't interested in a fast buck. This deal could be strung out nicely. He kept his face blank.

"Sure, John. I'll sign anything you want me to." He realized by Richardson's quick look that his tone had been a bit too casual. "Obviously, the sooner, the better," he said earnestly.

Richardson picked up the telephone and issued instructions to his secretary. Then he reflected for a moment. It was a promising start to a promising deal. Why then did he feel a sense of violence, of positions being taken, of a carving up of something invisible? He should be delighted. Instead he had a sense of trepidation, a gambler's thrill, only more. And banker that he was, he felt that somehow he was missing part of the gamble.

He lapsed into polite chatter. After a few minutes of small talk, his secretary brought in copies of the confidentiality agreement. Richardson checked it, then signed one and gave the others to Cassie, Frazer, and Eva. They all signed, keeping a copy for themselves and giving one to Richardson. Then Eva got to her feet, singlehandedly closing the meeting. Lunch would have been an anticlimax after the tension of the meeting. Instinctively, she chose to leave now. The rest of them stood.

Eva addressed them all formally. "Thank you so much for hearing me out. I've taken enough of your time." She shook hands and turned to go.

Frazer turned to Cassie and Richardson. "Thank you both for a most enlivening morning. It really has been fascinating. I'm sure we can do something here."

Almost telepathically, Frazer and Eva turned together and walked from the building. For a while they walked in silence, caught up in private thoughts, uninterested in the formalities of polite conversation. Frazer spoke first.

"That was quite a performance."

"Thank you." Eva gave him a quick sideways glance.

They walked down Savile Row side by side. When they paused at the corner, Frazer hailed a passing taxi and turned back to Eva. She held his look, acknowledging the question in his eyes. She paused, as if taking time to deliberate, head to one side, eyes on him. Then, at length, she inclined her head in unspoken agreement. She felt her chest tighten and her breath quicken. Frazer held open the cab door for her. She stepped in. They sat at a distance from each other in the back of the cab. Frazer gave his address, then turned to her.

"Tell me, are you really interested in diamonds? You spoke very well, quite convincingly. The perfect promoter of a deal. But somehow, I can't quite see you getting your hands dirty. You gave me no history, no background—you just appear from nowhere with this wonderful proposal, and I can't quite help wondering who you are and where you came from and what you want."

For a while Eva said nothing. She gazed out the window of the taxi, then at the floor. Then she raised her eyes to his.

"Does it matter? Judge the proposal on its merits, not mine."

Frazer laughed. "But you're all bound up together, proposal and proposer. How can I separate you?"

"That's your problem, not mine. You assess the returns, quantify the risks, decide."

"And are you part of the risks?"

"Of course I am," she said lightly. "The promoter of the deal always is."

"And how would I quantify you?"

"I don't think you could even begin to."

"Why? Do you think I don't understand women?"

She laughed. That's all he thought it was—the conflict between men and women. "Oh, I'm sure you understand them very well."

"So what's the risk, then?"

She averted her face. "What indeed?"

They lapsed back into silence, covertly watching each other, watching bodies and faces, a touch away. Each desired the other. Their presence together in the taxi was a tacit acknowledgment of that, and neither chose to hide it, but with the desire was a coldness. They sat at opposite ends of the seat, leaning against the doors, facing each other not in warmth but in scrutiny, almost like fighters sizing up the opposition.

He saw a woman coolly beautiful, desirable not in

union but in conquest. There was nothing soft, yielding, or generous about her. Her selfish desire was not tempered by regard for him. He knew that, could see it in her as clearly as she could in him, but it made no difference. His desire was equally selfish. Her pleasure would be incidental, furnished by her own imagination and by the requirements of his ego. For his own sake, he did not like to disappoint women. He shut off his mind and let his eyes linger on her, anticipating the pleasure ahead.

She removed her jacket. Her bare arms were slim, well-muscled, and tanned, with a faint covering of golden hair. Her lips were full, her eyes large, watching, coolly waiting. It was this absence of warmth that above all else excited him. It allowed him to ignore the formalities, any veneer of niceness. It gave him a rare chance to reveal himself.

Such openness on her part told him all he needed to know. Why she was like this he neither knew nor cared. Women were attracted to him for many reasons: money, status, good looks. Some women were attracted by his reputation for a certain promiscuity, cruelty, and lack of care. Half of them probably wanted to test their own powers in an ultimately futile attempt to reform him; others were simply self-destructive.

Some, like this woman, attempted to put on a mantle of hardness, approaching him as he did them, for convenient sex and a quick mind spin. Few were able to keep up the facade. He enjoyed teasing out these relationships until the women did ultimately soften and fall for him. The mental conquest was in many ways so much more satisfying than the physical one. And he couldn't help but derive some pleasure from their unhappiness on being abandoned.

He wondered how long it would be before Eva's self-conscious indifference began to turn into need, then love. Perhaps it would take longer than with most, but it would happen.

Eva watched him smiling at her. She studied the confident pose, the loose limbs, the half-closed eyelids, the casual regard he bestowed on her. *He has no doubt that he will seduce me,* she thought. *And quite right.* She wanted nothing but desire to register on her face, though she fought to quell the other feelings that threatened to surge to the surface.

It would not strike him as unusual, her immediate consent. Many women would sleep with him for many reasons, though none for hers. He would be blinded by his own vanity and complacency. She almost laughed. All she had to do was act. And the acting wouldn't be that difficult. He was physically desirable, and she was grateful for that. But there was something else, which even she, with her acute powers of perception, failed to realize—an attraction that went beyond the physical, that had more to do with the contents of her mind than his. But she didn't see it, couldn't have named it if she had. Certain things were best not looked at, and there was much, of necessity, that she had forgotten, like an amnesiac victim of shock. And so she went with him in a form of self-imposed blindness, which made it all so much easier, smoother.

The taxi was nearing the end of its short journey. It slowed and turned into Wilton Place. Eva and Frazer got out, and Frazer paid off the driver and led Eva into his house. She followed him into the sitting room. He sat down. She dropped her jacket on the chair but remained standing, her back to him, gazing out at his garden, her body in the same posture, poised between flight and rest, in which he had first seen her an hour ago. He noticed her blue cotton shirt, taut across her body, her brown legs, the calves slim, the muscles well delineated. He got to his feet and walked up behind her. He touched her shoulders lightly at first, then ran his palms down her arms, back up again, and forward to her throat. He felt her lean back against him, pushing her chest forward and her hips back, straining against him. His hands traveled down to her legs. He took hold of her skirt and pushed it up around her waist. Then she turned to face him, keeping pressed against him. For a second he caught sight of her eyes, and then they closed as her mouth tilted up to meet his.

For that second he froze in surprise and confusion. Such a look he had never seen, could not define. Then, as she moved against him, desire took over, shutting out all else, and he kissed her, feeling as he did the intoxicating thrill.

She smiled as she slid down his body and onto the ground. The floor, covered with a thin silk rug, dug into her hips, shoulder blades, and head. She felt the sun on her face, smelled the heavy scent of wisteria in the air, and felt him, the contours of his body, the smell and taste of his skin. She felt the air, warm against her naked skin as he took off her clothes, and then she felt him, skin on skin, eye to eye.

Behind her closed lids, Eva's eyes flickered with disgust, hatred, and desire. As she let herself go, she felt the blissful escape, release, and compulsion, simultaneous and torturously sweet. That he could give her this sensation, that she could take such feelings from him, acting all the while, intensified it all. But some well-hidden part of her knew it wasn't acting. It was the natural response as well as the necessary one.

ELEVEN

Andrew Stormont sat in the back of his official Rover, being driven back to his office after a meeting at Whitehall. As the car approached Vauxhall Bridge, the new SIS building bordering the south of the Thames at Vauxhall came into view. It had been completed in the spring of 1994 and occupied for just over a year. Stormont had watched the building go up and found it ludicrous. Now its over-made-up gaudiness made him think of a happy tart, and he smiled as the car approached it.

Designed by the postmodernist architect Terry Farrell, the building, known as Vauxhall Cross and quickly nicknamed the Green Goddess by staff, was a confection of cream stone and pistachio-green windows rising in four tiers from the riverside. Several large atria were cut into the building, creating light and space. There was none of the quiet neoclassicism of Thames House, the new Millbank home of MI5, the Security Service. Vauxhall Cross was monolithic, almost like the old Eastern European security fortresses, just a little more restrained by a self-conscious democracy. It was, however, impressively reinforced. The windows were impregnated with metal, the rooms lined with lead. There were wet and dry moats. It was designed to be bugproof and bomb-proof, functional, for all its frivolity.

Stormont thought it ironic that the *Secret* Intelligence Service was headquartered in such an exhibitionistic building. One of the more novel decorative touches was a row of yew trees on the fifth-floor river side. The trees had been flown in from Italy and acclimatized in Scotland, Stormont was told. He supposed the building made a statement about the SIS's going forward grandly, publicly avowed, into the twenty-first century: a wishful message of power, independence, and a certain defiance.

There were many who sought to curtail the intelligence empire, who thought it was a declining force, redundant in the brave new post–cold-war world. Stormont found their willful naïveté pathetic. The intelligence services would always be needed. Human nature didn't change; people would always retain a wish to destroy, to subvert, to win, and to profit, regardless.

Stormont read through the overnight reports on his desk, then got up, stretched, and walked around his office. It smelled of espresso and Turkish cigarettes from Davidoff. It was stark, functional, with gray carpet and white walls. A sharply angled metal sculpture about three feet high, loosely modeled on the human form, was the only adornment, beautiful but bleak. If Stormont ever felt in need of comfort or softness, there was no evidence of it in his office.

He preferred not to blur the edges of his secret and public existences any more than they were already. In his undercover role he assumed various guises, which sometimes coincided with his so-called real, outside life. Sometimes in his outside life, especially when it came to his dealings with women, he utilized all his considerable talents for secrecy and deception, both for the sake of his professional life and for his own selfish, purely personal reasons. While his lives did occasionally leak into each other, this was generally within his control. So it was with a sense of annoyance that he found Eva and Cassie occupying what he considered a disproportionate part of his thoughts.

He would have liked to see the two women together again: old friends, possible business partners, united by convenient ties and by a strange rivalry. He wondered at this rivalry. They were contemporaries, of course, rivals in beauty and achievement. Professional and sexual jealousy could be a potent mixture.

Suddenly Giles Aden, Stormont's deputy director of counter-proliferation, came into the room. Aden was a slight, dapper man, a background man struggling for prominence. He always wore immaculately cut suits with gaudy ties and stood with the bearing of a tailor's dummy. At forty-two, he had the body of a skinny schoolboy, maintained by clandestine visits to the gym. To flaunt these visits would betray excess vanity. The vanity already suggested by the suits and the bearing was quite sufficient to indicate his sense of self-worth. That it was somewhat forced he failed to see.

Aden was extremely intelligent, a natural cynic armed with a usefully negative disposition. This made him the perfect deputy, ideal for shooting down his superiors' less workable ideas. He was a restraining presence, not a creative one. He would never step into his boss's shoes.

He stood in Stormont's office, looking up at

him. Stormont sat down, indicating that Aden do the same.

"So?" he asked, seeing in Aden a coy smugness.

"Any news of Eva?" the deputy asked.

Stormont leaned back in his chair, stretching out his legs, clasping his hands behind his head, elongating his frame like a snake uncoiling.

"Not as yet. But I shouldn't worry, Giles. She'll string us out for a while, never can resist it, but she'll call in sooner or later."

"What d'you think she's up to?"

"Who knows? Could be anything. Give her her head. Best thing."

"And the project? Do you think Frazer will go for it?"

"I'm sure of it."

"Why so sure?"

"It has its merits."

"And what are they?"

"Eva Cunningham and Cassie Stewart."

"Incidentally, are there really any diamonds there?"

"As you say, incidental. Nice bonus, though, for Eva, and the Firm, if there are."

"And if the project does make money, will you let Eva keep it?"

"That rather depends."

"On what? She does expect it. You know that."

"Oh yes, I know. But that's just one of many variables, isn't it?"

"I'd be a bit careful with Eva."

Stormont sat forward, drawing his legs in, fixing his eyes on Aden. "It's control she needs, not care. And I rather think we have that, don't you?"

Aden got up to leave. He paused on his way, unwilling to back out.

"By the way, Cassie Stewart—your earlier comment. You don't have anything extra in mind for her, do you?"

Stormont lit a cigarette. "I'm not sure. I think I'll play that one along a bit, see how things turn out."

TWELVE

Eva lay in Frazer's bed, faintly aware of distant sounds—cars hazy in the warmth, birds settling down in the trees outside, a faint strain of music coming from a neighbor's house. Frazer had got out of bed very quietly a few moments earlier and walked on light feet across the room and out. Exhausted by their frenzy and the heat, they had, hours earlier, made their way upstairs to bed. Frazer had fallen asleep immediately, with the ease of someone used to unfamiliar bed partners.

For a while Eva had feigned sleep. Her mind was unquiet, pulling against itself in so many directions that she had to consciously shut it down, gently will herself into calmness.

It felt as if they had slept for hours. Eva glanced at the clock on the bedside table. It was nine in the evening. She lay still for a while, gazing up at the white ceiling. She felt a certain satisfaction, partly physical, partly from her very presence in his bed, her quick entrée into his life. And she felt contempt for him, mixed with a hatred so profound she felt it would corrode her skin. She knew of his capacity for ruthlessness, knew that it served for him the dual purposes of expediency and amusement. But she felt no fear, no uncertainty. She had waited so long for this moment, had dreamed of nothing else for long periods when all she had was time and her desire for revenge.

Stormont had aimed her at Frazer like a missile. For years she had been aimed. Now the fuse was lit. It was a long fuse, slow-burning but inextinguishable. Whatever Stormont wanted, whatever hidden motivations he might have—and Eva knew he would have a concealed agenda —she too had plans, and while Stormont was using her, so was she using him. For the time being they needed each other. The beauty of her current role was that it gave her the opportunity to destroy Frazer, if she chose to, and rid herself of Stormont. She didn't quite know how yet; the mechanics of the plan would evolve. But she relished the uncertainty, the wastelands of the mind in which she operated so well. She smiled to herself, and very quietly slid out of bed.

Naked, she walked across the darkening room and paused at the doorway. Then, silently, she walked downstairs until she heard Frazer's voice, muted behind a closed oak door. She paused outside, standing with one knee cocked, her pose relaxed but her ears straining to hear the words that filtered through the door. She must have been about ten feet from Frazer, yet it was almost impossible to pick out individual words. He was speaking quietly, it seemed to Eva deliberately so. But while words were indistinguishable, his tone of voice registered: cold, unyielding, demanding. It seemed almost as if he were threatening someone.

Abruptly the voice ceased, and Eva heard the creaking of a chair. With loping steps, she moved toward the kitchen and found the fridge. She opened the door, took out a bottle of mineral water, and drank greedily. She kept her pose relaxed as she heard the footsteps behind her, then appeared to jump, spilling water down her breasts when Frazer spoke to her.

"You're awake, then." His words were light, laconic, but he was watching her intently.

She gazed at the water trickling down her body and smiled uncertainly, half embarrassed. "You frightened the life out of me."

He walked up to her and ran his hand along her damp stomach. "That's what you get for creeping around."

"I wasn't creeping around. I'm starving and parched. In case it escaped your notice, I didn't have lunch, or dinner."

His face softened fractionally, back into complacent ease. "No. Of course. Would you like to eat now? We could go out, or my housekeeper could make us something."

Eva smiled and kissed him lightly. "That's very kind, but another time, all right?"

A faint, almost undetectable look of surprise registered on his face. "Of course. You'd better give me your telephone number." He walked off toward his study and returned with a slim navy address book. *You bastard,* thought Eva. *Adding me so obviously to a list of names.*

He opened the book. Blandly, devoid of expression, she recited her number. Then, without looking at him, she went to the sitting room to retrieve her strewn clothes. She dressed rapidly. He stood in the doorway watching her. She turned her cheek to him and let him kiss her; then she left.

Outside on the street she paused for a second, breathing deeply. Then she lit up a cigarette and walked home. The streets were quiet in the lull between the rush hour and the exit from restaurants, theaters, dinner parties, pubs. A few people walked dogs or just walked, enjoying the warmth of an unseasonably hot April. There was no breeze. It was one of those almost Mediterranean London evenings. The smell of pipe smoke hung in the air. Eva could see some way ahead an old man, stooped, walking, with a careful gait but head up, pipe in hand. She passed him, saw the look of simple contentment on his face. She inhaled deeply, loving the tang and the warmth. It made her think of pine forests and the South of France, a long time ago. She felt as if she could be anywhere.

For all she was English, London was not home; nor was anywhere else. And she was on an assignment. That always suspended reality, created an artificial world of her making. As she left the quiet streets of Belgravia and headed for the King's Road, she still felt as if she were playing a part. Eyes watched her as she passed, taking in the lithe stride and proud head, but she felt invisible and wondered to what audience was she playing.

She arrived back at her dark house. All the houses on her road were lit up, with sounds of laughter and music coming from gardens at the back or windows open to the street. Hers was silent, but as she took her keys from her handbag and let herself in, she smiled at the ritual—her house, to enter and leave as she pleased. She walked to the bathroom, shedding clothes as she went, and stood under the shower until every trace of Robie Frazer was washed from body, skin, hair, and mouth. Then she climbed into bed, exhausted, and fell into a troubled sleep.

Just over a mile away, on Sloane Avenue, Xu Nan sat on the edge of his bed, his eyes fixed on the wall opposite. His most recent conversation with Robie Frazer had lasted three minutes, a couple of hundred seconds that seemed to wipe out years, to rewrite the past and circumscribe the future. Smooth words; the suggestion of violence in the tone; a terrifying subtlety. Time was his no longer. Frazer was waiting, expecting delivery. And if he said no? Unthinkable.

He wished he could just freeze, turn to stone, never have to move again. Or return to the balm of routine and trivia, where he might enjoy his home, go to work, do his job, drink coffee, and talk on the phone, with nothing to think of but that. What comfort in dullness and routine, and the sleeping of the mind. A lost comfort, craved by splintered nerves.

He could not sit still, alone. Moving with manic jerkiness, he left his house, got into his car, and drove to work in Holborn.

The regularity of the drive, the familiar landmarks, the sense of normality, calmed him slightly. It was an odd time to appear at the office, but he could rationalize that. He told the three security guards that he had forgotten his wallet. The guards, knowing and liking him, did not challenge him but let him pass. After he had disappeared into the lift, they exchanged looks of suspicion.

"Drunk?"

"Could be. Didn't really seem it. Odd, though."

"Give him five minutes. He'll probably be right out, but if he isn't . . ."

"I'll go," said Jack, the oldest one.

After waiting five minutes, Jack went off to check on Nan. He walked with a slow professional beat, up to the lift, to the third floor, around the atrium to Nan's office. He found Nan just sitting there, in silence and semidarkness, the desk light shining into his eyes. He seemed oblivious to the light, as if all his senses were turned inward. After a while, reluctantly, he turned his head toward Jack. He met his eye, then looked away again.

"Found your wallet, then, did you?"

"Never lost it."

"Didn't think so." Jack sat down on the edge of the desk. "You're not really working, either."

"No."

"So, er, what is it?"

Nan turned and looked directly at him. He shrugged, impotent and helpless. "I don't know. I shouldn't be here at all." He got to his feet. "I'm going now." He patted his jacket violently. "And I've got nothing on me, no papers, nothing. You can check if you like."

Jack gave him an appraising look. "That's all right, Mr. Xu. I don't think you have." Random checks of employees, especially those in sensitive areas, were commonplace. Employees who acted suspiciously would be checked immediately, but there was something in Nan's demeanor that made Jack believe him. It was the look of someone who had lost, not stolen.

Outside, Nan got back into his car, started up the engine, and accelerated away. He drove with reckless disregard, like an automaton, almost unaware of the other traffic on the road. He didn't hear the blaring horns, didn't see the avoiding swerves. Through luck, he arrived home unscathed.

Inside, he went straight to the kitchen. He filled a watering can and began to water his plants. They were lined up along the window shelves like hungry children. He watered them well, stroking a few leaves as he passed. Then he returned the watering can to the kitchen and wiped down the surfaces where he had spilled water until everything was neat. Then the noise in his mind that the mechanical task had kept at bay returned, driving out reason. He felt at that moment that there could be no refuge from it. His autonomy had been stolen, his freedom taken, leaving him with nothing to lose. He picked up the telephone and rang Robie Frazer.

Frazer was sitting in his study, glass of Armagnac in hand. He felt a sense of good fortune, of promise. Eva and the diamonds, glittering things, both to be his. The ringing of the telephone broke the spell.

He picked up the receiver. The voice babbled into his ear before he said a word.

"It's over. I can't do it anymore. You lied to me, you trapped me, now you threaten to—"

"Now, Nan, let's not get overly emotional about this. I—"

"Fuck you, 'overemotional.' I'm not doing it anymore. Tomorrow I'm going to hand in my notice." Nan's voice shook with emotion. Now it trailed off into silence. He was unable just to slam down the phone. He still looked for something from Frazer, a sanction or a show of anger, some sign that the blow aimed had drawn blood.

For a while there was silence. When Frazer spoke, his tone was surprisingly gentle.

"I've put you under too much strain, Nan. I can see that now. I'm sorry. I hadn't realized. It's too much to ask of you to keep doing this. You're right. You shouldn't do it anymore." He paused, heard the exhalation of breath, felt his words working. "If you love your job, why not stay on? You don't have to resign. You'll be free to do what you want now."

There was a pause before Nan's voice came back, uncertain, the anger undirected now because of Frazer's startling compliance. "I don't know. I can't think straight. I just feel as if I want to get away, make a clean break, leave tomorrow."

"Yes. I can understand that." Frazer paused. "You might, of course, feel different after a few days. Perhaps it's better not to be too hasty. Why don't you take a few days off, give yourself time to think?"

Sleep. That was all Nan wanted to do—to go to bed for days. Frazer could feel him weighing his words. He waited calmly.

"Yes, I think I might. I'll just stay at home for a few days."

"That'll be good. A bit of rest. I'll go now, give you some peace, but don't forget, if you need to talk, I'm here."

There was a grudging silence, better than the anger of a minute earlier. Frazer put down the telephone gently, careful not to break the fragile peace he had created. He stared out the window, his face reflected in the blackness of the glass. His features were rigid, his eyes unwavering.

He sat quietly for a few minutes, as if composing himself. Then he picked up the phone and called Le Mai in Hong Kong.

"I'd like you to come over on the first plane."

"I'm on my way."

THIRTEEN

Eva Cunningham thrashed against the sheets twist-
ing round her body. Dreams and nightmares
merged, caressing her, torturing her. She wrenched herself free and awoke, sweat rolling down her bare skin. She
gasped in lungfuls of air, then concentrated on slowing
her breathing, calming herself.

Light filtered through the curtains. She glanced at the
clock on her bedside table: 8 A.M. She lay still for a while
as calm returned, savoring the feel of the sheets against
her skin, moving her limbs around freely, meeting no
barrier of bone or flesh. Her nightmare came back to her.
Frazer loomed in her mind. She tried to think logically,
to banish her fear.

Mechanically, she replayed events in her head. The
meeting with Frazer at Case Reed. Frazer's house. Sex
with Frazer. Here the smooth flow of thoughts faltered.
Emotionally, the sex had been tolerable. She was surprised by the treachery of her own body, at how it had
fallen asleep beside him. She had wondered when she
awoke in his bed if she had betrayed herself in sleep. All

day, every day, she filtered her words, but at night, asleep, did the filter still work? Did she talk?

There had been suspicion in his eyes when he found her in the kitchen, but that, she felt sure, had more to do with his guilty conscience than with anything she might have said. His muted conversation in the study was designed not to be overheard. If he thought she had overheard, so what? His intelligence and insight would be blurred by vanity. Hidden agendas were his preserve. She was just for sex. He would look no further, see no further. As long as she was careful, she would remain invisible, and by training and inclination she was extremely careful.

She got out of bed, walked downstairs, and went through her morning routine of music, exercise, and shower. Forty minutes later she emerged dripping from the shower, put a brightly colored sundress over her damp skin, and returned to the sitting room. East-facing, it caught the morning sun, which streamed in through open windows to form a pool of light on the floor.

She sat cross-legged in the center of the sunlight and called Stormont. It was eight-forty-five. He was at home in Old Church Street, eating breakfast. He glanced at the telephone, his official line, as it rang, and waited a short while before answering it, as if to divine who was calling. When he spoke his voice was brusque, rough, but there was in the exaggerated gruffness a hint of humor.

"Hello?"

"Stormont. I'm reporting in."

His voice developed a sudden warmth. "Ah, Eva."

She started off quick and businesslike, coffee and cigarette at hand. "I went home with him. Everything as you'd imagine—house quietly grand, him vain and egotistical. No surprises, no chinks. Only thing was a quiet conversation he had in his study while he thought I was asleep. Couldn't hear the words, and I can't be sure, but it sounded like he was threatening someone. After the phone call there was just this little bit of nastiness, not directed at me particularly, but it was there, like a residual nastiness to the world, left over from whatever he had given the poor person he was speaking to."

" 'Poor person'—you sound almost sympathetic."

"I would be, wouldn't I?"

"I rather suspect it was cohort, not victim, on the other end of the line."

"Get an intercept."

"Be patient. In the meantime, will Frazer bite?"

"Up to me, isn't it? I'll keep you posted."

Cassie arrived at work at twenty to nine and walked past John Richardson's office toward her own. She nodded at Richardson as she passed, only to be stopped by frantic gesturing to come inside. She walked in and took a seat to hear him saying on the phone, "Robie, Cassie just came in. I'm going to put you on the speakerphone, O.K.?"

"Fine," came back Frazer's voice, cool and modulated. "Morning, Cassie."

"Morning, Robie."

"I was just telling John that I think it's a most interesting deal you've come up with. I'd like to find out more. Obviously, I can't commit at the moment, but if it turns out to be as good as it sounds, you can count me in."

"Excellent," replied Richardson, smiling at Cassie. "We'll start putting things together."

"Incidentally, what exactly would your role be, and who would you represent?"

Richardson turned to Cassie, who leaned across the desk toward the microphone at the top of the telephone.

"We'd be coinvestors alongside you and Eva. We'd decide the best way to go, rights issue or takeover. We'd put the nuts and bolts of the deal together, the documentation, the due diligence, any overseas advisers, that sort of thing, although I'm sure you'd probably want to do some of your own due dili anyway."

"Oh, I'd leave all that sort of thing to you," lied Frazer, glad for the reminder. "So you're good old-fashioned merchant bankers, facilitators, deal-makers, risk-takers, none of this overlegalistic subdivision of interest that all the big banks seem so fond of."

"We do everything, don't we, Cass?"

"If it looks good."

"Call me soon," said Frazer. "If this thing is going to happen, I want it to happen fast."

"So far, so easy," said Richardson as he cut the line.

"Mm." Cassie looked vaguely preoccupied.

"What is it?"

"Oh, nothing really. I was just wondering if it was time to pay Owen Quaid a visit."

"It is really, isn't it? We can't go much further without being totally comfortable with your friend Eva, can we?"

Cassie spread her hands on the table and stared at her fingers. "No. We can't."

"How well do you know her?" Richardson had asked the question several times. He was not seeking the comfort of repetition. Cassie knew his approach, soliciting different information with the same casual question.

"How well do you know anyone? I think I know her. She's capable, intelligent, she seems to know her subject, she has fire. She can be coolly rational and passionate. She

showed us both sides yesterday. It was amazing, the transformation, the switch."

"She was cool with Frazer, wasn't she?"

"Cool? Didn't you see her at the beginning of the
meeting? She seemed to switch on for him, really flash
her beauty."

"She's a beautiful woman."

"But I've never seen her like that. I've never seen her
wear makeup or jewelry, or smart clothes."

"She'd have to dress up for a meeting, wouldn't she?"

"It was more than just dressing up. Then there was
that game with the diamond."

"Quite a game. Which reminds me. I hope she
makes that official announcement soon, to the exchange,
about finding diamonds."

"Oh, I'm sure she will."

"There are rules, Cass."

"Of course there are. And she'll know what to do
with them."

"Follow them."

"Well, that's one option, isn't it? Hey, c'mon," she
said, seeing Richardson's frown. "There's no such thing
as the perfect client. There has to be a flaw, doesn't
there?"

"I suppose so," said Richardson, wondering about
his and Cassie's.

"She is a bit of a wild card," continued Cassie, "but
then, so is Frazer. They're well matched. As long as we
can control them."

"Do you think you can?"

"We'll see, won't we?"

* * *

Cassie returned to her office and closed the door. She dialed Owen Quaid, then sat back, eager to hear his voice.

"Quaid." There was a rush of traffic around him as he spoke. He was walking through Berkeley Square.

"Owen, your services are required formally by Case Reed. Can you come by?"

He smiled into the sunshine. "Where? Your office?"

"Good a place as any."

"I can think of better."

"The resourcefulness of a private dick. I'm sure you can, but we'll settle for my office. Two this afternoon."

"It's always urgent with you, Cass. No tomorrow, or next week. I'm surprised you didn't ask me to come round now."

"All right. Come round now."

"I'll see you at two. I'm not that easy." He rang off before she could have the last word.

In his study in Wilton Place, Robie Frazer made a brief telephone call. He didn't bother to identify himself. He said simply, "Find out all you can about a young Englishwoman—Eva Cunningham, lives in London. And a bank called Case Reed. Focus on two people there, John Richardson and Cassandra Stewart. I want daily updates. Stop when you've run out of dirt."

Owen Quaid listened to Frazer's words with quiet horror. He allowed himself just a fleeting pause. Anything longer would have aroused suspicion. Any hesitation was bad enough, but he had to have just that split second to think, to weigh up his options, his loyalties. No time. Instinct answered for him.

"I'll get onto it." He shut off his phone with a grimace and a "fucking hell" to the world.

Frazer put down his telephone and immediately dialed again. "Eva. Good morning. How are you?"

His voice was light, teasing, loathsomely confident. She answered smoothly, "Oh, fine, fine." She covered up her distaste and contempt for his arrogance and overfamiliarity in ringing anonymously, assuming that she would recognize his voice, that she would have been imagining the sound of it, waiting for his call.

"I was wondering if you'd like to have dinner tonight."

"Tonight?" Eva couldn't resist a slight hauteur. She smiled to herself and said nothing more.

"You don't strike me as the type who fills her calendar months ahead with cocktail parties and charity evenings. You seem rather more spontaneous." He said the last bit with a smile in his voice, and Eva had to laugh.

"Touché. That makes us both spontaneous types."

"Oh, I'm a type, am I?"

"No more than I," she said levelly.

"Ah. I'm reprimanded. So would you like me to pick you up around nine?"

"No, thank you. I'll come to you." She didn't want him within a hundred paces of her home.

"As you wish. I'll see you at nine, then." He hung up, muttering, "Difficult bitch."

Eva frowned and lit a cigarette, drawing the smoke down deep into her lungs. She felt her bitterness bite into her. She couldn't do this as one person. She'd have to split off, become someone else, dig up another part of her. She got up from her chair by the telephone and walked to the mirror in the hall. She drew back her hair from her face, turned her head slowly from side to side, and studied herself dispassionately, as if looking at a stranger.

FOURTEEN

Andrew Stormont arrived at Vauxhall Cross at nine. He greeted Elsa, his secretary, on the way in.

"Morning, Elsa. Ask Aden to come in, would you?"

"Morning, Andrew. I'll go get him."

Aden appeared a minute later. "News?" he asked as he walked through the door. He took a seat opposite Stormont. Methodical by nature, he always tried to mirror Stormont's brevity and curtness in his company. This was his chosen form of defense against what he saw as Stormont's somewhat rude decision not to engage in pleasantries. His boss could be discursive and charming. He had seen that performance many times, but it was never bestowed on him.

Stormont took a sip of the coffee Elsa had just brought in, bitter espresso in a bone china cup. "Like some?" He nodded at his cup.

"No, thank you. Stomach rot."

Stormont hid a smile as he bent over his coffee. Aden's attempts at brevity always sounded forced. Still, anything was better than the interminable Foreign Office-style ramblings his deputy had favored when he first started working for him. Stormont did not particularly like Aden, but he respected his ability. Aden was thorough, painstaking, a good complement to his own more mercurial approach, which, he acknowledged, left gaps.

"News. Eva telephoned me at home this morning. She went home with Frazer after the meeting yesterday and slept with him."

"Did she now? That was easy."

Stormont said quietly, almost with menace, "Not easy. You know as well as I do what that must have taken out of her."

"I don't think she'd give you the high ground, Andrew."

"She wouldn't. But that doesn't detract from her being bloody good."

"Or bloody bad."

Stormont stared at him, saying nothing.

Aden quickly raised a hand. "Just joking."

Stormont continued evenly, "She's established contact, a way in. Apparently he made a somewhat threatening call to someone."

"Do we know the contents?"

"No. We don't."

"Need more than that, don't we?"

"Yes," said Stormont, detached now, eyeing Aden as he would eye a fly in his whiskey. "Carew won't sign a warrant on thin air." Carew was the foreign secretary. His signature was required on SIS requests for warrants to intercept telephone conversations.

Stormont continued, "I'm not going to go to him unless we know we'll get approval. They won't be falling over themselves to tap a man in Frazer's position—pillar of the establishment, multimillionaire, generous contributor to the Thatcher Foundation. They'll need some decent dirt."

Aden said with the appropriate hesitancy, "We could always go the other route—use a freelance, unaccountable, deniable."

"I'd rather not, at least for now. We'll expose ourselves enough going after Frazer. Better go by the book, just in case anything goes wrong."

"You think it might?"

"Who knows? There isn't a natural path to this one. It could go off in a number of directions. In the meantime, we need material. But we'll get it. Eva will get it."

"You have great faith in her."

Stormont looked past him, and for a few seconds Aden knew he had lost him. He watched Stormont's eyes focus on some distant memory that seemed to expand and fill his world for those few seconds. Then Stormont turned back to Aden and said sharply, "I do have great faith in her. And yes, she'll deliver."

"If she doesn't go crazy first."

"If she was ever going to do that, don't you think she'd have done it a long time ago?"

Aden looked away.

FIFTEEN

Cassie Stewart bent sideways, scanning a bookcase full of files in Case Reed's extensive business library. After five minutes she grabbed a file from the bottom shelf: VSE, the listings policy and procedures manual for the Vancouver Stock Exchange. "Brilliant," she muttered, carting it off to her office like a war trophy.

For one hour solid she read, immersed, undisturbable. Then she slammed the file shut with a cunning smile, got up, and went into Richardson's office.

"John, I've come up with a plan for Genius. If you think it sounds all right, I'd like to get hold of a broker in Vancouver, run it past him, and line him up."

"You don't waste time, do you? All right, out with it."

He sat in silent admiration as Cassie outlined her plan. "Sounds good to me," he said when she finished, "but you're right. You will need to check it with a Vancouver pro, and we do need a broker. In fact, I know just the man. He owes me a favor or two. Chap called Sam Brimton. Real Vancouver insider, knows everyone in the market. Made a fortune. Very sharp. You want to be a bit careful."

"Don't worry."

Richardson gave her a quick warning look. "I'll call Brimton after lunch, first thing his time. I'll tell him to expect to hear from you." He scribbled down a number on a yellow Post-It and passed it over. Cassie pocketed it.

"Thanks, John." She backed out quickly, before he could issue any more warnings.

Back in her office, she called Eva. "Eva, it's Cassie. How are you?"

"Hi, Cass. I'm fine, wonderful, sitting in a sunlit room with a huge breakfast." She paused to chew. "What could be better?"

"Sounds perfect. Lucky you. Listen, Robie Frazer rang this morning, said he wants to go ahead, subject to the right strategy, due diligence—you know, geological reports, project evaluation, all that. You must really have made an impression."

Eva laughed to herself, then spoke with real enthusiasm. "That's wonderful, marvelous. So what do we do now?"

"Put together a strategy, a business plan, you and I together. Then I become an expert in the diamond business."

"Piece of cake."

"What are you doing now?"

"Apart from breakfast, not a lot. Why?"

"Could you come in this morning? Then we can get started."

"Yeah, sure." Eva glanced at her watch: ten-fifteen. "See you in about three quarters of an hour."

"See you then."

Strange the way things turn out, thought Cassie. Eva the

entrepreneur. Almost unbelievable, and yet in the flesh she had been so convincing.

Eva left her breakfast half eaten, headed for the bedroom, and changed out of her sundress into a long, tailored, black linen dress and matching grosgrain slingbacks. She brushed her hair, tied it back, grabbed the geologists' reports and all the various bits of paper on the project McAdam had given her and left for Case Reed.

She walked into Cassie's office half an hour later. Cassie was working, deep in thought, didn't see her approach. Eva went in slowly, studying her—so self-contained, serious, yet there was a lightness about her, an ease. She was bent over some papers on her desk, concentrating, yet there was no furious frowning. Instead a faint smile curved her lips, touching her eyes. The lightness of an open life. For a brief second Eva envied her lack of contamination, her freedom. The moment passed. She smiled and walked through the open door.

Cassie looked up and jumped to her feet. "Eva, hi."

They kissed each other.

"Wonderful to have hooked Frazer, isn't it?" said Cassie. "Well done."

"Mm. Wonderful. But we still have to hook him good and proper."

"We will." She paused. "You must really have impressed him."

Eva saw the quizzical look in her eyes, sensed something beneath her apparent innocence. She passed it off with a faint shrug.

"By the way," Cassie continued, "I'm sorry I didn't really brief you about the meeting. I was planning to, but I rather felt I was intruding with you and your friend Stormont."

"Why think that?"

"Oh, I don't know. He's not a lover, is he?"

"Since you ask, no. Why? Should he be?"

"He's attractive."

"Lots of men are."

"Not like him."

"Got to you, did he, Cass?"

"I wouldn't lose sleep."

Never do, thought Eva. Quickly she moved on. "Anyway, what do we do with Frazer? What's the next step?"

"We put together such a brilliant package he'll have to sign up. And cough up." Cassie's voice was brisker now, businesslike.

"Tell me what we need."

Cassie pulled her chair from behind her desk and sat alongside Eva. "We need a nice short business plan. A history of the project, how it was found, copies of the licenses with the Vietnamese government, copies of the tests done and the results, details of the money raised, how much money has been spent, on what, how much money is left in the company, what you plan to do with it, and how much it will cost to do the bulk sampling, sink the mine if it comes to that, and do all the other necessary work to bring this thing onstream. Then we have to outline the strategy. How we plan to take over the company, how much it will cost. Then we propose different exits. If the bulk sampling were to look good, we could sell out at that stage to one of the big mining companies. We could sell out in whole or in part. There are various options. And we'll have to say a bit about the diamond industry, the cartel, distribution, how the diamonds would be sold."

Eva knew exactly what was required, had been fully

briefed in the quick induction to the financial world Stormont had secretly arranged for her, but still she sat back, impressed by Cassie's fluency.

"No sales spiel? No projections of revenues, of how much money we all might make?"

"That's what all the big banks do, produce reams of paper with worthless calculations of the future and pages of hard sell. Frazer would laugh. No one has a clue how this project will turn out. It could make us a fortune, it could lose us a fortune. We don't know. That's the nature of the risk. We're gambling. No point pretending otherwise."

Neither Cassie nor Frazer could possibly know the full nature of the gamble, thought Eva. Perhaps, in turn, she didn't either.

"Caveat emptor—buyer beware. So what next? Assuming Frazer agrees, what do we do?"

"We take over the company."

"And how exactly do we do that?"

"We send a draft notice of what's called a stock exchange takeover bid to the Listings Department of the Vancouver exchange. Then the exchange will implement market surveillance to check for any monkey business."

"Like what?"

"Like insider trading."

"So no monkey business."

"Not necessarily. Anyone engaging in anything a bit dicey is best advised to do it before the draft notice is sent to the exchange."

"Ah," said Eva. "I see."

"Just joking," said Cassie. "So," she continued more soberly, "the exchange then accepts the draft notice, and the bid is deemed to have begun."

"How much will we offer for the shares? How much do you think they're worth?"

"Doesn't matter what they're worth. We'll offer enough to satisfy people's greed but not enough to make them suspicious. If the shares are trading at four before the bid, we'll offer six. That should do it."

"What if someone else decides to bid once they see the company's in play?"

"First of all, you're a director of the company. You will recommend to other shareholders that they accept our offer. That carries a certain weight. And second, to-gether you and McAdam own twenty-five percent. That gives us quite a head start."

"No, it doesn't. I wouldn't rely on McAdam's siding with me."

"Why not?"

"He went a bit funny after Vietnam, after jail. We had a falling-out."

"Is that public? Do people know about it?"

Eva nodded.

"And does McAdam know about your desire to see Genius taken over? Does he know you came to see us?"

"No. He doesn't know a thing."

"Perfect," said Cassie, to Eva's surprise. "We can turn that to our advantage. It means he's not a concert party, someone who's deemed to be acting in concert with you. It makes a big difference, because if we lumped his holdings with yours, if he were acting in concert with you, neither you nor we could buy any more shares in Genius without triggering a takeover bid. The rules say that if any purchases made take a single holder or a con-cert party to a holding of twenty percent or more, then the takeover bid requirements come into force. Your holding of ten percent means we and Robie Frazer can buy, together, up to ten percent of Genius before triggering a bid."

"But why the need to buy any more shares before the bid?"

"Two reasons. As I said, it gives us a head start on any subsequent bidders, and we almost certainly pay less for the shares we buy before the bid than those we buy after. After a takeover bid is announced, the share price invariably rises."

"So who buys the shares before we make the bid?"

"Case Reed buys five percent, Robie Frazer buys five percent. Then, with twenty percent between us, we launch our bid for the remaining eighty percent."

"How do the mechanics work?"

"Case Reed and Frazer set up a private company to make the bid. We own the company fifty-fifty. Then, when we've bid, you exchange your share of Genius for ten percent of the new company. So Frazer and Case Reed both hold forty percent and you hold ten percent. The percentages may vary, according to how much of Genius we end up with, but those are the rough proportions."

"Sounds pretty smooth."

"Yeah, in theory. It's bound to get a bit dirty. It always does. But we'll handle that as it happens. The first thing to do is get the business plan written, send it to Frazer, call him in to a meeting, get him to agree to everything, then start buying."

"By the way," asked Eva, "will you bring anyone else in?"

"I'd rather not. Gets too crowded, too many people fussing around." Cassie smiled. "I might put some of my own money in, if you don't mind having me as a coinvestor."

"As long as you can live with the risks."

"If Case Reed can, I can."

"But that's someone else's money."

Cassie paused. "Are you trying to tell me not to put my own money into this?"

"Of course not. Just don't put in more than you can afford to lose."

"Eva, for a promoter of this deal, you suddenly sound very negative."

"You're an old friend, Cass. I believe in this deal, but I also know the odds. The risks are enormous."

"I'll take my chances, unless you're trying to tell me I shouldn't."

"No, Cass. I'm not. Go ahead. Put your money in."

"I will."

Eva smiled, almost sadly, it seemed to Cassie.

Cassie jumped to her feet. "I've got to go to the loo. Back in a sec."

Eva watched her disappear, trying to keep her face neutral, her thoughts veiled. She glanced around discreetly, aware of Cassie's secretary sitting outside the office, ten feet away. Nothing of any interest was accessible.

The telephone rang and rang. The secretary picked it up on her extension just as Cassie was returning.

"It's an Andrew Stormont for you."

Eva stiffened. The secretary had spoken quietly, but Eva's hearing was acute. She saw Cassie glance surreptitiously toward her, as if wondering whether she'd heard. Then she took the call, standing at her secretary's desk.

Cassie spoke quietly, softly, but her words were still discernible. She sounded surprised and pleased. "Oh, hello." She listened for a while, then said, "I won't have

much time. O.K. Quarter to one, here, see you then."
She put down the phone and returned to the office.

Eva watched Cassie's beautiful, normally guileless
face, guarded now. So it begins, a game still not out-
grown.

SIXTEEN

Eva and Cassie immersed themselves in writing the document for the next hour and a quarter. Emma started typing it up and photocopying all the licenses and geological surveys. Eva lingered for as long as possible, giving Cassie a chance to tell her that she was having lunch with Stormont.

At twelve-thirty, Cassie glanced at her watch. "I've got to make some telephone calls, overdue. And we're just about done. If I have anything else, I'll give you a ring."

"Sure," said Eva, affecting a small frown of disappointment, waiting a moment.

Cassie began to tidy up her papers. With genuine reluctance, Eva got to her feet.

"O.K.," she said, breaking the short silence. "Busy girl. I'll leave you to it. I think I'll go for a walk in the sunshine, buy some clothes, lunch, do what ladies of leisure do."

"Make the most of it," said Cassie, apparently oblivious to the barb. "It won't last much longer. Incidentally, are you happy with the deal, with my plan?"

"Sounds ingenious. I'm quite happy."

Eva walked out swiftly onto Savile Row. She bought a *Standard* from a newspaper stand and headed for the café on Clifford Street, selecting a seat that just gave her a view of the entrance to Case Reed. She held up the newspaper before her face, eyes peeping over the top. She saw Stormont arrive at twelve-forty-five. He was carrying a large Fortnum & Mason bag. She had never observed him from a distance, never seen him as a stranger would.

Inside Case Reed, the receptionist announced that Stormont had arrived. Cassie took from her bag a small hand mirror in a silver case. She brushed out her long, fine hair and put on lipstick. For a moment she studied herself; then she snapped the mirror shut, dabbed scent at her temples, and walked down to Stormont.

He stood waiting with his back to her, studying one of the paintings that adorned the walls. Cassie observed the strong figure, the confident, casual pose. She walked up silently and moved to touch his shoulder. Aware of her presence, he had started to turn, and looked into her eyes as she touched him. She drew back. They smiled, and then he moved forward to kiss her on both cheeks. Her hair lightly brushed his face.

"Cassie, good to see you. I'm so glad I managed to lure you out."

She smiled.

He nodded toward his bag. "I got some things from Fortnum's. Thought it would be a good day for a picnic. Better and quicker than a restaurant, since you're pinched for time."

"What a lovely idea."

They walked out of Case Reed into the sunshine, reflecting brightly off the pavement. Across the street, Eva watched them, noting their eager footsteps, the way their bodies inclined fractionally toward each other. She watched until they disappeared, then put down her paper and left the café, walking away briskly in the opposite direction.

Cassie and Stormont headed for Hyde Park and found a large tree. Cassie sat leaning against the trunk. Stormont half sat, half lay opposite her. He took off his jacket, loosened his tie. She removed her jacket, a navy linen blazer, to reveal a sleeveless navy slip dress, cut above the knee when she stood but riding high up her thigh as she sat. His eyes rested on her as she moved about, getting comfortable.

Cassie seemed oblivious to his scrutiny until she looked up and met his smile with one that fully acknowledged his observation, the underlying attraction, and said in return, *Fine, go ahead.* He felt a quick surge of sensation, mental and physical, flowing deeply through his body. He opened a bottle of champagne, vintage Taittinger, and filled two tall glasses.

"You travel well," she said, taking a glass and a long sip.

"Oh, there's more," he said, taking out foie gras, brioches, smoked salmon, and salad.

They ate for a while in contentment, enjoying the moment, wondering what it augured.

"Interesting idea," said Cassie, arching an eyebrow.

"What?"

"A picnic, not dinner in a dark restaurant."

He felt a pleasant jolt of surprise again at her lack of pretense, at her open acknowledgment of latent seduction.

"Would you like dinner in a dark restaurant?" He leaned toward her as he spoke, his eyes on hers.

She looked away. "We'll see." After a moment she turned back to him. "So how do you know Eva?"

"Our families know each other. I met her when she was about three." He paused. "It feels like a long time ago."

Cassie let the false note ring—fear of aging, what a poor cliché. She studied the strong, lithe body, the force in the eyes, latent now but still shining through. The passage of time, the loss of power, seemed a prosaic fear for a man of forty whose years could only have added to his attractiveness, as far as she could see. It was implausible, ignoble, a convenient but unconvincing blind. She glanced at her watch and rose smoothly to her feet.

"I have to go. My meeting—"

He jumped up. "Of course." He quickly gathered up the remains of the picnic. "I'll walk back with you."

As they walked, he felt that somehow she didn't want his company. She was preoccupied, walking quickly, glancing toward him rarely. Her thoughts seemed to be focused inward, but also cast out to someone beyond him. Her meeting, perhaps? Whatever, whoever it was, it would be pleasant. He could sense the anticipation in her. He was surprised and pleased to feel the pangs of a sudden irrational jealousy.

They arrived at Case Reed in what both pretended was a companionable silence.

"I'll leave you here, then." He looked down into her clear blue eyes, so clear, so clean, despite the secret musings. Again he felt the pull of desire, stronger than he remembered. But then, it always was, the desire for the next conquest.

Cassie stared up into his eyes, flickering with private thoughts. She turned toward him as he leaned forward to kiss her. He held on to her shoulders, not releasing her after the kiss, keeping his mouth close to her face, speaking into her ear.

"Would you like dinner?"

She smiled, and seemed to step outside her preoccupation for the first time since the picnic.

"I would."

He took his hands from her shoulders, and she turned and went inside.

Stormont watched the door slam behind her. He glanced up and down with a sense of heightened clarity, then crossed from Savile Row to Clifford Street and entered the espresso bar. He sat at a table facing the street and picked up a *Standard* someone had left lying there. Half concealed, looking over the top, he took up watch.

A waitress hovered with her best smile. "What can I get you?"

He waved his hand to send her away, then remembered himself and glanced up at her. "Double espresso."

She started to say that he would have to order food, but something in him pushed her away. She hurried back with his coffee, then left him alone.

It was five to two, five minutes before Cassie's meeting. The lunchtime pedestrian traffic outside Case Reed was heavy. A few secretaries and executives strolled up, tapped in the door code, and gained entry. Stormont leveled bored, disinterested looks on the office detritus.

At five past two he watched a man walk down the street toward Case Reed. In jeans and a loose jacket, he moved with catlike ease and confidence—not with the insolent swagger affected by so many jeans-clad men of his age, which Stormont put around thirty, but with a confident grace. As he came nearer, Stormont could see him smiling the same half-concealed smile of anticipation that Cassie had worn, with a touch more discretion, ten minutes before. The man paused before Case Reed and rang the bell. He waited for a moment, spoke into the intercom, pushed against the door, and disappeared inside.

Stormont got to his feet, took out three pound coins, left them on the table, and walked out. He crossed the street and turned into Savile Row, to his car, where his driver was waiting.

SEVENTEEN

Cassie sat in her office, waiting for Owen Quaid. At five past two, Emma appeared with him. He walked toward her, smiling his deep smile. Cassie watched him, taking in the jacket, the white shirt, the blue jeans, covering but still revealing the familiar muscular body. She looked up to his face, the blue eyes flecked with green, the rich brown hair, not cropped like a banker's but not long. Somewhere in between, like a grown-out haircut. Her eyes came to rest on his lips.

She got to her feet as he came into her office. Emma tried to look away with a frown of disapproval as he took Cassie's shoulders and pulled her right to him and kissed her lips. Cassie laughed and after a pause drew back, her blood racing.

"Sit down." She gestured to the seat with exaggerated formality.

He sat, knees out wide, leaning across the desk to Cassie. "You look spectacular." His voice carried the strain of his American mother, of his twenty years in New Orleans. Even though he had lived in England for the past ten years and had a British father, the American intonation lingered, giving a caressing drawl to his words.

Cassie thought briefly of Stormont and his courtly reserve, which, to her surprise, fared well in comparison. Quaid was intoxicatingly explicit in everything he said and did to her. Such a release after the inadequate fumblings, physical and verbal, of the companions of Stormont, the men of his type. Still, Stormont, with his hooded eyes and quiet formality, had got her in the vein too.

"How about a walk?" asked Quaid in a low voice.

She threw up her hands. "I can't. We can't."

He studied her for a while, playing with the image of her, formal in her dress before him. He exhaled heavily.

"O.K. Business. I put my professional services in your hands. What do you want of me?"

"We have a new venture, a new candidate."

He watched her closely. There was excitement in her voice; there always was with a new deal. But today there was something else too, a slight hesitation, a rare awkwardness.

"Tell me," he said gently.

Cassie was surprised at the tenderness, which he usually showed only in bed.

"A woman I know. We were friends at Oxford. Haven't seen her in years. We're still friends, though. She's brought us this amazing deal."

"Her name?"

"Eva Cunningham."

Quaid reached into his pocket for a pack of cigarettes and his lighter. His face was hidden as he bowed over the flame and lit up. Cassie went to fetch him an ashtray. She came back. He inhaled deeply.

"What do you want?" he asked.

"The usual. What does she do? Who does she see? Who does she talk to? Any dangerous habits? What does she spend her money on? If it's practical, how much money does she have? You know. The usual," she snapped.

"This bothers you, doesn't it?"

"Of course it bothers me. She's a friend. I hate it. But it's a risky enough deal without exposing ourselves to personnel risks. I know Eva, but Case Reed doesn't. And anyway, how well do you really know your friends, especially ones you haven't seen for eight years? I'd do anything to get around this, but I can't."

He let her talk on, burying his disquiet beneath hers. After a while she stopped and asked him, "What's wrong?"

"I'm bothered by what you're saying. It bothers you, it bothers me."

She reached across her desk and squeezed his hand. "It's tricky. We'll just have to muddle through."

He was silent for a while. "You could get someone else to do it. It might be better, distance things a bit." Concerned, considerate—it was a plausible suggestion. He held out a vain hope.

She shook her head. "No. If anyone's going to do it, I want it to be you."

His breath sank in his lungs, and he exhaled heavily, despite himself.

Cassie looked up, alarmed. Openly they watched each other's troubled faces.

"What's bothering you, Owen? There's something from your side, not just mine. What is it?"

"There's nothing. Nothing beyond what you've told me. That's enough, isn't it?"

She shook her head. Whatever it was, if there really

was anything, she wasn't going to get it out of him. She'd seen that clamlike expression before.

He went on briskly. "You'd better tell me about this deal. You mentioned its being risky. All your deals are risky, I know that. It's what you do. It's tacit, but you mentioned it specifically, even if in passing. What is it?"

"You're right. In this case you'd better know. We're thinking about coinvesting with a Hong Kong–based businessman—you might know of him, Robie Frazer—in a project in the Far East. A diamond venture in Vietnam." She paused to check his reaction. His eyes were on her, watchful, waiting. She told him about the deal, about Eva and Granger McAdam, the whole story. When she finished, he was speechless for a while.

"Fucking hell," he said finally. "What the hell kind of deal is that?"

She answered with equal force. "It's a very promising deal. Highly profitable, potentially. It could put anything we've done in the past in the shade."

"And you want to help out an old friend. How the hell did she find a diamond mine in Vietnam? What was she doing out there?"

"That's not really your concern, is it?"

"Of course it is, and you know it. How am I supposed to give you a reasonable analysis without some history? What do you want? Eva Cunningham got up today, had breakfast, made a few phone calls, went to the hairdresser's, bought a pair of shoes?"

They glared at each other across the desk. After a while, other feelings rose up, and in unison they found themselves laughing.

"Oh God. What a mess," said Cassie.

"No kidding."

Again Cassie saw the briefest flash of some hidden worry pass across his face. He was quiet for a while.

"It's important to you, this deal, isn't it?"

"It is."

"Well, here's what we'll do. I'll investigate Eva Cunningham. I'll get you a report, verbal and written. I'll spare you any irrelevant personal details, anything embarrassing but unnecessary for your purposes. All right?"

She nodded, and waited for something that hovered between them.

"Just be careful. We'll both have to be careful."

"Why? What do you mean?"

"You don't want her finding out that you're having her spied on, do you?"

"No. I don't."

"So we can't take the risk that she might see me tailing her and then see you and me together another time."

Cassie felt a quick bleakness. She had never thought of Quaid's withdrawing from her.

"It's all right," he said, watching her. "We can still see each other. We'll just have to be very discreet."

Outside, on the street, he cursed himself. For her sake and his, he should walk away, never see her again, give her a fictional report destroying Eva's character, destroying the deal. But he was too drawn to her, in a nightmare mixture of love, concern, and the desire to protect her from things she had no inkling of. A fleeting thought of comfort came to him. Perhaps he wouldn't have to invent anything to destroy Eva. With any luck, she would be rotten anyway. Unlikely, he reasoned. Eva was Cassie's friend. She couldn't be corrupt.

★ ★ ★

Cassie blocked off her uneasiness and tried to be dispassionate. She focused on what she had to do. Soon she lost herself in the addictive thrill of the deal, becoming a general with painted nails, sitting in her office planning a financial war. She thought of it more as a game. Most often victory went to whoever bent the rules most successfully while being seen to be staying within the boundaries of the law. There was so much room for inventiveness, creativity, and stealth. It was not merely numbers on paper. Much depended on correctly anticipating the reactions of others. The human element gave it unpredictability, heightened the risk and the scope for manipulation. The game was half the thrill; the other part was money, disguised in various forms—venality covered by the flash of a stone. Still in the ground, the diamonds blinded.

Cassie picked up the phone and called Sam Brimton.

An assistant put her through. Brimton's voice was slow, ironic.

"So you're John Richardson's protégé, huh?"

"That's right."

"And you want to play the Vancouver market?"

"I do."

"How can I help?"

"I need a Vancouver broker. Case Reed might take a small stake in a resource company, perhaps in a few days. We may also need a merchant bank adviser. We may or may not mount a takeover bid for this company at some stage."

"What you're telling me is that you've just told me nothing. That you haven't given me any inside-type information."

"That's exactly what I'm telling you. I'm also asking you if you'd like to be our broker."

"Well, I'd be honored."

"Good. That's settled, then. Now you can tell me, in your official capacity as broker, whether my scheme is kosher." Cassie outlined the strategy she'd agreed on with Richardson and Eva, without mentioning the company name.

"Sounds good to me."

"I'll have a meeting in the next few days, get everyone sorted out. Then I'll give you a call with the company name and buying instructions. In the meantime, we need to set up an account with you. Perhaps you'd get your assistant to call mine to sort out the details."

"Yeah. I'll do that." He paused for a second. "Listen, Miss Stewart, if all this goes ahead, I'd be a bit careful. This market's not like London. It's pretty wild, with all sorts of unscrupulous operators, lots of manipulation. You don't want to get burned. You'll want to make sure that what you know about this company is the whole picture. You don't want anyone knowing more than you do, being able to set off rumors and manipulate the price. They don't need hard facts to do that. It happens just on a whisper based on nothing, but by the time anyone figures that out, it can be too late. You'd better put yourself in a position where you know everything, down to what color toilet paper they use." He stopped, and then said lightly, "Of course, it wouldn't do you any harm if you knew a bit of bad news, if that came out before you launched your takeover bid."

"You're not suggesting a bear raid, are you, Mr. Brimton?" When speculators deliberately spread bad, false news about a company in order to buy its shares cheaply, having sold them earlier at the higher price, it was called a bear raid. This practice broke all stock exchange rules, but the profits that could be made regularly overrode legal scruples.

Brimton laughed, but his voice contained a warning. "I'm doing nothing of the sort. I'm just filling you in on common practice, that's all. Giving you a flavor of the exchange. There are a lot of cowboys out here, Miss Stewart. You can't always fight clean if you want to stay ahead of the game."

"Thanks for the warning."

"You'll need friends out here if you're going to be serious. You'll need to be prepared."

"Thanks for the offer, Mr. Brimton. That's just what you're for."

"I'll do what I can. You could do worse. We could all do worse."

Cassie hung up. A bargain lay between them, dormant now but ready for her to pick it up anytime she chose. She wasn't sure what it was, nor what the cost would be, but the benefits would be there, she was sure of that, and she believed Brimton's warning that she would need friends. She realized too the wisdom of his warning that in a market where so many play dirty, you handicap yourself by playing clean. If someone had to play dirty, better it was Sam Brimton than Case Reed, even if they were connected.

She felt herself wondering at her progression from naive graduate eight years ago to eye-opened practitioner now. She wasn't sure quite what the practice was, but she could see a slide, feel an easing of scruples. Eight years ago she wouldn't have had such a conversation. But it was no use being squeamish in her world. If you wanted to thrive, you had to play by the rules, and often enough that meant breaking them, or allowing them to be broken on your behalf while you looked primly away. Only this time she didn't want to look away. She wanted to see it all, from the center. She saw the same desire in Eva, saw too the same legacy, a jagged energy, excitement injected with fear.

EIGHTEEN

Eva dressed for her date with Frazer in a pale blue linen shift and tan slingbacks. She put on lipstick and scent. She needed no makeup. She was tanned, her eyes and skin were clear and smooth, her hair was glossy. She smiled at her reflection as she turned before the mirror. Good bait, a good rival.

She arrived at Wilton Place at ten past nine. Frazer greeted her with a kiss and a glass of champagne and took her out into the garden at the rear of the house. They sat in weathered wooden chairs beside a matching table. He took her arm in his hand and ran his fingers along her skin. Eva masked her unease.

He paused suddenly and appeared to scrutinize her inner arm down to her wrist. "What's this? What have you done to yourself?" He ran his fingers over patches of slightly discolored skin running along the inside of both forearms.

Eva kept herself from flinching. "You have very good eyesight."

"Well?"

Eva felt a sudden anger rising. She wanted to rip her

arm away and shout at him, *Plastic surgery! Skin grafts to cover my trackmark scars. It didn't take too well, and I burned the skin in the sun one year. It doesn't tan the same as normal skin. Satisfied?* She forced the anger down and answered levelly, "I had a skiing accident in Val D'Isère. Fell on a horrendous black run. Rutted snow ripped through my ski suit and scraped off my skin and a layer of flesh." She paused. "They said I was lucky not to have bled to death. Someone had, apparently, a week before, on the same slope. The ice cut through his arteries." She shrugged matter-of-factly, as if retelling an ancient story.

He grimaced. "So you have those scars."

"Yes," she said quietly. "I have those scars. It was two years ago. They haven't gone. Still, I was lucky."

He watched the darkness in her eyes. It seemed to him that she had thrown a mantle of gloom over herself.

He touched her face. "Everybody fears death."

She looked away, saying nothing. He reached forward and kissed her arm, running his tongue over the darker skin, shockingly gently. Eva felt dizzy in a maze of conflicting emotions. After a while Frazer stopped, and still holding her arm, his head bowed, he smiled up at her. Eva touched his hand, then reached away from him, down to her bag on the floor. She took out a packet of cigarettes and lit up.

She exhaled, blowing the smoke away from him, averting her eyes. What had passed between them was a powerful, complex intimacy, outside the realm of convenient sex and the simple, well-tried rules that accompanied it.

"You like ugliness, do you?" she asked.

"It can be intriguing, don't you think? There can be something quite bland about perfect beauty."

"What do you think of Cassie Stewart, then? Is she a perfect beauty?"

"She's very beautiful." Frazer watched Eva closely. "I haven't had the chance to study her, to see if she has any hidden scars. But I wouldn't call her bland."

"No. There's a cleverness to her beauty, a jaggedness almost. It's something new, strange. It wasn't there at Oxford."

"What changed her?"

"How do I know? Eight years have passed. Enough for a lot to happen to all of us." Eva found herself straying dangerously. She lightened her voice. "It's probably just me. I've changed, see things differently."

She leaned forward and kissed him, fully and slowly. When she drew back, there was hunger and desire in his eyes. She smiled as she felt him under her control.

"When's dinner? I'm starving."

"Any time now. We're eating in. My housekeeper's cooking." He glanced at his watch. "She'll call us in a minute."

The evening passed in a pleasant haze of wine and food. Neither of them spoke of the deal. It seemed to Eva that Frazer wanted to separate her and the deal. She could be a lover and a business partner, but not at the same time. He made love to the woman, talked business to the business partner. She was happy to play along.

Frazer was a good host; he had all the easy charm of a lover confident in his role, unencumbered by emotion. Their earlier intimacy was quietly forgotten. Eva fought herself less, allowed herself to enjoy the warmth of the evening, sitting outside in the garden, eating good food, drinking good wine, listening to and telling amusing stories.

Frazer told her nothing that was directly useful, just

harmless anecdotes about Hong Kong and London, a cynical but indulgent businessman's conversation. It was amusing, but almost deliberately bland, the quality he so clearly despised. He was on guard, but not specifically against her. Eva thought it was probably the generic watchfulness of a man with secrets, or with a desire to avoid the intimacy implicit in any depth of self-revelation. It was a good proxy for a dinner conversation, and it would have satisfied many on Frazer's circuit, who simply wanted him to play the Frazer they knew and admired. But it left Eva frustrated, edgy, wanting but not yet daring to probe beneath the surface. She was not yet sure of herself, feared her questions might come out hard. She wished for a moment that she had Cassie's lightness of touch, but then, it was easy for Cassie. She had nothing to hide, was unburdened by secrets or hidden agendas. She didn't have to act.

Eva felt her body tense, so she pushed Cassie from her thoughts, emptying her mind of all but Frazer. He had the lightness of touch, yet he was so deeply contaminated it filled every pore. Eva studied him. Perhaps he didn't feel contaminated. He could simply be amoral, with a psychopathic lack of conscience. Or else a good actor. Eva looked off into the distance. She didn't know which was worse.

She wondered too what he saw in her—someone who was light and happy, with nothing to hide, or did he suspect that there was something deeper, and that she was an actress, good or bad? She would have to throw him something, a bone of self-revelation, for he would be looking for it, if only out of academic interest. He would give her nothing of himself, but would inevitably want to extract something from her, some emotional dependence. Egos such as his fed on their ability to extract from others that which they would not give themselves: a zero-sum game. They took what you gave up. That thought sobered her, and she took his hand across the table.

"Let's go to bed." The acting was easy there, increasingly redundant. Her body took over with frightening ease.

She awoke the next morning at seven, slipped out of bed, and showered. When she came back into Frazer's bedroom, she looked with distaste at her linen dress lying crumpled on the floor. Her eyes went to Frazer, still sleeping. She walked quietly across the floor to his dressing room, adjacent to the bedroom. Wardrobes flanked two walls. Against the third were two tall chests of drawers. She opened the wardrobes first: rows of suits and trousers and jackets. Lined up on shelves were jeans, folded shirts, and jerseys. She took out a pair of jeans and pulled them on over her naked body, tightening the belt to the maximum. She looked over the shelves again quickly, trying to find a T-shirt. She tensed as she heard Frazer behind her, but she continued her casual rummaging, standing with one leg bent, head to her side as if she were trying to figure out what to put on.

"What are you doing?" His voice was uncharacteristically sharp. She turned to face him.

"Can't find any damn T-shirts. Don't feel like putting on last night's clothes." Apparently oblivious to his sharpness, she walked half naked toward him and kissed his lips.

He smiled, but his voice remained harsh. "You should have asked me. I'd have found you something."

"I didn't want to wake you. Thought it might put you in a bad mood. And I was right, wasn't I?" She spoke teasingly. "You are in a bad mood. What are you worrying about? That I'll find some woman's clothes tucked away?" She relaxed as she saw the amusement in his eyes. "You needn't worry. I'm very broad-minded. I know I don't have a monopoly on you."

He laughed and she felt the tension ease.

"Now, where's that T-shirt? I can't go home like this."

He turned to a chest of drawers and pulled out a plain white T-shirt and handed it to her.

She pulled it on. "Thank you."

He watched her tuck it into his jeans. His clothes hung loose on her, but still the contours of her body were visible, the firm muscles. He imagined her smooth skin. She looked more appealing than ever in his ill-fitting clothes. He pulled her toward him and ran his hands over her body, pushing down the loose jeans, lowering her to the floor.

An hour later he watched her dress again. "You hungry? Margaret will make us breakfast."

"A proper fry-up?" she asked hopefully.

"Have it every morning. The hell with cholesterol."

They sat down at the dining room table ten minutes later, easy again with each other. Eva tucked into bacon, fried eggs, tomato, sausages, and mushrooms. Margaret brought in coffee unblinkingly, clearly accustomed to seeing women at breakfast. There was probably a regular traffic of new faces, thought Eva. That was her best cover.

Women were curious. All but the most scrupulous or least interested poked around in wardrobes and bathroom cabinets, looking for signs of other women—face cream, perfume, shoes, dresses. Frazer would connect her rooting around in his wardrobe with a familiar pattern. She also had the added excuse of wanting a change of outfit. She had discovered nothing, but she had established a workable precedent, covered by the foibles of her sex.

She glanced at Frazer, who was buried behind the *Times*. She could just see his eyes. He seemed perfectly relaxed, happily devouring his breakfast.

Margaret came in almost silently. She stood beside the door, saying nothing, waiting until Frazer turned to her.

"Telephone."

He got up and followed her out. He closed the study door behind him and picked up the telephone.

"Yes?"

"It's Le Mai. I've just arrived at Heathrow."

"Come straight here."

When Frazer returned to the dining room, his early-morning languor was gone. Eva could sense his impatience. He finished his breakfast with a clatter of cutlery, pushed his plate away, and looked half expectantly at Eva, who was eating still. He got up, walked over to the window, and stared out at the garden. Eva took her time, apparently unaware, flicking through the *Daily Telegraph* with bored indifference. Then she got to her feet, walked over to him, and kissed his cheek. "Goodbye." She turned to go.

Frazer, to her amusement, looked surprised, as if he had not expected such a clean exit.

Owen Quaid watched Eva leave Frazer's house. He sat low in his rented car, an anonymous burgundy Mondeo. He expected her to find a taxi. She lived half an hour's walk away and would no doubt be tired this morning. She walked out of Wilton Place, through Wilton Crescent toward Belgrave Square. He watched her wait at the side of the square. He drove one full circuit and returned in time to see her climb into the back of a cab. He was sure she would return home, just wanted to check. He allowed a three-car gap between them and set off in pursuit.

The cab stopped outside a newsagent's on the King's Road. Quaid pulled in some way back and watched Eva come out of the shop with a plastic bag of newspapers and a few bulky items, which looked like a pint of milk and a loaf of bread. Nicely predictable.

He followed long enough to see the taxi turn into Langton Street, then he turned around and headed for his office in Notting Hill.

Once there, he made a telephone call to a small company that sold the usual information: medical records, itemized telephone and credit card bills, bank statements.

"How soon?" asked the man at the other end of the line.

"Now," said Quaid.

"Yeah, sure," said the man, hanging up.

Eva went through her usual exercise routine. Thirty minutes later, clearheaded and sweating, she rang Stormont. His secretary answered.

"He's in a meeting. But Giles Aden is here. He wants to talk to you."

Before Eva could object, Aden came on the line. "Eva. I've been wanting to speak to you. What's up?"

"Get Stormont out of his meeting, would you, Giles?"

"Well, Eva, I'd like to, but he's with—"

"I'm not interested in his appointments, Giles."

Aden bit back an answer and disappeared to get his boss.

Stormont came on the line a minute later. "Eva, what's going on?"

"I need a telephone intercept, Stormont. I have a feeling Frazer's up to something, but I need a damn sight more than physical surveillance to pick it up. A room bug would be nice too. We're wasting time otherwise."

"O.K., Eva. I've resisted it so far because no foreign secretary likes to sign interception warrants for a man of Frazer's ilk. But you're right, we are wasting time. I'll put a warrant request through to Carew today."

"Great. It will help to establish one thing, at least."

"What's that?"

"That Frazer has something to hide. I doubt we'll pick up anything really incriminating, since Frazer's very careful. He appears to talk candidly, but he doesn't really give himself away. I'll bet he works on the assumption that his telephones might be tapped. We'll probably just get some vague conversations where he hedges himself, but you never know, we might get some leads. How long will it take?"

"Could get authorization today, with a bit of luck. Then we pick the right time to go in."

"Do you want me to do it? After all, I have access."

Stormont was silent for a while. "Bit risky. If you got caught, it would demolish your cover. But you are well placed."

"Get the stuff to me. I'll do it."

"O.K.," said Stormont after another pause. "I'll have it sent around now. In the meantime, don't let Frazer get distracted. Keep the diamonds on the agenda, and watch out."

"Don't worry."

"You'll have to be careful, Eva."

"For God's sake, Stormont. As if I wouldn't be."

"I know. I know you will be. It's just that we both know what he's capable of."

NINETEEN

Owen Quaid fidgeted in his office, chain-smoking half a packet of cigarettes before grinding out the last one, jumping to his feet, and striding into the office of his colleague, Paul Black. Black was a sharp, cool thirty-five-year-old with wavy black hair, a long bony nose with a bump in the middle, watchful blue eyes, and a prematurely wrinkled face. Whiskey, cigarettes, and a lifetime's undercover work had left their mark.

The two men had joined forces four years before, partly as an experiment. Both had been independent operators who became overstretched. Neither had known, or admitted knowing, much about the other. Theirs was not a world of resumés and references. Each man had relied on what he managed to find out about the other and on instinct.

Quaid knew that Black had worked for over a decade in the Far East. What exactly he had done there he didn't know, and he knew better than to ask. Neither man wished to trade revelation for revelation. There was always the danger that in swapping anecdotes, competitiveness would get the better of wisdom and reserve. Discretion was a rule of their business, one they chose not to break. There was another reason too, almost congenital after more than a decade's practice: discretion slipped seamlessly into habitual concealment. It was not solely their preserve. In many lives discretion cloaked mistresses, bank accounts, lies. But in their case, professionally it was necessary and a good cover, and the boundaries blurred. Within these constraints they trusted each other and worked well together.

They had a profitable operation, working for a small group of clients. They were generally commissioned by one business partner wishing to check out another. They investigated financial and personal probity. Individual psychology was as important as bank accounts, and they had to be equally adept at accessing and reading both. They used freelancers for intensive work like surveillance, where sheer numbers were needed. They lacked the resources of the large corporations with worldwide operations, like Kroll, but they offered an anonymity that Kroll, for all its discretion, could not. Kroll was almost an establishment in itself, or perhaps a counter-establishment. Quaid and Black could be used by people who chose not to acknowledge their need for such services to an outfit as prominent in the business as Kroll.

Black and Quaid were small enough to remain almost invisible. Their company was called Black Property Services. Invoices, apart from the size of the figures, looked innocuous enough. The office, in a residential district of Notting Hill, was airy and relaxed, a good foil for the clinical efficiency of its occupants. For all his laid-back grace, Quaid was an ingenious investigator who could by charm and cunning obtain the most protected information. He knew well the network of secrets for sale, the bent bank clerks and medical records officers, the computer hackers only too eager to demonstrate their skills. Quaid knew too how to seek out the black holes in people's lives, knew when to look below the innocuous cover; he had a real instinct for it.

He walked quickly into Black's office. Black looked up, took a long sip of coffee, and pulled a cigarette from a packet on his desk. Every move was casual, relaxed. He sat smiling, waiting for whatever bad news lay behind the tension that came into the room with Quaid. Whatever it was, Black's manner seemed to suggest, it was no problem, nothing to trouble him.

Quaid sat on the edge of Black's desk and said bluntly, "We have a problem. I've paddled myself so far up shit creek I have to keep on paddling or sink."

Black raised his eyebrows and his smile faded, but he said nothing.

"A conflict of interest—two parties on either side, each investigating the other. I've accepted the commission, both commissions."

"Who?"

"Robie Frazer and Cassie Stewart."

"That's quite a feat, Owen. Has your brain gone AWOL, or d'you just get bored with life?"

Quaid smiled for the first time that morning.

"What's it all about?" asked Black.

"A diamond discovery in Vietnam. Cassie has a friend from Oxford, Eva Cunningham. Cunningham has spent the past eight years in the Far East, on the hippie trail, apparently."

Black's eyes registered a question, but he said nothing.

Quaid continued. "Cunningham hooked up with this American geologist who thinks he's discovered diamonds north of Hanoi. Cunningham bailed him out of prison, a local fracas, and got a ten percent stake in the diamond site in return. She brings the deal to Case Reed. Needs more money to do more tests. Case Reed invites Frazer in as coinvestor. Cassie asked me, much against her will, to investigate her friend Eva. They obviously think Frazer is above suspicion."

Black interrupted with a barked laugh.

"Yeah, rich, isn't it?" said Quaid. "But in Cassie's defense, perhaps she just thought that if a man on Frazer's level did have any secrets, he would hide them so well it wasn't worth my even looking."

"Come on. Who cares? There are a thousand financial institutions panting to do business with Frazer. All they care about is his prestige, his ability to make a ton of money. They all hope he'll gild them with a bit of his Midas touch. When you get to Frazer's level, no one cares what you might have done in the past, how you made your money. It's called the sanctity of wealth. No one wants to look any further. They're all dazzled into respect, seduced by greed."

"I can't argue with you. Cassie's not the dazzled type, but it wouldn't occur to her to doubt Frazer. She's way out of her league. Case Reed is way out too. Cassie's never come across anyone like Frazer before. She has no experience to go on. She thinks she's being prudent by having Eva checked out. So anyway, I agree to investigate Eva. But a few hours before that, Frazer rang me, asked me to investigate Case Reed, John Richardson—Cassie's boss—Cassie, and Eva Cunningham. I said yes automatically."

"You didn't have much choice, with Frazer."

"Not a whole hell of a lot. I would have kissed goodbye the best part of the business if I had refused." He was silent for a while, sensing Black's eyes on him. "And I have to admit, I wanted to find out what was going on. Felt I might be able to protect Cassie in some way. Then when Cassie told me about the site in Vietnam and Eva and Frazer, what could I say? If I refused to help, what explanation could I give? That it was a conflict, that I was already investigating her for Frazer?"

Black ground out his cigarette and lit another. "You could have told her. It wouldn't be unprecedented for an investor to investigate his coinvestors."

"No, true. But it would say a lot to her about Frazer's mentality. If she is going to get involved professionally with him, I'd rather she had no inkling of how he really operates. She might start asking awkward questions. You know how curious she is, and how perceptive. It's much safer for her if she suspects nothing, thinks Frazer's just another client, albeit a vastly rich and talented one."

"All right. Against all our best professional interests, you take a position based on personal considerations. We've all done that. You can guess what I think of the wisdom of it, but I won't question your decision. We're not automatons. We all do unwise things for personal reasons. That's why you and I have a business. But it's going to be bloody difficult to control. You want to protect Cassie, but if Frazer even gets a suspicion we're acting on both sides, it will be dangerous for all of us. And if he discovers you and Cassie are having an affair . . ."

"I'm wise to that," said Quaid, picking up the implicit warning. "I told her that just in case Eva gets a clue that she's being investigated by her old Oxford friend, we want to keep a low profile—that we can't risk Eva's connecting the two of us."

"She bought it?"

"She did."

"You know the safest thing to do, to protect Cassie, is to trash the deal, get Case Reed to drop it."

"I thought of that, but Cassie's all gung-ho, and I can hardly trash Frazer. She'd ask me what I know."

"What are you going to tell Frazer about Cassie?"

"Oh, a nice sterile report, all the usual data. Cassie has nothing to hide anyway."

"Everyone has something to hide. Her affair with you, for example. Have you thought about her telephone records? Your number will be all over them."

"If Frazer wants to check them—and I doubt he'll be bothered with that kind of detail once he's read my report—I'll have to reveal that we do the odd piece of work for Case Reed. It's a risk, but no way would Frazer think we're acting against him."

"No," agreed Black. "It wouldn't occur to him that we'd be so totally insane." He paused, gazing off into the distance. "Eva Cunningham bothers me. I'll be interested to see what you dig up on her. Hippie trail in the Far East for eight years? That raises a few questions, to say the least. Then bailing someone out of prison. What did that cost? Where did she get the money? What exactly is she doing? It's quite a transformation, from hippie to entrepreneur. And not some corner shop. Somehow or other, she's got herself in the big league. I'll back you all the way in this, Owen, but I won't pretend to like it."

TWENTY

Le Mai traveled from Heathrow to Belgravia by taxi. He paid off the driver at the south side of Belgrave Square and walked the short distance to Frazer's house in Wilton Place. He carried only a small canvas roll bag—efficient packing in expectation of a short stay. Whatever he had to do for Frazer would be quick, urgent. Despite the Tai Pan's customary languor, the curtness of the instruction to come to London immediately betrayed the urgency.

Margaret opened the door to him. She nodded and stood back to let him pass.

"The study?" he asked.

"Yes."

Le Mai knocked, waited for Frazer's "Yes," then went in.

Frazer was standing in his habitual pose, looking out at the garden unseeingly, his eyes merely seeking farther horizons. He turned to Le Mai and regarded him with a mixture of admiration and proprietary carelessness.

"We have a problem with our friend Xu Nan."

"Unreliable?"

"Yes." Frazer took a key from his pocket. "Safe deposit box—you know where. Plans, keys. Get someone from Chinatown if you need help. Come and see me when you've finished. Stay in a hotel in the meantime."

"Quick?"

"Quick."

Giles Aden left his desk at twelve-forty-five to hunt for a decent sandwich from a street café in the no-man's-land of Vauxhall Cross. He didn't want to eat in the staff restaurant, wanted instead the privacy of his office and a chance to still his uneasiness. Instead, impulsively, he took a detour via Andrew Stormont's office.

Stormont was talking on the telephone. He saw Aden hovering and waved him in, cutting short his conversation.

"What's up?"

Aden took a chair, taking time to rearrange its position, gathering his thoughts.

"It's Eva. I'm not sure about the wisdom of letting her install the bugs. Really could blow the whole thing."

Stormont looked at him for a while before speaking. Aden wore the ferret face of the disingenuous, concealing something behind the guise of an honest worry.

"It will only blow the operation if she's discovered," Stormont finally said. "And I want more than a telephone intercept. I want a device in the house. Someone has to do it. The risk that outsiders without her kind of access will be caught is much higher. Sure, there's a risk with Eva. It's called a calculated risk, playing the odds. Now what's really bothering you?"

"As if you didn't know. It's Eva. I know what you'll say about how good she is, but you're placing an awful lot of faith in her playing straight—unless, that is, you have some contingency in place you're not telling me about."

Stormont laughed. Aden was becoming bolder and edgier by the minute.

"I do have a contingency I haven't told you about." Stormont said it with a smile, but still Aden grimaced at the deliberate humiliation. "Not that I expect it to appease you, particularly."

Aden broke his contemplation of his shoes and looked up in surprise. He waited for Stormont to elaborate.

"Cassie Stewart and Eva are close. They'll get closer still working together on this deal. She's a bright woman, Cassie—seems very perceptive."

Aden wondered how Stormont knew enough of her to make such a judgment.

"But there's something else there, between those two women. Some sort of tension."

"What kind of tension? Jealousy?"

"That would be the simplest explanation. But mutual jealousy? It tends to go just one way."

"If one is jealous of the other, the other will sense it and will react in some way."

"Very often the object of the jealousy is completely unaware of it—the last-to-know syndrome. But there is some kind of problem between them. They're old friends, in many ways quite different characters who've led very distinct lives since Oxford, but circumstances have thrown them into the same arena again. They seem to circle around each other. They watch each other carefully, choose their words about each other carefully. It's not quite as light and spontaneous as it might be. Eva has stepped into Cassie's territory, and they can't help but compete."

"Hang on a minute. You don't mean to say you've seen them together, that all three of you have met?"

He saw the answer in Stormont's hard, smiling eyes, in the look of contained amusement.

"You must be mad, throwing yourself into the equation. If Cassie Stewart mentions to Frazer that she met you and Frazer has you followed to this building, which everyone in London knows is the Firm's HQ, you could blow Eva's cover to smithereens."

"Neither Frazer nor anyone else can trace me to this building. First of all, as you know, Munro drives me everywhere, and we check for tails. We'd never come near here with a tail on us. Second, for the duration of this operation I shall use an outside base. From tomorrow, I'll be in Tooley Street."

"Either way, you shouldn't be seeing Eva, except in a safe house. And certainly not Cassie Stewart."

"I know the rules, Aden. If I don't always follow them, it's not through forgetfulness."

"Why break them?"

"Because I have to see Eva, to see that she's all right."

"And no one else could do that?"

"Only you, the chief, and I know of her role in this operation. As you know, she won't see you, and having the chief run an agent is hardly practical. That leaves me. And I wouldn't choose to have anyone else try. How could they get to know her, understand her, all her background? She just wouldn't have it. She wouldn't trust them, and they wouldn't know how to handle her or what to look for."

"You mean if she's gone back on heroin?"

"I think that's extremely unlikely, but I have to be sure. And I have to follow everything closely, make sure she doesn't take unnecessary risks."

"Why should she?"

"Her tolerance of risk is way beyond normal. She almost revels in it. We both know that. I have to rein her in. I can't do that from a distance."

"Which brings me back to my original question. Why use her if it's all so tricky?"

"Because I want Frazer, and Eva'll get him."

"All right. I can see you'll never be persuaded otherwise. But why see Cassie? How can that be justified?"

"Seeing her is another way of keeping tabs on the operation, and on Eva. Cassie's loyal to Eva. Eva is not particularly loyal to Cassie, but then how could she be without splitting herself in two? But I think in a while Cassie will begin to see Eva differently, get closer to her and move away at the same time. Then she'll begin to talk more freely about her. Cassie is our unwitting contingency."

"Have you told the chief?"

"He knows what he needs to. If I break the rules, I take full responsibility."

"For putting both your beloved Eva and Cassie at risk?"

Stormont wondered at the bitterness in Aden's voice. Professional reservations he could understand. But this was a new note, almost personal, and it struck a warning chord, which Stormont registered, filed away. He watched Aden resume a mask of watchful respect, as if he realized he had gone too far.

"Eva and Cassie are already at risk. My intervention is designed to reduce the overall risk, even if it introduces new, smaller risks. It's playing the odds, Aden. You can't always manage people or operations according to the rulebook. I've always operated this way, you know that."

"I know that." He knew too, the implication—that

Stormont had been spectacularly successful in his operations so far. But this one was different. It involved risks that even Stormont didn't know about. That gave Aden a perverse satisfaction, and he found himself smiling. *Arrogant bastard,* he thought, getting to his feet, almost wishing that Stormont, the mastermind so smoothly, blithely playing his characters, would have cause to falter one day, to realize that perhaps he had been wrong, his vision had been blinkered by his own desires.

Stormont watched Aden disappear. He would never make an operative. He was utterly transparent, easily provoked. Stormont knew it was too easy a game, riling his deputy, but he couldn't resist it. He pushed Aden from his thoughts, picked up his telephone, and called Cassie.

"Cassie, it's Andrew Stormont."

"Andrew. How nice." She sounded pleasantly surprised, but there was a hint of teasing as they played the old game. Who telephones whom, with what gap in between? Stormont knew he had telephoned sooner than coolness required, and Cassie's deliberate surprise confirmed that she knew it too.

"I was wondering about that dinner. Perhaps you'd like to join me tonight?"

"I'd love to, but I can't."

"Tomorrow, then?" Stormont was surprised at himself, breaking another rule of sexual engagement with his undisguised persistence.

"Tomorrow would be lovely."

If she too had been playing strictly by the rules, she would have pretended to be busy for weeks, never admitted to being free on a Friday night. At best she would have mumbled something about having a cancelable arrangement, about how perhaps she would be able to see him. She probably did have an arrangement, which she would now cancel. The fact that she had accepted immediately, without any dancing around, gave him a quick twist of pleasure.

"What time would suit you?"

"Nine?"

"Perfect. Would you like me to pick you up?"

"Yes, thank you."

"What's your address?" he asked, knowing it already, adept with the lie. She told him and rang off.

She felt the quick thrill of complication. Other women's men. It was like playing with other people's money. You could do it with more detachment, and once there were costs to be borne, someone else would pay. Stormont wasn't supposed to be Eva's. Both protested the innocence of their friendship, too much perhaps. Echoes came back to Cassie. She had played with Eva's men before, but there had been no consequences then. Eva was so self-contained. Nothing touched her.

TWENTY-ONE

Cassie felt restless all afternoon. She was trying to write up a preliminary report on Eva's project, but she found her mind wandering and kept taking breaks to gossip with her secretary or go to the coffee machine.

She left at six and walked in the warm sun to Knightsbridge. The early summer sun had brought out a bouquet of short dresses. She looked down at her business suit, which skimmed her legs three inches above her ankles—fashionably long, but dowdy. Surreptitiously she slid one hand along her waist and hip, feeling the firm contours, curious, as if she were touching someone else.

She came to Harvey Nichols, source of much of her wardrobe, and walked on. She stopped before Miss Selfridge and went in. Blaring music and racks of short dresses greeted her. She selected an armful and headed for the communal changing room. She stripped down to her underwear, observing in the mirrors the discreet glances of the other women. Smiling, she pulled on a succession of dresses and selected three, two with short sleeves and one with thin straps, all cut high on her thighs. Armed with her purchases, she caught a taxi and headed home.

David Wilson was clanking pans in the kitchen when she arrived. She shouted "Hello," darted in to pour herself a glass of white wine, and retreated rapidly. David followed her, a glass of wine in his hand. He flopped down next to her on the sofa.

"I need a break. I think I might have been a bit ambitious. But it's all in the oven, so too late now." He looked doubtful. "We can always get a take-away."

"I'm sure it will be just fine."

David sipped his wine in a contented silence. He watched Cassie drink a little wine, get up, water the plants, come back, switch the television on and off twice.

"Cass, for God's sake, sit down. You're like a cat on speed."

"I know. Sorry. I've been leaping about all day."

David gave her a searching look and found her averting his gaze. "O.K. What's up? Business, or a man?"

"I don't believe you sometimes."

"Yes, you do. Especially when I'm right. So which is it?"

"All right, I'll tell you, if only to stop you going on all evening."

He leaned back, arms folded, a look of satisfaction on his face.

Cassie took another drink, smiling a private smile that David knew had nothing to do with him.

"Well, it all seems to revolve around Eva," she began. She was staring into space and missed the look of apprehension that crossed David's face. She carried on in the same tone of happy enthusiasm. "Her deal is very exciting. I really have a good feeling about it."

"And? What else revolves around Eva?"

"I met a friend of hers the other day. We had lunch yesterday. And we're having dinner tomorrow night."

"I thought you were going out with that idiot James whatsit tomorrow."

"I was. But I canceled him."

"That's unlike you. You never normally cancel if you can help it."

"No. Not normally."

"So who is he?"

"He's called Andrew Stormont."

"And what does he do?" Anxiety cut through his voice now.

Cassie let it go, used to his inquisitions about other men. "You know, I have no idea what he does. We didn't discuss it."

"And he's nice, decent. You like him?"

"I don't know about nice or decent. He's attractive, intelligent, and he has a sort of hard-edged integrity. He's quite a powerful character, disturbing in a way."

"Why disturbing?"

"There's a hell of a lot beneath the surface. It's almost as if there's a ruthlessness behind the integrity. I wouldn't want to be on the wrong side of him."

"And you're thinking of getting involved with him?"

"I don't think he'd show that other side with women. He's not the type to see women as adversaries, the enemy, even if they're attracted to him. He's not a misogynistic playboy."

"Be careful, Cass. He sounds like a bit of a handful."

"I think he might be."

"What happened to your natural caution? What happened to 'guilty until proven innocent'?"

"I'm bored with playing it safe. Anyway, it doesn't always work. You might give yourself a long time to get to know someone and lull yourself into a sense of security because you think you know him. But you never do, not until some catastrophe rips off the veneer, tears him open, and what you discover is quite different from what you imagined." She smiled gently, with a quiet wisdom that seemed to have crept up on her. "There never are any guarantees. You just take your chances, play the odds."

The telephone rang, cutting off his reply. David answered it.

"For you. It's Owen."

"Owen, hi. How are you?"

His voice jarred her. "We have to talk. Not on the telephone. Can I come around?"

She paused for a second, unnerved by his tone. "Sure. Come around now."

She put down the phone, emptied her glass, and poured another. David watched her with a worried frown.

"What was that all about?"

"I don't know. But it's not going to be a bundle of fun, whatever it is."

"You've got him investigating Eva, haven't you?"

David knew that Case Reed used private investigators on clients. Cassie had always had a need for confidants, and she told David most things. He knew about her friendship with Quaid, had met him at the house several times, and rather liked him. He would have felt different if he had known about their affair, and for that reason, Cassie had kept it from him.

She nodded. "I had no choice. I don't like it one bit. Some people would love the chance to discover their friends' secrets, the things they try so hard to hide, but I'd rather not know. I prefer to give them the benefit of the doubt. Everyone has a dark side. If we knew about it, it would change the relationship. It's like eavesdropping— you never hear anything good about yourself. But I have to find out as part of the due diligence. I can't make an exception of Eva just because she's a friend."

David nodded. Conscious of her unease, he just listened. Using Quaid for Eva was distasteful, and nothing he could say would convince Cassie otherwise.

They had finished the bottle of wine by the time Quaid arrived. He walked slowly into the house, his normal exuberant vitality absent. Cassie led him out to the garden. He sat down next to her on the grass.

"What's going on?"

"Some information on Eva has started coming back. There's no easy way to say this, Cass. She's a heroin addict."

"Eva? Oh, come on, that's ridiculous."

"It's a medical fact. She was treated for it four years ago, in a specialist clinic in western Scotland. Cured now, as far as junkies ever are."

"How do you know?"

"I read her medical records, her doctor's notes."

"How the fuck did you get hold of those?"

"In the usual way, Cassie. It's standard procedure. You know that."

"The hell with standard procedure. God, I hate this. Are you absolutely sure, Owen? There's no chance you could have got this wrong?"

"None."

"I don't want to know this. I'd rather not be having this conversation."

"You can't stick your head in the sand, Cass. I couldn't withhold this. It is material, even if she's cleaned up now, which she seems to be."

"Why would she do it? If anyone ever had everything, it's her."

"You're joking, aren't you?"

"Hardly. She's rich, intelligent, beautiful, confident. She has some great house in the country, or her family does, and a gorgeous brother—I used to go out with him. He was in my year at Oxford. They were very close. Beautiful mother, I've seen pictures of her. Pretty nice setup. Maybe that's it. Perhaps everything was just too perfect. She just had to go and muck it up."

"I don't think it was quite like that."

Cassie looked at him, puzzled. He spoke with an odd gentleness, and his eyes were patient, tolerant, like a correcting father.

"How was it?"

"You're right in part. She did live an idyllic life. Until she was twelve. Her mother left then, went to live in South Africa with some man. Nine months after that, Eva's eldest brother, who was twenty-two at the time, killed himself. The father then withdrew completely, but he saw that Eva and her remaining brother, Johnnie, had money—Johnnie much more than Eva, incidentally. She was expected to marry well."

Cassie stared at the ground. "I really got it wrong, didn't I? Got her wrong. I had no idea. She never spoke of any of this, and neither did her brother. You'd never have guessed if you knew them. It did all seem so perfect, and she seemed so smooth, so invulnerable, as if nothing had ever happened to her." A trace of anger mixed with the remorse in her eyes. "How the hell did you find out all this?"

"I went to the village on her family's estate today. Had lunch in the pub, spoke to the landlady. She loved Eva, said she was a gorgeous kid, really friendly, never above herself, you know. Then after all this happened, they never saw much of her. She and Johnnie spent nearly all their time together, never went to the village like they had before."

"I still can't believe it. When I met her she was so wild, so happy. She would do the most outrageous things." Cassie had a distant look on her face. She was speaking mechanically, more for her own benefit, it seemed, than Quaid's. "We went skiing once. There was never a slope she wouldn't ski down. We were in a group of ten, all very good skiers. After a while, none of the others would go with her. I only went so far. She really came alive, throwing herself down slopes that weren't really slopes. All off-piste, more like cliffs. She really loved it."

"That doesn't sound too happy to me. More like someone desperately trying to forget. Sounds like she put on quite a show."

"It wasn't a show. Not all of it. She made herself that way, so strong."

"Better than cracking up."

"Why the heroin, then? She seemed so together, as if she must have got over what happened."

"Do you ever get over that sort of thing? I think the best most people hope for is just some way to keep going."

"So the heroin was escape, and a bit of rebellion? She always had that streak. She liked risks, excitement, putting herself outside society. It's very exciting on the edge, stepping over the edge, testing yourself, perhaps even trying to destroy yourself, seeing how much you can take. I always had that sense about her. I never really saw anything to prove it, but I knew. I only had to see her across a room to know she was a risk-taker. That's one of the things that makes her so attractive, that scintillating vitality and the way she plays so loose with it."

Cassie was speaking into the air. Then she turned to Quaid. "When did it start?"

"From what I gather, about eight years ago. About six months after she left Oxford."

"And she's been clean for four years?"

"Looks that way."

"It started in the Far East, I suppose. It's easy to get hold of it out there. In some places it's part of the culture," mused Cassie.

"What are you going to do? Will you tell Richardson?"

Cassie sucked in her cheeks and began to chew at them. "She was an addict. She's clean now. She's obviously trying to turn her life around. How can I tell Richardson? I can't do that to her."

"So you'll lie to Richardson?"

She nodded.

Quaid made up his mind. He'd have to lie to Frazer too.

TWENTY-TWO

Eva spent Thursday evening alone. She sat at home, listening to a recording of *Don Giovanni*. At eight she ordered a delivery of chicken tikka masala from a neighborhood Indian restaurant. She drank two cans of Heineken with it, and when she finished she turned to cigarettes and black coffee.

Despite the music and the smell of spices and tobacco, there seemed to be a void in the house. Eva sat very still, concentrating. She didn't use the telephone, and it didn't ring. She had told very few people that she was back in London. She didn't want the distraction of friends, didn't want the obligatory drinks and welcome-home parties that would have followed. She didn't want the unnecessary expenditure of effort in maintaining her cover before a host of curious friends and new acquaintances asking, "What did you do in the Far East? What are you doing now? Going into business? How interesting. Tell me more." Like all deep-cover agents, she wasn't sure where the cover ended and real life began. In her they were entwined. Her life was cover; her heroin addiction had been cover, a cover that went too deep, took hold. Good cover often did, often became difficult to shake off when no longer needed. It was impossible to live a life of deception and not be tainted. The strain of keeping cover, of masking oneself—in the intelligent, talking banalities; in the happy, faking sadness; in the strong, feigning weakness—was sometimes so great it was almost easier to remake oneself in the required mold. The problem was then how to unmake.

Eva lit a cigarette and felt herself begin to sweat slightly. The English summer suddenly felt humid. Her four years of addiction came back to her, the ecstasy and the despair. She knew seconds after the drug first entered her bloodstream that she would become addicted, knew the future of it, had seen it around enough to know what would follow. In every moment but those blissful hours when the heroin kicked in and soothed her, banishing every concern, she felt a heightened sense of looming catastrophe, felt the struggle of the battle ahead, almost began to ready herself for it. She hadn't known what would trigger her going clean. She had never sensed that it would be another catastrophe, that she would have to handle two simultaneously.

She smiled grimly. The heroin was beaten. The shockwaves of the other catastrophe were still rippling out. Now she was fighting her way back to the epicenter, to the source of the shock. Only this time the balance of power was reversed. Robie Frazer knew nothing of her save the guise she had manufactured for him. He knew nothing of the danger that slept beside him in his bed.

The telephone rang, making her jump. She leaned across and picked up the receiver from the table next to the sofa.

"Eva, it's Robie."

"Robie, hello." She sounded pleasantly surprised.

"I was wondering what you were doing tomorrow night. I have to go to the country on Saturday morning, but I thought we could have a good dinner on Friday night, talk about diamonds, celebrate the end of the week. You know."

"That sounds like a lovely idea. Shall I come around at nine?"

"Perfect. See you then."

Frazer put down the telephone, relieved by the prospect of distraction. He had not heard from Le Mai since their meeting that morning. Waiting never came easily. Le Mai never disappointed, but still . . .

The comfort of logic was cold, no balm to emotion, and Frazer's mind fixed quickly on Eva, on her physicality and the warm oblivion of it. Sex blocked out all rational thought, all irrational worries. Her mere company entranced him, and when she was gone and he wasn't reliving the physical sensations, he found himself speculating about her. Her quiet self-sufficiency was frustrating. She seemed to have none of the vulnerabilities of other women. She never asked when she would see him again, never telephoned him, never sought to clarify what she was in his life. Most women would seek that out, even as early in their acquaintance as this. But she did none of that. On the surface she seemed content to let him have her on whatever terms he chose, a passivity he found surprising in someone who exuded strength as she did.

He wondered what she did want. His money, he supposed, for her diamond venture. That was the simplest explanation, and the most convincing. It still left him unsatisfied. He would try to rattle her tomorrow, to see what he could shake up. By that time he should have a preliminary report from Quaid.

* * *

After her brief conversation with Frazer, Eva went out for a walk. It was nine o'clock. The sky was darkening, but the streets were bright, lit by illuminated shop windows and streetlamps. Chelsea was warm and comforting, and Eva felt herself part of the moving throng of walkers. The disjointedness and detachment that she had felt for so long seemed to be ebbing. The constraints of her cover were easing. Parts of her that were perfect for the task were coming to the surface, and they were real. This whole exercise was not just about Frazer. It was to Stormont, of course, but as Stormont knew, it was much more personal to her. Frazer would be her catharsis. She would trap him and hand him over to Stormont, and that would be the end of it for her, the end of Frazer, and he would no longer taint her future as he had her past.

She felt restless suddenly, wanting things to move faster, wanting to move them herself. The thrill of risk, the lure of what she had to gain, did not begin to justify what she had to lose if things went wrong. But still, happily, she had made her choice, and she now would live and die by it, if necessary.

TWENTY-THREE

Stormont rang Eva first thing Friday morning using the Vodaphone digital transmission system, for security reasons. This system turned words into numbers which were sent electronically to local exchanges, which then put them on the land line. The numbers were automatically jumbled up. Anyone scanning the airwaves to intercept conversations would just get beeps. The Vodaphone system was terribly difficult to decrypt. Although neither Stormont nor Eva would run the risk of talking freely on it, it allowed for basic communication.

Eva had just finished her exercise routine and was slightly breathless when she picked up the phone.

"I'm not interrupting anything, am I?" asked Stormont.

"No," said Eva, regulating her breathing. "Exercise."

Stormont had a quick image of her alone in her flat, of her glowing muscles and smooth skin. He banished it before it could develop.

"How's the deal going?"

"Not bad. My friend has it all worked out. I'm waiting for the next official meeting. I'll encourage her, get her to set it up."

"Good. You'll be pleased to hear that our friend signed the intercept warrant. Bit reluctant—rang me directly to ask if we really did have good reason for going after such a paragon."

"But you convinced him."

"I did. The intercept should be active this afternoon. And we have the backup all ready for you to place the room bug. We'll have the recording checked twice daily."

"Good. I got the device yesterday afternoon. Nice equipment. I'll place it tonight, if all goes well."

Stormont was silent for a few moments. Then he spoke with surprising gentleness.

"Be careful, my friend."

Owen Quaid rang Frazer with his preliminary reports just before lunchtime. He sat in his office with Paul Black listening carefully by his side, his ear locked to an extension phone.

"All clear on all the parties so far," said Quaid. "Nothing stands out. Nothing abnormal. No financial irregularities. Nothing personal—nicotine, alcohol, lovers, but none to excess and no one troublesome."

"Indulge my curiosity a little. Who are they? Any background stuff?"

"Cassie Stewart comes from a small village in the west of Scotland. Modest background. Made quite a bit of money in the City, has a nice house in Chelsea. She's done well, but not too well. Nice girl, people seem to like her. No skeletons I could find." He moved on quickly. "Richardson is just what you'd expect. Farm in the country, house in Trevor Square. Eton, Guards regiment, then the City. Again, he's well liked, although one thing did crop up a few times. He's supposed to be extremely sharp, much more than he seems."

Frazer laughed. "He's a lump of lard with a fragment of brain attached. The only thing sharp about him is his razor. Give me a break, Quaid."

"I'm just reporting what we picked up from his contemporaries."

"They still think anyone who works is sharp. Tell me about Eva. I don't expect anything of interest about Cassie and Richardson, but Eva's different. I would have expected there to be something."

Quaid and Black exchanged a frown.

"Well, she essentially disappeared off to the Far East for eight years after earning a good degree at Oxford. She taught English to children in remote areas in Vietnam, Laos, and Thailand. She financed herself with family money. She comes from a rich family. Father doesn't really do much besides shoot, read, and fish. Not that close to Eva. They're not estranged, just distant. Mother living in South Africa. Ran off a long time ago. One brother, who will inherit the bulk of the estate. Eva has a house in Chelsea, registered in her mother's name. Apart from that, and a small allowance, she has to make her own way. She drinks, smokes, but not a problem. Seems to keep to herself."

"That's all rather bland."

"I could spice it up for you. But you're not paying for fiction."

Frazer was silent for a while. "I'm wondering about surveillance on her, a full team, for a week."

"If you like."

Frazer smiled. "Yes. I'd like." He hung up.

"Shit," said Quaid. "We're probably going to have to

invent something juicy." He had not told Black about the heroin. Black had no idea that he had just lied to Frazer.

"He's really looking for something, isn't he?" said Black. "It almost sounds like it's a sport to him. It seems to go beyond the requirements of checking out a business partner."

"They're having an affair."

"There's too much personal shit flying around," said Black, looking hard at Quaid. "Too many lies. This thing just gets worse and worse."

When Black left the office, distancing himself, Quaid picked up the telephone and began to call his list of free-lancers. He organized a team of twelve for round-the-clock surveillance for seven days. They would work in shifts, six on, six off, starting the following Monday.

Frazer sat in his office, strangely disappointed. Eva didn't fit her conventional background. Something else had molded her.

The telephone rang, interrupting his thoughts. Le Mai spoke curtly, a hint of worry in his voice.

"Our friend has gone to the country. We don't know where. We're told he'll return on Monday or Tuesday."

"Try to find him. Keep someone here in case he comes back early."

Frazer went to lunch. He didn't drink—he didn't trust his mood.

Cassie sat in her office trying to decide whether she was hungry, whether she should force herself to go out for a walk and a sandwich. She laughed inwardly as she thought of arriving home last night laden with new dresses, in a spirit of happy ignorance. The excitement she had felt had pointed to challenges and risks ahead, with the deal and with Stormont. But it had felt controllable.

She had felt as if she knew the parameters, could predict and anticipate events. The news of Eva's heroin addiction changed all that. It revealed a wildness in Eva beyond what she might have expected, beyond her experience. And now it forced a schism. She would have to lie to Richardson, and she had the feeling that like most lies, it would breed.

She had always led an open life, not needing to hide or conceal things. That gave her a certain freedom and strength. Now she felt she was losing both. She had a sense that she was crossing into an alien territory, one she had always known about but had consciously avoided.

The clearheaded commitment she had felt to Eva and the deal was now clouded. She could let the deal languish. But it would be uncharacteristic of her, and Richardson would be suspicious. Her normal pattern was either to kill deals or to commit herself wholeheartedly. She would have to mask her lies—lies of omission, but lies just the same. Even if her motives were good, she couldn't feel the same about the consequences. She no longer felt sure of her ability to predict them, or to deal with them. As much as this troubled her, it excited her. She felt something else too: the beginnings of a sense of guilt toward Eva. Guilt for misjudging her, for not handling her and her brother more generously. She had never sensed their pain, never thought to give solace. She had simply enjoyed their aura of excitement and glamour without pausing to look deeper.

She got to her feet and walked into John Richardson's office. She sat down opposite him.

"We have to get this diamond deal moving."

"What do you need?"

"More background. I need to know more about diamonds, the business."

Richardson thought for a while. "There's a friend of mine who might talk to you. He could tell you all you need to know and more. Let me call him, see if he'll help."

When Cassie returned to her office, Richardson called his friend Aubrey Goldstein. After a brief exchange of pleasantries, he came to the point.

"Aubrey, I need a favor. We're looking at a diamond deal here. My colleague Cassandra Stewart is running it. She wants to know more about the industry. I thought perhaps . . ." He left the request delicately trailing.

"You know as a rule I don't like talking to anybody. You know what I'm like about discretion."

"I know. I wouldn't ask unless I had absolute faith in Cassie. She's discreet."

"Since it's you asking, and since you give me reassurances like that, I can hardly say no. But I'm not sure how much help I'll be."

You'll talk, thought Richardson to himself. "Thanks, Aubrey. I really appreciate it," he said.

"What's she like?" asked Goldstein quickly. "Will I like her?"

"She's intelligent, warm, funny. You couldn't not."

"Hmm." Goldstein sounded unmoved.

"She's also quite beautiful."

"Is she now?" Goldstein smiled to himself. "Well, give her my number. Tell her I'm expecting her call."

Richardson went to Cassie's office and reported, "He'll talk to you, on a confidential basis."

"Goodness, he sounds terribly mysterious."

"They all are in that business."

"Who is he? What's he do?"

"His name's Aubrey Goldstein. He's written several

books on diamonds. Knows everything you might want to know and more. Other than that I can't tell you."

"Can't or won't?"

Richardson seemed not to have heard. He opened his address book and scribbled a name and number on a yellow Post-It. He handed it to Cassie. "He's expecting your call."

Cassie looked at Richardson carefully. He was studiedly relaxed. She pocketed the number, deciding not to quiz him further.

"I'm thinking of calling a meeting for Monday—you, me, Eva, and Frazer," she said. "I spoke to Brimton. He had no problems with my plan. I've appointed him official broker. He's waiting for buying instructions from me."

"How much money do we need?" asked Richardson.

"For stage one, to buy a five percent stake, a hundred thousand shares at six dollars a share, we need six hundred thousand Canadian dollars. The brokerage account is set up. All I need is the cash." Cassie smiled across the desk.

"So it's make-your-mind-up time?"

"Yes."

"O.K. Now tell me how you see this deal. Tell me why we should go ahead—that is, if you think we should."

Cassie was silent for a moment. "I think we should go ahead, but with a clear understanding of what we're getting into." She paused again, wondering if the lie, the concealment, was visible on her face. She studied Richardson, who watched her without reaction.

"Prospecting for diamonds is super-high risk. Investing in Vietnam is super-high risk. We have industry risk and country risk up to our eyeballs. On the other hand, when diamond deals go right, the returns are huge, more than anything we've ever seen on any other deal we've done. And Vietnam could well become the hot new market. A lot of money is pouring into the country, and more's waiting on the sidelines. If our deal works and Vietnam remains stable, we'll have queues of investors wanting to buy in.

"Then we have Robie Frazer, the man with the Midas touch. His involvement alone, when it's made public, will enhance the value of this deal, and, more important, we have his expertise and contacts. He probably knows scores of investors who would jump to buy into anything he touches. And we have Eva, who is passionate about this deal and seems to be putting everything into it. That passion goes an awfully long way. This whole venture will be extremely complex. There are bound to be heaps of problems. We want someone on the ground with Eva's energy and drive to steamroller things through. So I'd say the potential up side more than outweighs the down side, but everyone has to accept that we're really just gambling. If we can live with that, we should do the deal."

"I can live with that. The mineral reports so far look very promising. I agree with what you say about Eva and Frazer. I know about the problems. Go ahead. We'll do your deal. I'll make sure the money's there."

Cassie grinned. "Brilliant. That's wonderful."

Richardson was warmed by her enthusiasm. "I'm assuming, by the way, that Eva and Frazer will go for your plan."

"Oh, they'll go for it."

"I'd be a bit careful with those two, Cass. You don't want to take anything for granted." He got to his feet. "I have to go to lunch. Set up the meeting for Monday. I'll be there."

As he walked out of her office, he turned and studied

her for a moment. "Everything's all right, isn't it? For a second there you looked a bit strange."

"I often look strange, John—always have. Everything's fine."

Cassie sat quietly, relishing the moment. She felt as if she had just started a race. Jubilant, high on adrenaline, she phoned Frazer, promised to have her business proposal couriered to him that afternoon, and set up the meeting for ten o'clock on Monday morning. Then she called Eva.

Both Frazer and Eva bit. They were perfectly smooth and polished, but still their hunger cut through.

Next she called Aubrey Goldstein. "Hello. Could I speak to Aubrey Goldstein, please."

"Who's calling?"

"Cassie Stewart, from Case Reed."

"Ah, Miss Stewart. I'm Goldstein. You'd like to talk about diamonds?" The voice was oldish, wise, and wry.

"Yes. I would."

There was a pause and Cassie could hear papers rustling. "I have to go away on Monday. Does it have to be before then?"

"Yes, ideally. If you could squeeze in some time . . ."

"Well, I was just about to have lunch. I'm sure my housekeeper can stretch things. Would you like to join me?"

"I'd love to. That's very kind."

"Not at all." He gave her his address. He looked forward to her visit. Like most beautiful women, she would not be suspicious of favors, would merely expect them as beauty's due.

TWENTY-FOUR

Cassie arrived in Holland Park at one-fifteen. Aubrey Goldstein lived in a large stucco-fronted house on a quiet tree-lined avenue. His books and his consulting must pay well, Cassie thought. As she rang the bell, she noticed two security cameras angled down from the third floor. She felt herself being scrutinized. Then a voice spoke over the entryphone.

"Yes?"

"It's Cassie Stewart."

Seconds later the door swung open. A short thickset man with gray hair and bright blue eyes stood facing her.

"Miss Stewart. I'm Goldstein."

Cassie extended her hand. He shook it firmly.

"Come in. Would you like a drink? There's cold white wine in the fridge."

"Love one," said Cassie.

Goldstein led her to the kitchen and poured out some wine. He attended to her with the charming awkwardness of someone used to butlers and housekeepers. They made their way out to a flagstone terrace at the head of a large, well-tended garden. A wooden table had been laid for two. They sat down, and the housekeeper brought out grilled fish and salad.

"I hope this is enough for you," said Goldstein with an apologetic smile.

"It's lovely," said Cassie.

His eyes rested lightly on her face as she spoke. Suddenly she felt very alert. She took a sip of wine.

"So you want to know about diamonds?"

"That's right."

"Fascinating stones." He pushed his plate aside and leaned back in his chair. The hardness Cassie had seen in his eyes disappeared, and he took on an avuncular gentleness.

"The word 'diamond' comes from the Greek *adamas,* meaning 'I tame' or 'I subdue.' Throughout history, there's always been a sense of fight with diamonds, of victors and vanquished. The stones were revered as talismans as far back as 800 B.C. in India. They're supposed to provide fortitude, courage, and victory in battle, and constancy and purity in love. Some legends have it that diamonds lose their magical powers when the wearer sins, and the stones then carry the sin as a curse." He smiled. "The histories of famous stones read like adventure stories and fairy tales—murders and curses, daring men and beautiful women. Not much has changed, except perhaps the advent of daring as well as beautiful women."

Cassie felt oddly disconcerted by this comment, which sounded like a threat.

"It's a risky business you're getting into," Goldstein continued.

"That's what we do."

"I don't think so. Don't think I'm being rude, but whatever you've done before won't be anything like this, won't be any sort of preparation."

Cassie looked questioningly at him.

"Look, I don't know what specific questions you have for me, but the best I can do for you is prepare you, tilt the odds very, very slightly in your favor."

"That would be helpful."

"You don't have much of an ego, do you? Not in the bad sense. Most pinstripes would protest about how much they know, then bore me with explanations of all the deals they've done."

"I've got as much of an ego as anyone. I just know when to control it."

Goldstein leaned back in his chair and drank his wine. "All right. I'll tell you. There's the official perception of diamonds—a girl's best friend, a good investment, the oldest thing you will ever hold in your hands." He paused, then said almost diffidently, "Did you know they're millions of years old, some of them? That's why they're supposed to represent eternal love. They're as old as eternity. Anyway"—his voice became more business-like—"then there's the official money-making side—it's a huge business. Annual sales of diamonds amount to over forty billion dollars. Investors reap huge profits from a successful venture, with equity returns of over one hundred percent. Then there's the background to the profits, the Central Selling Organization, crudely known as the cartel. About eighty percent of the world's annual production passes through the single channel, as the CSO is also known. These diamonds are sorted, graded, and sold at Charterhouse Street, in the City of London, De Beers's main base outside South Africa. It's a six-story, modern glass building, built like a fortress. On every fifth Monday of the year, a select group of diamond dealers, known as sight holders, is invited to the second floor at Charterhouse Street to collect a sack tied with a ribbon.

Inside is a cardboard box. Inside the box there is a kind of envelope, called papers. The uncut stones within a paper are similar and belong to one of the hundreds of classes into which the CSO sorts its supplies. Each box contains stones worth on average between two and five million dollars. The buyer buys or not at the price shown on the box. There is no negotiation, and it is not wise to decline to take a box. It is an extremely efficient, well-disciplined system, and it has to be. There is a considerable excess supply of diamonds in the world. There are huge stockpiles. If the CSO did not restrict supply and set and support prices, prices for most grades would fall dramatically.

Cassie's eyes widened.

"It's a brilliant operation. Over the past sixty years the CSO has done for diamonds something that eluded the oil producers of OPEC and even the cocaine barons of the Medellín cartel. It had the muscle and nerve to impose its own order on the market, and it built a syndicate not for weeks or months but for decades. There have been lapses, of course—the time a London dealer decided to buy his stones outside the cartel in Angola, the time Zaire decided to try and go it alone, the time Moscow flooded the market to pay for its adventure in Afghanistan. But in this club, tantrums have tended to be short. Until now. The Russians are causing trouble again. Millions of pounds' worth of some of the finest Russian diamonds keep appearing on the market outside the single channel."

"Why would the Russians do that if it lowers world prices?"

Goldstein smiled. "They want a seat on the De Beers board in South Africa and a hand in running the CSO in London."

"Will they get it?"

"Wait and see. But it's destabilizing, another risk for you to be aware of."

Goldstein poured some more wine.

"And the other risks?" Cassie asked.

Goldstein paused. The faint smile on his lips made him look benign but for his eyes, which she could feel probing her. As someone who read others well, Cassie could sense the skill in him and again felt disconcerted. But he took a sip of wine, and the scrutiny eased. He seemed to have made some sort of decision.

"There's a lot more you should know, in case you run into it, and the chances are that you will."

The quiet familiarity with which he spoke about troubles to come increased Cassie's uneasiness. She reminded herself that he was a writer, a friend of John Richardson's who was here to help her.

"The diamond business is used for many reasons besides the obvious. For example, stock-price manipulation, if the company concerned is quoted. For months, sometimes years, the price is sustained on hope while testing is done. Hope can be twisted very easily. Then there are those who are supposedly on the side of the angels who use the diamond trade for their own purposes." He saw her questioning look. "The intelligence services. They are close to De Beers—they exchange favors."

"How?"

"Simple. Diamond prospectors have a reason to travel all over the world, into Russia, Angola, South Africa, anywhere. They have long periods of idleness, perhaps when they're waiting for test results to come back. They have plenty of time to do whatever it is they want to do. And a good cover."

"And the favors in the opposite direction?"

"The services can help to ensure that certain supplies

of diamonds that might otherwise bypass CSO channels come back under control."

"For instance? Who would be hostile to the cartel if it's in so many people's interest to see it continue and to cooperate with it?"

"The Americans," he said simply. "The CSO is illegal there, because of the Sherman Antitrust Act. It contravenes American laws on monopolies. I've already told you about the Russians. They want a larger quota of world sales and more influence within the CSO. Then there are the smugglers, who cannot go through the established channels."

"And how might they rechannel these supplies, the intelligence service ?"

Goldstein laughed. "You'll have to work that one out for yourself. Use your imagination and then some. Look for the logic and then apply it to a different cause. Look for a wild card, an inconsistency. It will almost always be there. Look for an element of the unpredictable, the illogical, almost the self-destructive—that's the best cover of all. And, my dear, look out for yourself. That's the best advice I can give you." His eyes were, for a second, almost gentle.

Lunch was over. Goldstein got to his feet, reached into his jacket pocket, and took out a card. "This is my secretary's number. She'll be able to put you through, wherever I am." He gave Cassie the card and led her to the door. "Give me a call if you need any help. Oh, incidentally," he asked, opening the door for her, "where is your deal, somewhere interesting?"

"Yes," answered Cassie, distracted by the undertones of his offer of help. "Vietnam."

She wondered for a moment if it had been wise to tell him where the site was. She had a sense, which she couldn't pin down, that it was a mistake. He was saying goodbye. She shook his hand, they parted, and she walked down Holland Park Road. She thought of all the warnings, from Richardson, Brimton, and now Goldstein. They were piling up like dead flies in summer.

Goldstein watched her till she disappeared, then closed his door and picked up the telephone. He dialed long-distance, then spoke without announcing his name.

"A bit of news about the Vietnamese deal. It's come to London, to a venture-capital house called Case Reed."

There was a silence. Then a firm voice answered.

"Follow it. We'll wait. There'll be time. You're on full consultancy with this. The usual deal."

TWENTY-FIVE

At seven in the evening, Eva went for a run. She ran for an hour around Battersea Park. The blossoming trees lining the river were shedding their petals, and she ran along a perfumed carpet. It had been a warm day, and the park was full of people walking dogs, running, playing tennis and boules, or just lying on the grass. The normality of the scene was oddly reassuring.

She returned home sweating heavily, loving the feeling of easy effort, of her body working so readily at her will. Inside her house she did forty pushups and a hundred situps. After stretching and cooling down, she took her pulse. She always liked to check. She remembered checking it years ago when she did her special firearms training, shortly after joining the SIS. She had needed to get fit then. Holding a handgun steady was much easier with a low pulse rate. Around fifty-five beats per minute was ideal. Then Eva had got hers down to fifty-four. Now it was fifty-one.

She showered and dressed carefully for her date with Frazer in a shortish, swirling black silk dress and black shoes. It was amusing putting on all these smart, grown-up dresses after so many years of living in jeans and shorts. She glanced at herself in the mirror and looked almost with surprise at her reflection. She wondered what Frazer saw when he looked at her.

She checked the small package that had arrived by SIS courier the previous afternoon: one power socket transmitter. Indistinguishable from an ordinary socket, it contained miniature electronics within a functioning standard U.K. double-switched power outlet. The transmitter would operate continually once installed, using the main power supply. It operated on narrow-band FM, on a frequency range of UHF 365 to 455 MHz. It would pick up all conversations in the room in which it was placed.

Eva wrapped it in a handkerchief and put it into her handbag. She snapped the bag shut and locked up her house, then made her mind go blank, emptying it of all but the most inconsequential thoughts, so that she felt nothing, so that Frazer would be unable to pick up any nervousness or excitement or fear.

She arrived at his house at ten past nine. He kissed her.

"You look wonderful. Glowing."

"Thank you. I've just been for an hour-long run. That's probably it."

"An hour? Bloody hell. Remind me never to go for a run with you." He led her out to the garden, where a bottle of champagne stood in an ice bucket on the wooden table. He handed her a glass and studied her as she stood drinking, looking at the throngs of rosebushes in full bloom.

"You're incredibly fit, aren't you? You're in superb shape. I thought that the first time I saw you, standing with your back to me. I remember thinking you looked like an athlete, about to run. You're what we call battle-ready."

Eva sat down on the wooden chair. "Battle-ready? Yes, I am, I suppose. I have a lot to do."

"And what might that be?"

She looked at him in surprise. "The deal, of course. The diamonds. This could be so big. Way out of my league, really. But with your help, yours and Case Reed's, I think we can do it, don't you?"

"I'll help you, as much from self-interest as anything else. I too happen to think it could be very big. But I want to know why you're doing it." He sat down opposite her, resting his arms on the table, leaning toward her. "I want to know what you're about, Eva. Why this deal— why do you want to do it, and what are you doing with me?"

She laughed. "You sound like an ingenue. I'm having an affair with you. I would have thought that much was perfectly obvious."

"I figured that much out, but not much else. You puzzle me. Most women seem to want something beyond an affair. Oh, there are always the one-night stands, less so now, and they die with the morning. But you're not one of those. Then there are the relationships. And the women, however subtle, look for signs on my side, ask me the question I just asked you. But you don't ask any questions like that. You walk blithely into an affair with me, even though it could complicate this deal that means so much to you. Why?"

Eva sighed. "Look, you don't know much about me. It's fair enough that you ask, especially since we might be business partners, so I'll try to tell you." She reached into her bag for her cigarettes. Her handkerchief, containing the bug, was lying next to them. Carefully, she took out the cigarettes and lit up. She inhaled deeply, blowing the smoke up into the evening air.

"I don't think about these things very much. I don't go in for self-analysis. Most things I do spontaneously, instinctively. I trust my judgment, and if I want to do something, I do it. I don't think much about the consequences. I handle them when they come. People worry too much, spend hours trying to preempt the future, figuring out how to deal with it. Most often they're wrong. They focus so frantically on what they think might happen that when something different does, they're completely thrown and go into a tailspin." She paused and studied his face. "Do you understand what I'm saying?"

He refilled their glasses, looking at her with a new expression, one of pleasure, curiosity, and regard.

"I think I do. You live in the moment, trusting in yourself, not worrying about anyone else. But this deal doesn't fit with that, does it? You have to plan, you have to try to control the future, prevent problems before they happen."

"Exactly. That's one of the reasons I'm doing it. I've never done anything like this before. I want to try it, see what happens. Then there are all the other things."

"What other things?"

"Now we get into the introspection." She took a long drink of champagne. "I need to do something, put down some sort of a marker. For years I've done very little in the conventional sense. I've taught English to children in all these remote little villages all over the place. It's great fun, a wonderful way to live, but not forever. I'm thirty now. I feel ready for something different. And, to put it bluntly, I need to make some money."

She shrugged. "It's the same old story. My family had quite a bit, but my father was never very careful with it at the best of times. My brother will inherit the house and the bulk of what's left of the money. My father has made provisions for me, but much less. I'm a girl, expected to marry well and have my husband provide. That scenario isn't for me. But that's all right. I would have been able to live quite simply on the interest of the capital that was supposed to have been put aside, but then my father got hit by the Lloyds disaster. He was in one of the very bad syndicates, lost a bundle. I don't know how much, but enough to eat into what he had provided for me and my brother. It's virtually drained what he was going to leave me. So you see, it's very simple. I'd never been bothered about money. Now I am, especially since I've found something that could produce quite a lot. It's such a wonderful chance for me. I could never go and get a normal nine-to-five job. I'm not cut out for it. So if you wonder why I'm focused, why I don't leak all over you like other women apparently do, it's because my mind is on my project. That's all I really want. Do you see?"

He reached across to touch her arm. His eyes were warm and surprisingly compassionate. There was a look of understanding in them.

"I see better than you could imagine. I was the second son. When my father died, my elder brother inherited everything. Suddenly I went from this very privileged life to being shut out, effectively—to being in my brother's shadow, with no money to speak of. We want the same thing, you and I. Our 'fuck you' money. I happen to have made mine, but it's never enough, it just feeds my appetite. You're just starting out. Wait and see. It becomes addictive."

They smiled at each other. Eva put on a look of tacit complicity and understanding, as if they were suddenly partners, on the same side. She got to her feet.

"Excuse me. I've got to go to the loo."

She took her handbag and walked into the house, breathing deeply to calm her nerves. She went through to Frazer's study. She paused for a second, listening. Then, very swiftly, she took the package and a small screwdriver from her bag, unscrewed the power socket under Frazer's desk, and replaced it with the bugged socket. She dusted off her prints with her handkerchief and put the original socket into her handbag. Then she went upstairs to Frazer's bedroom, took off her clothes, and got into his bed.

After five minutes he went looking for her. He found her and smiled slowly.

"What's all this?"

She drew back the sheet. "I don't really want dinner, do you?"

He took off his clothes, looking at her all the time. The passion came naturally, surprisingly, exhilarating them beyond anything they had come to expect.

The telephone rang at midnight, waking them both. Frazer grabbed it with a groan.

"Hello? Yeah, hang on. Give me a minute."

He replaced the receiver and turned to Eva, kissing her lightly. "Hong Kong. This is going to be long and boring. Go back to sleep. I'll talk in the study."

Eva said sleepily, "Don't be too long."

She feigned sleep when he returned. She lay still, feeling him toss and turn remorselessly. She smiled in the darkness. In a few hours, if the telephone intercept had started as Stormont promised, she would be able to know the exact nature of his long and boring call.

TWENTY-SIX

At the same time that Eva arrived at Robie Frazer's house that night, Andrew Stormont drew up outside Cassie's. He looked at the pretty facade. It seemed to be the perfect house for her. When he rang the bell, he heard a furious barking and Cassie's voice, stern in admonition.

"Nesta, shut up. Stop making such a racket."

She opened the door, laughing. "Sorry about my dog. She feels it her duty to protect me."

"Wise dog." He leaned forward to kiss her, catching a trace of delicious scent, heavier than the one she had worn the other day.

"Come in." Nesta jumped around his ankles as he vigorously rubbed her neck. "Would you like some champagne?"

"Love some." He would normally have been driving to his house in the country at this time on a Friday night. It was strange to be here in London, on a date with this beautiful woman, so young in her short dress, so painfully desirable.

"This is David Wilson, my housemate," Cassie said,

gesturing to a long-limbed man who uncurled from the
sofa to extend a languid hand and a regard somewhere
between politeness and scrutiny. "David, this is Andrew
Stormont."

The two men shook hands, said curt hellos.

Cassie uncorked the champagne and poured out
three glasses. Stormont glanced at the bottle in approval.
He took the glass she handed him, sat down in a deep
armchair, and stretched out his feet on one of the Persian
rugs. He allowed his surroundings to enter his conscious-
ness slowly. Cassie seemed to be in everything around
him, in the fineness of her possessions, in the air of happy
normality, of a house well lived in, well enjoyed. There
was none of the sterility of someone else's interior design.
He felt sure that Cassie had chosen everything herself.

He suddenly felt a yearning for her happy openness,
her uncluttered lightness. And he mourned it. Whatever
happened in this operation, Cassie would not be unaf-
fected. He couldn't predict what would happen; he
would have to design events himself as they unfolded.
Neither could he protect her. He couldn't be the dog
barking at her enemies.

David Wilson clearly saw himself in that role, but he
was not much of a protector, Stormont thought, casually
studying him. Committed, but probably inept. Cassie
would have to fight her own battles. He wondered how
she would fare, and found himself comparing her strength
with Eva's. Eva was formidable, a fighter well trained and
ready for battle. Cassie wouldn't know what the hell had
hit her if things went wrong; she wouldn't have the experience.

At Cassie's request, they went for dinner to Rakes,
the dark basement restaurant that always reminded Cassie
of a tart's boudoir—a perfectly nice boudoir, one with

excellent food, but still a place of sex, of assignations. She laughed to herself and wondered what Stormont wanted —besides sex, of course. There was a sense of a broader purpose about him.

He sat before her in a dark suit and a pale blue shirt. His clothes were perfectly made, like the body beneath. Everything about him was firm and strong—body, voice, face, mind. His will, too. She saw it beneath the surface, latent, waiting, operating now behind the charming armor, the impeccable manners, the glowing interest he showed in her. His will never protruded in the guise of ego or arrogance, the qualities she most despised in men. But it was there in his smile, in his unspoken confidence, in his curiosity.

They scanned the menu and ordered, and then he slipped into a stream of questions. He asked under the pretext of getting to know her. The questions were friendly, conversational, but Cassie sensed a hidden earnestness, an intent. As a rule, she disliked questions, saw them as a shortcut to discovering someone. Many men asked them in the belief that they were showing interest, allowing their women to talk about themselves, which they deemed a favorite pastime. But she preferred more oblique methods. Had she not been so drawn to Stormont, becalmed by his seductiveness, she would have evaded the questions with a yawn and a change of subject. Instead, she watched him watching her as if he were trying to work out a puzzle.

"Quite a fierce housemate you've got. Seemed to watch over you like a dragon."

"Why is everyone so interested in him?"

"Everyone?"

"Oh, Eva was asking about him too, wanted to know if he was my lover."

"And is he?"

"No. He's just a friend. Is that so strange?"

"You strike me as independent, successful. I wouldn't have thought you needed a housemate."

Cassie shrugged. "I'm not very good at living on my own. I never have been."

"Why not?"

She looked away as if debating which answer to give. Then she turned back to him and spoke, her voice low. "I hate lying in bed hearing noises, wondering what they might be. I don't like the way an empty house echoes when I walk in alone. I feel safe with someone else in the house. And I enjoy it. David's great fun. Can you understand that?"

"Yes," he answered gently. "I can." He wanted to ask her why she had these fears, where they came from, but she looked away, as if to shun further questions.

"It's just a bit surprising," he said, drawing her back to him with his voice. "A bit at odds with this image you have—the super-slick City woman."

"You said it yourself. It's an image."

"But tell me, why did you go into the City? Bit of a snakepit, isn't it?"

"It can be a snakepit, if you allow it. The big banks are worse than Case Reed. I only stayed in the City proper for four years, long enough to get a good training in all sorts of things. Then I went to Case Reed. It's much more civilized—no real office politics. I'm given a free rein, allowed to do what I like, more or less."

"But it's still the City, even if it isn't in the Square Mile. What's the attraction?"

"Risk."

"You like it?"

"Why shouldn't I?"

"Your life seems so well run, so in order, so open. Risk seems alien to you."

"That's why I can afford it. I welcome it."

"Why?"

"It gives me something to pit myself against, to measure, to predict, to play with. It's not random risk-taking. It's all calculated. Risk, return—the banker's maxim."

"So you never take risks just for the hell of it?"

"Why should I? What would be the point?"

"That's very rational, very clearheaded."

"Look, lots of people seem to like playing that game, getting themselves into trouble just to see if they can get out again."

"And you don't need to. You know you could get out, so what's the point."

"Something like that. Or perhaps I'd rather not put it to the test without good reason."

The waiters cleared one course and brought the next. Cassie used the interruption to scan the restaurant, deliberately letting the conversation lapse. Enough analysis.

"How's your deal with Eva Cunningham going?" asked Stormont easily.

Cassie paused for a moment and studied him openly before answering. "Not much has happened yet. I've called a meeting for Monday. Things should start moving then."

"Will you finance her?"

"Her, the site . . . We'll do something."

"And how will you do it?"

"Come on, Andrew. That's insider stuff. You don't really expect me to answer, do you?"

He shook his head. He hadn't expected any detail, just wanted to test her capacity for discretion.

All the while, as he spoke, as he listened, part of his

mind was with Eva, wondered how she was getting on with Frazer, hoping and fearing for her.

"Now," said Cassie, finishing her lamb. "You've asked me a lot of questions about myself, but it's been very unequal. I know almost nothing about you."

"What would you like to know?"

"Oh, what you do might be a start."

"What do you think I do?"

She studied him. She was silent for a long time. Although he was used to doing the same thing to other people, Stormont was surprised at his own discomfiture. He saw what Eva meant: Cassie's watchfulness was acute.

Finally she spoke. "You could do any one of a number of things. You could be in the City, or a businessman. You could be a psychiatrist, or some sort of highbrow journalist. Or, somehow or other, you could combine all those things. You seem a bit like a dilettante, only you're too intense. You do something that's very important to you, and only my psychiatrist theory squares with that. But I know you're not a psychiatrist. You're too vicious."

He laughed. "What am I, then?"

Her conversation with Aubrey Goldstein rang in her head. "I don't think you really want me to answer that."

"Why on earth not?"

"Because I think you're a spook."

Stormont laughed again, lightly and smoothly. It was, thought Cassie, the reaction of either a man with nothing to hide or a man secure in his lie, even when confronted with truth.

"You do me a great honor," he said, "investing me with all that hidden glamour. The truth is much more prosaic. I dabble in property, I'm afraid."

"You disappoint me."

"I'm sorry. I'll do my best to make up for it." His

eyes dipped from her face to her throat, then to her breasts. He looked up to see her watching him. Her eyes showed a half-contemptuous satisfaction at his predictability.

"Incidentally, what the devil makes you think I might be a spy? Do you know any? Do I resemble someone?"

"As a matter of fact, you do."

"Who? And how do I resemble them?"

"You have a look about you, in your eyes. They appear to be open, but you're guarded as hell, and watching all the time. Watching, but revealing nothing but what you choose to. I've seen it before, this behavior. We all do it when we're lying, but it switches on and off with the lie. With you, it's permanently switched on, as if you have to mask your life."

"Ingenious. But wrong."

"Fine. I'm wrong but ingenious. Let's forget all about it. You go on being a property speculator and trying to make up for it. I'll try not to be ingenious."

They looked at each other, both aware of a new ambivalence in their feelings for each other, hostility as strong as desire.

Stormont dropped her off at midnight. He parked his car outside her house, keeping the engine running. He kissed her lips once, lightly.

"I'll see you soon," he said. She stepped from the car.

He felt an unaccustomed frustration. She was distant and intimate at the same time, elusive but disconcertingly perceptive.

At home, sitting in his study, whiskey in hand, Stormont was still thinking of her. Was she that perceptive, to call him a spy, or was she just guessing, teasing? Did she know something? He sipped at his whiskey. The whole operation was dangerously volatile. And he had a strange sense that Cassie Stewart would prove more of a threat to him than he could know. But however perceptive she was, there was still so much she could never work out. Whatever threat she posed, he could match it with ease.

TWENTY-SEVEN

Cassie awoke luxuriously late, at ten, on Saturday morning. She threw on jeans and a tight T-shirt and went to the new delicatessen that had just opened near World's End on the King's Road, where she bought two plain and two almond croissants, orange juice, and milk. David had appeared in the kitchen in the bottom half of a pair of pajamas when she returned.

She stuck the croissants under the grill for a minute, then carried them piled up on a plate into the sitting room. David followed with coffee.

"Did you have a nice evening?" he asked.

Cassie nodded, her mouth full of croissant. "Fine. What do you think of him?" She knew it was an unwise question. David ripped apart boyfriends and suitors without invitation, but she was curious, and he was almost always accurate.

He took a while to finish his croissant. "I think he's a wolf. He hid his teeth when he was here. But he's hunting you in a big way. I'd hate to see the look in his eyes when he's alone with you in the dark. I'd probably kill him."

Cassie laughed. "A wolf—hmm. What do you think he does for a living?"

"Probably one of those City types. He has that sort of well-refined ruthlessness about him. Why d'you ask? You don't normally ask. And why are you looking like that? You have a funny look on your face, Cassie."

"Do I?" She seemed suddenly distracted. It was clearly not an unwelcome distraction, for she was smiling, although it struck David as a not particularly pleasant smile.

"Cass, you look as if you're plotting someone's execution."

Stormont rang Eva at eleven. She had just returned from Robie Frazer's house. She picked up the telephone with her customary brusqueness.

"Hello." It was a challenge, not a greeting.

"How did you get on?"

"Easy. All in place by nine-thirty. At midnight he had a call that he had to take in the study. Might be promising."

"Good. I'll get transcripts and tape copies to us both as soon as possible. Aden and a team of listeners are going through the intercept and device recordings now, filtering out what might be important."

"And you? Any news?"

Stormont paused. He had to tell her about seeing Cassie. She would find out anyway. There was no reason for Cassie not to tell her. Better if it came from him.

"Some strange news. I saw Cassie Stewart last night." He left a pause, allowing for her reaction. She was silent. He continued, feeling a slight trepidation. "We had dinner, were chatting quite happily. She asked me what I did. I said guess, and she did."

"What do you mean, she did?"

"She said, very slowly and deliberately, that she thought I was a spook."

"What?"

"Don't worry, I finessed it. But how the hell did she hit on that?"

"Not from me. If that's what you're wondering."

"I didn't think that for a second. But how the hell did she make that connection?"

"How do you think?"

"Damned if I know. I think she's bright, usually keeps it dimmed. Then all of a sudden, it came on, full beam. I felt as if I were in a spotlight."

"I told you there was something about her—this quiet watchfulness."

"She said I reminded her of someone who was a spy."

"Who's that?"

"She wouldn't say."

"She couldn't mean me, could she? I mean, we're hardly similar."

"She might have meant you. She described this look in my eyes—like a permanent mask, designed to conceal everything, to cover my life."

"Shit. She's right on the mark there."

"You have that look too, Eva. We all do, if someone knows what to look for."

"And how on earth might she know what to look for?"

"Beats me. I think we've underestimated her."

"So what do we do?"

"Carry on as we were. What can we do? Apart from watch her like a hawk. You know, I think she said it very deliberately. It almost felt like a warning."

"About what?"

"I don't know. To watch out. Perhaps just to watch out with her personally—you know, not to fuck her around, because she is too perceptive for that, would cut me off at the first sign of misbehavior."

"And?" asked Eva, picking up on Stormont's half-finished answer.

"I asked her about her deal with you. She told me very politely to shut up, that it was insider stuff, that I knew that so why was I asking. I think it was a warning about the deal, to me and to you. You're the link to me. She knows we're friends."

"Will you tell me, Andrew, how your seeing Cassie fits in with this operation? I hope you don't intend to use her to spy on me."

"Why would I do that? I trust you, Eva. I don't need to spy on you."

Eva said nothing.

"Be careful with her, Eva. I'm not sure what kind of game she's playing, but I think she might be trickier than we bargained for."

"We're on the same side, remember? We all want to make money from this deal. And, anyway, more to the point, you be careful. You're the one she thinks is a spy. Have an affair with her, fine. Just leave me out of it, and for God's sake don't mess up this operation."

Her voice bit across the receiver. She rang off, giving him no time to answer.

The transcripts and copies of the recording arrived at twelve; one copy of each was delivered to Eva and to Stormont. Stormont also received a report enclosed by Giles Aden, who was overseeing that side of the operation.

The quality of the recording was perfect. Both Stormont and Eva listened to it immediately, absorbing every word and nuance as if the conversation were being spoken at first hand.

Frazer spoke first. "Where have you been, Chin? I've been trying to reach you for days."

"Business. What's the problem?"

"Nan is no longer of use. You'll have to wait a bit longer for your information."

"What's happened with Nan?"

"He won't cooperate."

"What will you do?"

"We're dealing with it now."

"You mean it hasn't been dealt with?"

"It will be." ·

There was a long pause. When Ha Chin spoke, his voice was cold, unflinching.

"It better be. You fucked up, Frazer. You picked the wrong man."

"It was a risk. It happens."

"Not to me. We shouldn't even be having this conversation."

"It's secure."

"How can you be sure? Especially now. You're getting sloppy, Frazer."

"No. You're getting paranoid. You're losing your grip, Ha Chin. I have a sweep every week. Later today, as it happens."

Stormont rang Eva immediately. His words were fast, urgent.

"You've got to get that bug out of there immediately. It could blow you sky high. Sounds like you've got a few hours at most."

"He's supposed to be going away for the weekend. I could ring, check he has gone, then pretend to his housekeeper that I've forgotten something." Eva was perfectly calm, her clarity sharpened by the imminent danger. She was fully aware of the consequences if Frazer discovered the bug.

"Do it now," said Stormont.

Eva rang Frazer's house. Margaret answered the telephone and informed her that Frazer had just left.

"Thank God you're in," said Eva. "I left something behind this morning, terribly sorry. But would you mind awfully if I popped round to get it?"

"I'll be here," said Margaret tightly.

Eva rang off, picked up her bag from the night before, and caught a taxi to Wilton Place.

Margaret answered the door and stepped aside with a cold smile. *She must hate me,* thought Eva. *She thinks I'm just another tart after Frazer's money.*

"I think I left it in the bathroom, upstairs."

Margaret looked her up and down. "What is it?"

"My contraceptive pills. They're in a long pop-out packet, sort of grayish and—"

"I know what they look like. Go ahead. Look for them." Margaret turned and walked toward the back of the house.

Eva watched her disappear, then walked quickly and silently through the hall to the study. She prayed the door was unlocked. It was. She closed it softly behind her and moved to Frazer's desk. She bent down, unscrewed the power socket, and replaced it with the original. Then she let herself out, ran upstairs, and walked slowly back down. She reached the hallway just as Margaret reappeared.

"I can't find them. Perhaps they fell out somewhere on the street."

Margaret gave a hard little smile, as if to say that's where they and everything else belonged.

Eva was at the door. Margaret followed her, held it open, and closed it firmly behind her.

Eva called Stormont the instant she arrived home.

"Got it. The housekeeper was there, grumpily let me in."

"Good, but it's still just damage limitation. She'll tell Frazer you were there, looking for something. It's unlikely he'll link that to his comment about the sweep being done today, but not inconceivable."

Eva started laughing.

"What's so funny?"

She answered between gusts of laughter. "It's just that I told his housekeeper that I'd left my contraceptive pills behind. She'll think it's all part of some devious scheme to entrap Frazer."

"It is. And I wouldn't take it so lightly."

"I don't. This will just make them look in the wrong direction."

"You do play dirty, don't you, my dear?"

"I thought you liked it like that."

There was an odd pause. Eva had the unfamiliar sense that she had disconcerted Stormont. When he next spoke, his voice was formal.

"Your device picked up a conversation between Frazer and an associate at eleven-thirty this morning. Aden just sent a copy round posthaste. You should receive one any second. Listen and ring me back."

The recording arrived five minutes later. Eva sat down to listen. She heard a door closing, then Frazer's voice.

"Still no sign?"

The second voice bore a heavy Hong Kong Chinese accent. "No. But we're ready."

There was a short silence, then Frazer spoke again. "What's on your mind?"

"Is there any chance that he might leave a letter with his solicitor, something to be opened in the event of his death? Revenge from beyond the grave, naming you?"

Frazer laughed as if it were a joke. "Foul play would never enter his mind. He thinks I'm a friend. Besides, his solicitor is mine." He paused. "If you're really worried and it won't jeopardize anything, you could always go in tonight, take a look at his papers, see if you find any evidence of other solicitors, anything strange."

"Yes. I'll do that."

"Stay away from my house. Best not to be seen. I won't be here anyway. I'm just off to the country. Call me there if you have to, but be careful."

There were scraping sounds as chairs moved, then silence.

Eva rang Stormont immediately.

"Good stuff."

"It is. You don't recognize the voice, do you—Frazer's henchman?"

"No" said Eva, casting her mind back. "I've never heard it before. I don't know him." She spoke the truth, as she knew it.

"What's your reading of the conversation?" asked Stormont.

"The Chinese is obviously a hit man, or has been brought in to oversee a hit. Question is, who?"

"Well, at least it can't be you. Some man who's gone to ground." There was a long pause before Stormont spoke again. "This is good news and bad. Now we have something to use, the beginnings. But it's a warning, too.

Frazer's still a killer. Your little game with Margaret might distract him, but he'll still be suspicious of you. You can't even begin to let him think he might have reason."

"I know."

"The worst of it is, you'll have to go in naked now, with no protection, no devices. You'll have to get your information firsthand. The more you need protection, the less we can give it. We can't afford to risk letting Frazer find anything incriminating." There was another long silence. "The risks are rising, Eva. I don't want to sound alarmist, but you know you can drop out at any time if you're not sure about this."

Eva felt a jolt of surprise. She had never for an instant thought that Stormont might give her a way out at this stage. It made her instantly suspicious.

"What's going on, Andrew? I've no intention of walking away from this. You know that. And I'm quite happy going in naked, as you put it. I've done it often enough before. I'll be careful."

"You'll have to be," said Stormont grimly. "You and Frazer. You say I never give you any background, never give you the big picture. Well, I'll give it to you now. Do you know who Ha Chin is?"

"Tell me."

"On the surface he's a high-ranking politician and an extremely successful businessman—hotels, office blocks, computer software."

"And underneath?"

"Everything you can think of. Commercial secrets, drugs, and arms. He has quite an organization. He's utterly ruthless. Kills for convenience, any threat. That puts Frazer directly into the firing line, and if Frazer thinks you know about Ha Chin, then you're a target too."

"Fine. Then they're both targets. If I can deal with

Frazer, I can deal with Ha Chin. They've both got blood on their hands. It wouldn't be a tragedy if they happened to spill each other's."

"That's not part of the plan, Eva. We want Frazer alive. We've established that he does business with Ha Chin. That's a major breakthrough. If we get hard evidence of Frazer's trading secrets, drugs, or weapons with Ha Chin, it might be enough to get Frazer to cooperate with us. Don't forget, that's what it's all about. And when we've got what we want from Frazer, who knows what will happen, what the Chinese might do to him. But until then we need him alive."

Until then, thought Eva—as if there would ever be a time when Stormont and the Firm would withdraw their tentacles voluntarily.

TWENTY-EIGHT

Cassie awoke at six on Monday morning. She showered, washed her hair, and dressed quickly. Then she went down to the kitchen, put the espresso maker on, and fed the cats and Nesta. Nesta followed her, puzzled by the excitement she could sense in her mistress.

Cassie took her triple espresso out to the wooden table in the back garden and sat in the quiet early-morning sunlight. It was lovely to be in the garden, alone and peaceful and awake, when half the world was asleep, oblivious to the beauty of the tranquil morning. It made her feel as if she had scored one point in an invisible game.

She sat for an hour in the sunshine, replenishing her coffee from the pot kept hot on the stove. By the time she left for work at seven-thirty, her mind was electric.

She took a taxi and arrived at Case Reed at seven forty-five. For two hours she worked with clinical efficiency, checking all the details of her plan, making sure there were no legal, tactical, or financial errors.

At nine forty-five she walked into Richardson's office. He smiled at her as she came through the door, letting his eyes soak her up. She was wearing a swirling blue-patterned silk skirt cut a few inches above the knee, a crisp white linen shirt, a wide. blue belt, and high blue shoes. And she was wearing serious jewelry—a sapphire and gold bracelet and matching earrings. Her hair was drawn back into a long ponytail, revealing the contours of her angular face, sculpted like cut glass.

"You look well," said Richardson, restricting himself to necessary understatement. "All ready for the meeting?"

She gave him a dazzling smile. "I am. I want to present Eva and Frazer with a fait accompli. I don't want to waste time discussing a million ways to do this deal. They can do it my way or not at all. If we are going to deal with those two, we have to do it on our terms."

"You sound rather suspicious of them."

"No, I'm just being prudent. They're both strong characters. This deal is going to be difficult enough without giving them their head."

"We have to trust them, Cass."

"Of course. But it doesn't do any harm to be one step ahead, to protect ourselves as much as possible."

"You almost speak as if they are adversaries. Who are we fighting here?"

"No one. We're all on the same side. We all want to make money. I just want to be sure we do it in the most effective way."

Richardson's intercom buzzed. "Robie Frazer's here," said the receptionist.

"Send him up." Richardson turned to Cassie. "The money's ready. Everything's in place. Good luck."

"Thanks," said Cassie. He had handed her a piece of rope the length of a noose. They exchanged a quiet smile and got up to go to the meeting.

Robie Frazer awaited them in the boardroom, stand-

ing with his back to the door. Cassie let her eyes run up
and down the lithe, tall body, standing casually, confidently, in an attitude of disregard. After a moment he
turned, to Cassie first, holding her eyes, acknowledging
her scrutiny. Then he nodded to Richardson, a curt
greeting.

The door opened and Eva Cunningham walked in.
The other three paused in their greetings to accommodate her. As she kissed Cassie and shook Richardson's
hand, Eva was aware of Frazer, gauging his reaction to her
while he thought her attention was elsewhere. She went
to him, shook his hand, looked into the blue eyes. He
took her hand and squeezed it, let his fingers trace over
hers as he removed his hand. In his eyes were desire,
admiration, the customary hardness, but she couldn't see
suspicion.

Eva took her seat and lit up a cigarette. Frazer sat next
to her. Cassie looked at them, side by side at the polished
rosewood table. Although they sat about two feet apart,
their bodies were inclined toward each other. They sat in
silence.

Cassie took a seat opposite, next to Richardson; *Battle ranks,* she thought. Occasionally in such meetings she
would deliberately sit with the other side, but it only
increased the tension and confusion. The importance of
the human geography of a meeting room always amazed
her. The company, the business at hand, could be of the
utmost sophistication, but the behavior patterns hadn't
evolved since the Stone Age. There was a veneer of pol-
ish, that was all.

Cassie's secretary came in, bringing coffee and mineral water. Cassie continued to study Eva and Frazer.
They looked at ease but charged. There seemed to be a
complicity between them, a silent understanding. Still

their bodies inclined toward each other, although Eva's head seemed to be pulling in the opposite direction, as if she were drawn to Frazer and repulsed at the same time. Their movements were fractional, almost invisible, but to Cassie they were signposts, tiny fragments of the invisible picture she was trying to discern.

It was easy, as she had said to Richardson, to unify them all with the motive of making money from the deal. Their hunger for money, hers included, was tangible. But there was no sense of unity in the air. Instead there seemed to be conflicting motives. Perhaps it was just her, looking for hidden agendas that didn't exist. Perhaps Aubrey Goldstein and Sam Brimton had poisoned her with idle suspicions. She looked again at the two faces opposite, hard, purposeful, smiling their pleasant smiles, which seemed to her at that moment utterly unconvincing.

The coffee was poured, and everyone sipped and settled down. Cassie began to speak.

"Here's my proposal. If you agree, we can get this deal moving today." She left unsaid her implicit threat: agree to my proposal or else we drop the deal. She continued, cool, fluent, confident of her material.

"I propose that we set up a new company to bid for Genius. Eva will inject her ten percent into the new company in return for a five percent stake. Eva's stake will be diluted because we, Case Reed and Robie Frazer, will each put ten million pounds into the new company. That should see us through the bulk sampling. If we need more, we can fund it along the way. Then Case Reed and Robie, using the new company, will each buy a stake in Genius of five percent—four point nine percent, to be exact. The share price is four dollars. I suggest we bid six. At that price, the stake will cost us just under six hundred thousand Canadian dollars.

"Together, we constitute a concert party, and our holdings will be aggregated. The four of us together will own just under twenty percent. A holding of twenty percent or more triggers takeover-bid requirements. Once we have our holding in place, we make a bid. I would recommend a stock exchange takeover bid. We notify the Vancouver exchange Listings Department of our intentions. When they accept our notice, the bid starts. We have to pay cash using this method, so we have to be able to demonstrate our financial wherewithal. A letter from our respective bankers should suffice.

"Assuming the takeover goes smoothly and we've taken the company private, we start the bulk sampling. After the bulk sampling is done, assuming the results look good, we can look at taking on a joint-venture partner to help fund the construction of the mine. We might want to sell out totally. Alternatively, we might decide to bid in such a way that we leave enough Genius shares outstanding to enable us to preserve a listing. That might come in handy. We could use it to raise more money for the project, or to reduce our own holdings if we see a big enough profit. That way we could effect a partial or total exit at any time, if the share price warrants it. I have the paperwork all ready to set up the new holding company, a private company. The directors will be the four of us."

Cassie watched their minds turning over her words as she spoke. Frazer and Eva each looked faintly surprised when she pushed across the documents for them to sign.

"You can consult with your lawyers if you need to, but it's really quite simple. The documentation is straightforward. The underlying risk is not—diamonds in Vietnam. But I think we've all had enough time to mull over the risk. It's a punt. We either take it or we don't. There's only so much we can do to foresee the risks. We can deal

with them as they emerge." She paused, her eyes going to
them each in turn. "Case Reed is happy with the risks.
We are ready to go ahead."

She let the question hang. She would apply no pressure: take it or leave it.

Eva leaned toward her. "Say we sign your documents,
get your company, *our* company, up and running. Then
what?"

"It will take a couple of days to get the documentation completed. We'll have to agree on appointing a Canadian merchant bank in Vancouver to organize the
takeover for us. We can't do it—we need someone well
versed in local market practice. We'll need a broker too,
in case we want to do any buying as a prelude to the bid,
or in conjunction with it."

There was silence around the table, broken finally by
Robie Frazer.

"Vancouver's a tricky market." He leaned back in his
chair, eyeing Cassie.

"We can take care of it." Cassie smiled. "Trust me."
She felt three pairs of eyes upon her, saw the intrigued
looks as they wondered what secret schemes she might
have. All three knew better than to ask—at least not in
such a public forum, where the conversations would all be
on the record. But there was an irony in her promise to
take care of them. "Trust me" had been corrupted in
City parlance to mean "Trust me if you dare; buyer beware," or, at worst, "Fuck you."

They looked at the clear blue eyes, smiling innocently
at them. There was around Cassie Stewart an aura of
cleanliness, of scrupulousness. No one would doubt her.
Still, there had been in her words not only promise, an
assurance, but something else, almost undiscernible—a
threat.

Frazer spoke again, first to Cassie. "I'd rather take the company private. No outstanding shares. That just complicates things, dealing with minority shareholders."

Then he turned to Eva. "I've been meaning to ask you. Who actually runs the technical side of things at the site?"

"An Australian contracting company called ConCo. They do all the technical stuff. Granger McAdam and I oversee things."

"Does Granger make many day-to-day decisions?"

"Not anymore. He's a bit too close to the bottle for that."

"Are you set on your contracting company?"

Eva felt that a position was being taken. She tried to discern what it was.

"Not necessarily. Why?"

"Oh, I just thought you might consider using a contracting company I know of. It operates throughout Asia. First-class reputation. I might be able to get better rates than you now have."

Eva regarded him for a while without speaking. "Talk to Michael Rise—he's the company accountant in Vancouver. He has all the records of costings." She checked her address book and scribbled down a number, which she passed to Frazer.

Cassie watched Eva's easy compliance with surprise. She had expected proprietorial defensiveness.

Frazer turned back to Cassie. "You have your own broker lined up for Vancouver?"

"We do. Sam Brimton, at Brimton, Dixon. You have one you can use?" Cassie smiled. "Or would you like an introduction?"

Eva grinned at Cassie's impudence.

"Thank you, that's very kind," said Frazer. "I have my own."

"Of course you do," said Cassie.

"You're very confident, aren't you, that we'll do this deal?" said Frazer.

"Shouldn't I be?" asked Cassie.

Frazer said nothing. He looked at her for a moment, then took a fountain pen from his pocket, signed Cassie's documents, and pushed them back to her. Eva turned to look at him, then at Cassie. She too signed and pushed Case Reed's copies back across the table to Cassie, who gathered them up like trophies.

The first maneuver was completed—a declaration of intent, an act of incorporation, unifying them all in a common purpose. This was the starting point. If there were any divergent purposes, they would start here.

TWENTY-NINE

Eva and Frazer left the meeting together.

"How about lunch today?" asked Frazer when they were outside. "I have a few things to do first. Shall we meet, say, at one, at the Savoy Grill?"

His eyes were veiled, as always. Any new suspicions he might harbor were undetectable. But that gave her no confidence that they did not exist.

"Lovely. See you there," she replied. They kissed cheeks and walked off in opposite directions.

After about thirty seconds, Eva glanced once over her shoulder. She saw Frazer moving away, easily picked out his tall body, his smooth, confident stride. Even from a hundred yards he stood out. In a street of pinstripes, he did not fit in; immaculate as he was, he could never blend with the crowd. There was an arrogance and a carelessness to him. More than his physical attributes, it was his air of purpose, combined with his disregard for those around him, that set him apart. Physically, he occupied more space than most. He did not hunch his shoulders or weave through the crowds. He walked a straight line, forcing others to break step, to navigate around him. He strode on, careless of their accommodations.

Eva looked down at her green dress, which was striking, well cut. She stood out. But just as easily she could efface herself, and no one would notice her passing. She could blend, be invisible. Frazer chose not to. He set himself up to the world as a target, in the mistaken belief that he was invulnerable. Perhaps one small part of his subconscious did it to invite a challenge. Eva didn't know. She watched him till he disappeared into a side street. Then she turned and headed for Bond Street.

Two hours to kill. Days, weeks . . . She hated the waiting, wished for the commencement of whatever loomed. She knew something would happen, something beyond the plan prescribed by Stormont. Operations always took on a life of their own. The thing was to turn whatever happened to your advantage.

She turned off Bond Street into Brook Street and walked up to Hanover Square. She crossed into the park at the center of the square and sat down on a bench under the shade of a plane tree. At eleven, there was no one in the park save a couple of elderly male alcoholics, who lolled gently on their benches, nursing their cans of beer. A sparse traffic of office workers and shoppers walked briskly past, seeking a flash of greenery.

For an hour Eva sat motionless on her bench, a beautiful woman, poised and collected, her thoughts invisible to the world. For a while the alcoholics watched her, an oddity in their midst; then, as their eyes grew accustomed to her, they looked away, and soon forgot she was there.

At twelve, she got to her feet and left. The alcoholics, startled by the sudden motion, saw her once again, smiled at her smile, watched her pass and disappear. Another sudden motion made them look around. A man they hadn't even noticed had got up from one of the benches and was moving with a slow, casual gait after her.

They frowned at him as he passed. "Weirdo," muttered one. They had liked her, felt in her a deep warmth, sensed that she was on their side. This man they did not like, and they knew too that he was not on her side. "Bastard!" shouted the other.

Eva heard the distant shout, felt the hostility in it. She didn't turn but carried on, walking past Fenwick's, past a row of brightly lit windows. She glanced in, seeing alongside the wax mannequins her own reflection.

She watched the early lunchtime crowds milling before her. Glancing across the street, she saw a sea of advancing faces. She turned off Brook Street onto Bond Street and went into the main Fenwick's entrance, then lingered by the Chanel counter just inside. She tried out lipsticks on her hand, holding them up to her lips and eyeing them in a hand mirror. She bought two of them, paying with a credit card, and looking around, bored, as the sales assistant processed the sale. Casually she let her eyes rest for just a split second on all the people within view. Then she turned, pocketed her things, and walked back out onto the street.

Farther down the street she repeated the exercise; in Fogal, buying stockings, in Smythson, buying writing paper, across the road in Yves St. Laurent, a quick scan of the racks and out again. By this time she was sure. She was being tailed. She walked on in the sunshine from Mayfair to Piccadilly and down to the Strand.

She arrived punctually at one at the Savoy Grill. The maître d' advanced on her as soon as she entered. When she announced that she was with Robie Frazer, his silent approbation threatened to overwhelm every gesture. Covering her amusement, she followed his ceremonial progress to a table at the center of the restaurant, where Frazer was already installed. As she walked, she was aware of heads turning discreetly, of an almost imperceptible hush. The quiet attention lavished on her was, she knew, as much a function of whom she was lunching with as of her looks and sex. She was the only woman in the room. She remarked on it to Frazer as he got to his feet and kissed her cheek.

"I feel like an exhibit."

"You are rather, aren't you? But I would have thought you were used to it by now."

"Oh, I'm quite used to the attention I attract, but I'm not used to the attention I attract by virtue of lunching with you."

"Oh, I wouldn't have thought that would augment it at all. They're all looking at you because you're beautiful. I have nothing to do with it."

"You're being falsely modest. Look around, see them watching you. You're the center of attention here, Frazer, and you know it."

He smiled, shaking his head.

"You know, I hadn't quite realized what a draw you are. There is virtually a boardroom full of the great and good in here, and yet it's you they're all interested in. You're the star here. You're the in-house entrepreneur, the billionaire of the day. Why are you wasting your time on a two-bit diamond mine in Vietnam?"

He leaned back in his chair, studying her with a smile. "That was quite a speech."

"Well, are you going to answer me?"

"Why ask me that now, when we're all signed up?"

"I suppose it never struck me before. I'd never seen this reaction to you."

He paused and took a sip of wine. "It's not about a

two-bit diamond project in Vietnam, and it's not about money. The money is incidental now."

"Well, what is it, then?"

He sighed heavily, disliking the introspection but drawn by the lure of ego, by a residual need to be understood. He answered as if he were giving her a gift.

"It's the risk, it's the unknown, it's something to do. I don't need to make money anymore. But it amuses me. It's a test, like running the hundred-yard dash at school. You can't win too often. But you do have to play with the odds to get the same kick. Easy money bores me now. There has to be some quirk, some risk beyond the run-of-the-mill. And I need the prospect of a decent return to balance that. I haven't degenerated to the stage of pissing my money away just for the sake of it. I'm not vain enough to think that everything I touch turns to gold. So many successful businessmen fall victim to that one, believing in their own invulnerability, almost praying to be proved wrong. I don't gamble mindlessly. I look for greater risk matched by greater reward. Your diamond project fits that. You know as well as I do that if this thing comes off, we could be sitting on hundreds of millions of dollars a year."

He paused. "And there's something else about this deal."

"What?"

"Diamonds, Vietnam, you, Cassie Stewart. The combination intrigues me. Take today, the meeting. Cassie Stewart walks in and presents us with a fait accompli, but she dresses it up as a challenge, almost saying, 'Invest if you dare, trust me if you dare.' She's playing some kind of game. You're probably playing one too."

"What about you?"

"I'll wait and see what you and Cassie get up to."

"She is playing a game, isn't she? What d'you think it is?"

"I don't know yet. But I'll find out. So put her on warning."

"Put her on warning yourself. I'm not her guardian angel."

"No, I suppose not. By the way, Margaret said you came back on Saturday, that you'd lost something."

His voice and face showed only casual concern. The mask didn't reach his eyes, which remained set on her, hard, unyielding. *His ego will break him,* thought Eva. *He never can resist showing that he is no fool. Test me, watch my reaction. Fine. Just don't give yourself away in the process.*

"Yes. I did lose something."

"Your contraceptive pills, apparently."

"That's right."

"Did you find them?"

"No." Eva kept her eyes on his.

"So what did you do?"

"I rang my doctor. She telephoned a prescription through to my local chemist."

"Well, that's all right, then, isn't it?"

Eva inclined her head.

"What if it hadn't been?" he asked with an air of curiosity. "Would you have a child, Eva?"

Her eyes slipped away from him.

"Well?"

She looked back. "Hypothetical, Frazer. It's not relevant."

"Indulge me." His eyes traveled over her body. "It would look good, wouldn't it?"

Eva forced herself to keep her eyes on his face. She regarded the sensual features, the eyes that had seen her revealed in passion.

"Don't play games, Frazer. It's boring. You might find a woman you can't buy off one day. Then you won't find it such an amusing little academic exercise. Just count yourself lucky that you don't have to pay for another abortion."

"You assume that's what I'd want."

She leaned toward him. "I'm not interested in what you want. The sooner you understand that, the better."

"Oh, Eva. How you protest. I don't think you're nearly as hard as you try to be."

THIRTY

Cassie returned from lunch with John Richardson at three. She sat in her office drinking her sixth espresso of the day. A bare pad of paper and an unopened fountain pen lay before her while she moved the pieces of the deal around in her head. Some things were better not committed to paper. Facts belonged on paper. Suppositions, calculations, predictions of human behavior, and tactical nudges all sooner or later translated into profits if you were right, losses if you were wrong. They could become numbers but never words.

She busied herself with some paperwork, then, at four, she called up the Vancouver Stock Exchange on her computer through a new service she had subscribed to the week before. Today was the first day it had come on line. Her eyes scrolled down the screen till she found Genius. Four dollars a share. She checked the cash notification Richardson had sent her in the internal mail. She had six hundred thousand Canadian dollars to play with. It was time to buy.

Filled with the prickling excitement that always came with buying and selling, she picked up the telephone and rang Sam Brimton in Vancouver. "Sam, it's Cassie Stewart."

"Cassie. How are ya? Are we going to deal?"

"Hope so, Sam. Where d'you have Genius, say ten thousand shares?"

"Genius, eh? Don't go in for half-measures, do you?"

She laughed. "I try not to."

"I presume you're buying."

"That's for me to know and you to work out."

"Shit, Cassie. It's not the most liquid of stocks. Ten thousand will move the market. You know that."

"Too bad."

Market professionals habitually asked for prices without revealing whether they were buying or selling, because the brokers on the other end would amend the price to suit themselves if they knew whether or not they would be asked to buy or sell stock. Cassie knew she would get a better price by asking Brimton to quote blind.

Brimton took an educated guess. "Well, you're bound to be buying. Three sixty to four sixty."

"That's quite a spread. And it's four on the screen, Sam."

"Not for buying a half-percent stake in the company. And if my memory serves me right, you're looking to buy five percent for starters. You'll have to be prepared to pay a lot more than four dollars a share to get a holding that size."

"We'll see, won't we? I'm just dipping my toe in the water. I may or may not deal again."

"Four sixty, Cass."

"Not interested, Sam. Four forty-five and you've got a deal."

There was a long pause. Brimton knew her game,

knew that as a matter of principle she would try to nego-
tiate him down. He had increased his quote by ten cents
to allow for that. But she had seen through that and
shaved off another five cents. He laughed. He knew he
could get hold of Genius shares cheaply enough. The
company had done nothing for a while, and the market
was bored.

"O.K. Done. You buy ten thousand Genius at four
forty-five, normal settlement."

"Done."

"Welcome to Vancouver, Cass."

She cut the line and gave her secretary the transaction
details to process. Then she sat back and waited. She
wondered how long it would take for the news to spread,
first from Brimton to a list of deserving recipients of favors, then down and down, greasing the market until the
favors ran out. She waited and watched. Within minutes
the share price had gone to four and a half dollars, then to
five. She laughed to herself as she saw the price rising,
watched her private predictions play out on the screen as
the Vancouver insiders bit.

She made a few phone calls, refined her plans. The
afternoon passed in the turn of a head. Just before she left,
at seven o'clock London time, she checked her trading
screen.

Genius's share price, inscribed in green all afternoon,
which signified an upward trend, had just turned red.
Over the next ten minutes, Cassie, motionless with anger
and dismay, watched the price fall to two dollars.

She rang Brimton. "What the hell's going on?"

"I don't have a friggin' clue, but it's sure as hell nothing to do with me."

"No, this trend wouldn't be. I know that. No an-
nouncements?"

"None."

"Is someone doing a bear raid?"

"Smells like that to me."

"I want to know who and why, and if it's not that, then what the hell is it? I know about your contacts in the market, Sam. Why do you think I appointed you? If anyone can find out what's going on, you can."

"I'll do my damnedest. There's a lot of money down on this one."

If Cassie's calculations were right, Brimton would have bought into Genius at around four dollars, in the expectation that Case Reed would sooner or later stage a takeover, making the price shoot up. But now his investment had halved in a matter of minutes. For his own sake as much as for hers, he would want to find out what was behind the drop.

"You were lucky not to have bought your full five percent," he said.

"You could say that."

"Pretty clever, is what I'd say."

"You're not suggesting I had anything to do with this, are you, Sam? After all, you said yourself that I don't know how the market works, that I'm an outsider. Only an insider could swing this. If it is a bear raid."

"That's true, but it's not exactly bad news for you, is it?"

"I've just lost twenty-five thousand dollars in my first foray in your market. That's not exactly good for my credibility, is it?"

"That depends who's looking."

"And how devious their minds are? Look, Sam, we could go on like this all night. Call me at home if you hear anything." She gave him her number and hung up.

She locked up her desk, avoided John Richardson, and went home.

Brimton rang her at nine London time.

"It is a bear raid, getting nasty." Brimton's voice was hard. "You have a friend named Eva Cunningham, yeah?"

"I might."

"Yeah, well, the story goes she strings you along with some phony data, gets you to agree to a takeover. It's merely a device to raise the price of the stock, enable her to sell her stake, make some money, pay off her debts. Apparently the project took all her money, is a real dud, and she's going bankrupt."

Cassie was silent.

"Not implausible, is it?" asked Brimton.

"Don't be ridiculous. It's a good story, sufficiently plausible to make the market buy it. Whoever's behind this is no fool, but I promise you, it's not Eva Cunningham. Do you really think that I, and Case Reed, could be used by her like that?"

"If you gave me a cent for every time I'd seen something like this, I'd be a rich man."

"You are already."

"Exactly."

Cassie put down the telephone and rang Eva.

"Eva, Cassie. There's a bit of a problem. I'd like to discuss it with you, now if I may."

"Sure. Go ahead."

"Face to face. I'll be there in five minutes."

"What's happened?"

"Stock-price manipulation. Someone's fucking around with the price of Genius stock, and with us. That's what's happened."

* * *

Cassie took a taxi straight to Eva's. She looked around the house with surprise. Beyond the bare minimum of furniture, the rooms were almost empty. The only signs of life, of passion, were the many Persian rugs scattered throughout the rooms and the music collection. Eva had, Cassie noticed, a highly sophisticated sound system and dozens of CDs lined up. But there was no clutter in the house, and there were no photographs.

"Where are your books?" she found herself asking, remembering Eva's collection at Oxford: reams of books on many subjects, none of which Eva was meant to be studying.

"Ah, my books. Still in storage." Eva had no wish to explain that to her, books more than anything made a home, and London wasn't home—not now, not under these circumstances.

She poured two large whiskeys. "So tell me." She regarded Cassie carefully. There was a coldness in her she hadn't seen before.

"It's very simple," said Cassie, taking a long gulp of whiskey. "Someone has started a rumor that caused the price of Genius to fall from five dollars to two. My belief is that whoever it is sold at five and bought back at two. It's called a bear raid. It's artificial stock-price manipulation, and it's illegal."

"Hang on a minute. When I last checked, a few days ago, the price was four dollars. Then suddenly it increases to five dollars, then falls to two dollars? At the risk of sounding naive, I always thought there was such a thing as an objective value, a sort of underlying value that couldn't be manipulated."

Cassie grimaced. "That's the theory, at its purest, but it doesn't work in the marketplace. Value is in the eye of the beholder. People are not always logical, rational. Markets are just a collection of individual psychologies, and are just as susceptible as any mass of humanity to self-delusion, panic, and hysteria. Look at Polly Peck. One day it was worth billions of pounds, the next day virtually nothing. The same with Maxwell. The trappings of value aren't too difficult to create. Everyone wants a success story. If something approximating one appears, they all leap on it, turning it into more of a success story, and so the bandwagon rolls on. You might even know it's a bandwagon you're on. That doesn't matter, as long as you jump on and off early, as long as a queue of people are still ready to jump on after you and buy your shares from you at an inflated price."

"But surely people see that. How many times can you pull that off?"

"Never underestimate people's capacity for ignorance in the face of greed. I've seen it so many times, you can't imagine. Dangle the prospect of making ten million pounds in front of someone and he suspends his critical faculties. It's almost as if the dream is more important than the reality. Nothing must be allowed to interfere with the dream. That's the mind-set so common all over the country. City sophisticates are just as vulnerable."

"So how do you get around that?"

"You have to have a permanent professional cynicism —never give anything or anyone the benefit of the doubt. Guilty until proven innocent. Anyway, I'm digressing. The success story, the bandwagon, the share price rising to the stratosphere—finally someone takes a really hard look at it and begins to see the flaws, starts pointing them out. Suddenly everyone tries to sell, the herd instinct takes over, and the share price plummets. This can happen in minutes." She shrugged. "What's the true value of the stock? It's worth what someone will pay. That's not always a rational decision, but it's often predictable, if you understand market psychology. And if you do, you can manipulate the market. For a little while."

"It's quite incredible. Everyone always thinks the financial markets are so scientific and high-tech, with all the computers and telephones and trading screens and God knows what."

"No. That's just the trappings, the infrastructure. It's not cold and technological. It's driven by instinct and emotion."

"And how does it work with Genius? What's the rumor they're spreading?"

"The story is that you've duped Case Reed into believing that there's value in the Vietnamese site when in fact there is none. That you've created this takeover ploy just to make the stock price rise, so that you can sell your stake and make some money. Apparently you're bankrupt and are desperate enough to do anything to get some cash."

Eva stretched out her hands before her and studied her nails. Cassie could see a vein pulse in her forehead.

"So someone I've never met invents a story about me, trashes my name around the marketplace—"

"Your name and mine."

"You think there might be some truth in the story, that I might be the one behind it."

"I'm not sure what to think. I sometimes wonder how well I know you. What were you really doing in Vietnam, Eva? Now that I think of it, your hippie-trail story does sound farfetched."

"You were ready enough to believe it when you thought you were going to make money. Is this what a little hiccup does to you? Christ, Cassie. I never had you down for a paranoid."

"Don't fuck around with red herrings, Eva. I'm not remotely paranoid. Perhaps this little problem has just given me some perspective, made me see a little more clearly."

"If a problem like this troubles you, perhaps you should think about the whole deal. I thought you were used to high-risk transactions. If you're going to come running to me with hysterical accusations every time there's a slight difficulty, perhaps we shouldn't be in business together. I'm not going to nanny you."

"I don't need nannying. I need the truth." Cassie stared at Eva.

"Christ, that's the last thing you need. You've never been one for unpalatable truths, have you, Cassie? Everything's always so light and bubbly and frothy. You can't see the truth for the haze of saccharin you spin around yourself."

"And you're so hard and tough. Eva, who's seen it all, done it all, confronts everything." Quaid's words came back to her as soon as she shut her mouth. Too late she remembered Eva's childhood, what she knew of her life.

Cassie was shocked by how easily the anger had spilled from both of them, but just as quickly, Eva's seemed to recede.

"If it helps you to think that, then go ahead," Eva answered. She then sat patiently, seemingly at ease with the lengthening silence. Cassie found it intolerable.

"I'm sorry, Eva. I suppose all this shook me up. I didn't mean for things to come out like that."

Eva smiled. "Yes, you did. And I would have asked the same question about Vietnam. I have lived an unconventional eight years. I'm surprised you didn't ask more questions earlier."

"I was your friend. I didn't think I had to."

"You're also a banker."

Against Eva's understanding, Cassie's resistance collapsed. "O.K. Let's put aside the personal stuff." She slowly regained her composure. "Let's start again. I told you the bear-raid story to see whether it triggered any ideas about who might be doing it. It could be your friend Granger McAdam, for all I know."

Eva responded as if nothing untoward had passed before. "Why should it be him? He wants the price to be as high as possible."

"Maybe. How the hell do I know who it might be? It doesn't make sense on any rational grounds. My broker in Vancouver would have suspected that Case Reed was planning to take over Genius as soon as I appointed him and gave him my buying instructions. That would have filtered out into the market pretty quickly. It should have raised the price and kept it up. The price did go up, as I predicted. Then, all of a sudden, it plummeted."

"Wait a second. What happened to confidential information? You seem very unconcerned about what is effectively inside information seeping out and insider trades being done on the back of it. It almost seems as if you orchestrated it yourself."

"Vancouver lives on inside knowledge. I knew that there was a good chance that any broker we took on would leak the news to his friends. Giving someone this kind of business is doing him a big favor. I did Brimton a favor in return for future ones from him. And don't look so shocked. We're going to need all the favors we can get if this thing is going to work. Brimton warned me that Vancouver was dirty, that the deal would be messy."

"Cassie, what the hell are you up to? You talk about all these favors passing hands. Isn't all this illegal—aren't you breaking the law in all this?"

"What have I done? Appointed a broker, that's all. I can't take responsibility for what happens after that, for what he then does with the information. And you can be damn sure I'll be just as careful with any favors he does me in return. And don't get all squeamish here. This is for your benefit as well. What did you expect this to be like? Nice and clean and straightforward?"

Eva surprised Cassie by looking at her with something approximating admiration. "No, I didn't expect this to be nice and clean. It's quite a jungle, and you're quite an operator. But my dear, however clever you've been, there's someone out there one step ahead, doing something that makes no sense to us but you can bet your last cent it makes a hell of a lot of sense to him. And as for all your favors, they haven't exactly helped our case."

"You're not entirely right," said Cassie suddenly looking meditative. "I didn't focus on this when I heard the news, but from our perspective, this could all be very helpful. It might mean that we can take over the company for considerably less than might otherwise have been the case."

"What you're trying to say, rather politely, is that if it isn't you and it isn't me, then it might be Frazer."

"I'm not really saying that. I don't think this is his style. It's too obvious and too clumsy."

"So we're back to square one. Someone with no obvious interest is doing something that makes no obvious sense."

"That's about the size of it," said Cassie. She got up to go. "But we'll find out who it is. Nobody like that stays invisible forever."

THIRTY-ONE

Le Mai sat in an anonymous gray car parked at a meter, waiting. Another man, recruited from the Hong Kong Chinese community in Soho, sat next to him, his eyes scanning the other side of the street. Both men wore baseball caps that shadowed their faces. Neither spoke. Only their eyes moved.

Le Mai recognized Xu Nan's red BMW at thirty yards. He saw it driving down Sloane Avenue toward him, checked the license plate, and nudged his companion. In silence, both men watched the car swing left and turn into the entrance to the underground garage. They watched Nan insert his pass into the barrier machine, saw the bar rise up and Nan's car disappear.

They waited ten minutes, then stepped out of their car, crossed the street, and walked down the ramp into the garage, turning their heads down and toward each other to conceal their faces from the security cameras. The cameras would record only two men walking, their faces obscure.

They took the service lift to the seventh floor, got out, and paced along the main corridor, looking around.

It was eleven o'clock at night. The corridor was deserted. They paused before Nan's door and listened. They heard music, loud enough to cover the sound of the key in the lock—Frazer's duplicate key. When he had bought the flat for Nan, he had had a set of keys made for his convenience, for a contingency such as this.

The door to the flat swung open. Nan, standing in the sitting room, turned pale with shock. A scream began to form, but before the sound came out, Le Mai moved across the carpet and covered Nan's mouth with an acrid hand that stank of sweat. Nan struggled for a moment before fear stilled all movement. The other man went behind him and bound his hands with silk. He was surprisingly gentle. He had no wish to leave marks for the police, or traces of fabric.

There was a strange economy to both men's movements. Le Mai removed his hand from Nan's mouth and very quickly replaced it with a wad of silk, which he pushed in until it blocked off breath and sound. There was terror in Nan's eyes, and incomprehension. Both of the other men wore gloves, a garish yellow, almost fluorescent in the half-lit room. Nan stared in horror at them.

Le Mai drew a pistol from inside his jacket and pointed it at Nan. Nan felt his trousers grow suddenly warm as, uncontrollably, he began to urinate.

"We want you to write a little letter, Nan," said Le Mai, looking around. He saw a pen and some paper on a table next to the telephone and brought them over. "This will do. Shall I tell you what to say?"

Nan swung his head wildly in a frantic no.

"Just to encourage you . . ." Le Mai nodded to the other man, who removed a pair of pliers from his bag. Le Mai followed Nan's terrified eyes. "It really would be better if you cooperated. You will die either way—with or without extreme pain. Which would you rather? It's all the same to me."

Nan looked from one to the other and saw with inescapable certainty the resolve in their eyes. They wore it almost lightheartedly, as if it were no big thing. Their indifference to what they were about to do unhinged him. He lunged toward Le Mai, who moved nimbly back. Nan spun around, off balance, and knocked one of his plants from a shelf on the wall. Its china pot shattered on the wooden floor.

Le Mai swore and reached down into his bag while the other man grabbed Nan's arms and held him rigid.

"Will you write?" asked Le Mai, holding a syringe and needle up to Nan's face, moving it slowly toward his left eye. "Just for your information, the syringe contains sulfuric acid. The needle will feel like a caress compared to the acid."

Nan began to wail, the sound muffled by the wad of silk in his mouth. He took the pen and paper Le Mai held out to him.

"Where's your wallet?" asked Le Mai.

Nan nodded to a side table across the room. Le Mai fetched the wallet, opened it, and withdrew a credit card.

"Make sure your signature matches the one on this credit card, will you?"

Le Mai began to dictate. His hand trembling wildly, Nan wrote. "I am sorry," the note said. "I couldn't help it."

As soon as Nan signed, Le Mai snatched the note, studied it, and nodded. The other man picked up the broken plant and pot and put them into a bag. He took out a handkerchief and dabbed at the few spots of soil that lay on the wooden floor until they were gone. Then both men took hold of Nan and led him out to his balcony. At the last moment, they unbound his hands and took the wad from his mouth. Then they pushed him, head first, over the edge.

The body landed with a sickening thud. The men went back through the flat, checked that the corridor was empty, and let themselves out. No one saw them as they made their way to the service lift and down to the underground garage. Four minutes after murdering Xu Nan, they were in their car, driving away down Sloane Avenue. On the other side of the building, a crowd gathered around the body on the pavement. A trickle of blood appeared at the corner of the corpse's mouth, sickeningly red on the cracked concrete.

THIRTY-TWO

After Cassie left, Eva sat quietly in her armchair, sipping her whiskey, going over their conversation from every angle. Then she rang Stormont.

"Can we meet?"

"Of course. But rules this time. We need to be more careful."

"You're right. The club?"

"See you there."

The club was Stormont's personal safe house, unmonitored, unused by anyone save him and occasionally, on his express permission, one or two others.

Stormont walked out of his house onto Old Church Street and caught a taxi. He changed taxis twice, circling around on foot to make sure he had no tail, before arriving in a dark street in Soho. He descended a flight of stairs into a basement jazz club, where he walked through the main room toward the lavatories at the back of the building. There a door opened onto an alleyway. Stormont let himself out and walked to the end of the alleyway, up to a dark painted door. Taking a key from his pocket, he unlocked the door and let himself in. He switched on the light to reveal a sitting room and a small bathroom and kitchen down a short hall. He sat down on a dusty sofa on the far side of the room and waited.

Meanwhile, Eva went to her bedroom and picked out a suitable wardrobe: short black suede skirt, white silk shirt, black stockings, high black shoes. She put on red lipstick and heavy black eyeliner. She surveyed herself in the mirror, wondering what Stormont would make of her. Then she grabbed her handbag and cigarettes and walked out onto the street.

She walked slowly down the King's Road, looking for a taxi. On her way, she paused to look in a few shop windows, casual, relaxed, as were the other evening strollers, and her tails. There were two of them, a man and a woman, pretending to be a couple. There would be others too, she knew, ahead of her, and more in a car, waiting for instructions. She had to lose them without being seen to do so. Only a professional would have picked up the tails, and she couldn't afford to be seen as such.

She thought quickly, then hailed a passing cab and gave the address of a private drinks club in Mayfair. Ten minutes later, the taxi dropped her off in front of a five-story house. She rang the doorbell. A man opened the door.

"Hi." She gave him a dazzling smile. "This is really embarrassing. I'm meeting a member for drinks. I'll know his face, I'll recognize him all right, but I can't remember his name. I met him really late last night." She looked vaguely embarrassed. "You know how it is."

The man laughed, gave her a raking glance up and down. "Yeah. I know how it is." He held the door wide open to her.

"Thanks." The door slammed behind her. Her tails, she knew, would not be members of this club and would not be able to gain access. She made her way quickly to the ladies' room in the basement. There she locked herself in a cubicle and, straining the seams of her skirt, climbed out a window. She ran up the basement steps and out onto a back street, then walked as fast as she could without attracting attention. She hailed the first cab she saw and told the driver to take her to Regent's Park. All the way, she checked for tails. There was no sign. Just to be sure, she paid off the cab, walked around, took another one. Only when she was convinced she was clear did she give the driver the address where she was meeting Stormont, in Old Compton Street.

When she arrived at the jazz club, she took the same route as Stormont, through the club, out to the door at the end of the alleyway. She knocked lightly. Stormont opened the door, stood aside, let her in. Then he closed the door, leaned back against it, and studied her.

"You certainly dressed the part."

She turned slowly before him, hands on hips. "You like it?"

He meant to laugh along with her obvious teasing, but the air stayed in his tense lungs. He let his eyes rest on her in unconcealed appreciation. Her clothes promised what her bearing forbade. All that showed was beauty, and a kind of feline grace.

"I do like it. Very much."

She moved to a chair at the end of the room. "We have a problem," she said, substituting one tension for another.

Stormont pulled a chair from the side of the room and sat down opposite her.

"Cassie came around this evening, quite worked up. Apparently someone is doing a bear raid on Genius. The share price went up to five dollars today, then fell to two." She told Stormont about the rumors, and about the insider trading and Cassie's sanguine acceptance of it. She left out the anger that had passed between them. "We'd all rather like to know who's behind it," she concluded.

Stormont pulled a packet of cigarettes from his pocket and offered one to Eva, then got up and took a bottle of Glenlivet from a bookshelf, along with a couple of glasses. He dusted them off with his handkerchief and handed her one.

"Trouble with these safe houses, they're totally safe from any form of cleaning."

He poured out whiskey for them both, lit her cigarette with his flamethrower of a lighter, then lit his own.

"Who do you think's behind it?"

Eva shrugged. "I really don't know. Cassie, Case Reed, and Frazer all have an interest in lowering the price of the stock. I know it's not me. It could be Cassie. Outlandish as it is, I wouldn't put it past her. The more I see of her, the sharper she seems. She sits there like Little Bo Peep, with a very crooked crook."

Stormont laughed.

"She's not quite the innocent she pretends to be," Eva continued, "but I don't really think she's behind it, or Frazer. I'll judge better when I talk to him about it, monitor his reaction. It doesn't seem to be his style, but who on earth else would want to do it? I can't see a good reason."

"Well, watch it, look out for all angles. Someone is up to no good here, and we can't ignore the fact that the attack is aimed at you."

"Yeah. I don't like that bit. I'll live quite happily with accusations of what I've done, but what I haven't done . . ." She paused. "That's the first thing."

"There's more?"

Eva took a sip of whiskey, and said evenly, "I'm being tailed. I discovered it today, after my meeting at Case Reed. I think it must have started today, but I can't be sure. There are six of them, a full team. Professional, but by no means invisible. They've been careful, but I don't think they know I'm a pro. They've taken only those precautions they would with any Tom, Dick, or Harry. So I've picked them up easily enough. Don't worry, they have no idea I saw them. They were following me again this evening." Stormont started to speak, but she raised her hand to interrupt. "I lost them. They think I'm in a private club in Mayfair. I'll go there again via the back route when I leave you, then exit by the front door, and they'll be none the wiser." She saw him relax a little, but tension stayed in the taut muscles of his face. She continued, "But who the hell are they, and what are they looking for?"

Sitting with Eva in this dingy room, Stormont felt a strange intimacy. He was strongly drawn to her, and sensed in her a flicker of reciprocity, even though she covered it. There was an excitement too in knowing that the game had started. To plan their response, they had all night together, alone with the beat of the jazz club rhythmic on the walls, pulling at their senses.

He looked at her features glowing in the half-light. He saw in her eyes the same excitement he felt, the thrill of an invisible fight.

"It's started quickly." He drew on his cigarette and took a slug of whiskey.

Eva nodded.

"What do you think?" he asked her.

"I would have thought that here, the most obvious answer is the correct one."

"Frazer."

"Yes."

"And your logic?"

"He has something to hide. He knows he is exposing himself to me by doing business with me, by having an affair with me, so he decides to do a quick check. He either finds something that shouldn't be there and decides to follow up with physical surveillance, or he finds what we intended him, or anyone else, to find—nothing. He decides that doesn't square with what he thinks of me, so he decides to dig deeper."

"Which do you think it might be?"

"I'm working on the assumption that my cover is secure. I wouldn't be sitting here otherwise. I think Frazer's ego and curiosity make him think he knows better than my empty reports. What do you think?"

"I think it's ego and curiosity and a natural inclination to be suspicious. How do you want to play it?"

"Same as before, as if nothing's changed. I'll sharpen myself up invisibly, cover it all with sex."

"Do you enjoy it? Sex with Frazer?" His words came out hard, unemotional.

She leaned toward him. "I enjoy sex, Andrew. I might even enjoy it with you."

The laugh came now, and he reached for his whiskey and drained the glass, his eyes on hers all the while. He got to his feet and walked slowly past her chair to the bottle. He refilled her glass and his, replaced the bottle on the shelf, then leaned down to her, his lips almost touching her ear.

"Perhaps you should try it."

She turned her head so that her lips were a fraction away from his.

"Perhaps I shall sometime." She brought the glass to her lips. He moved away, back to his chair.

"We could watch the surveillance team," he said, as if nothing had passed between them, "but it's a hell of a risk if they spot it. Whoever it is will show his hand sooner or later. Almost certainly Frazer. Just keep watching."

"Frazer's certainly up to something. It feels like he's positioning himself. At the meeting today, he asked me if I was happy with the contracting company running the site. I gave him an open answer, to see what he'd say. He asked me if I might consider using a company he knows, said they were very good, suggested he might be able to get better rates from them."

"And what did you say?"

"I said I'd be delighted, told him to talk to the company accountant. No surprises if he comes up with a very competitive quote."

"Then what?"

"I'll have to sack the current contracting company, let in Frazer's people."

"They're a front company, presumably."

"I would think so. There'd be no link between him and them on any visible shareholders list. It will all be done through nice little nominee accounts in the Caymans, something like that. Anyway, what it means is that Frazer's moving in, has some plan of his own."

"Looks that way."

"I suspect he'll want to go out there, sooner or later."

Stormont sat up straight in his chair. "We'll discuss that before you go anywhere. You would be horribly exposed in Vietnam. I'm not even sure I'd sanction it."

"If he's planning on doing something dirty, that's where he'll do it. I can't very well stay at home."

"We'll see what happens if it comes to that. But keep me informed. The last thing I want is you going AWOL with Frazer."

Eva smiled, giving him a disconcerting look of acceptance, as if whatever happened, it would be all right; she was ready. It was not blind confidence; it came from another vein, one Stormont could not detect. He watched her in silence for a while before he spoke.

"You need to get Frazer's guard down. I think you should do something illogical, unpredictable."

Eva looked questioning.

"Are you very cool and clinical in your relationship with him?"

"I suppose so. He commented on it. Said I wasn't really like other women."

"Be like them. Reassure him. Ring him at one in the morning. Ring him now, tell him you're on your way."

"I can't do that. I've never done that in my life—gone chasing."

Stormont laughed. "You'd be surprised at the number of women who do. You want to make him complacent, Eva. If you behave like other women, he'll think he has a hold over you. That will reassure him that you're just like all the rest. Otherwise you're a threat."

"If I make him feel complacent, he'll become bored. He'll look for another, more challenging conquest."

"It's a delicate balance. You're too far on the challenging, threatening side." Stormont glanced at his watch. "Have either you or Cassie spoken to him about the bear raid?"

"I haven't. Cassie was fit to be tied. I imagine she will have."

"Ring him now. Arrange to go and see him later. Tell him about the bear raid, charm him at the same time. You'll be hitting him from two different directions. See if that reveals anything."

Eva got to her feet, picked up the telephone, and

dialed. It was twelve-thirty. Frazer answered after three rings.

"Robie, it's Eva. I'm at a club, the company's boring . . ."

Stormont could hear Frazer laugh. He watched Eva, who was half-lidded, full-lipped, and smiling slyly. He couldn't hear what Frazer said next, just Eva's reply.

"I'm on my way."

She put down the telephone, walked over to Stormont, leaned down toward him, and pressed her hands on her thighs. She kissed his lips, leaving them covered in a swath of red.

"I'd better go, do what you said."

He didn't get up. "Eva, we can't meet again unless it's an emergency. You know that, don't you?"

She looked down at him for a second, saying nothing. There was a brief break in the inscrutability in her eyes. "I know." She turned to go. He watched her let herself out and disappear.

For three hours Stormont sat in the dingy room, in case Eva's surveillance team had followed her to the club and decided to examine everyone who left shortly after her. He got up to go at three-thirty, taking with him the smell of Eva—of her skin and the perfume she wore—and the faint taste of her lipstick still on his lips.

THIRTY-THREE

Robie Frazer sat in his drawing room, the full-length windows open to the garden. At his side was a bottle of whiskey. He drank slowly, savoring the smooth burn. He thought of Eva, of her coming to him now, openly, with no invitation or pretense of dinner or a drink. This was the first chink in her cool facade. It would have bored him in other women, would have been a predictable move. In her, it was so unforeseen that it only added to his excitement, to his need for her.

Le Mai sat opposite him, studying him. Frazer had never looked so alive to him. His face showed a curious mixture of satisfaction and hunger. Although he was lounging in his chair with his legs stretched out, his muscles seemed tensed, as though he were ready to spring up at any moment.

"You'd better make yourself scarce," Frazer said to him. "I have a woman coming. Sleep in the blue bedroom, and stay out of sight."

Le Mai got to his feet. "Special woman?"

Frazer seemed intrigued by the question. He studied Le Mai while he thought. "Yes. In her own strange way."

"Very beautiful?"

"Beautiful, all right. But that's the least of it."

Frazer sat up slowly. Le Mai took the cue for his dismissal, left the room, and went upstairs. In the blue bedroom he stood in the darkness at the window, looking out, waiting for Frazer's special woman. He saw a taxi pull up and a woman get out. She paid off the driver, then walked up to the house. Le Mai watched her. After the door had opened and Frazer had let her in, Le Mai remained staring down at the spot where she had stood, her image captured in his mind.

Frazer shut the door behind Eva. She stood before him in her sexy outfit, like a promise. He pulled her to him, pressed her against the wall with his hands, and kissed her, keeping her there with her back against the wall. He gazed into her eyes as he held her. She seemed to have about her the presence of another man. It shone from her eyes, like a taunt, goading him to erase its presence. He made love to her there, staring into her eyes till they closed and her face contorted. Then he took her upstairs, laid her on his bed, covered her with a sheet, and got in beside her. They fell asleep almost immediately, their faces glazed by the moonlight shining in through the open windows.

In the room two floors above, Le Mai sat on the window ledge. He had listened to them, soaked up every sound. He imagined the woman with nothing but the cool air on her skin. He imagined her eyes, and wondered how they regarded Frazer. With passion, or with hatred?

Frazer awoke at seven the next morning. Eva lay next to him, turned slightly from him, her features still. He studied her face, the strongly drawn features. Even at rest there was a tension to her face. There was no placidity to her. Physical satisfaction gave her a smile of triumph, a catlike complacency. It did not make her calm, render her soft or yielding. Always there was this resistance, this turning away, even in sleep. However much she might desire him, whatever pleasures she might take from him, he felt certain that she could turn on him, spit at him, walk away in a second, leaving him somehow damaged. He sensed that she had the desire to wound. Many women had that, especially the beautiful ones whose beauty had been abused too many times. They sought to redress the balance. But that didn't fit her desire to scratch. He couldn't imagine her allowing herself to be abused by anyone, couldn't see that she would have anything to avenge. Yet still there was a sense of violence about her. Not that it worried him; it just alerted his senses.

Suddenly she woke. She saw him watching her and her eyes widened, then half closed as she pulled his face down to her breast and held it there. He felt the softness below his lips, felt a dizzying sensation creep over him, both desire and contentment, as sexual and maternal comfort mixed.

They lay for half an hour awake, until the ringing alarm broke the silence and their stillness and she sat up.

"I need more jeans and another T-shirt. I'm not going home like this." She gestured at the clothes lying by the bed.

Frazer laughed and got up. As she watched him walk to the dressing room, it struck her that he and Stormont looked quite similar. It was more than mere physicality; there was an overlapping quality—the brilliance, the talent, the watchfulness. The difference was in the way they used it. Frazer returned with clothes for her and dropped them at her feet. Suddenly she took hold of him and pulled him to the floor, not even fighting for a second the physical compulsion that for the duration obliterated all else.

By the time they had showered and breakfasted, to Margaret's silent disapproval, it was eleven o'clock. They were still at the breakfast table, reading the newspapers, when Margaret announced that Cassie Stewart was on the line. Frazer was gone for five minutes. When he returned, Eva studied him carefully, smiling benignly when she observed that he was scrutinizing her in return.

"You've heard about this bear raid?"

"Cassie told me about it last night."

"Why didn't you tell me?"

"Oh, I suppose I could have. Last night, when I arrived, or this morning, when I awoke. My words would have been a bit disjointed, a bit irregular and breathless, but apart from that, there really was no reason why I couldn't have told you. Sorry. I'll remember next time."

He surprised her by looking sheepish. "Save business for the boardroom, I think."

"Since you brought it up," said Eva, "let's pretend this is the boardroom for a second."

"O.K."

"Would you mind explaining to me what the hell's going on? I mean, you're an old hand at all this kind of thing, and Cassie's in the business, but it's all a long way from what I know. It's a bit disconcerting to sign a deal in the morning and have all sorts of monkey business start in the afternoon, with someone or other spreading rumors about me, trashing my company."

"I'm as much in the dark as you are. I'm familiar with this kind of game, but I honestly don't have a clue who's playing it, or why. It's really odd, because it seems as if someone is almost doing us a favor. The lower the price drops, the better it is for us and our takeover—as long as it's dropping for spurious reasons, not good ones."

"I've told you all a million times, it's a good deal, but it's risky. This rumor is absolute crap. You can check my share certificates, check with my bank. I haven't done any trades in Genius."

"It's all right. I believe you. I tend to know when people are lying."

"Well, that's good, because I don't think you're lying either. But that doesn't get us very far. You're not doing it, I'm not doing it, Case Reed isn't doing it, so who is, and why?"

"What makes you so sure Case Reed isn't doing it?"

"Do you really think it's their style? Can you imagine John Richardson ever doing anything dirty?"

"No. But I don't think your friend Cassie Stewart is the pure, innocent little thing she pretends to be."

"You overestimate Cassie." She hoped Cassie hadn't told Frazer about her favor-trading with her Vancouver broker. She had a sense that it would behoove Cassie to veil her cleverness from Frazer. She would have to find a way of suggesting it.

"Perhaps. But I tend to agree with you. I don't think it's Case Reed."

"Can you find out? There must be ways of finding out these kinds of things."

Frazer studied her for a moment. "There are. I'll make a few inquiries. It's your baby—I can understand your being upset. And I don't like being messed with, either."

THIRTY-FOUR

Cassie confronted Richardson first thing Tuesday morning. "We have a problem with Genius. Someone seems to be doing a bear raid."

Richardson raised one eyebrow slightly, but other than that, he was impassive. He waited for her to explain. When she had finished, he was silent for a while.

Cassie felt calmed by his self-control. Richardson always acted as if whatever the problem was, calm reflection could solve it. There was never anger, or bitterness, or resentment at mistakes made, just concentration as he planned a solution.

"Eva and Frazer come on board, and almost immediately this bear raid starts," he finally said. "I can't believe that Frazer would be so unsubtle as to incriminate himself in that way. That makes me think he's probably not behind it. As for your friend Eva, it seems a little beyond what we know of her. But I wouldn't trust her entirely. I have in this transaction because we have the same interests. But she and Frazer have every reason in the world to do this if they think they can get away with it."

"Perhaps Frazer feels immune," Cassie replied. "No

one would believe that he could incriminate himself in this way, so we all assume he must be innocent."

"That's entirely possible." He paused. "Did you talk to Aubrey Goldstein?"

"Had lunch with him. He was very helpful."

"I thought he might be." Richardson watched her, as if waiting.

Cassie thought fast, answered slowly. "He asked me, just as I was leaving, where the diamond site was."

"And you told him."

"I said Vietnam, but Genius isn't the only diamond site there. I didn't think I was giving too much away, didn't think he'd use it. Shit, John, I'm sorry if I blew it, but I didn't see Goldstein that way. And I was careful—I gave him just one clue, admittedly one that slipped out."

"Or one he pulled out."

"You don't really think it's him, do you?"

Richardson surprised her by smiling. "He's just another candidate to add to our list of suspects. We can't really rule anyone out, can we?"

"Apart from ourselves." Cassie laughed, despite his now impassive face. "What are you going to do?" she asked quickly. "Will you talk to Goldstein and Frazer?"

Goldstein—a man of silence, clenched as a stone when he needed to be. And Frazer, sharp and slippery as ice. Confrontation would achieve little.

"Let me think."

Sometime later, Richardson made a telephone call. "Peter, John here. I know it's short notice, but I was wondering if I could stop by for a few moments. As soon as possible. Good. Thank you."

He put down the telephone and left his office. He took a short taxi ride, and got out in front of a large, anonymous-looking building, the home of one of the largest private investigative agencies in the world. He announced his name to the receptionist, then took the lift to the fifth-floor office of Peter Bawden, the managing director.

Bawden greeted him with a handshake. "Coffee?"

"Yes, please."

Richardson waited until the coffee arrived. He took a sip and replaced the cup delicately in its saucer.

"I'd like you to take on an assignment. I need a report very quickly. I don't have the luxury of time. You needn't worry about getting all the facts. They'd be in pretty short supply even if you did have time. If this individual does have something to hide, he'll do it bloody well."

"What do you want, then?"

"Your opinion. Hunch, hypothesis. Any facts or stories you can come up with."

"You'll act on that?"

"I might have to."

"It sounds as if you've already made up your mind."

"No, I haven't. Something's happened, made me wary. It seems to have punctured a hole in my image of this man. I got a glimpse of something, a feeling." He waved his hand. "I'm starting to sound like Cassie Stewart, with all her intuition."

"She gets it right, though, doesn't she? What does she think?"

"I haven't asked her, but she's been behaving oddly lately. I get the feeling she's holding something back."

"Who is this man, John?"

Richardson sighed, prepared himself for disbelief. "Robie Frazer."

Bawden was silent. He took a sip of his coffee and

regarded Richardson over the rim. The two men were old friends. They had been at university together, and Bawden's firm regularly did investigations for Case Reed.

"You'd better tell me what the problem is. No one would ask about Robie Frazer on the off chance."

"Will you take the assignment?"

Bawden paused for a while. "We'll take it."

Cassie saw Richardson return to Case Reed. He seemed strangely quiet. He walked into his office with his head down, shutting out his surroundings. She wanted to go in and talk to him, but a sense of his reserve held her back.

Instead she went out to the café on Clifford Street and bought her third espresso of the day. When she got back, she drank it down and rang Owen Quaid.

"Owen, take me to lunch, take me to dinner, do something with me, will you? I'm going half mad here."

"Oh, my poor baby. What's your wretched house-mate doing today?"

Cassie brightened. "He mentioned something about doing some research at Kensington Library. I think he goes there to pick up girls. Apparently it's rife there."

"You don't say. So your house is empty?"

"I think I'll tell my secretary I'm going for a long lunch."

"See you soon, my lovely."

Cassie caught a taxi and arrived home five minutes before Quaid. She opened the door to him and drew him inside the hall with a kiss. He pulled her to him, so that she could feel the seams of his jeans pressing through the thin silk of her skirt, could feel every contour of his body against hers, as legible as Braille. He kissed her as if he were parched, and she responded. She always responded, but she never started anything. She asked for nothing from him save what he gave voluntarily.

He dug his fingers into her arms and watched her as he kissed her. Her eyes flickered open and closed. She looked like a cat, and was probably as fickle as one, but he was here now. He led her upstairs to her bed. As he laid her down, he felt her eyes on him. Wide eyes, warm, and focused only on him. What did she think? Did she, like him, cover need and love with laughter? It was always light and happy when they were together, as if by silent agreement. He wondered whether it was naturally like that or whether it was because of some kind of aversion to pain. Just laugh, look for nothing beyond lust and laughter. He took off her clothes, marveling at her pale body, and thought caved in to desire.

An hour later they sat in her garden with a bottle of chilled Chablis, crisp and cool on their parched palates. Nesta and the cats sat peacefully at their feet, basking in the midday sun.

"My darling, you sounded a bit rattled on the telephone this morning, and much as I would like to think otherwise, I know it was more than just missing me," Quaid said.

"I did miss you. I do feel unwell if I don't see you." Always the teasing eyes when she spoke of feelings. "But yes, there was something else." She told him about the bear raid. "I don't like feeling out of control."

"Have you spoken to Eva and Frazer?"

"Yes. But I really don't think they have anything to do with it."

"Mm." Quaid frowned.

Cassie looked at him questioningly. "Owen, there's something you know about all this—the deal, or Eva, or Frazer—that you're not telling me. I know that you'll have a very good reason for not doing so, and that I have no right to ask. But it's impossible for me to sit here knowing that you know something that I don't and not want to find out. So whatever it is, will you please tell me?"

Quaid took his cigarettes from his jeans pocket and lit up. He blew the smoke over Cassie's head.

"Oh, Cass. You're becoming a real pain in the ass. Curiosity and perceptiveness are all very well, but sometimes it's better just to let things be, not to go around digging under stones the whole time."

"I can't help it. Once you've seen under a few stones, your imagination gets going."

"I know. Professional suspicion. You must have caught it from me."

"Probably. Anyway, are you going to tell me?"

"I shouldn't, Cassie. I'm breaking nearly every rule in the book just thinking about it. It's not some little game. The consequences are serious, much more so than you could imagine. You're messing around with something you really shouldn't touch." His voice had become angry, but suddenly, as if resigned, he spoke softly. "If you insist, I'll tell you. There's only so much I can do to protect you." He didn't add that he was putting himself and Paul Black at risk too.

"Oh, for God's sake, Owen. This all sounds so melodramatic. Either you're going to make me laugh or you're going to scare me." Cassie reached across to him and touched his cheek. "I know I can be difficult, awkward. But whatever you tell me, you can trust me absolutely. I'm worried by this deal, especially now, with this bear raid. There's something really weird going on, and not just with the bear raid. I'm not sure what it is. Perhaps my imagination really has run wild this time. But I have this strange intuition that there's the diamond deal and then there's something else completely, another picture. I can almost see the outlines, but I can't pick out the details."

Her words came out in an accelerating rush, ideas forming as she spoke, half-perceptions crystallizing into words.

Quaid gripped her hand and squeezed it. "Hey, slow down. Tell me exactly, no matter how strange it sounds."

"There's nothing to tell, nothing more than I've already said. That's the thing. It's just a load of suspicions, all swirling around. And a feeling of uneasiness, of being in the dark. I hate it."

"O.K. I'll tell you what I know. It won't answer all your questions, but it might fill in something. The reason I was so hesitant about this deal right from the beginning was that before you asked me to work on it, Robie Frazer called and asked me to investigate Eva, John Richardson, and you."

"Me? Why the hell would he want to investigate me? Or Richardson?"

"Why shouldn't he? You investigate your business partners. Working for an apparently reputable institution rather than for yourself doesn't make you clean, it just makes it easier to hide the dirty bits."

Cassie's face was hard with anger.

Quaid continued, "When Frazer asked me to investigate you, I had no choice. I suppose I could have said no, but he's one of my biggest clients, and he doesn't appreciate being turned down. I also wanted to try to control the process. If I'd said no, he simply would have got someone else to investigate you. I know it's a violation. I knew how upset you'd be. But if anyone was going to investigate you, I thought you'd rather it be me."

"I'm not so sure I wouldn't have preferred it to be a

complete stranger. Having a lover know all your secrets is everyone's nightmare."

"Not when you have nothing to hide."

"Christ, Quaid, everyone has secrets." Cassie paused, then asked unflinchingly, "So what did you find out about me? What did you tell Frazer?"

"Not much. That there was really no dirt on you, nothing compromising, no dodgy secrets."

"That's it?"

"Yep."

She laughed, it seemed to him almost with relief. "God, it makes me sound so boring."

"Skeletons are glamorous only to those who don't have them. They just mean you've taken risks and got it wrong. You've taken them and got it right. That's the difference."

"Thanks, Owen. That's a nice way of putting it. I'm nothing special at picking the right risks. I've just been lucky—I've never had to risk very much. That's all. There's no point in dressing it up."

"Keep it that way, then, Cass. Anyway, the point is, Frazer was satisfied with the report I gave on you, and on Richardson, incidentally. But he just refused to believe the clean bill I gave Eva. Because you weren't going to tell Richardson about her heroin addiction, I couldn't tell Frazer, and without that, Eva looks pretty clean. Unconventional, but not particularly suspicious. But Frazer just wouldn't have it. He's been having an affair with her— perhaps that's made him extra-suspicious."

"What? They're having an affair?"

"Not altogether surprising, is it?"

"No." She spoke slowly. "I can see the attraction."

"Yeah, I'm sure you can, but leave Frazer to her."

"Why d'you say that?"

"Why d'you think? Jealousy." Quaid moved on quickly. "So anyway, Frazer was convinced there was more to Eva, so he asked me to put her under twenty-four-hour surveillance, to see what I could dig up."

"And what did you dig up?"

"This is one interesting lady."

"Why? What's she been up to?"

"Well, it's not just what she does, although that's interesting enough. It's everything about her, the way she does things."

"Tell me. Exactly."

"O.K. Exactly. At six-thirty yesterday morning, she got up and went for an hour-long run around Battersea Park. Then home, till eight-thirty. Then she emerges all dressed up, goes to a patisserie on the King's Road, sits at an outside table in the sunshine, has two pastries, one orange juice, and two cappuccinos. Then it's off to Case Reed for an hour. Then she goes for a walk and sits in a park in Hanover Square for an hour, does a bit of shopping on Bond Street, and has lunch at the Savoy Grill with Frazer. Home for a few hours. Next she goes to this place called the Biedecome or something, a judo club by the Fulham Road. She does judo for an hour and a half. Serious judo."

"How serious?"

"Let's put it this way: she could kick the shit out of me. O.K.?"

"Jesus. So after the judo?"

"She goes home for a few hours. Next thing, you arrive at her house, in a storming hurry by the look of it. You leave, then half an hour later, around eleven, she emerges, dressed to kill, and goes off alone to a private drinks club in Mayfair. We don't know who she met there—we couldn't get in. She leaves after a couple of hours and goes to Frazer's house, where she spends the night."

Quaid waited for Cassie to speak.

"It's incredible. She does all these things, has this packed life—one hour solitary, the next teeming. She seems to appear in so many different guises, has so many surprises. In some ways her life's almost spartan—the running and the judo and the sitting on a park bench for an hour. But then the breakfast, and the lunch at the Savoy, and the shopping, and the drinks club, and the sex with Frazer . . . So many different sides."

"I know. It is amazing. She does everything so beautifully, calmly. It's as if she were putting on a performance."

"Perhaps she was. Perhaps she knew she was being followed."

"I don't think so. She gave no indication."

"She wouldn't, would she? Not if she were any good."

"What do you mean, any good?" Quaid asked, his voice sharp.

"Oh, I don't know. I don't know what I mean. Nothing, probably."

"Yes, you do. Come on, out with it. You can't expect me to level with you if you just clam up when it suits you."

"It's not as if I know anything. I just have all these suspicions."

He waited stubbornly.

"All right. Just don't laugh if I sound like a crackpot." She tried to make light of it, but there was no humor in her words. "I had a conversation the other day with this character who is an expert on diamonds. He's a friend of John Richardson's. Anyway, he told me about diamonds, what he called the official picture, and then he seemed to give me a sort of warning."

"What d'you mean?"

"Well, I'm not sure myself. He started talking about all the other things that go on in the diamond business. About all the people who use it as a cover."

"Such as?"

"The intelligence services."

They were both silent for a long time. Finally Quaid asked, "And where do you make the link?"

"I don't know. I can't help wondering if Eva doesn't have something to do with the intelligence world."

"Why should she?"

Cassie didn't answer immediately. She was going to mention Andrew Stormont and her suspicions about him, but something made her decide to keep quiet about that. Instead she talked about Eva.

"There's a lot more to Eva than she lets on. I just have this feeling about her. And it is a bit strange, going to the Far East for eight years, being a hippie, becoming a heroin addict, then finding this diamond site and going all serious all of a sudden."

"It's not all that outlandish. It just doesn't fit in with your world, with the conventional world. It's unusual, but there's nothing necessarily sinister in that."

"I know. And it's not as if I'm judging her. I'm not. As for the unconventionality, I couldn't care about that." She was quiet for a while. "Then there's Frazer. Perhaps he's in intelligence?"

Quaid laughed. "No. Not on your life."

"Why? Why on earth not?"

"Look, all Frazer cares about is money and kicks, preferably intertwined. He's totally amoral—there'd be no commitment to any side. Sometimes they can use that, the services, but not in Frazer's case. He'd be impossible to trust."

Cassie put down her glass and glared at Quaid. "Hang on a minute. Are we talking about the same Robie Frazer here? He's supposed—"

"Wake up, Cass. Forget what he's supposed to be. How do you think anyone makes a billion pounds as quickly and as invisibly as he did?"

"What's he done? How did he make his money?"

"Why do you think he asked me to check out you and Richardson and Eva?"

"Tell me."

"It's very simple. Because he has something to hide and wants to be sure that his prospective business partners are just that, nothing more. Look," he said, switching his tone, "what do you want out of this deal with him and Eva?"

She looked at him, surprised by his cold practicality. "I want to make money, I suppose. I'm interested in the project, in diamonds, in Vietnam, and I'll admit, I want to make money."

"Focus on that. Don't worry about Frazer, or about Eva. Don't worry about what they might have done or what they might do. If you must go ahead with this deal —and from where I sit I can't see that anything I say will stop you—then just concentrate on making money. Frazer probably wouldn't be in it if he couldn't smell money, so you should have your chance to make some too. Take it, sell up, and get out. Walk away at the first chance, do you get me?"

"Why else would Frazer be in the deal if not money?"

"Who knows what goes on in Frazer's mind? With him, things are never straightforward." He lapsed into silence. Cassie was looking past him, her mind jumping from thought to thought.

"Why on earth would the intelligence services want to get involved in a deal like this anyway?" she asked suddenly.

"Who knows? No reason. Just your imagination. But listen, Cass, if for any reason they are involved, don't be under any illusions. They'll do what they do with no regard for you. If anything strange starts to happen, the best thing you can do is run like hell. In the meantime, for God's sake pretend that you have no suspicions about anything, that you see no evil, et cetera. Do that, and get out as soon as you see the chance of making this money you're looking for. All right?"

Her eyes rested on his. He could see her mind working, but she said nothing.

Cassie said goodbye to Quaid and returned to the office. She felt as if she were moving in fog, sensing rather than seeing her way. She turned on her screen and checked the price of Genius; still two dollars. She called Brimton.

"Any news?"

"Nope. More of the same, but the story hasn't gained any momentum. Price is stuck like treacle."

"Good. I'll get the rest of my stake. What price for eighty-nine thousand shares? Sorry it's an odd number, but I can't take my stake above five percent."

"What the hell are you doing, Cassie? As your broker, I should advise you as well as do trades."

"Sure you should. And I've made up my mind. Give me a price, Sam."

"I hope you know what you're doing. You might come to regret this."

"That's my problem."

"It's your money to burn. Two and a half."

"Done. I buy eighty-nine thousand Genius at two and a half."

She knew she'd have to pay considerably more than the screen price to build up such a large holding, but two and a half was cheap compared to the six dollars she'd been prepared to pay at the outset. The situation had changed with the bear raid, but part of her couldn't help feeling that that was a smokescreen. She put down the telephone with a smile. The potential rewards had just shot up. So had the risks.

THIRTY-FIVE

Eva and Frazer had just finished lunch and were reading in Frazer's sitting room when Margaret walked in.

"Someone to see you."

Frazer, half lying on a sofa, got to his feet and followed her silently from the room. Eva watched him go, heard the door close and the murmur of soft voices. Another door closed and there was silence.

Le Mai was waiting in Frazer's study. He watched as the Tai Pan came in and sat down.

"What is it?" asked Frazer.

"I'm not sure, not certain. It was a long time ago, and people change. But if I'm right, then we have a problem. You have a problem."

"Where? Who? Stop talking in riddles, Le Mai."

"Here. In London."

Frazer listened while Le Mai told him his suspicions. The anger showed in Frazer's eyes, in a kind of dull shutting-down of feeling, so that all that was left was intense coldness. He got to his feet and returned to the sitting room.

Eva glanced up when he entered. She saw him look at her, and away. She watched him sit down, pick up his paper, flick the pages, and read. She watched his eyes moving over the print and knew he wasn't taking in a word. His elaborate display couldn't begin to conceal the rage that had walked into the room with him. Eva felt it like the heat from a nearby fire. Like him, she scanned the newspaper, praying that unlike his anger, her fear was contained. The effort of sitting in a chair with a sated smile on her lips almost made her sweat. She willed her skin to coolness, breathed slowly, deeply, and soundlessly. Out of the corner of her eye she saw him rise and walk over to her. He reached down and took her bare arm in his grip. His touch felt like a brand. He pulled her up to him.

"How would you like to take a little trip?"

She put down her newspaper. "Depends where, when, and with whom."

"Hong Kong, this afternoon, with me."

"Now why would you want to do that?"

"Because I have a business to run and I've been away too long. And I thought we could take a detour through Vietnam, see your site."

Another turning point, another wrong step she knew she would take.

"All right. I'll come. Give me an hour to pack and I'll meet you back here."

"No time. If we leave now we can catch the afternoon flight. We can buy everything you need in Hong Kong. My driver will wait for you to pick up your passport on the way to Heathrow."

And I'll have no chance to tell anyone I'm leaving. Stormont's warning rang in her head. Suddenly the assignment had turned real. Alive to the danger, Eva kept her voice light.

"I'll have to do a lot of shopping, Frazer. I hope your credit card can stand it."

"Oh, I think so." He called Margaret. "We're leaving for Hong Kong."

"I suppose I'd better ring Cassie," said Eva, stretching. "She's already freaked out enough about this bear raid. If we disappear on top of it, she'd really throw a fit. You'll have to talk to her too." She paused. "By the way, what do we tell her? I mean, going off together, all of a sudden—she might think it a bit strange."

Frazer walked over to the window to gaze out at his garden.

"What does it matter, in the end, what she thinks?"

Eva walked up to him so she was almost touching him.

"It matters to me. I'm trying to raise money from her. I cannot afford the luxury of disdaining her opinion."

"You're also trying to raise money from me. Why do you need her?"

"I should have thought that was perfectly obvious. She introduced me to you. I owe her a certain loyalty, and I wouldn't have known how to proceed without having a merchant bank advise me."

"But you don't really need her now, do you, Eva? What if I said I'd bankroll you all the way, have my own bankers advise you?"

"Isn't that called a conflict of interest, Robie? Don't you think I might need just the slightest protection from you?"

For a moment they stood eyeing each other, saying nothing. Frazer turned away.

"Call your protectors, then, for what they're worth."

Eva dialed the number. Frazer moved forward and switched on the speakerphone. Eva stood impassively.

"Cass, it's Eva. Look, Frazer and I are off to Vietnam to go and see my site. I think he wants to make sure that it really exists."

There was a pause before Cassie asked, her voice sharp, "When are you going?"

"Er, this afternoon, to Hong Kong."

"And to Vietnam?"

"Vietnam?" Eva glanced at Frazer. "Tomorrow, probably."

"You don't sound very sure."

"I don't have the international timetables in my head. I'll let you know when I get there."

"What the hell are you up to, Eva? We're trying to run a deal here. There are things we'll need to talk about, not least this bear raid. Must you go now?"

"Frazer wants to look at the site. That's fair enough, isn't it?" Eva's voice softened. "I'm not being deliberately difficult, Cass."

There was a slight pause, then a faint puzzlement in Cassie's voice when she spoke. "Neither am I. And it is reasonable for Frazer to see the site. But this is all very sudden. We're supposed to be partners now, all of us. You don't just go running off without consulting us."

Frazer broke in. "It's Robie Frazer here, Cassie. I'm afraid I have lots of businesses to attend to, all over the world. You don't really expect me to consult you each time before dealing with them, do you?"

"I'm not interested in your business portfolio, Robie, just this deal. We have a major problem here, with the bear raid. I don't want to get any more nasty surprises, or this deal might start to slip."

"Perhaps my checking on the site will reassure you, then. Incidentally, have you heard any more about the bear raid?"

"Nothing. The story's still doing the rounds. We'll let it ride for the time being. It's in our favor in the longer term, as long as the trend reverses. But don't forget, we're all in the red here. I bought stock before the price fell. I'm assuming you did too. It's not the size of the loss that matters so much. It's the principle of being messed around. I don't like it, and I presume you don't either."

"Not my favorite pastime."

Cassie ignored him. "Listen, Eva, if you must go, then keep in touch. Ring me from wherever you are, will you?"

Unwittingly, Cassie had thrown her a lifeline.

"I'll call you. I promise. Happy now?"

"Not exactly."

Eva and Frazer sat beside each other in the back of Frazer's chauffeur-driven Bentley.

"Where to?" asked Frazer.

"Langton Street." Eva forced in deep, silent breaths, hating every hundred yards as Frazer drew closer to her house.

"I'll come in," he said, jumping out of the car after her when it stopped in front of her house. She froze and started to turn and glare at him, but then carried on, going through the motions of feet on steps, keys in locks. She felt Frazer standing behind her and had an overwhelming desire to thrust her heel into his shin. She pushed open the door.

"I'll just get my passport."

They walked into the sitting room. Frazer watched her open a desk and take out her passport. He looked around. For all the strength of her personality in the flesh, he felt nothing of it here. Like her history, like Quaid's reports, there was a void.

"Shall we go?" she said.

They left the house and Eva locked up. She had had no time to call Stormont. She hoped that Cassie would tell him, that somehow it would slip out in conversation.

They sat at the front of the plane, in first class. Now that Frazer had her on board, he seemed almost indifferent. He read, ate, drank, slept, occasionally threw a word to her carelessly, as if she were his captive audience. Eva felt her anger begin to grow, not for herself, but for the girl she might have been, who might have sat there next to Frazer with high hopes, bathed in ignorance.

THIRTY-SIX

On Wednesday evening, local time, they arrived in Hong Kong. Frazer walked through the airport as if untouched by the long flight. The babble of Asia rose around them, not the baying of poverty but the confident voices of wealth, of aspiration. Diamonds, emeralds, and carousels of gleaming luggage greeted them left and right.

Eva walked at Frazer's side, just a fraction behind him, noting the looks he attracted. He seemed oblivious to the attention. She felt eyes on her too: curious, hostile, envious. She was the consort of the Tai Pan, her position revealed by his casual neglect of her. And Frazer was the Tai Pan, had inhabited that persona almost as soon as he had boarded the plane. In London he showed a trace of reserve, of humor. In Hong Kong, that mask was stripped to reveal harshness, the *noblesse* without the *oblige*. Eva, despising him, forced her body to follow his, forced her steps to match his.

His driver was waiting in an old slate-gray Rolls-Royce. They weaved through the traffic, past other Rolls and Mercedes and Porsches and BMWs, gleaming horsepower in a concentration seen nowhere else on earth.

Eva looked up at the skyscrapers that walled in the road. To her, Hong Kong was a Far Eastern Manhattan, only more extreme in its poverty, its wealth, its enterprise, the ringing of steel on steel and the dull thud of ball on brick as buildings went down and up, almost before her eyes. The darkness felt like a backdrop, a stage-managed setting for the neon that glowed and pulsed, for the strips like static lightning that lit the spires of the skyscrapers in Central. New York had nothing on Hong Kong. Here there was only one focus: money. And it was as tangible as the smell of decay that rose from the harbor, as the heat that lunged at them when they stepped from the air-conditioned airport into the air-conditioned car.

Eva turned to Frazer, who sat leaning slightly away from her, gazing out.

"Why no helicopter?"

"I prefer the road. I like the drive from the airport. It's a form of acclimatization."

She watched his eyes roaming over the tenement buildings, their windows lit by ghastly blue neon; over the luxury high-rises topped by swimming pools; and, as they climbed to the Peak, over the big houses lit like birthday cakes. All the while in his eyes and in the clench of his jaw was the same excitement, a look of appetite and of readiness.

They arrived at his house—the large white house that clung to the hillside, the house that Stormont had watched from a distance. A housekeeper and a butler, both Hong Kong Chinese, greeted Frazer on the driveway. He led Eva inside.

"Kim will show you to your rooms."

Kim, the housekeeper, walked silently ahead up the curving staircase. Eva glanced around: marble, chandeliers, mahogany, rugs, paintings—a panoply of wealth, Eastern ostentation barely restrained by English austerity. Flowers and light were everywhere. But there was no gaiety.

Kim paused at the end of a long hallway. "Your rooms."

Eva walked through the open door into a sitting room with rich, aged, dark wood floors, a ceiling fan, Chinese rugs that were threadbare in patches, oil paintings of flowers, nudes, gardens. It was a woman's room, a mistress's room. The bedroom was even more so, in richer colors; it had ocher instead of white walls, a large carved wooden bed, empty wardrobes.

Eva turned abruptly at a sound from the sitting room. Frazer appeared at the bedroom door. She felt a flash of sickness at the look in his eyes—a look she had half expected to see now, had been waiting for. He walked toward her, took hold of her shoulders, and pushed her back on the bed. He pulled up her dress with one arm, pressing the other hand on her chest. She stared into his eyes, inches from hers, and saw the coldness, the look of possession, a small boy's sick pleasure in pulling the wings from captive flies.

Eva maneuvered for space under him. Suddenly she brought her knee to his groin in one smooth blow. He leaped back, doubled over. She got up, smoothed down her dress, and waited for him to recover. When his breathing eased and he moved to take a step toward her, she drew back her hand and slapped his face, a single strike which shattered the silence in the room.

"Don't you ever touch me like that again. I'm aware that this must be something of a tradition for you, an induction into your Hong Kong life. Some girls probably like it like that. I do not. Do you understand?" Her voice was quiet, controlled, the words delivered with a force that chilled his desire. For a while he just looked at her, as if seeing her for the first time. Then he walked away.

Eva waited for the slam of the door, waited for her breath to return to normal. There was no sound save the echo of disappearing footsteps. She walked through to the sitting room, to the open door, and slammed it with such violence that the door frame shuddered and a hairline crack raced downward.

She was left alone that night. The butler sent up a tray of supper for her. Untouched, it grew cold in the sitting room.

In the bedroom, Eva stood before the window, looking down to Central and the skyscrapers and out to the South China Sea beyond. She wondered how much that one touch of Frazer's, a touch of hate, of humiliation, might have destroyed.

She was awakened the next morning by a knock at the door. She sat up quickly. "Come in."

Kim appeared with a breakfast tray, which she put on a side table by the bed. "Ned, the driver, will be ready for you in one hour. Mr. Frazer has instructed him to take you shopping. Apparently you need some clothes." Her eyes swept over Eva, who was obviously naked from the waist up.

Eva ate her breakfast, Frazer's traditional cholesterol feast followed by mango and papaya, all washed down by the usual excellent coffee. Then she showered and put on her only clothes with a grimace of distaste. At one minute to ten, as instructed, she walked out of her sitting room, down the hallway, down the stairs, into the main hall, and out of the house.

A Eurasian man was leaning against a racing-green Aston-Martin parked in the drive.

"Ned?"

He nodded.

"Shopping time."

They drove down from the Peak to the crowded mayhem of Central, where Ned parked in an underground garage. Together they took the elevator to ground level.

Outside in the raging heat, Eva turned to him. "You escort me, and you pay for everything, right?" *And you shadow me, making sure I don't escape or make any phone calls.* She studied his athletic build, the strength in the sinewy body, and imagined pitting herself against him.

"Right."

"Well, we might as well have some fun, then."

First stop was Chanel. She bought an entire new outfit, down to shoes and bag, and walked out wearing it, with no underwear. Next she bought underwear and swimsuits, toiletries, another day outfit, three evening dresses at Valentino, luggage at Vuitton, jeans, T-shirts, and shoes she could run in from the Gap. All the while Ned watched over her, scrutinizing her purchases.

At lunchtime Eva consulted her watch. "I'm hungry. Do you have permission to take me to lunch?"

Ned looked disconcerted. " 'Anything,' he say, Mr. Frazer. He say to get you anything. Lunch is anything, no?"

"Lunch is definitely anything." Eva headed off to the Chinese restaurant at the Peninsula. Glowing in her Chanel suit, she was seated immediately. Ned followed, his appetite overcoming his uneasiness in the unfamiliar surroundings.

Eva finished lunch at two-thirty. "Good. That was excellent. Now just a bit more shopping."

Ned nodded, resigned. His uneasiness returned abruptly when Eva paused for a second outside Bulgari, the jewelers, then marched in. He followed her.

She leaned over and whispered in his ear, "Let's see how good that credit card is, shall we?"

He looked worried. Large-eyed, he watched her pick out a watch with a gold and platinum band, a matching bracelet, a ring, and earrings. Finished, she turned to him.

"That should do it."

The total came to two hundred and ninety thousand Hong Kong dollars, about twenty-nine thousand pounds. Ned came forward with the credit card and handed it over. Eva leaned on the counter and watched with interest. The sales assistant took the card with a smile and began the fuss of processing it. To Eva's amusement, it all went through. She wondered just how large Frazer's credit limit was.

The assistant presented the payment slip to Ned, who signed it awkwardly. Eva walked out with her purchases. They were a measure of security, a small contingency fund she could turn into cash, although much less than had just been expended. She had seen a pawnbroker's earlier on and memorized its location.

"Home now," she said to Ned.

There was no sign of Frazer when they returned. Eva watched Kim hang and fold away her purchases. Then she picked out one of her four new bathing suits, changed into it, walked through the house swinging a towel over her shoulder, and headed for the pool on the lower terrace.

She dropped the towel on the hot flagstones and dove into the cool blue water. For over an hour she swam back and forth, until her body felt as fluid as the water. Then she got out and lay on the towel on the flagstones for an hour, turning after half an hour, bronzing front and back, enjoying the stones, hot and hard beneath her, and the sun, scorching her skin, ripening her bones.

At six o'clock she returned indoors and slept for an hour. Then she showered, dressed in one of her new outfits, a long silver-gray silk sheath dress, and put on her new jewelry. At eight o'clock she sat on her bed and waited.

Minutes later she heard the creak of the sitting room door and the tread of hard-soled shoes on the wooden floors. Frazer appeared.

Eva got up slowly from the bed and walked toward him. She paused before him, letting him look at her, her eyes smiling as his traveled over her body and face. She saw that he was moved by her beauty. She kissed his cheek.

"Thank you for all this."

"Are we quits now?"

The more she spent, the less he would have to be forgiven. She had guessed the equation.

"We're quits."

He took her arm, his fingers light on her bare skin. "Let's go down and have a drink."

They drank champagne in the drawing room and talked lightly, inconsequentially, but still Eva could feel the tension. Kim announced dinner. Frazer got up and went into the hall, followed by Eva. As they were making their way to the dining room, a man came out of another room. His eyes went straight to Eva and stayed on her. Frazer turned to her, his face a mask.

"Eva, I don't believe you've met Le Mai. Le Mai, this is Eva Cunningham."

Le Mai came forward, stretched out his hand, and shook hers. In her heels she was six inches taller than him. She looked down at him as he took her hand and barely inclined her fingers around his as he grasped hers. She looked as if any movement in his direction would be a wasted effort. Then she withdrew her hand and glanced at Frazer as if bored, waiting to get on. Her high heels felt like stilts, about to topple her.

Frazer turned back to the man. "Goodnight, Le Mai."

Slowly, Le Mai removed his gaze from Eva, bid Frazer goodnight, turned, and walked away.

All through dinner, Eva played her role. She talked, smiled, and ate as if nothing had happened. She fought with all she had to keep the fear from her eyes. She glanced down at her clothes. She stroked the silvery silk, remembering rags, remembering her shrunken body. She could recognize herself still, but she lived with herself every day through the transformation. The grand lady and the junkie. The after and the before. Would Le Mai make the connection?

At ten-thirty Frazer got to his feet. "A drink in the library?"

"Yes, thank you."

Frazer stood back as Eva left the room first.

"My lipstick," she said, smiling over her shoulder as she headed upstairs. He nodded and continued to the library.

Eva stared at her face in the bathroom mirror. She

concentrated on reapplying her lipstick. Her hand shook, and the lipstick line blurred on her skin. She dabbed away the color. She would always look the same. She should have known that nothing could disguise her eyes. Le Mai had recognized her. She had seen the hatred, and the pleasure, in his eyes.

She went into the bedroom and looked out the window. She was thirty feet up. As she began to release the catch, she heard a sound and turned. Frazer stood in the doorway.

She heard her voice, struggled to keep it low. "God, it's stuffy in here. I need some fresh air."

He walked over and took her arm. "We'll have our drink on the terrace. You can breathe there." He led her downstairs.

"We'll leave for Vietnam tomorrow. All right with you?"

THIRTY-SEVEN

Eight hours behind, London was taking tea while Eva Cunningham went to bed in Hong Kong.

"I'm worried about Eva." Andrew Stormont clumsily replaced his cup in its saucer. The cup tilted, spilling thick Turkish coffee over a report. "Fuck it," muttered Stormont, mopping it up with his handkerchief. "Nearly three days, not a word and no sign."

Giles Aden raised one eyebrow, simultaneously conveying smugness, unease, and a sense of the reckless inevitability of events. Something bad was always going to happen.

"Oh, for God's sake, stop looking so smug. Ring Angus Fawley. Get him to find out where Frazer is. That might tell us something."

"What are you going to do?" asked Aden.

"I'm going to make a date with Cassie Stewart, see if she knows where Eva is."

Cassie snapped up the telephone when it rang.

"Yes?"

"Cassie?"

"Who's this?"

"Andrew Stormont."

"Oh, Andrew. Hi."

"It *is* you. You sounded strange."

"Bad day. Bad week, come to think of it."

"Why don't I cheer you up with a wonderful dinner somewhere?"

Cassie glanced moodily at her calendar. Uncooperative pages stared back.

"I seem to be busy forever."

"Well, in that case, how about tonight? If every night's as bad as the next . . ."

Cassie frowned again at her packed schedule. There was no comfort, no distraction in what she had planned. She felt an odd need to see Stormont.

"All right. You can pick me up at nine."

Stormont put down the telephone with a sense of relief.

Aden came into the room. "Fawley just called me back. He spoke to Frazer. He's in Hong Kong." He paused to deliver the punchline. "He's leaving for Vietnam tomorrow. A bit of business to see to."

"I'll bet Eva's with him," said Stormont. "He's obviously put her in a position where she can't ring in."

"Perhaps she's just being ultra-cautious."

"I'm sure she has reason to be."

"So what's he playing at?"

"You want the spectrum?"

Aden nodded. He leaned back, hands folded in his lap.

"He could be testing her, in the normal male way. Trying to whisk her off, cut her off, increase her dependence on him. It's not altogether implausible. She's the kind of woman men want to do that to. Her independence is a challenge. It would act like a gauntlet to a man of Frazer's arrogance. That's the best gloss."

"And the worst?"

"What do you think? Call station in Hong Kong, Saigon, and Hanoi. Have them look out for Eva and Frazer. No surveillance, just discreet observation. But caution them. Unless they have absolutely no choice, they must do nothing that brings them to Frazer's attention. We just can't risk him seeing them, seeing the picture." He added, almost as an aside, "That is, if he hasn't already."

"You think he has?"

"I think he might be wary of something, but then he's congenitally suspicious, has a lot to fear. I don't think he knows anything. I don't think he has any specific suspicions. If I did, I'd have no choice but to pull Eva out immediately." There was a long silence. "We'll continue on the assumption he hasn't."

"You're exposing Eva in the meantime. There's no way you can be sure he hasn't found out something. The evidence suggests he has."

"The evidence suggests that Eva fears he might have suspicions but isn't sure herself. Presumably she went with him to Hong Kong voluntarily. She hasn't pulled herself out. That gives me some comfort."

"Perhaps she can't get out?"

Stormont shook his head. "I'll trust it to her for a little longer. She can mold his suspicions one way or the other by her behavior. I thought she could handle it at the outset. I still do. But we have to be ready to pull her out. Warn the stations. No details. Just have them ready."

"You think it might come to that?"

Stormont didn't answer.

THIRTY-EIGHT

Sam Brimton rang Cassie just as she was calling up Genius's share price on her computer. The price had risen, prompted by her earlier purchase, to $2.55, but it had stuck there stubbornly.

"Any news?" she asked him.

"Not a squeak, babe. None of our normal boys are responsible, that much I know. It's a market outsider. That's what makes it so strange."

"How strange?"

"Well, insiders stick together. Normally they're quite happy to split on an outsider—you know, admit who started the rumor, sort of tell us what they're up to. But not here. Nothing."

"And?" asked Cassie, discomfort rising.

"And that means deep shit. Whoever is behind this is not the kind of person who gets split on. Cover me?"

"If you mean do I understand, the answer is yes."

"Oh my. We are in a bad mood."

"No kidding. What do you expect, giving me all these warnings about some shadowy mastermind?"

"It's ugly. I warned you."

"That's a great comfort. What am I supposed to do in the meantime?"

"Not a lot you can do. Wait for him to show his hand."

"Just sit around?"

"Yup."

"I hate being passive."

"Don't have much choice, do you?"

"Don't count on it. Your mastermind doesn't have a monopoly on surprise."

"What's that supposed to mean?" Brimton spoke to thin air. There was a click of the receiver and she was gone.

Cassie walked out to her secretary. "Emma, could you get hold of a telephone number in Vancouver, please, for a Granger McAdam?"

Emma came back minutes later with the number. Cassie picked up the telephone and dialed.

A hostile male voice answered after the tenth ring. "Yeah?"

"Granger McAdam?"

"Who wants to know?"

"My name is Cassie Stewart. I'm a friend of Eva Cunningham."

"That fuckin' bitch. Bad start, girlie."

Cassie sat back abruptly in her chair, almost reeling from the malice in his voice. But at least it was the right McAdam.

"I thought she was a friend of yours."

"Friend?" He spat out the word. "Oh yeah, some friend. Kiss of death." Cassie's shocked silence seemed to goad him. "You want my advice?" His voice rose, under-cut by an edge of hysteria and what sounded like liberal use of the bottle. "Steer clear."

"It's a bit late for that. We're business partners."

"Don't tell me—something's gone wrong."

Cassie began to feel a deep disquiet. "You could say that."

"So what d'you want with me?"

"Information."

"And why should I tell you jack shit?"

"Have you looked at Genius's share price lately?"

"What d'you think I do all fucking day? Crapped out, two and a bit dollars."

"How would you like to sell out your entire stake for four dollars a share?"

His answer came back like a whiplash. "Five and it's yours."

She hadn't expected him to want to sell, couldn't believe he would give up so easily. Neither could she quite believe that she was offering to buy his shares for herself, with her own money. Money that she didn't have. She pushed on, not wanting to stop and analyze what she was doing.

"Information first. Then you've got a deal. At four fifty."

There was a long pause. Granger looked around his filthy flat, at his unkempt body and clothes. He felt the despair of lost hopes seeping through him. The mine, for all his dreams, had brought him nothing good. Finally he spoke, his voice dead.

"O.K." He took a slurp of cold coffee from last night's cup. Time to sober up. "Ask away."

"I know you're going to lie about this, so I'll discount what you say accordingly, but tell me about the site. Are there really diamonds there that can be mined profitably?"

He snorted. "Yes and yes. There are diamonds there.

I know it. I've never seen such good indicators. But that's the least of your worries."

"What do you mean?"

"I mean Vietnam and Eva Cunningham. I mean bear raids and lies."

"You're talking in riddles."

"I can't explain." His voice was plaintive. "Things happen in riddles. When I found the site, it was like a dream. Then everything started to go wrong. Eva Cunningham comes along, and accidents start to happen. She comes on like a saving angel, but she don't feel like that, you know? Something about her. She saves me from this trouble which seems like a nightmare and then walks off with a chunk of my stake in the site. Next thing, the value of what I have left is cut in half, and surprise, surprise, there's Eva again. The rumors say she's going bankrupt and has this scam going. So you see, it almost doesn't matter about the diamonds. There's all this other shit going on, and it's stronger than the diamonds. The diamonds should make a ton of money, but all they've done is lose me money." He gave a quick, bitter laugh. "Until now."

"Tell me about Eva," said Cassie.

"Eva." He spoke her name as an exhalation. "God knows. She's everything all mixed together. Good and bad. I don't know what she's doing, I just know it's something."

"Making money, perhaps?"

"Could be. But I think there's more to it than money."

"What more?"

"I don't know." His voice whined with powerlessness. "Look, I've got better things to do than talk about Eva. Are you going to buy my shares or not?"

"I'll buy them. Three hundred thousand shares at four fifty. One million, three hundred and fifty thousand dollars. My bank will fix it. Payment in thirty days, at the end of the settlement period. O.K.?"

"Can't you settle immediately?"

"I don't have that kind of money sitting around in my current account, Mr. McAdam." She didn't have that kind of money anywhere.

"But you can get the money, right?"

"I can. If I don't, you simply hang on to the shares. So you have nothing to lose. But don't worry. You'll have every last cent in a month. Where do you want payment?"

He held his breath for a second, not quite believing that she would go through with it, reluctant suddenly to abandon his dream, however tarnished.

Cassie waited through the silence and heard, finally, a long sigh, like a relinquishment of hope. "Bank of Nova Scotia," he said wearily, adding the account number. "They hold the share certificates too. Talk to Mr. Robert Thomson."

"I will."

His voice was bitter and soft. "I hope you have a lucky charm, girl. You'll need it to turn this one around."

"I'll be all right."

"Yeah, sure. But just in case you're wrong, don't say I didn't warn you."

Cassie put down the telephone, Granger's warning ringing in her ears. The verbal trade was as good as binding. Effectively from now, the shares were hers. Although she had executed large and risky trades for Case Reed, she had never risked her own money like this before. She could lose everything. The odds on that, according to all the available facts, were high. But the share price could rise dramatically during the next month and she could sell for a substantial gain. The odds on that were slim to anorexic. But still, with some ineradicable instinct, she felt it would happen. She felt the wild excitement of the true gambler, where the lure of risking all is every bit as strong as the draw of money. It wasn't everything, it wasn't life or death, it couldn't kill her. The money could come or go. It would do so again.

She jumped to her feet and strode into Richardson's office, where she perched on the arm of a chair. Richardson was talking on the telephone. He looked startled by her sudden arrival. Her body seemed to pulse with excitement. He cut short his conversation.

"I've just bought three hundred thousand Genius shares."

The receiver clicked into its cradle.

"What? From whom? At what price?"

"I bought Granger McAdam's stake. All of it. Four fifty a share."

Only Cassie's history at Case Reed and his respect for her kept John Richardson from an outburst. He sat at his desk, fingers interlinked, eyes on her in silent contemplation.

"I'm missing the logic. I know it must be somewhere, but I'm afraid I can't see it."

"That makes two of us. I can't see it either." She gave the faintest of smiles. "But I know it's there."

Richardson's reserve began to crack. "I think you'd better tell me what the hell you're doing, Cassie."

She leaned across the desk, her eyes bright. "Look, I know this must seem a bit mad to you."

Mad, he thought, eyebrows raised, watching her, waiting.

She went on. "My only defense is instinct." She raised a hand as he tried to interrupt. "I know I've always been the logical one, put my faith in numbers, and yes, that's paid off. My decisions have been right, and we've made a lot of money."

She needn't repeat her track record, he thought. We all know how good she is.

"I'm not saying this as any plea for clemency, I'm just trying to explain what's going on in my head. I suppose I decided that we weren't going to get anywhere by playing according to reason and logic. Suddenly that seemed so worn and sterile and fearful. And I think if we did play it that way, we would lose the money we've already spent. I didn't like the odds, so I went about changing them, doing something out of character, unpredictable, perhaps to shake them up in our favor."

"And how is that supposed to work?"

"I don't know. It's part gauntlet, part device. Somebody is manipulating the share price, controlling events. How? By spreading plausible rumors. By having the gravitas to make people believe those rumors over a number of days. Why? To make money, I presume. If we sit back and do nothing, we just play along with his"—she paused—"or her scheme. So I decided to do something, to create the illusion that we too had a game plan. This should confuse our mastermind, because on the surface it isn't rational, so he will think we know something that he doesn't." She smiled. "We turn the tables on him. Not to mention that when Robie Frazer's involvement and the discovery of diamonds at the site become public, the share price will almost certainly rise."

Richardson took a cigar from the humidor on his desk. He twirled it, circumcised it, and made much show of lighting it. After a few luxuriant puffs, he laid it to smolder in an ashtray.

"You weren't supposed to play a wild card, Cass. What's got into you?"

"Wild card? Yes, that's exactly what it is. And no, I'm not supposed to play it. That's what everyone bargained on. And now they're wrong."

"And what happens now?"

"We wait."

He was silent for a while. "Who, incidentally, is this everyone?"

"I only wish I knew." She paused. "Do you know? Have you found out anything about the bear raid?"

"Give me time." He was an infinitely patient man. He played the game of time better than anyone she knew, exhausting everyone else.

"What are you going to tell Eva and Frazer?" he asked. "We have a big problem now. We hold just under twenty percent alone. Together with Eva's and Frazer's holdings, that carries us to just under thirty-five percent. Twenty percent or more triggers the takeover-bid requirements. We're obliged to bid now."

"Not necessarily. You cannot be in concert with someone who's incommunicado. Frazer and Eva are in Hong Kong, probably in Vietnam by now. Eva rang me on Tuesday to say they were leaving. She promised to keep in touch."

"Hang on a second. Both of them are in the Far East together, effectively incommunicado?"

"I told her it wasn't a good idea to go off at the moment."

"They're having an affair, aren't they?"

"Yes."

"What the hell are they doing running off at a time

like this?" He glanced apprehensively around his office, suddenly distracted. "I'll have to tell the other partners that they own another three hundred thousand shares of Genius at nearly twice market value."

"No, you won't."

"Look, Cass, there's only so far I can go to—"

"Case Reed doesn't own the shares. I do."

"How the hell can you buy them? You don't have that kind of money."

"No, I don't. But I hope to sell them on at a profit before the account clears in thirty days."

"And what makes you so sure you can sell for a profit within thirty days?"

"As I said, news of the diamond discovery disclosure and of the involvement of Robie Frazer. The man with the magic touch. And I just have a feeling. Something will happen."

"Christ, Cass. I don't know what's got into you. That's a lot of faith to put into female intuition. And why the hell buy the shares yourself? Why didn't you come to me, try to convince me to buy the shares for Case Reed? I hope this isn't getting personal in any way."

"What do you mean?" asked Cassie sharply.

He took a while searching for a diplomatic answer. "You and Eva Cunningham—some kind of game between you."

"Funny game."

"My thoughts exactly."

"There's no game. Just business. I bought the shares myself because I had no right to commit you and Case Reed there and then. I was talking on the telephone to McAdam, and it just seemed like the perfect time to do a deal with him. There was no time to confer with anyone. I knew if I made him an offer there and then, he would take it, and he did." She paused. "And I just wasn't sure it was fair to increase Case's exposure to Genius any more. We've lost money already. It's my deal. I'm responsible. I didn't want the loss to get any bigger."

"So you decided to take that risk yourself."

"Double or quits."

"Only it's not double, is it? It's more like tenfold. And if something goes wrong, you haven't got a hope in hell of paying for those shares."

"I have my house."

"Oh, for God's sake, Cassie."

"Don't worry. It won't come to that."

He said nothing, just looked at her with leaden eyes. She hadn't been burned yet, didn't know what it was to come out on the wrong side of a risk that was too big. To her, it was just a thrill she thought she would never have to pay for. Despite her perceptiveness, she still had the sense of omnipotence of a child.

"So what's next, Cass? We have all these shares now, and whatever you say about the technicalities, we are in spirit a concert party with Eva and Frazer, and we're bound to make an official takeover bid. But you don't seem to want to do that. What are you waiting for?"

"I don't know. There's something going on in the background. I suppose I'm trying to stir it up so it'll show itself."

"If there is anything like that, perhaps it's better hidden."

"I don't know. Just give me a bit of time. And if you or Case Reed want some of the shares, I'll sell them at cost. I'll offer them pro rata to Robie Frazer, at cost plus a suitable premium."

Richardson got up from his side of the desk and perched alongside Cassie. "You're very blithe about all this. Be careful, Cassie. You don't want to mess around with Robie Frazer. And I'd be rather careful of your friend Eva too."

"What d'you mean?"

He raised an eyebrow. "I think you know exactly what I mean. It takes just one look at her. I think she could cut up the lot of us if she chose, including Frazer." He regarded her in silence for a while. He wished he shared her confidence. "I'll give you your time, Cass. A few days. Just be careful."

THIRTY-NINE

Andrew Stormont arrived at Cassie's house at nine sharp. Nesta met him with much barking, leaping, and yowling, but his response seemed oddly automatic to Cassie. His face was perfect, all cool planes and remote eyes. He was physically beautiful. She had not really seen it with such clarity before. He seemed this evening to have been stripped of a layer, as if he had had something taken from him. She felt a pulse of desire and decided not to be too difficult.

She smiled at him as he kissed her cheek. "Would you like to come in for a drink?" she asked.

"Table's booked for nine, so thanks, but we'd better go."

"I'll just get my bag." So what? thought Cassie, collecting her bag and keys from the sitting room. Why the hurry?

They ate at a new restaurant on the Fulham Road which Stormont said he wanted to try. He still seemed oddly detached. His eyes were focused, but not on Cassie.

"Why the bad mood earlier? Problems at work?" he asked after they ordered.

"Yeah. One of my stocks is behaving strangely. A bit of manipulation, I think."

"And what can you do about that?"

"Legally?"

He laughed. "If you prefer."

"Well, legally, not a lot. It's difficult to prove."

"So what do you do?"

"Why should I do anything? Surely it's a fait accompli?"

His eyes warmed for the first time that evening. "You don't look as if you've just been squashed by a fait accompli."

"I did something illogical."

"Why?"

"As an experiment. And because it seemed like the right thing to do."

"Is this on your deal with Eva?"

"Oooh, curiosity."

There was a silence. She felt tense. "No, it's not," she lied.

"How is your deal with Eva?"

"I don't know, really. She rang me on Tuesday, told me she was off to Hong Kong and Vietnam with our coinvestor to look at her site."

"And does the coinvestor like it?"

"Don't know. Eva promised to keep in touch, but I've heard nothing from her or the coinvestor for two days, so I don't know what's going on. It's bloody inconvenient, actually."

"Why don't you ring her?"

"I tried. But I haven't managed to speak to her. I

rang the coinvestor's housekeeper in London, asked where I might get hold of him. She said she thought he was just about to leave Hong Kong for Vietnam. So I rang Hong Kong. I spoke to a housekeeper there and asked for Eva. She said that Eva couldn't come to the phone but that she'd leave a message telling her I'd called. I haven't heard a word back."

Stormont felt chained to the table. He waited for courses to come and go, all the while his mind elsewhere, seeing only Eva.

Cassie watched him. "What's going on?"

"Going on?"

"Oh, come on."

"I don't know what you're talking about."

For a long time they stared at each other, both unyielding. Finally, Cassie spoke.

"It's late. I think I'll go home."

"I'll take you."

Stormont called for the bill, then drove her back to Markham Street and walked her to the door. He kissed her goodnight. They stood eye to eye, unflinching, holding back questions, fears. As he returned to his car, he felt as if he were carrying nitroglycerin—any small movement and the air would explode.

Back home in Old Church Street, Stormont called Giles Aden.

"Eva is with Frazer. Apparently Frazer is just about to leave for Vietnam, presumably with Eva. Eva telephoned Cassie before leaving England, promised to keep in touch, but Cassie hasn't heard a word for two days, seems worried. She left a message in Hong Kong, but Eva hasn't called back."

"I've spoken to the stations. They're on discreet lookout, but no sign of Eva."

"Are they ready?"

"They're ready. Do you want them to go in?"

"No. Not yet. We're still in the game."

FORTY

Eva slept badly. Suddenly she jerked awake. Frazer was standing at the foot of her bed watching her. She sat up quickly.

"We leave for Vietnam in an hour. We'll fly in my jet."

His jet, with no recourse to other passengers, no help.

Frazer moved to leave, then, at the door, turned back to her. "I hope you're prepared."

"Prepared?"

"You'll need a bit more than Chanel in that terrain."

Waves of nausea rose in Eva's stomach. "Don't forget, Frazer. It's home territory to me."

His eyes rested on her for a second, mocking. Then he turned and walked out.

Eva jumped out of bed. She stood still, naked in the middle of the room, as if taking bearings. Then with long strides she walked to the window and looked out. She noticed Ned standing on the terrace below and another man walking along slowly, with the unmistakable gait of patrol. For a while she stood still, weighing up the odds.

Escape, which would prove her guilt, would probably fail. The alternative was to go along with Frazer, wait for a better chance to flee, and discover what she could in the meantime. She made up her mind and headed for the bathroom. After showering briskly, she dressed in one of her new outfits, a cream linen suit with a long split skirt and high suede mules. She put on her jewelry and began to walk toward the door but stopped suddenly, as if at an afterthought, to kick off her mules.

On bare feet she walked down the marble staircase and headed into the bowels of the house. She swung open the door into the kitchen, causing Ned and Kim, who were sitting drinking tea, to look up sharply.

"I'd like some coffee, please, Kim. In fact, I'd like the whole works, the usual fry-up," she added, seeing the look of indignation on Kim's face. It would be wise to eat while she could.

Kim got slowly to her feet. "Coffee on the stove. If you want, you can take some now. I'll bring your breakfast up later."

"Thank you."

Kim poured coffee into a pot and milk into a jug and placed both, along with cup and saucer, on a tray, which she handed to Eva.

"Bring the rest up as soon as possible, could you? We don't want to keep the Tai Pan waiting." Eva swung back through the green baize door.

As she was approaching the main staircase, the murmur of voices seeped from a side room. She stopped to listen.

"We found an old army base we can stay at, about two miles from the diamond site. It's empty. We arranged to take it for a year, paid off the relevant people. It's ours. It's perfect."

"Good. Don't have too many people there. Don't want to attract too much attention."

Le Mai's voice, and Frazer's. Eva walked on quickly, back up to her room. She placed the tray on her bed. She stared for a few moments at the telephone on the bedside table. She prayed it was still connected. Any calls she might make would be recorded, she felt sure of that. But it was a risk she had to take. She knew the precariousness of her position, knew how badly she needed a lifeline, however tenuous.

She picked up the receiver and dialed. It was 12:15 A.M. in London. She prayed Cassie was in. The phone rang and rang. Just as she was about to give up, Cassie answered. Eva kept the relief from her voice.

"Cass, hi. Sorry to call so late."

"That's all right. I just got in from dinner, was in the bath." Cassie too felt a flash of relief. She asked quickly, "Where are you?"

"Hong Kong. We're just leaving for Vietnam, Frazer and I. It's so exciting, going back to the site. And Frazer's been incredibly inventive. One of his functionaries, Le Mai, has taken over this old army base about two miles from the site, can you imagine? All I need is a pair of fatigues and a jeep and I'll feel like a female Rambo." She laughed. "All I've got is a bunch of Chanel I bought on a mega–shopping trip yesterday."

"Designer Rambo," said Cassie, her relief turning into puzzlement over Eva's frothy torrent of words, all so uncharacteristic. Before she could say anything more, she heard a slight intake of breath, then Frazer's voice.

"Who are you talking to?"

His cold, despising tone cut through her. She felt a quick flash of fear, her own and Eva's.

"What's going on, Eva?" she asked.

Eva's voice came back, taut with fear. "Nothing. I have to go."

Click and she was gone.

FORTY-ONE

John Richardson was alone in the office when Peter Bawden called. It was 8 A.M. He glanced with curiosity at the telephone. People knew not to disturb him until after nine. He picked it up and listened, then got to his feet and hurried out of his office, putting on his jacket as he went.

Ten minutes later he sat in Bawden's office. Bawden looked uncharacteristically tense.

"What I'm about to tell you goes no further. If you do take any action as a result of what I'm about to tell you, you'll have to think up a good explanation for it. Anything but the truth, which would compromise you, me, my entire organization, and several highly valued sources."

"Take it as understood."

Bawden paused. Then, in a quiet voice, he began to speak. "We've been conducting an investigation on behalf of one of the defense contractors. They called us in because they suspected that an employee was selling details of their computerized weapons guidance systems. Our brief was to identify buyer and seller. It came down to

one man, a Hong Kong Chinese named Xu Nan. For
some time he had been living beyond his means. His bank
account details, in Switzerland, confirmed large, irregular
payments. Whoever was paying covered their tracks well.
We haven't managed to identify them. It seemed we had
only half a case, but four days ago Xu Nan was found
dead on the pavement. He had apparently jumped from
his seventh-floor flat."

Bawden seemed to take a long breath. "The police
are investigating. They know nothing of our own investigations, and neither will they, but it seems they do suspect
foul play. They have forensic teams crawling over the
place. We don't know what they've found, if anything,
but their presence is reason enough for suspicion. Then,
last night, one of my people obtained a copy of this."
Bawden handed Richardson a photocopy of a handwrit-
ten letter.

> *I don't know who will read this, besides my solicitor, or
> what good it will do. None to me, because I will already be
> dead, my condition for the opening of this letter. But I will say
> it anyway. For years, since I was a child, Robie Frazer has
> given me money. At first it was to pay for my education. I was
> a talented child, and he made sure I was well educated. I
> thought it was pure charity until, six months ago, he asked
> me to provide him with details of my work in weapons systems
> at General Engineering. I refused, but Frazer made it clear
> that I had to do what he wanted. So, over the past six
> months, I have passed on details of our weapons development
> programs to Frazer and have been well paid for it. Recently I
> tried to stop this, but I fear what will happen to me if I do not
> do what Frazer wants. I appointed this new solicitor, and gave
> him this letter, because for some time I have suspected that*

Frazer will try to kill me, or have me killed. And now I am dead.

The letter was signed "Xu Nan" and dated three weeks earlier. Richardson handed the copy back to Bawden. For a while, neither man spoke.

Richardson got to his feet. "Thank you, Peter. I know how many rules you've broken to tell me this."

"What are you going to do about your deal with Frazer?"

"Wreck it—invisibly, so he'll never know what's happening. Get out."

"Cost you a lot?"

"Not as much as it cost Xu Nan."

Cassie was in her office when Richardson returned to Case Reed. He walked in without greeting her and took the chair opposite her desk around to her side so that he sat almost knee to knee with her.

"I'm going to tell you something you will never repeat, to anyone. You will never appear to act on it. You will never give any indication that you knew or know anything about it, even if it becomes public knowledge."

Cassie looked at him with growing alarm. She had never heard him speak in this tone of voice, never seen him so still.

"You're scaring the wits out of me, John. Whatever it is, I'll never let on, O.K.? Now say what you have to say."

He took five minutes to tell her. Every word seemed to take her away from herself, from what she knew, until she felt, ludicrously, that this was not really happening, that her imagination had finally gone out of control. Only her horror seemed real, and the look in Richardson's eyes.

Finally she spoke. "What happens now? Will they go after Frazer, these people with the letter, whoever they are?"

"No. They have no interest in getting the police involved. It's the last thing their client would want. They don't want to be seen to have poor security, not where military secrets are concerned. And no one could ever convict a man with Frazer's resources on this. If Xu Nan was murdered, no one would be able to tie it to Frazer. He'd have henchmen for all that, and if necessary, they'd do time for him."

"But what do we do?"

"I want to think about it very carefully. As soon as is practical, and in a way that is not at all suspicious, we sever our ties with him." Richardson got to his feet. "We'll talk later."

Cassie watched him leave her office. She sat completely still, every sense unnaturally alert. She thought of Eva, somewhere in Vietnam now with a man she didn't know, an extremely dangerous man. She thought of the fear in her voice when they spoke the night before. Eva had told her where she was going with Frazer—some camp near the site.

Almost compulsively, blocking out thought, Cassie opened her filing cabinet, took out the Genius file, and flicked through it till she found the map of the site. She stared at the map for five minutes, seeing contours, labels, names of alien places. She felt herself responding to some unknown prompt, whose voice spoke so loudly it drowned out reason. She had to go to Vietnam, warn Eva, and get her away from Frazer, if it wasn't already too late.

She picked up the telephone and spoke to her travel agent, giving him quick instructions. He booked her on the first flight to Hanoi and reserved a room at the Metropole for her.

She waited until Emma had left her desk, then collected up her bag and walked out of her office. She took the back stairs so she didn't have to pass John Richardson. On the street, she caught a taxi back to her house. She asked the driver to wait and ran upstairs to her room to pack.

As she was carrying the suitcase down the stairs, David Wilson shuffled from his room, wiping the sleep from his eyes. "Where are you off to? Why aren't you at work?"

"Vietnam. Hanoi."

"What the hell are you going there for?"

Cassie sat on a step and let the case tumble to the foot of the stairs. David squeezed down next to her.

"I'm going to see Eva and her site."

"She's out there?"

Cassie nodded.

"Where? Where are you staying?"

"I haven't quite got all the details fixed," said Cassie evasively.

"Hang on a minute. This isn't fucking Brighton. You don't just show up and hope for the best. And what's the hurry? Yesterday I heard you making plans for the weekend. Now you're off halfway across the world." He took hold of her shoulders and turned her toward him. "What the hell's going on, Cass?"

She glared at him but made no move to throw off his hold. "I don't know. That's what I'm going to find out."

"That's not an answer. For God's sake, Cass, you can't just go trooping off to Vietnam."

She got to her feet. "Look, I'm going." Her face

hardened, warding off his words. He could sense her implacability.

"At least let me come with you."

She paused, disconcerted by his concern. She stooped down to kiss his cheek.

"I'll be fine, David. Please don't worry." She walked to the suitcase lying at the bottom of the stairs.

David sighed, watching her. Her movements were oddly stiff. He walked down to her.

"I'll stay put, if that's what you want."

"That's what I want."

She kissed him again. He hugged her tightly, then let her go.

The telephone rang just as she was walking out the door. She grabbed the receiver in annoyance.

"Hello!" It was a shout, not a greeting.

"Cassie, hello. It's Aubrey Goldstein here."

"Oh, Aubrey, hello."

"Are you in the middle of something? Am I disturbing you?"

"I'm just going to catch a flight."

"Ah. Anywhere interesting?"

"Vietnam."

There was a brief silence. Cassie waited agitatedly. Then Goldstein spoke, his voice smooth and seductive.

"To Genius's diamond site."

"I don't suppose that took too much deduction."

"No. You, Vietnam, diamonds, Genius. I don't believe in coincidence."

"Neither do I." She thought of the bear raid, of Case Reed in the red, and her voice hardened. "What can I do for you?"

"I know someone who might want to acquire some Genius shares."

Cassie paused for a second, forcing herself back into the business mode. "Does he want control?"

"Possibly. He has the resources."

She knew she had to get rid of her shares. If Case Reed wrecked the deal with Frazer, Genius's share price would plummet.

"Tell him to go to the Metropole Hotel in Hanoi. We can discuss it there if he's really interested."

"I'll tell him."

There was a click and she was gone.

Goldstein dialed another number. "I think we might have a deal on Genius. Stewart wants someone to meet her at the Metropole in Hanoi."

"Does she now?" The voice was wry, jaded, cold with distance and the customary contempt born of always being right, of knowing the outcome in advance. "You'd better go, then. She might be a bit softer there. It's a long way from home, not a congenial environment for a woman alone. Do what you can. Get her shares. It's a good time to buy, with the shares so low. She and Case Reed have probably been burned pretty badly."

"No doubt."

"I'll leave the details to you. Do what you have to."

FORTY-TWO

The faxed report from Heathrow was lying on Andrew Stormont's desk when he returned to his temporary office in Tooley Street at five that afternoon: "Cassie Stewart left country 11 A.M. Flight TG915 to Bangkok, connecting Hanoi. Arrive Hanoi 12:20 local time. Subject traveling alone. One suitcase."

Stormont had alerted Special Branch at Heathrow and Gatwick to be on the alert just in case Cassie traveled anywhere. It had paid off. But the small satisfaction it might have brought was overshadowed by the fears that her flight to Hanoi suggested. He crumpled the fax in his hand and threw it at the bin, then dialed Cassie's number at Case Reed.

Her secretary answered. "Cassie Stewart's office."

"Could I speak to her, please."

"Uh, she's not here."

"Do you know where I could contact her?"

"Is this business or personal?"

"Personal."

"She might be at home."

"Might be?"

"Er, I'm not exactly sure."

"It's important I talk to her."

"She'll probably be back here soon. She—"

"Has she been in the office today?"

"Yes. She was in first thing."

"Thank you." Stormont cut the line and called out to Aden, who, thanks to Stormont's temporary move, was cramped in a tiny office ten feet away.

Aden appeared in an excited flurry. "What's happened?"

"Cassie Stewart has flown off to Vietnam on some private mission. Apparently she went into Case Reed first thing this morning. Then, without telling them, she disappeared. They don't know where she is."

Aden took a seat. "Why would she do that?"

"It's my guess she had another conversation with Eva, or maybe even with Frazer. Something they said must have seemed off-base. Not so much that she got really scared, or I doubt if she would have gone. But something must have come across as odd, especially for her to go out there without telling Case Reed, who, after all, are supposed to be running this deal."

Aden shook his head. "Doesn't work. I think we're missing something."

Stormont thought for a while. "You're probably right. But I think what we do have is the possibility that Eva somehow alerted Cassie to the fact that something was wrong. She didn't terrify her, but she did worry her. Now, for what? Did she want Cassie to go careering off to Vietnam? I doubt it. It's much more likely that she hoped Cassie would mention something to me or that I would call Cassie to find out discreetly what had happened to her after she failed to get in touch. Eva's using Cassie as a conduit, only Cassie has ideas above her station, decides to become more of a participant than any of us predicted. That's the missing bit. Why has she stepped over the line?"

"Perhaps she heard something at Case Reed?"

"Possibly. But what? Cassie doesn't engage. She watches, deliberates, deciphers what goes on with incredible accuracy, but as far as I can gather, she always stays on the sidelines."

"Hang on a minute. She's a banker, for God's sake. A venture capitalist. She invests money in high-risk transactions. That's hardly standing on the sidelines."

Stormont gave him a contemptuous look. "That's her job. Civil servants and politicians who close down casualty units kill people, but they never put their hands around people's necks and squeeze. Cassie takes risks for a living in an air-conditioned office with wall-to-wall carpeting, then she goes home to her beautiful house in Chelsea. Her risks don't touch her. She doesn't live them."

"O.K., O.K."

"But you have a point," added Stormont, surprising Aden. "She's gone to Vietnam. It's not in character. Something we don't know about must have made her do it, must have been a catalyst."

"So what is it?"

Stormont got to his feet. "We can speculate forever." He hit the intercom. "Elsa, I'd like to get to Hanoi, please. All speed."

Elsa buzzed him minutes later.

"You'll have to go commercial, I'm afraid. The air force boys are being difficult buggers. Apparently there's nothing free until tomorrow."

"Forget it. I'll go commercial."

"The fastest route, leaving now, is via Hong Kong.

I've booked you on the Virgin flight this evening, departing Heathrow at eight-thirty, arriving Hong Kong at five tomorrow afternoon. You connect at seven with Cathay Pacific to Hanoi."

"Good. Thanks, Elsa."

"What are you going to do?" Aden asked Stormont.

"I don't know yet. Be another catalyst. Throw myself into the pot."

"You'll probably find it'll all have blown up by the time you get there."

"Oh, I don't think so. Everybody's still lining up, still trying to work out which side everyone else is on. I think I'll arrive in time."

"In time for what?"

"You said it yourself. The explosion."

FORTY-THREE

As Cassie Stewart's plane was coming in to land in Hanoi, Andrew Stormont's was flying over Saudi Arabia and Aubrey Goldstein's was waiting on the tarmac, being serviced for its flight in three hours' time from Heathrow.

Cassie gazed out the window as her plane began its descent. All she could see spread out below was red earth, dark like dried blood. In parts it bunched up into hills, stubby, pointy little hills. As the plane lost altitude, the ground flattened out, and Cassie was able to pick out paddies, wet green marshes stretching to every horizon. She could see people dotted around, and oxen, and tall, dull green trees spreading lavish leaves in a canopy around them, staving off the heat.

The plane landed smoothly and taxied toward the terminal building, which was low, new, concrete, functional, and ugly. She collected her bag from the overhead compartment and her book, Graham Greene's *The Quiet American,* from the seatback in front of her. Was it still Greene's Vietnam? Beguiling equally in beauty and violence?

Steps clanked against the door, making her jump. People filed out. She stood in line impatiently. Head up, eyes searching, she stepped from the plane. Humid, vibrant air enfolded her. She walked down the steps and across the baking tarmac into the terminal building, which, to her surprise, was air-conditioned.

WELCOME TO THE SOCIALIST REPUBLIC OF VIETNAM, said a sign. She felt as if she were witnessing something of history, one of the last selfacknowledged socialist states. She wondered how long it would be before Vietnam accepted capitalism, which already gripped its economy if not its politics. The Americans had just lifted their embargo, and business was booming. But still the sign was there, proud and prominent: the socialist republic. Cassie wondered what it would be like outside the enclave of the airport. Like East Berlin before the fall? She had been there in 1987, felt the corrosive suspicion in the air, the gray cold, the hostility of the officials, the sense of watchfulness, a closed, dark excitement. But here the culture and mindset were different, unknown. There were few European links, and there was no Caucasian empathy, no antipathy of unequal familiars.

Of Vietnam, she knew not a thing. She felt suddenly as defenseless as a child. Her only point of reference was Eva, and Frazer too, she supposed. She wondered what had happened in the long hours since she had last spoken to Eva.

She waited for her luggage. A thin tanned man with long hair tied back in a ponytail waited next to her.

"Where are you going?" he asked casually. His eyes were kind.

"Hanoi—the center, I think."

He glanced at her clothes. "Don't let the taxi drivers rip you off. Don't pay any more than fifteen dollars."

"Thanks, that's handy to know. Where are you going?"

"Up-country somewhere. I'm a photographer. I wander around, kind of looking for stories."

"Exciting."

"Yeah. Beats the tube."

Cassie felt unreasonably cheered by this slight contact. She turned back to the luggage carousel, grabbed her suitcase, and nodded goodbye to the ponytailed man.

At customs and immigration, an unsmiling Vietnamese flicked through her passport and visa documentation, looking back and forth from the papers to her. Finally she was through. She hauled her suitcase out to the front of the terminal.

The concrete teemed with people, some waiting patiently, others shrieking as they spotted relatives and friends, yet others shouting good-humoredly to clear a path. Cassie could hear no individual voices, just a cacophony. It was not hostile; it seemed generically friendly, but it was so loud and invasive, along with the heat, that she felt overpowered.

Two local men stood still at the center of the crowd, watching the newly arrived passengers fight their way out. When they saw Cassie, they exchanged a nod and pushed their way through the crowd toward her.

"Taxi, madam?" one of them said, reaching out for her case.

"How much to the center?"

"Twenty dollar." His broad smile revealed two black and two missing teeth.

"Too much. Fifteen."

"Fifteen? I'm a businessman. I run a business. Fifteen not enough."

"Then no thank you," said Cassie, trying to move on.

"O.K. Fifteen. Fifteen dollar," said the man hurriedly. Cassie handed over her case. Pleased with her bargaining ability, she had no idea she was onto a sure thing.

The two men led her to a rusting black Lada. One opened the door for her, then slammed it behind her with great force. "Door not close easily," he said, grinning at her startled face. He got into the driver's seat and his companion got in beside him. They turned and grinned again at Cassie, who managed a slight, uneasy smile.

The two men spoke to each other in Vietnamese. Occasionally they glanced back and smiled, but there was no comfort in their faces.

They passed through a landscape the like of which she had never seen before. There was chaos everywhere. Cars, trucks, motorcycles, bicycles, oxen, and carts thronged the dirt road, weaving madly. Horns blared continuously. Cassie could not look ahead for fear of impending collision. Somehow, by skirting the road, sometimes to the extent of clinging to the steep banks on either side of it, the vehicles avoided collisions, but her nerves remained braced.

On either side of the road were rice fields where women worked bent double, their heads shielded by conical hats that Cassie had thought were worn only in films. Oxen grazed on patches of grass with a strange calmness about them, as if they cared for nothing save the grass, which would always grow, and the sun, which would always shine.

They drove on for miles through this landscape. Cassie wondered if they were disappearing into the depths of the country, or if sooner or later signs of a metropolis would emerge amid the pastoral poverty. At last they did.

The sloping banks gave way to gutters and the fields to scattered houses, which as the miles passed drew closer together. The gutters flowed with brown liquid, dammed up in parts behind refuse. People squatted in conversation or in silent contemplation of the circus around them. Children and dogs played. Houses lined the road, tall and thin, stone mostly, decrepit, with peeling yellow and orange paint. Piles of bricks lay stacked up, and new construction abounded. Shops open to the street sold bottles in neat rows. Street sellers sat by mounds of fruit: apples, oranges, bananas, and melons.

Cassie gazed out the open window, her hair blowing around her face. Trucks roared by, leaving the metal taste of diesel in her mouth. Her skin sweated in the heat and was sticky to the touch. Her creased clothes clung to her.

She was overwhelmed. She felt utterly alone in an alien culture, devoid of all the props of Western civilization, stripped of her own resources. Her lack of strength frightened her, and to her surprise and horror, she felt panic mounting. She forced her breath into a steady rhythm, inhaling deeply, but she couldn't stick to it, and soon she was snatching again at shallow breaths. She felt as if she were hardly breathing at all.

Surely there was more to her. She must have more innate strength. She wished she could look for it, but she was too frightened to try.

The car rolled on. The track was bumpier now, the traffic thinning out. Once again open countryside surrounded them: rice fields, cows, ducks, rivers. They crossed a succession of latticed bridges. She tried to withdraw into some sanctuary within herself, to switch off all feeling. But the panic remained.

She glanced at her watch. They had been driving for over an hour. She had no idea where they were going.

She sat, eyes closed, and waited. She felt the bumps rock her through the thin suspension. She heard an increasing tide of horns and engines.

Suddenly the car came to a halt. She opened her eyes.

"Metropole Hotel," said the driver with a grin, seeing her discomfort as a huge joke. From his innocent perspective it would be, she thought, handing over fifteen dollars. All of a sudden she felt like laughing. Here she was, safe. Yet her imagination had for a time crippled her. With reason?

She wondered about Eva. What was she doing? Cassie tried to sense her presence but felt nothing.

The driver handed Cassie's case to the doorman. Then he and his accomplice got back into the car and drove off. In a side street half a mile from the Metropole, they parked and went into a house. The driver telephoned, speaking perfect English.

"We picked her up. She's safely installed at the Metropole. Jumpy as a cat."

"Watch her, then. And watch who's watching her. We won't be the only ones. And don't let anything happen. Not yet."

FORTY-FOUR

The Metropole was a large white colonial-style structure on a dirt street lined with trees. A row of hexagonal clocks hung in the foyer, showing the time in Paris, Moscow, London, New York, and Sydney. Apart from the slight exoticism suggested by the Moscow clock, the hotel was furnished like any five-star hotel anywhere in the world, all marble and chandeliers. But there was none of the sepulchral calm found in some grand hotels. Cassie sensed a strange urgency. The guests wore looks of excitement, of anticipation, and walked with a visible air of purpose.

A beautiful Vietnamese woman in a long tunic split to the thigh, worn over trousers, all in pale yellow silk, approached. She smiled and led Cassie to her room. Cassie closed the door behind her and looked around. It was almost dark inside, as the sunlight was kept out by wooden blinds of dark wood. The same dark wood lined the floor and the lower half of the walls. The rest of the walls and the ceiling were painted white. A large bed with gleaming white sheets stood against one wall. Opposite was a large gilt mirror.

Cassie threw back the blinds and opened the windows. Noise and sunlight poured in. She leaned out, smiling in delight at the melee below. Taxis and cyclos picked up and deposited guests in an almost constant stream. Cyclo drivers plied for trade by aiming their craft at pedestrians, shouting "Ride?" and "Yes?," some with force, some with faint hope. It was interesting to see who responded to which kind of blandishment. She would go for the soft ones, she decided. Children and dogs ran around, oblivious to the heat. Old women squatted on the ramshackle pavements, taking shelter under the shade of the sprawling trees, and all the while a Grand Prix took place, with bicycles, cyclos, motorbikes, cars, and pedestrians jostling for position, hooting and shouting ceaselessly.

Cassie turned from the window, shed her clothes, and took a long shower. Dressed in a long print skirt and white T-shirt, she went down to reception.

"I need to hire a car and a driver tomorrow."

"No problem. Where would you like to go?"

"I'm not sure exactly where the place is," she said, and the concierge gave her a tolerant look. "It's near a village called Lang-son, eighty miles northeast of here." Cassie knew that the diamond site was near this village, and Eva had said the camp was near the site, so Lang-son was the best pointer she had. "It's an old army camp. I don't know what it's called, but there can't be that many in that particular area."

"We use a variety of different drivers for special occasions, trips. I'll talk to them, see if anyone knows your army camp." The concierge couldn't resist pronouncing the last two words with particular care, his eyes watching her carefully.

"That would be very kind. I'd like to leave at nine in

the morning, and I'd like you to confirm everything as soon as possible, please."

"Of course, madam. I'll do what I can."

Cassie picked up a booklet guide to Hanoi from the reception desk and walked out onto the street. Now that she had arrived safely, her sense of alienation had vanished as quickly as it had come, to be replaced by curiosity.

The heat and noise of the streets took hold of her, sweeping her along. She walked along Ngo Quyen Street, past rows of sandy yellow and tawny orange houses overrun with greenery. The paint peeled and flaked, and parts of the stone structures looked precariously loose. All around Cassie saw images of fading beauty and grandeur, poignant houses with a past.

She paused at the roadside, trying to see her way across the barrage of traffic. It seemed impenetrable. Finally an old man, gnarled, wrinkled, nut brown, and smiling, grabbed hold of her arm and marched her across, leaving the traffic to pick its way around them. They got to the other side quite safely. Cassie thanked the man, wishing she knew the words in Vietnamese. With a brief nod, he went on his way. Cassie watched him till he was swallowed up by the crowds.

She meandered along the boulevards, walking according to whim, not noting her path. She would take a cyclo back to the hotel, so she had no fear of getting lost. She walked alongside a large lake with a temple on a little island close to the edge. It was linked to the shore by an arched red wooden bridge. She consulted her booklet and recognized the temple as the Jade Hill Pagoda. It was dedicated, she read, to Van Xuong, the god of literature.

She crossed the wide boulevard Vietnamese style, letting the traffic accommodate her, and found herself in a maze of narrow streets lined by tall, thin houses in various

shades of amber yellow, with the odd shocking flash of
turquoise, bright as the sky. Shops formed the ground
level of most of these houses. Many of the streets, or
sections of the streets, seemed dedicated to one trade—
children's clothes, shoes, underwear, tourist knickknacks,
cakes, cassette players, and sewing machines, many in use,
chattering away wildly. The air was rich with smells, a
mixture of drains, food, spices, dogs, joss sticks, jasmine,
exhaust fumes, dust, and gas cookers. People were having
what looked like impromptu picnics on the street, frying
up concoctions on their gas stoves, filling the air with the
tang of coriander, ginger, and chili. Women sat by little
trestle tables, drinking tea or selling melons and corn on
the cob from elaborate piles.

Cassie gazed at the faces around her. She walked on
—probably in a huge circle; she wasn't sure—and came
across a street of barbers. All she could hear was the *chink,
chink* of cutting scissors in the air. There must have been
forty to fifty barbers, all in a row under blue awnings.
Their customers, all men, looked very smart. Some wore
suits, others berets.

Cassie glanced at her watch. She had been walking
for two hours. She wasn't sure where she was, or where
the hotel was. She glanced around, looking for a cyclo,
trying to select from the score the neediest-looking. Distracted, she didn't notice the men watching her—two sets
of four, scattered among the crowds. She wouldn't have
suspected anything sinister in it even if she had seen them.
She was used to being noticed. She selected a cyclo and
flagged him down. He slowed to a halt.

"The Metropole," she said.

He nodded and waited for her to climb onto the
wooden seat up front, then laboriously pedaled off. Other

cyclos were hastily summoned and took up pursuit, invisible in the mass.

Cassie turned to look at her cyclo driver. He was almost half her size, but thin and wiry, probably immensely strong for his size, and fit. There was no fat on his limbs. She wondered what he had to eat in a day. She felt guilty, sitting before him in the tiny cart while he pedaled in the afternoon sun. But he seemed unconcerned; there was no bitterness to him, more a dignified resignation. Cassie disembarked at the Metropole, paid him extravagantly, and returned to her room to shower and change for dinner.

The concierge, who had seen her pass, was beginning to worry about how he was going to make his excuses to her. He had rung his usual selection of drivers, but no one knew of the army camp. Just as he was about to call her to tell her to forget about her rather unorthodox trip, a stranger rang him.

"Ngo Lung suggested I call you. He mentioned you were looking for someone to drive a guest to an army camp near Lang-son. I know the camp. I will drive your guest. I have a good car. Japanese, five years old, good suspension, air conditioning."

"You're a friend of Ngo's?"

"Ring him. Ask him about me. He'll tell you."

The concierge was silent for a while, pondering the wisdom of letting an unknown driver transport one of his guests. But the stranger had turned up like a lucky charm. The concierge did not relish the prospect of telling the beautiful Englishwoman that he had failed. And the man was a friend of Ngo's. That was easy to check.

"All right. Come here at nine tomorrow. The passenger's name is Stewart, Cassandra Stewart."

"I'll be there at nine."

The concierge rang Cassie. Once she knew that she would be going to the camp, the fear she had banished returned. Her room seemed unbearably small. She went downstairs to the bar. On one side were tables in the half-darkness, next to an open courtyard where a swimming pool glistened. On the other side were large, well-lit tables and deep sofas. Cassie chose a sofa. A waiter came. She ordered a whiskey sour. She drank it quickly and ordered another, letting her eyes wander casually around the bar, her ears pick up the strains of different conversations.

After her second whiskey sour she went through to the dining room. She scanned the menu and ordered what turned out to be an incredibly good dinner. She started with bittersweet fish soup, in a huge bowl that would have served four. Huge chunks of a variety of different kinds of fish, all unrecognizable, all delicious, floated in the soup. As she dug in, she encountered layers of delicate flavors. She felt a tinge of guilt as she conspicuously failed to do justice to it, leaving it half eaten, saving space for her next course, ginger chicken with coriander and steamed rice.

She carried on drinking whiskey sours, needing the strong, rasping taste. When her initial pangs of hunger were sated, she ate more slowly, taking time to observe her surroundings. There were a few women on their own, and men too; a few groups, a few couples, including one terribly glamorous one, man and woman matched for beauty. Everybody, even the glamorous couple, seemed to be interested in everybody else, and covert glances traveled back and forth.

Cassie felt not the least bit self-conscious to be sitting alone at dinner. Through her fear, she began to feel a wonderful sense of anonymity, one of the most seductive feelings she had ever come across. It brought with it a feeling of freedom, as if she could get away with anything. Now she felt the strength she had been afraid to search for hours earlier, on the long drive through the rice fields.

FORTY-FIVE

Andrew Stormont's plane arrived at 8 P.M. in Hong Kong, three hours late, having sat on the tarmac at Heathrow with a mechanical problem. There were no more connections to Hanoi that night. He would have to wait until tomorrow. With quiet fury he had made the preparatory telephone calls in London to change his arrangements. A car had been sent to collect him from the airport and take him to a safe house in Wanchai. Colin McKenzie, the head of station in Hong Kong, had been alerted and was there to brief him. He welcomed Stormont with a handshake and a gin and tonic.

Stormont sat straight in an armchair, grim, gray with lack of sleep. He waited for McKenzie to speak.

"There's been a lot of activity at Frazer's house, or among his known employees. Eight of them have flown out to Vietnam. Frazer was accompanied on the flight by the woman you alerted us to, blond, young, beautiful—Eva Cunningham. Something is going on in Vietnam. We got a report from Hanoi station. Frazer and his entourage are holed up in this army base about eighty miles northeast of Hanoi. Frazer and his men have spent a lot of time at the diamond site, a few miles from the base. The girl went along yesterday morning, but hasn't been seen since."

"Not much of a place for a girl, a jungle camp. Frazer's probably sent her home."

"We've no record of her going through any of the airports," McKenzie said bluntly.

Stormont looked past him, saying nothing. McKenzie watched him, seeing his stillness, his battening down of emotion.

Stormont scarcely saw McKenzie. He saw instead a picture of Eva—her face, her stance, strong and resilient. He closed his eyes abruptly, to banish the picture.

Cassie awoke the next morning at seven. She showered, dressed in loose cotton trousers, running shoes, and a T-shirt, and packed an overnight bag in case she would have to spend the night at Eva's army camp. When she went down to breakfast, at one of the other tables she saw a large group of people wearing identical T-shirts emblazoned with "Canadian Travel Agents' Educational Tour Vietnam 1995." So much for exoticism.

She ordered croissants, coffee, and coconut milk, but toyed with the croissants when they arrived. Her appetite of last night had been choked off by nerves. At five to nine she went to the front desk and asked for her driver. A wiry Vietnamese man came forward to introduce himself. His eyes rested on her in brief scrutiny.

She followed him out to his car. He held her door open. She stepped in. He closed it behind her with a slam, then got into the driver's seat, turned on the engine, and pulled out into the throbbing melee. As he drove, he said nothing.

After half an hour, her discomfort mounting, Cassie leaned toward him.

"It's the army camp we're going to, yes? You know it, I take it?"

He glanced over his shoulder and said in perfect English, "Oh yes, I know it." Silently, he continued to drive.

Cassie failed to find the comfort she sought in his words, feeling instead the sickening lurch of panic. She turned to look out the windows, at paddies and bent women and oxen and frail footbridges that swayed when a lone person crossed. Yet cows crossed too.

The silent Vietnamese drove on. They gained altitude slowly, leaving behind the open wetness of the paddies and moving into a landscape of trees and red soil. Cassie rolled down her window and let in a blast of hot air. It crept over her like sticky fingers. Quickly she rolled the window back up, shutting out the world beyond, so alien in sight, sound, and smell. She sat pressed back against the sticky plastic-covered seat and watched the jungle grow around her.

The car followed a scar of a track. Cassie could feel the heat beating through the roof, overpowering the air conditioning. She felt herself begin to sweat. Remorseless, the sun hung overhead, casting shadowless light straight down upon them.

Suddenly she sensed a change in the driver. He slowed the car and glanced once more over his shoulder.

"Soon we'll arrive. How long will you stay?"

"Don't know. Depends."

"On what?"

She didn't know herself. She was going to see, drawn by some instinct, hoping perhaps to prove herself wrong, to find that after all, everything was fine. Even though she knew it couldn't be. She frowned. He was awfully curious for a driver.

"On my mood," she answered sharply.

"I'll wait if you like. Otherwise, how will you get back?"

"Yes, wait for a while. I'll tell you if I want you to stay after I've talked to my friend."

"You have a friend staying at the camp?"

"Yes. She's expecting me," she added, as much for her own benefit as his.

Eva stood poised in a casual pose, senses straining, as she smoked a cigarette, blowing the blue smoke skyward, nonchalantly watching it till it blended with the jungle air and disappeared. She waited until she saw the last ground-based guard go into Frazer's makeshift office, then she dropped the cigarette and bent to tighten the laces in her running shoes. She glanced around one more time. There was a guard in the observation tower. She was shielded from him by a large lean-to full of sacks, but if she moved he would see her. She waited until he began to turn to check the far corners of the camp. Then she ran from the compound across ten yards of open ground and into the circling jungle. She hid behind a tree and looked back at the camp for signs of pursuit. Nothing. It was almost as if they meant her to escape.

All morning the guards had been distracted, fearful, tense with anticipation, neglectful. Their eyes had locked onto the distance beyond her. Over the last few days they had displayed the arrogance of jailers when they looked at her. They had let her walk around during the day, but she knew the exits were heavily guarded and impassable. At night they locked her in a room with barred windows. She had watched and waited for her chance to escape. But today to her puzzlement, the guards almost looked through her, as if she existed no longer. Frazer watched her with his usual coldness, but still there was a desire to wound in his eyes. Their status, as captor and captive, was tacit.

Now her body was braced, waiting. She looked around, not seeing danger but feeling it everywhere. She ran fast, but not freely. The jungle felt as much of a trap as the compound. Sweat slicked down her body. Anger would carry her on, would travel the two miles to the diamond site and beyond in the hundred-degree heat. They would discover that she was gone, she knew that. They might perhaps intercept her and stop her before she got to the site, but she had to see it unsupervised. See it and escape. She understood the strange behavior of the guards. They looked at her as if she were already dead. She had a sense that time was racing away from her. It made her run faster, as if she could outpace it.

On Frazer's instructions, she had dismissed the old contracting company and let in Frazer's men. The new crew had started work on the bulk sampling immediately, rushing around with a flurry of activity that seemed to her to call too much attention to itself, as if to disguise some other purpose. She forced her body faster, running through the jungle on light feet, the only sounds the screaming of displaced birds and her own breath.

The light grew brighter, and Eva knew she was nearing the clearing that housed the site. She slowed to a walk, then fell to her knees and crawled. She stopped behind a tree, just yards from the open ground, gaining a good unobstructed view. The wooden huts were groaning under padlocks. Observation posts stood at four corners. And the machines had come, great yellow giants that raked up the earth.

Today, as every day, the site bustled with activity. The giants dug. Fleets of lorries roared across the site, dumping the excavated rock and soil into two growing mounds, one large, one small, about forty feet from where Eva crouched.

Another lorry approached the smaller mound from a different direction. It was carrying a cargo of stones about a foot in diameter. Strange, thought Eva. There was no soil among the stones; they were clean. The lorry tipped up its back and released the stones onto the mound of soil. Eva watched in amazement as they bounced almost silently, with no crisp clash of rock. The lorry turned and drove away.

Eva looked around. The mound of earth and rock would give her a makeshift screen from the workers and the occasional guard she saw pacing around. She inched forward on hands and knees, up to the pile of rock and soil.

One of the newly delivered stones lay on the ground within reach. Eva picked it up. Her skin turned cold as she felt the surface: rubber, unyielding. Something was packed tightly within. She searched in the rubble for a sharp stone. Earth filled her fingernails, and sweat stuck her hair to her face. A rough stone caught her finger, drawing blood. She grabbed at the stone and began gouging at the rubber. She quickly cut a narrow scar, which she worked on till she finally cut through. As she held up the rubber rock, a thin trail of white powder trickled out. With a lurch of her stomach she recognized it. She didn't wet a finger, pick up a coating of the powder, and taste it. She knew it well enough—heroin. Frazer had turned her own trap against her. She could see his plan. He would ship the heroin-laden rubber stones and the soil samples to Australia, probably, under the pretense of bulk sampling. It was an ingenious scheme.

Her senses dulled by rage, she didn't hear the footsteps approaching, didn't detect the imminence of danger until it was too late, until the hand clamped on her shoulder and the pistol touched her head.

Moving only her eyes, she saw the hard dark glare of the guard looking down, a guard with a radio and a gun. Safety off, no doubt. The radio crackled into life. She heard the guard say in Vietnamese, "Frazer's woman is here. She's found the heroin."

Time slowed, as it always does with capture. Everything seemed unearthly still; all external sound seemed distant. All she heard was the rage inside her own head. All she felt was her own fear stretched out before her, and the quick, sickening loss of discovery, of the end of a game that she wouldn't relinquish but knew she would be forced to give up. She knew what would happen, but not how, or when. They were merely incidentals, irrelevant to her death, which was assured. Her last four years had been a gift, stolen from Frazer. Now he would steal time back. For a long while Eva stared into the distance. Then she turned to the guard. Every second now was a bonus.

A jeep pulled up beside them. Three other guards stepped out. One brought a rope, bound her hands behind her back. They motioned her into the jeep. She climbed into the back. Two guards flanked her. Two sat up front. They drove along the track through the jungle back to the camp, to Frazer.

Eva looked at the trees, seeing every giant leaf in perfect detail. She looked up to the sky, huge and blue above her, stretching out forever, back to England, to her childhood home, to the empty shell she now called home, to Stormont. She saw his face as clearly as if it were before her, heard his voice, felt his presence, knew the tricks played by a distorting mind. She knew that she was utterly alone.

Frazer was waiting for her in his wooden room. A fan circled above his head, spinning the hot air, which lay on her like a miasma as she was led in. Frazer looked at her, saying nothing. Eva stood before him, unflinching. There was between them the same intensity they had shared in sex. But now the look in his eyes was of death. There was no pretense, no sweetly poisoned distraction. Eva stood rigid, poised to wound. Frazer stood casually, as if he had the luxury of time.

Finally he smiled, and she felt a spasm of sickness. His hands were clasped behind his back, and he seemed to be holding something. He spoke, his voice icy and smooth.

"So you found my heroin, Eva. You know all about it, don't you—used it, I believe, when you worked for me. Eight years ago. Le Mai thought he recognized you in London. Then, in Hong Kong, he was sure. I found it hard to believe at the time, that you had been a junkie, had recovered, had come after me so many years later. And I had you checked out too, when we first met. I had a private investigator on you. He gave you a clean bill of health. You sounded like just what you were supposed to be, an English teacher in Vietnam who got lucky and discovered a diamond prospect. Unlikely, but not implausible. But after Le Mai thought he recognized you, I had someone else do more background checks on you. He discovered the heroin addiction, and from that moment, my dear Eva, you were dead. You and the investigator who lied to me, Owen Quaid." He shrugged. "Quaid was having an affair with your friend Cassie. No doubt they teamed up to protect you. Not that it did much good, did it?"

She watched him, confusion mixing with her fear. How could he have found out about her addiction? Her records should have been expunged and replaced with clean ones.

He took a step closer to her. He seemed to be fiddling with whatever he held behind his back.

"Ah, Eva. Such a waste. So beautiful. You had so many good things . . . And great strength of will—not many junkies clean up. Not many manage that. But all in a good cause, wasn't it?" His lips twisted with sarcasm. "So you could come back and try to get to me, for MI6, am I right? I always knew there was an agent somewhere, buried in my organization. I thought I had her once—I set a trap. She was caught, hanged, so she couldn't have been an agent, could she? Her people would have plucked her out. I suppose you heard about it. She was a friend of yours, I believe." His eyes were mocking, goading her. "Still, a minor casualty, and I got you in the long run, my little spy." He ran his finger along her cheek, then recoiled. Her skin felt like ice.

He stepped back, looking beyond her. Then he laughed suddenly, and his eyes took on a quiet fury. "MI6's private war. Against me. They have to justify their existence, so they muddle about in the drug trade and the arms trade, try to keep tabs, try to get in the way occasionally if the outrage is too big even for them to swallow. And they send you to fight me. And what were you going to do with me, Eva? Spy on me and report back? A victory for conscience? We know who's doing what. We won't stop them. It just comforts us to know. It's the vacuum theory, isn't it? We can't remove them; otherwise, someone else will fill the vacuum of evil. Someone worse, perhaps. It's called containment, isn't it? An exercise in moral relativism." He took a step closer, his eyes bright, cutting into her. "That's what you're dying for, Eva. That's your empty cause, yours and MI6's. How does it feel to know you've wasted your life?"

He stopped abruptly at the look in her eyes, of hatred, of pride, of absolute defiance. It burned his blood. He looked away.

"You thought you could beat me, could come here and trap me and ruin me? Don't worry. I don't expect an answer." He came closer still. "We were going to keep you alive until Ha Chin came this evening. You could have amused him. But better to get things over with."

Two guards held her, one at either side. A third bound her arms and then her feet together. Then he took a leather belt and tied it tightly around her bare upper arm. A vein pulsed and rose. Frazer took his hands from behind his back and extended the syringe.

"A nice little overdose for you, Eva. The junkie once more. Most recovered addicts go back." He smiled. "A plausible death, don't you think?"

FORTY-SIX

The driver dropped Cassie at the entrance to the
army camp. She got out of the car, looked
around, and listened. An electricity generator whirred,
and smoke and the smells of cooking rose from a chim-
ney, but there was no one around. She walked toward a
large building at the center of the camp, where a door
stood open. As she drew close, she could hear a single
voice. She couldn't distinguish words, just the tone, the
sickening cadence. She forced herself to walk nearer, on
silent feet. She stepped through the doorway and tiptoed
along a corridor to the source of the voice. She stopped
outside the door, breathing heavily. The door was partly
open. She heard Frazer's words now, frighteningly clear.
She listened till she heard him pronounce Eva's death
sentence. Then, shaking with horror, she peered around
the door.

Frazer was injecting a hypodermic needle into Eva's
arm. Eva's eyes were shut, her body straining away. Cassie
screamed and jumped through the door toward Frazer,
knocking into him. The needle dangled from Eva's flesh,
then fell. A guard grabbed Cassie.

Frazer steadied himself. Eva glanced at the syringe on the floor. Only a fraction of the liquid was gone. She might just be all right. Still, she felt warmth and carelessness slipping through her. She tried to fight it but found herself opening up. Dry sobs racked her body as she felt the drug corrupt her.

Cassie struggled against the guard, who tightened his grip on her. Nothing she had heard about Frazer had prepared her for this. She stared at him with incomprehension. Before she could form any words, he spoke to her.

"Cassie Stewart. A bit far from home, aren't you? Would you like to explain what you're doing here?"

His voice was ironic. He seemed unmoved by the horror, as if he were used to it.

Cassie stared at him, until, slowly, the words came.

"What are you?"

He laughed. "The same man I always was."

Looking at his eyes, at the utter lack of doubt in them, Cassie almost felt paralyzed with futility. Part of her still had to ask the question, as she searched frantically for a scrap of normality. "How could you try to kill Eva?"

"Perhaps you missed that part, did you? She found out rather too much about me."

"So you just silence her?"

"It's necessary."

Cassie had never felt pure hatred until that moment, never knew the violence of it. "You bastard. Do you . . ."

Frazer took a step toward her and slapped her in the face.

"Shut up. Tell me how you got here."

Cassie felt her head reeling, but through the rage and

pain her mind worked fast. "What difference does it make?" she said bitterly. "A driver dropped me off."

"He's gone?"

"Yes." She gestured at the overnight bag by her feet. "I had thought I might stay for a couple of days. I would hardly ask him to wait, would I?"

Frazer examined her for a minute, as if trying to detect a lie. Cassie hoped he might believe her, hoped that her absence might trigger some sense of alarm in the driver, who might do something, anything, to help them. Frazer turned to the guards.

"Look around. See if you can find any evidence of a driver lurking about. If you find him, bring him in. Lock these two up. Ha Chin arrives in five hours. We'll deal with this before then."

Cassie and Eva sat on a dirt floor in a stinking room with no windows. Arms and legs bound, they faced each other.

"Oh, Cass, why on earth did you have to come here?"

Cassie's voice was deadened by shock. "I learned something about Frazer. Some people think he killed a research scientist who was selling him military secrets. I wanted to come out to warn you about him, and something you said, or the way you said it, when you telephoned from Hong Kong . . . I thought you were frightened of Frazer."

"I was."

"When you said you'd be staying at this camp, I thought it was because you specifically wanted me to know."

"I did. But I didn't want you to come out here."

"Who, then? Ah, I see. Andrew Stormont."

"Did you tell him about the camp?"

"No. I didn't tell anyone. My housemate knows I came here, and my travel agent, but no one else." Cassie paused. "He's going to kill us, isn't he?"

"Yes."

"And it's true what Frazer said? That you're an agent for MI6?"

"There's not much point in denying it now." Eva looked away. "It's a relief not to have to lie anymore."

"We all hide things, Eva. You don't have a monopoly on secrets, just because you create them for a living. Why don't you just play your role convincingly if it's worth playing, let the world underestimate you?" Bitterness came as hope left Cassie.

"Sooner or later we all crave understanding."

"I knew you were an addict, if that's what you're talking about. I knew that much."

Eva stared at the wall beyond her. "That's what puzzles me. Frazer spoke about this private investigator who found out about my addiction but didn't reveal it to him. He said you and the investigator, Quaid, were having an affair, kept the heroin stuff from him to protect me. He told me in detail, this great long lecture. Wanted to show me how clever he was, how much he'd found out. He couldn't stop himself from trying to impress me even when he was about to kill me."

"I didn't think it was relevant, you and the heroin."

"That was kind of you, but it's not the point. Your investigator found it in my medical records, did he?"

"I think so."

"It shouldn't have been there. The Firm was supposed to make sure it wasn't there. They create what they call a legend for agents. They make sure your cover is as perfect as possible. My cover meant no addiction. I was supposed to be clean. If my addiction was left in my medical records, it means someone did that deliberately, knowing that if Frazer discovered it, it would blow my cover. Burn me."

"Burn you?"

"Kill me. Someone in the Firm wanted me dead."

Cassie stared at her despairingly. "Who? And why?"

"It could only be one of three people. I suppose I'll never know now. And why? Who knows. There's always a maze of reasons for anything those people do. I knew I was up against Frazer. I never knew I had to watch out closer to home. The worst thing is, Frazer's right, all that stuff about moral relativism. The Firm never meant to kill him; they just wanted intelligence. I was supposed to be a conduit, passing it along. Frazer would have been a link in a chain. Men like him should be stopped, but they're so big, so corrupt, so plugged into the system, they're the new untouchables." She looked at Cassie. "I would have done it. It's too late now."

"How did all that work? You talk about being a conduit, about intelligence. What is all this really about?"

"Two things, what SIS wants and what I want. The Firm wants Frazer, wants to get close to him. They think he's corrupt. But they don't want to shut him down, just to get close enough to get some dirt on him, to blackmail him into spying on the Chinese. He has extensive dealings in China, knows all the big players. It's all in the name of counter-proliferation. The Firm wants him to report back on China's weaponry program, who it sells arms and capabilities to, particularly nuclear and chemical." She paused. "The diamond site was designed to trap Frazer."

"What made you think he'd go for it?"

"Everyone has a weakness. It was a question of playing on his."

"And?"

"Curiosity and greed. He's made a fortune, but that doesn't matter. Making money is his thing. He has to keep doing it, and diamonds have the potential to bring in huge amounts of money. And there was something else about the diamond mine. It served some other purpose too, some kind of favor. I don't know how that all fits in."

"And Case Reed and I? How do we fit in?"

"You were just convenient, I'm afraid. We couldn't approach Frazer directly, so we got a mutual friend to recommend that he do business with a number of small British venture capitalists. We picked two terrible ones and Case Reed, guaranteeing you'd look good. Then I told you about the diamond site and left the rest to chance. Only it wasn't chance. It was calculation."

"And how did you calculate I would act? What was my weakness?"

"You promoted the deal for me. Your weaknesses were greed and competition."

"Competition?"

"It's always been under the surface. I knew you would act on it, continue to act on it."

"What the fuck are you talking about?"

"It doesn't matter now, Cassie." Eva looked away, weary with the futility of it all.

"So you hate me, and you used me in this scheme of yours. Well, I'm getting my comeuppance, aren't I, Eva?"

"I don't hate you, Cass. I never wanted you to get hurt. I tried to warn you off the deal once." Eva smiled gently through the haze of heroin, through her sense of isolation. "You were the best person in the right place. It was as impersonal as that."

"You still set me up, just like you set up Frazer."

"Welcome to the world, darling. Not your venture-capital world, where the only risks you take are on paper, where you sit safely around a board table and talk about risk, where the worst that happens is that you lose some money, and very rarely your own. It's always someone else's money, isn't it, someone else who takes the risks while you sit by and watch and follow at a safe distance? Always safe, always protected—'ring-fenced,' as you call it. Only you can't ring-fence yourself forever, can you? And you didn't want to, did you? Something inside you sensed this risk, and you ran after it. You ran just as fast after it as I pushed it to you. You were hungry for it, desperate for adventure, desperate to bring something unpredictable, unquantifiable into your life."

She paused for a moment, studying Cassie's face. Hostility, anger, and a strange compassion moved back and forth between them with no lull. It was as if, conscious of the lack of time, they pared their reactions down to seconds, with no grudges borne.

"Now you have your excitement," continued Eva. "How does it feel?"

"You tell me. You brought me here."

Eva suddenly seemed to shrink. "I know. And you'll never know how sorry I am for doing that to you."

Cassie's voice was strong, low, full of fury. "You've done it to yourself too. Doesn't that make you sorry? You glory in confrontation. There's nothing you won't face. You're compulsive, as trapped as any of the rest of us, caught between fear and your own false sense of bravado. You can't even see when you should get involved or when you should turn away. You just rush blindly forward and call it courage. Because it looks good, doesn't it? Fearless, brave Eva takes anything on. But only because you're running so hard you can't stop. And from what? You never stop for long enough to see your demons, let alone entertain them. You are just as escapist as I. You just dress up your fears a bit better."

"Oh, Cassie, I don't have the choice. You live your life safe on the other side. Nothing really terrible has ever happened to you, has it, until now? No truck looms out of the fog and hits you. No one steps out from behind a tree and rapes you. You were never an innocent casualty. How easy it is to have your benign worldview, your sense that personal responsibility is the answer to every question. Only someone who lives on the sunny side could ever believe that."

"You talk as if what's happened to you is just one piece of bad luck," Cassie retorted. "There was a certain inevitability to it. You were always self-destructive. We seal our fate day by day, year by year. You mold it."

"Don't you think I would have liked to have lived differently, to have looked at things from a sunny perspective, not to have been drawn to the blackness? You didn't see the ugliness in the world. After my family fell apart, I saw it too closely. It was as if I had a cataract darkening one eye. Everything I saw was cast in shadow. Even if I was skiing down the most beautiful white slope on a sunny day, there'd be a patch of darkness on the snow. I'd ski so fast, trying to escape it, but it was always there. Heroin was a way out of that. It was good cover, but it was also a beautiful balm, a rose-tinted poison."

Cassie stared up at the dark ceiling. "I hid too, in routine, but I couldn't sustain it. You're right, I was looking for something else. I felt this incredible sense of dissatisfaction, as if something was wrong. I suppose I was drowning in trivia, in the superficial. That's one of the reasons I was always drawn to you. You always did seem as if you had your own personal fight. You were always driven, restless."

"Well, we were both wrong, weren't we? We ended up at the same place. This is where it ends."

For a while the two women just looked at each other in silence, seeing in each other's eyes the mirror of their own despair. Cassie spoke finally.

"Or we could both be right. What would you do if we got away, if we escaped somehow?"

"We won't. Don't waste your time."

"No, I know. But just for imagination's sake, just to have something to hang on to."

Eva shifted position on the dirt floor. The rope bonds cut into her wrists and ankles.

"The ancient Greeks believed that a vow of revenge was a contract between man and God. It comes before everything else. Irrevocable."

"That was your plan, was it? You said MI6 had its own agenda and you had yours."

Eva nodded. "I'd come right back here. Do what I intended to do all along. I'd come back to kill Frazer."

FORTY-SEVEN

Andrew Stormont arrived in Hanoi in the late morning. He was driven straight to the embassy, at 16 Ly Thuong Kiet Street, where he sat in an air-conditioned room while the head of station, Charles Courtney, briefed him.

"Two of our men picked up Cassie Stewart at the airport yesterday and drove her to the Metropole. She checked in, went for a walk, had dinner, made no apparent contact of any significance. But she did ask the concierge to get her a driver to take her to Frazer's army camp at Lang-son. We found out about it and supplied our own man, Truong. He drove her there this morning. He radioed back half an hour ago to say that he had dropped her off. The place is normally lousy with guards, but they must have all been inside. No sign of Eva Cunningham, or Frazer. Truong was worried that the guards would come out and see him, so he had to move some way off into the jungle and hide his jeep. I'm not comfortable with it. He's been keeping a discreet watch on the camp for several days and says the guards have been jumpy as hell. I'm not quite sure what they'd do with him if they did discover him." He paused and tugged at his shirtsleeves. "I hope he's out of sight, but it makes direct surveillance difficult, so we don't have any real idea what's going on in the camp at the moment."

"How many guards are there?" asked Stormont.

"About ten. There were fewer. More seem to have arrived today, perhaps from the diamond site, because that's crawling with guards too."

"What d'you think's going on there?"

"Something unpleasant. All the guards are heavily armed, and there's a lot of activity. I know diamonds warrant security, but this seems excessive."

"If we had to remove someone from there . . . ?"

"Unless you have some way of walking in there as a friend and walking back out still friends, there'd be a bloodbath."

"There might be a way. If it's not too late already."

"You think it might be?"

"As you say, something's going on. They're gearing up."

"What d'you want to do?"

"Fist in a velvet glove. I'll go and talk with Frazer."

"I'm not sure I—"

Stormont interrupted. "I'll be the glove. You'll be outside the camp, with as many people as we can muster. I'll give Frazer a choice. Either he frees Eva or he'll have his bloodbath."

"And you'll be the first victim."

"I don't think it'll come to that."

"Russian roulette."

"No. The odds are worse, and the motivation is different."

"You know we can't match his force. Not in the time frame I think you're talking about. I'm not sure all of the men we can get will be as sanguine about the odds as you seem to be."

"They don't have to be. The threat from our side is a bluff. I just need enough people to give the impression of force on our side. If the bluff doesn't work, you can all get the hell out of there."

Courtney shook his head, but in wonderment, not refusal. He'd worked with Stormont in the field before, knew that side to him.

"I'll get as many people as I can. How long have we got?"

"Two hours."

Frazer looked across the table at Le Mai.

"How many times do I have to say it? It has to look like accidental death. A junkie's overdosing is acceptable. But now we have to deal with Cassie Stewart too."

"What about a road accident?"

"What? Just let them drive out of here and then hit them with one of our earth-movers? Don't be ridiculous. Eva could easily avoid that. She'd probably take out the other driver."

Le Mai smiled suddenly. "I'd almost forgotten. Something from the war. Grenade in the petrol tank. It would blow them sky high. Just as if they went over a mine. And everybody knows this country's still riddled with mines."

"How does it work?"

"Simple. You make sure the mouth of the petrol tank is wide enough, then you remove the pin from the grenade, slip an elastic band over the spring, and put the grenade in the tank. You fill up with petrol and wait. The petrol eats through the rubber band, and *bang*." The two men laughed in unison.

"Perfect. Set it so that it happens a bit away from here, perhaps a couple of miles."

"Can't make it quite that sensitive. It might go off too soon, blow us all up. One rubber band, ten miles, and a quarter of a gallon of petrol should do it."

"How long will it take you?"

"Five minutes. But how are you going to convince them to drive the thing?"

"I'll think of something."

FORTY-EIGHT

Eva and Cassie were sitting in silence in their darkened room when they heard footsteps approaching: heavy, slow, not the swift patter of the Vietnamese.
Frazer. Eva knew it was him before he opened the door.
Bolts twisted in rusty sockets and the door flew open.
Frazer stood, backlit by the sun, his features masked in the
bright glare.

"I thought you'd like to know. Your organization
seems to value you, Eva. They've been in touch. We
made what I think is a satisfactory arrangement for everyone."

Two guards came up behind him, pulled the women
to their feet, and dragged them out into the brilliant sunshine. Le Mai sauntered up. The guards cut the ropes
binding ankles and wrists.

"You're free to go, both of you." Frazer motioned to
a jeep standing five yards away. "Go to Hanoi. Get on the
first plane back to England."

Eva looked from her swollen ankles to Frazer's face,
as if doubting the freedom of one and the truth of the
other. He threw her the keys to the jeep. She reached out,

hands numb from constriction. She failed to catch the keys, which dropped to her feet. When she bent down, she felt a wave of dizziness. She was disbelieving but ecstatic with the promise of freedom. Part of her sensed she could be walking into a trap if she left, but to stay was suicide. She gripped the keys in her fingers and straightened up. She turned to Cassie, who was looking at her with an air of fear and disbelief.

"Go on. You're free. Go."

Eva forced one foot in front of the other, took hold of Cassie's arm, and got her moving. Wordlessly, they walked to the jeep and got in. Still the unreality gripped her. Dulled by the heroin, she dimly heard one of the guards whispering something in Vietnamese to his fellow. Then both of them laughed out loud. Something about mines. Her mind didn't register it then. She turned the key in the ignition, put the jeep into gear, and let out the clutch, spraying red earth into the air as she accelerated through the compound and out onto the road.

Frazer watched them go, feeling a strange anticlimax. He had expected her to turn on him, spit rage, lash out at him. Her silence disturbed him. It was almost as if she were expecting to see him again, as if she were merely postponing her response.

Cassie stared ahead, hair streaming across her face as Eva sped over the bumpy track away from the compound, toward Hanoi.

Eva wondered why she felt not released but as if she were somehow still in a trap. Through the heroin haze, her mind was filled with warning. She struggled to think. She didn't believe Frazer. It was unlikely but not altogether unbelievable that the Firm had negotiated her release. She could have accepted that. But less believable was the look on Frazer's face. She had seen his bloodlust, felt his yearning to kill her, saw the sick passion of it in his eyes when he stuck the needle into her. But he had shown no disappointment when he watched her get into the jeep and drive off. It was as if he still expected her to die. The words of the Vietnamese guard suddenly came back to her: "Watch out for mines." She slowed the jeep.

Cassie cried out, "What are you doing? Why're we stopping?"

The jeep skidded to a halt. Eva jumped out.

"Frazer wouldn't just let us go. He expects us to die. I could see it in him. He's set some kind of trap—the jeep, probably." She tugged at Cassie's arm. "Come on. We've got to get away from here on foot."

For a moment Cassie was paralyzed by the fear she saw in Eva's eyes, and then blindly she followed Eva off the track, into the trees at the side of the road. In silent single file they walked for five minutes, sweat streaming down their bodies. Then the hot silence of the jungle was shattered by the roar of an explosion. Birds screamed and flew from the trees. Cassie and Eva turned to see the jeep, now some quarter of a mile behind them, in flames. The stench of burning petrol filled the air.

Eva turned to Cassie, who was staring in horror at the flaming wreck. She grabbed her arm. "Come on. They'll come to inspect their handiwork at any minute. They'll assume we're dead, probably won't look for us very thoroughly. But the farther away we get, the better."

Cassie was motionless, a blank emptiness in her eyes. For a moment Eva despaired, fearing Cassie would stay rooted to the spot. She gripped her arm harder, till her nails cut into Cassie's flesh.

"Come on. Run!" She pulled at Cassie, who jerkily began to move, stumbling into a run.

They ran for over a mile, fast, until their lungs felt as if they were about to give out. When they finally stopped to catch their breath, they heard a dull rumble in the distance. They crouched in the jungle, watching the road, and saw a lorry laden with coconuts appear. A small, dark farmer sat in the open cab, singing at the top of his voice. As he approached, Eva stepped out into the road in front of him. He brought the jalopy to a shuddering halt.

In the jungle by the roadside, Cassie watched them speak, then saw Eva turn to her and beckon. She ran forward and jumped up with Eva into the back of the lorry, alongside the coconuts. The farmer shifted his vehicle into gear and drove off, resuming his singing at full pitch.

"He's going to Hanoi. He'll take us all the way."

Hanoi meant buildings, places to hide and be hidden, but their exhilaration at escape was muted by the fear that they were still a long way from safety. They traveled in silence. After a couple of hours, the plains gave way to the outskirts of the city.

Eva turned to Cassie. "Your housemate knows you're here. Anyone else?"

"Just David." Cassie had forgotten about her conversation with Aubrey Goldstein and his promise to send someone to Hanoi.

"He might have told someone," said Eva.

"What happens now?"

As the heroin receded, Eva was growing stronger. "A million things. Some controllable, some not. We have a fair chance of getting out of this, if we play it right." She didn't say that the odds were infinitely worse for herself than for Cassie. Cassie's were playable; hers were not.

Eva leaned forward and spoke to the farmer in Vietnamese. He executed an abrupt right turn, halting the traffic in his path, moving off the main road that led to the Metropole and taking a quiet side street around to the back. Eva turned back to Cassie.

"The Metropole will be crawling with people looking for me, you, or both of us. I don't want them to find me just yet. It won't matter if they find you, as long as you do exactly what I say."

Cassie looked at Eva for a while, considering the unspoken request for help.

"I know what you're going to do, Eva. I don't know how to, but I'll help you in any way I can," she finally said.

Eva nodded. She was silent for a while. "You could just go to the airport—collect your passport and go."

Cassie said nothing, just shook her head.

"All right, then. I am going to jump off in a street at the back of the hotel. I will go in and wait in the kitchens. The farmer will drive you around to the front of the hotel." She explained Cassie's part in brisk detail. "It should take you about four or five hours, perhaps overnight. Don't wait for me. Just get on the first plane home. Don't go back to your house, go to Case Reed. If I'm successful, I'll leave a message there. Then you'll be safe, more or less. If there's no message from me, ring the Foreign Office, ask for Stormont. Tell him everything. I can't say exactly what he'll do, but he'll be better than nothing."

"Will he? Someone in the Firm wanted you dead."

"Me, not you. And you can't fight Frazer on your own. Stormont'll be the best help you can get."

"Do you think he was the one who set you up?"

"I hope not, Cassie."

The lorry stopped. Eva glanced around, jumped down, and walked briskly away. Cassie watched her disappear. She didn't once falter, or pause to turn and wave goodbye.

The lorry turned and headed to the main street, to the front entrance of the Metropole. Cassie dug in her purse and gave the farmer fifty dollars. He looked at her bemusedly, gave her a little bow, and drove away.

Cassie walked quickly up the steps and into the foyer. She walked straight up to the reception desk, elbowing aside a group of businessmen patiently queuing for the receptionist's attention.

"I have a problem with the security of your hotel."

The receptionist looked up sharply from her computer. "I'm sorry?"

"Didn't you hear me? I said I have a problem with security. The driver you gave me took me off into the countryside and robbed me."

The receptionist glanced round nervously. "If you come this way, madam, I'll get the manager."

She rang a bell, summoning another receptionist, then led Cassie away from the open arena of the front desk into the manager's office.

"Our guest says she was robbed by one of our drivers."

The manager quickly took in Cassie's bedraggled clothes and disheveled hair. "I'm so sorry," he said, jumping to his feet. "What can we do to help?"

"He stole my money and my room key. I'm afraid he might have had an accomplice rob my room. I want your security people to check it out for me, and when they tell me it's safe, I want them to escort me back to my room. I don't want the police informed. Not yet. I want to try to sort this out quietly."

The manager nodded. "Of course, madam. We'll do it now." He picked up the phone and called security. A burly doorman and two plainclothes Vietnamese came quickly.

"What's your room number?"

"Three thirteen."

The manager spoke to the guards in Vietnamese. They exchanged a quick look, took a passkey from the manager, and disappeared.

They came back five minutes later. "We looked. No one. And your room looked in order too. I don't think anyone's been through it."

"I'll go to my room now," said Cassie. "But could you do this for me—could you have a guard posted on my floor? I'm worried he might come back, the thief." She paused. "Of course, I could go and stay in the embassy."

"No, no. That won't be necessary." The manager got to his feet and gave Cassie a spare key. "I'll have a guard posted."

"Thank you." Cassie got to her feet. She walked to the door, then paused. "Oh, I forgot to say. The man who robbed me was armed, had an automatic pistol."

Cassie turned and walked away, followed by one of the guards. She strode up the stairs and down the corridor to her room. Without pausing, she stuck the key in the lock, turned it, and threw open the door. Her room looked just as she had left it that morning. She looked at her watch: seven hours ago. If she could just stretch out her arm and pull herself back seven hours, she would find a stranger. She closed the door, leaving the guard outside.

At the bottom of her suitcase, she found a small white envelope: her contingency fund. She counted out three thousand dollars, put it in one of the hotel's envelopes, and concealed it in a handbag. Then she picked up her key and let herself out. When she had made her way through the hotel to the kitchens, she found Eva waiting, as she had specified, at the exit to a grubby back yard. She handed over the money, squeezing Eva's hand as she did so.

"Good luck."

"Thanks, Cassie."

Before she could say anything else, Eva had gone.

FORTY-NINE

Cassie returned to her room, took a shower, and dressed. She combed out her hair, which dripped warm water down her back, leaving a patch of darkness on her white linen shirt. She stood before the mirror attaching earrings, turning her face as she did. The contours of bone and flesh were thrown into relief by the severity of her hair, combed back from her face.

She picked up her key, went downstairs, walked through the lobby, and took a seat on one of the sofas. After looking around, she ordered a drink and sat back to wait.

A few minutes later, the first approach was made.

A Vietnamese sitting at the bar slipped quietly from his seat the moment he saw Cassie take hers. He spoke quickly and quietly on the hotel telephone.

"Stewart's here, in the bar, alone."

"Watch her," answered Stormont. "I'm on my way. Don't let her go in the meantime."

"Is that wise, coming yourself?"

"She has her suspicions anyway, and I want to pick everything up directly. Besides, she's controllable."

Stormont was dropped outside the Metropole ten minutes later. He walked in, saw Cassie, and slipped into a seat beside her.

Cassie couldn't just turn in feigned amazement, express surprise and delight, ask him wide-eyed what on earth he was doing here. So she waited for him to speak, knowing how much she was revealing by her silence.

He too was silent for a while. He watched her hand clasping the whiskey glass, seeing the crystal glittering as the glass shook.

"Where's Eva?"

She turned to him in surprise. The voice, the eyes, were so hard and sharp. She looked away. She felt his hand clench around her arm.

"No time for fucking around, Cassie. Where is she?"

She remembered Eva's voice, the instructions: just lie.

She spoke slowly, reluctantly. "All I know is that she said she had to see someone here in Hanoi."

"Who and where?"

"I don't know. She just said that she had to see someone, that it would take a few hours, and that she would meet me here for dinner."

"What happened with Frazer?"

"What d'you mean, what happened? I went to see them at the camp this morning, to check on the investment. I saw the diamond site. It all looked in order, so I came back. Eva said she'd had enough of Vietnam and wanted to go home, so she came back to Hanoi with me. The driver who took me out there had disappeared, so one of Frazer's men drove us back."

"I think you'd find it easier if you told me the truth."

"How many times do you want me to give you the same answer?"

Stormont watched her in silence for a while, wondering what it would take to make her speak.

"All right. Just answer me this. Is she safe?"

It was then that misery threatened to contort Cassie's features, unleash the tears. Eva was anything but safe. She took another sip of whiskey and averted her eyes.

"She went willingly, voluntarily. She made no big thing about it, just said, 'See you later.' She'll be here later. Just wait."

"When exactly is she coming back?"

Cassie suddenly looked up and noticed a man walking through the lobby.

"Aubrey."

Stormont watched the man halt in his tracks. He walked toward them.

"Cassie Stewart. I was wondering when I'd bump into you."

"Come and join us, have a drink."

Stormont got to his feet, eyes on Cassie. "What time is she coming back?"

"For dinner. She said to meet her in the bar between eight and eight-thirty."

Stormont nodded briefly to Goldstein, caught the eye of the Vietnamese watcher still at the bar, and walked away.

"Rather abrupt, your friend," said Goldstein, watching Stormont's fast exit.

"Busy man," said Cassie. She summoned the waiter and ordered another whiskey sour for herself, asking solicitously what Goldstein would like. He ordered a vodka and tonic, watching her closely.

When the drinks came, Goldstein turned to her. "About your diamonds . . ."

"You'd like them?" Suddenly she felt more than a

match for this man. She began to understand for the first time where Eva's strength came from—to see the most horrific things and not be destroyed by them made everything else easy.

Goldstein nodded.

"I wonder how far you'd go to get them, to get control of them," Cassie mused. "It's a legitimate business, but that doesn't rule out illegitimate practices, does it? There's so much at stake, isn't there? So much money to be made." Her voice suddenly became more direct. "It was you, no doubt, behind the bear raid on Genius. What was the purpose of that?"

"As you say, there's a lot at stake. I want control of this project, and to get that I need McAdam's stake. Let's just say he wouldn't have sold directly to me. But I thought he might be willing to sell to some other party, who would then sell on to me. It was a question of identifying that friendly party and then creating the environment that might encourage McAdam to sell. When you came to me talking about diamonds in Vietnam, I guessed it was Genius. I thought perhaps you would be the friendly party I was looking for."

"I can see all that," interrupted Cassie. "But why the bear raid? Case Reed lost money on that, and McAdam would surely be less likely to sell into a falling market."

"Case Reed's losing money was just bad timing. You bought too early, or the rumors and the bear raid caught too late. It was designed to make it easier and cheaper for you and me to accumulate stock, and to wear down McAdam. Falling markets make people panic. Knowing what I did of McAdam's character, I thought he'd panic and sell."

"He did."

"Case Reed bought his entire stake?"

"No. I did. I now control fifteen percent directly, another fifteen indirectly." She paused, took a sip of her drink, and sat back, almost bored. "I'll sell you the first fifteen this afternoon if you like."

"How much?"

"Four million pounds."

"You must be joking!"

"They found diamonds on the site. I saw a four-carat one. You know what that does to the value of Genius. Take it or leave it."

She turned from her drink and looked at him. Without moving her eyes, she raised her arm and called the waiter. "The bill, please." Then she got up and walked to the counter to pay.

Goldstein watched her moving away. She wasn't playing hard to get. Her departure was real. There was a finality to it. Deal on her terms or not at all. He got to his feet.

She was standing at the bar, signing her bill. He leaned toward her.

"All right. Four million."

She looked up at him. "And another four for the other fifteen percent when I deliver that."

"How will I know that you'll deliver? The value of the first fifteen percent is to a certain extent contingent on getting the other fifteen percent."

"You'll just have to trust me."

"And you me."

Stormont arrived back at the embassy ten minutes later. In Courtney's office, he asked, "Have we heard anything from Truong?"

"He's still skirting the camp. There's no sign of Eva."

"I spoke with Cassie Stewart. She's covering something up. She seems to think Eva's safe, that she's gone to see someone here in Hanoi. It's possible she's telling the truth, but I'm sure she's lying. The question is, why? It's almost as if she's covering up for Eva."

"Perhaps they're in league with Frazer somehow."

"Not Eva."

"What about Cassie?"

"No. She's malleable. She's not above her own brand of corruption, but not with Frazer, and never against Eva."

Stormont listened to his words—"no," "never," absolutes that he had seen overturned by fact so many times. Yet he could not doubt them now. The alternatives seemed, as they always did, unthinkable.

"So what are we going to do? Shall we still go to Frazer's camp?"

"Frazer let them go, at least let Cassie go, and I'm assuming he let Eva go at the same time. It is inconceivable that he would be holding Eva prisoner and Cassie wouldn't tell us. Something has happened to her. She's seen something. I don't think she's under any illusions about Frazer. She wouldn't leave Eva there without telling me. No. Eva's not with Frazer, she's off doing her own thing."

"And what's that?"

Stormont didn't answer. His eyes closed briefly and he shook his head.

Courtney continued, "Cassie says she'll be back in what, about three hours?"

"Eight to eight-thirty. We'll wait."

"And if she doesn't turn up?"

"Then we take Miss Stewart away to a quiet place and induce an explanation, which, with what I have in mind, will take thirty seconds. Then we pay a visit to Robie Frazer. Let's hope it's not overdue."

Half an hour later the telephone rang. Courtney spoke briefly, then handed the phone to Stormont. It was Truong.

"I've just worked my way round to the front of the camp, to the main entrance. You'll never believe who just went in."

Stormont waited.

"It was Ha Chin."

"Did you get any photographs of them together?"

"Half a roll."

"Then get the hell out of there. If they find you now, you're dead. Come straight here."

Stormont turned to Courtney. "There is no legitimate reason on earth why Frazer would meet Ha Chin, or allow himself to be connected in any way to him. We've got Frazer now."

"So what's the problem?"

"The problem is what Frazer does with anyone other than his own men who sees the two of them together."

"You mean if he catches Truong?"

"Or Eva."

FIFTY

When Eva left Cassie, she moved quickly through the streets. She was careful to walk among the throngs of people. They wouldn't conceal her, but their numbers would dissuade anyone from trying to train his sights on her.

She turned off Ngo Quyen Street onto Phan Chu Trinh. Halfway along the street she pushed open a door cut into a high wall of rusting corrugated iron. The door clanged shut behind her. She stood facing a large, partially asphalted yard. At the center, gleaming white, stood a helicopter. She smiled briefly and hurried toward a scruffy office at the side of the yard.

The man sitting at the desk, alerted by the clanging of the gate, watched her approach, puzzlement giving way to joy. He and Eva were old friends. They'd met in Hanoi when she had come back to the Far East, four years earlier. They had drunk together, complained about the heat and mosquitoes together. He flew his helicopters all over the country. She traveled to teach, but they found themselves in the same places often enough over the years.

"Eva." He jumped to his feet. "I haven't seen you for months. I thought you'd gone forever. You just disappeared. What ha—"

She silenced him with a kiss, full on his lips. "Long story, no time. I need your help. I need you to fly me to Halong Bay."

He took in her mud-stained clothes and uncombed hair. "God, Eva, I wish I could. I have a bunch of tourists scheduled for six. Full load."

Eva peeled off her Bulgari watch. "Hawk this. It cost twenty thousand dollars last week."

For a moment her thoughts traveled back to Hong Kong, to freedom, when nothing had happened. An illusory freedom. She snapped back. This was what she had been waiting for, however terrifying, however unreal it felt. Eight years had led to this. She felt suddenly just as she had at Changi, when she and Sun Yi were arrested. That one irrevocable wrong step. Then she had got away with it. Another step today, and again Frazer was the target. But today the odds were far worse.

Her watch clattered on the table. Tom stared at it.

"I don't want this. It's not the money, Eva."

She reached over and unbuckled his watch, an old Swatch model. "I'll need this. You don't mind, do you?"

He laughed at the ease of his submission as he held out his wrist and got to his feet. He shook his head, still smiling, but sobered as he saw in her eyes more than he wanted to know.

"Come on, then. I'll take you." He shouted over his shoulder to his secretary sitting in the back office, "Tell the six o'clock bunch that there was a mechanical problem and give them their money back."

They walked out to the helicopter. Tom held open the door for Eva. She got in, strapped herself in, and put the headphones on. The rotor blades began their soft whirr but soon picked up to a roar. In three minutes Hanoi dropped away below her, cut off by the air and the thrashing of the blades that carried her away.

Tom's voice came over the headphones. "Are you going to tell me what this is about?"

"No, Tom. I'm not. And you never flew me, all right? You haven't seen me. For your sake, not mine."

"Why? Why not for yours?"

Eva fell silent.

For the sixty-minute journey, she said nothing. Tom guided the helicopter over the landing patch at Halong Bay. The blades slowed above them and came to rest. Tom went through the full shutdown, then looked across at Eva. She was looking down, immobile, concentrated in herself, repelling questions or intrusion. Her shoulders were slightly hunched, as if warding off pain. He watched her for a moment. She glanced at him briefly, then swung open the door and got out.

Tom also got out and walked around to her. Before he could speak, she kissed him again, eyes shut, keeping them from him.

"Thanks, Tom. You'll go back now." She said it as an instruction, as a farewell.

His voice was obstinate. "Don't think I will. Rather stay here now. Think I'll spend the evening in the bar." Then he gripped her arm. "I don't know what the hell you're up to, Eva, but for God's sake watch yourself, O.K.?"

"I will."

She watched him head toward the beachfront bar where he always went, where they had drunk together over many sunsets. She pushed the memory from her mind and headed off in the opposite direction. She didn't see him turn and furtively follow her.

She walked through the busy evening streets, seeing familiar faces, receiving warm smiles, shouted greetings, and waves from old friends. She didn't stop, and no one tried to delay her, as they might have done. Ever sensitive, they saw the look of purpose on her face and let her pass.

Her house had been colonized, as she had expected, by a local family she knew. She greeted them at the door. She took her time with the materfamilias, the old grandmother, who shifted between embarrassment and gratitude for the house and for Eva's graceful reaction to their occupation. Eva went through the formalities of greeting the whole family, speaking her perfect, formal Vietnamese. Then she made her request.

"I've left some personal letters in a hiding place. Could I just have a few minutes to retrieve them?"

The grandmother ordered the family out and followed them without a backward glance. Eva thanked her, entered the silent house, walked to the center of the sitting room, and got down on her hands and knees. She hoped the family hadn't explored the house too intimately.

She found the rough-edged floorboard and edged her nails down the side. She felt splinters drive into her skin. The floorboard yielded. She put it aside and saw with overwhelming relief the small metal box. She opened it, just to check, and smiled. The Browning was there, lying amid five magazines of bullets. Enough. She closed the box and went back out to the grandmother.

"Your son, I believe, has a jeep."

The woman nodded.

"I was wondering if he might like to sell it."

The grandmother cackled and looked knowing.

"A thousand dollars?"

A halfhearted tirade followed. Eva glanced at the house, her house, and back again. The grandmother followed her eyes. Cheated out of a prolonged bargaining session, she gave way.

"O.K. Thousand dollars."

"Full petrol tank, please. And a toolkit. A strong pair of pliers. And a bag—something light, about this big." She sketched a shape about a foot square. The grandmother raised a quizzical eyebrow but also gave a quick nod. She shouted a message to her oldest son, who was squatting with his wife and children at the side of the house. He got up smartly and returned with the jeep five minutes later.

"Full tank, bag." He held up a small, muddy brown canvas knapsack. "And tools." He nodded to a toolbox in the back of the jeep. Eva opened it, tried out the six-inch pliers, and replaced them. She pulled wads of notes from her jeans and handed over the money. The son gave her the keys and dropped the knapsack in the back of the jeep. Reminded by a sharp dig of an elbow in his ribs, he handed the money to his mother.

They watched Eva get in the jeep and drive off. Then they returned to the house, pried up the floorboard, and stashed the money. Seeing the empty space where the metal box had been, the grandmother smiled.

"She took the gun?" asked the son.

"You saw her. What did you think she came for?"

Feeling a sickening premonition, Tom watched Eva till her jeep disappeared from view. Then he retraced his steps to the bar, to seek futile comfort in the flow of beer and the sound of laughter. He couldn't begin to guess what she was up to. He only knew from the look on her face that he couldn't stop her.

Eva drove away, leaving the evening bustle of Halong Bay. She headed northwest. In her mirror she saw the signs of civilization fade as she drove on, as two hours passed and night fell around her. The green of the jungle turned black at the roadside. Her headlamps made a tunnel of light in the darkness, dazzling her to everything outside their range. She was blind to the dark jungle. She was indifferent to all directions beyond the brilliant path stretching out before her.

The small voice of reason spoke to her on several occasions, telling her to turn back. She wondered where it came from, that alien voice. Stormont, perhaps—his logic? If he had been there, would he have gripped her arm, wrestled with the steering wheel? Officially, he would have done so. Privately, he might have let her pass, freed her to her own compulsions.

The road was deserted, the whole wilderness apparently empty, yet the evening jungle would be seething with life. How many eyes watched her pass? The hunting animals would be out now; the villagers would be squatting around a wood fire, cooking dinner. But no human eyes should be watching from the roadside.

She drove on, the roughness of the road rattling her bones. She watched the odometer and her watch carefully. When she was about twenty miles from Frazer's camp, she shut off the jeep's lights to accustom her eyes to the darkness. Anyone watching would hear the jeep, but in darkness it would present less of a target.

Her eyes grew accustomed to the lack of light. She picked out the worst bumps in the road, saw the trunks of the nearest trees. She drove on for another seventeen miles. Then, when she saw a slight break in the jungle, she pulled off the road. She guided the jeep through the trees and parked it about thirty feet from the road. Green and camouflaged even in daylight, it would be invisible from the road at night.

She took out her pistol, a Browning M 35 Hi-Power single-action automatic fitted with a silencer and a fourteen-round magazine. She loaded a magazine and walked back to the road. The red dirt glowed slightly in the light of stars and a crescent moon. Picking out a gnarled spot on a tree opposite, she braced herself, raised the pistol, holding it firmly in both hands, and squeezed her right index finger on the trigger. There was a dull thud as the bullet sunk into the bark. She fired off the rest of the magazine, a further thirteen rounds, then crossed the road to the tree. Her aim had been good, the pistol true. The bulletholes were clustered, some overlapping, in what remained of the small gnarled patch.

She loaded a new magazine into the pistol and put it with the spares into the knapsack. She added the pliers and a couple of screwdrivers, put the knapsack on her back, and shook it into place. Then she entered the blackness of the jungle.

For a while she stood still, training her eyes on everything within range, slowly picking out the detail as her pupils enlarged, straining for the hint of light.

FIFTY-ONE

Andrew Stormont returned to the Metropole at five to eight. He found Cassie Stewart in the bar, sitting up straight, impassive. He sat down without greeting her. A waiter took his order for a gin and tonic. He looked at Cassie's whiskey sour.

"How many of those have you had?"

"This is my third."

He watched her drink it slowly. They sat in silence, both staring straight ahead. To anyone who passed, they might have looked like a despairing couple who had run out of words, but there was no emptiness in their expressions. Cassie's eyes showed the effort of concealment, while Stormont's revealed hope and anger.

At eight forty-five, he drained his glass. "She's not coming, is she? Never was."

Cassie shook her head. Stormont took her arm.

"Let's go."

He pulled thirty dollars from his pocket and dropped the fluttering notes on the table. He led Cassie, unresisting, from the hotel.

Courtney was waiting in a car outside. He glanced at

Stormont, reading his instructions in his eyes. They drove to the embassy. Stormont took Cassie into a brightly lit room. It was stark, like a waiting room. It made her think of doctors and dentists and hospitals, of coldness and clinical smells.

Stormont gestured to a hardbacked chair at a square wooden table. Cassie sat. He turned his back to her and walked over to a shuttered window.

"If you lie now, you'll be responsible for the consequences. I think you know what I'm talking about. Perhaps I'll be proved wrong. If I were you, for your own sake, I'd pray that I'm wrong."

Cassie got to her feet, trying to throw off the sense of oppression she felt Stormont imposing on her. She walked over to him.

"What are you going to do? Give me electric shocks, inject me with a truth drug?"

He turned slowly and moved closer to her. "Oh, we can be much more imaginative than that. The possibilities for making life unpleasant are endless. You'd be surprised how easy it is, what a contamination fear can be, how it comes to infect each part of your life, rotting it all. There's no refuge from that."

"You presume a lot."

"Don't pretend you're suddenly immune to fear. No one is. And don't think I won't do it."

"Oh, I know." She looked at him with unconcealed rage. "But I'll spare you the fun. Eva's gone to Halong Bay to meet someone. That's all she told me. That is the absolute truth. After Frazer's driver dropped us off, Eva said she had to go and see a friend in Hanoi, get hold of a car, and drive to Halong Bay."

"What is she going to do there?"

"I don't know. She didn't say." She stared at him.

For the first time, fear came into her eyes. Stormont saw it clearly, could read what lay behind.

"We might be able to stop her if we go by helicopter." He paused. "Tell me, why did Frazer let you go?"

The lie was easier now that he had believed her once. "I told the whole world I was going to his camp to see him and Eva. I told him that as soon as I arrived. And besides, why shouldn't he let us go?"

Stormont just looked at her until she shrugged.

"All right. I know he must be up to something, otherwise this whole thing wouldn't be happening. But I don't know what it is, and what's more, he knows that I don't know what it is, so it would make sense for him to let us go."

Stormónt walked to the door. "You'll stay here at the embassy. It's safer."

Cassie suddenly remembered what Eva had said about her cover's being deliberately blown, about someone in the Firm wanting to kill her. She stared at the door Stormont had locked behind him. She had read his passion for Eva in his face. Impossible, then, that he should be the one who would want to kill her.

She sat on the carpeted floor in the corner of the room and waited.

Stormont spoke quickly to Courtney. "We need a helicopter, and night flight approval. I don't care how you get it."

Twenty minutes later Courtney returned from his office. "The Australian embassy has a copter and a pilot ready. Kicked up a stink, but they owed us a few favors."

Stormont, Courtney, and three of his men drove to the embassy heliport. The helicopter was waiting. They got in, said a brief hello to the Australian pilot, who,

keeping his silence, started up the machine and flew
through the quiet sky to Halong Bay. They arrived at
eleven. According to instructions, they fanned out and
began to look for Eva.

FIFTY-TWO

Eva moved more slowly as she drew closer to the camp. After she had walked for half an hour, she calculated that she was probably a mile or so away. She stopped when she saw a gleam of water on the dark soil. She walked over to it and felt her shoes sink to just below lace level. She fell to her knees, felt the mud yield. She reached down and took up handfuls, and rubbed it into her hair until blond turned blood brown. She covered her arms and jeans, rubbing mud into the fabric until it was filthy. She covered her palms and smeared mud over her face, carefully avoiding her eyes and mouth, until the camouflage was complete.

She walked on until she heard in the quiet of the jungle a faint hum—the electricity generator. Then she saw the haze of distant light filtering out from the camp into the surrounding darkness. Silently she walked forward until, about four hundred yards away, she could see the outline of the wire fence stretched high around the camp. The light from the observation tower glittered on the metal wire like flashing eyes.

The adrenaline began to flow. She glanced at her

watch. It was just eleven. She would lay up for another hour, hoping that by then Frazer and Ha Chin, who should have arrived sometime earlier, would be in bed. Frazer's habit over the past few days had been to retire to his room after dinner, at about ten-thirty. She had watched the strip of light under his door, seen it burn till after eleven. She visualized him reading. Perhaps he would stay up later, drinking with Ha Chin. Ideally, she should wait till the small hours, till three or four, when sleep was deepest, but she doubted she could freeze her clanging nerves and muscles until then. She also feared that the longer she waited, the greater was the chance of search and pursuit, by either Stormont's men or Frazer's. Sooner or later Cassie's presence in Hanoi would be detected by Frazer's men, who would then organize a huge hunt for them. And Cassie would only be able to deceive Stormont's men—possibly even Stormont himself, if he had followed Cassie to Hanoi—for a couple of hours. If Stormont had come, he would probably have guessed her plan, would intercept her if he could.

Her headlong thoughts stopped for a while as she wondered what his motives might be. What if he, unthinkably, was the one who had blown her cover? Why would anyone do that? Sheer hatred of her, a wish to see her die? Or perhaps it had been more impersonal, just a desire to warn Frazer of her role. Her death would then have been merely a consequence, not the objective. It was betrayal either way, an endless chain of death.

When her watch showed midnight, Eva got to her feet. She rubbed her muscles back into life and shook to move the circulation in her limbs. She smoothed back her hair, smelling the rich stench of the mud, like liver, like dried blood. She checked the pistol, stuck it into the waistband of her jeans, and looked around one more time, glancing back in the direction she had come. Then she turned toward the camp and moved forward stealthily through the trees.

From a distance of a hundred yards, veiled by the trees, she skirted the camp. The lights were bright, but there were shadows, patches of darkness where the light didn't reach. She looked for the guards who had patrolled day and night during her stay. There seemed to be three on duty, two who sat in a guardroom playing mah-jongg and one who roamed around, flashlight in hand, the bulge of a holster at his hip. The camp was quiet, unsuspecting. Whatever they feared, it wasn't her. She was dead. The quietness was evidence of that.

She watched the meandering guard. He took a roughly circular tour of the camp, taking about ten minutes for each circuit. Eva moved through the jungle until she was opposite the part of the camp that Frazer had colonized for himself. This was a single-story wooden building that had probably been the headquarters of the chief of the camp in wartime. Frazer's men occupied a long wooden building off to the right.

Two lights burned in Frazer's building, with a window of darkness separating them. Eva glanced around. The guard should be at the farthest point of the camp from her, screened from her by Frazer's building. She crawled quickly toward the perimeter wire and took the pliers from the canvas knapsack.

The wire was not electrified—she had tested it while she was Frazer's prisoner—but she still felt fear as she closed the jaws of the pliers around it. There was no flash of light, no jolt of power. Releasing her breath, she worked quickly until she had cut a small loop. She glanced around again. Still no sign of anyone. She squeezed though the hole she had cut and ran, bent double, across the open distance between the wire and Frazer's building. She crouched against the wood, about fifteen feet from the first light. She glanced around again. All clear.

She straightened up and peered through the small darkened window in front of her. She made out the white glow of enamel, of a lavatory and bath. The window was open. She pushed it gently, until it gaped two feet. Then she reached up a leg and slid it over the sill. Hanging on to the slight frame for support, she leaned back, pulled her other leg over the sill, and slipped into the room. Her feet landed silently on the dusty tiled floor. She half closed the window, then paused, listening for sounds. Her own breathing came back to her. She stilled it, straining for sounds through the walls. There was nothing. She pulled the gun from her waistband and held it ready in one hand. With the other, she squeezed down the metal door handle and edged the door open an inch.

She looked up and down the corridor outside. It was empty. She moved silently along until she came to Frazer's door. She reached her hand forward slowly, like a snake preparing to strike. Then, in one rapid movement, she turned the handle and threw open the door.

Frazer and Ha Chin were sitting on either side of a small table, playing chess. Ha Chin rose to his feet, his mouth opening. His hand knocked the table over as he reached toward a revolver on the floor.

Eva leveled her pistol at him and fired twice. Both rounds hit him in the chest. She watched his eyes widen with shock as he fell backward onto Frazer's bed. His blood gushed out, covering her in a fine spray. She turned to Frazer, who had caught the falling table and was steadying it with both hands. Softly he let it fall back into place. Those were the only sounds—the click of the table legs on the wooden floor, the dull thud of the bullets as they met skin and flesh, and Ha Chin's collapse.

There were no sounds from outside, no sign of pursuit. Eva stood in front of Frazer, every sense flaring at the stillness of death, the cloying smell of blood. She felt the heat of Ha Chin's blood as it slid down her face, over her forearms. She tasted the metallic tang of cordite from her pistol.

Frazer sat two feet from her, staring at her. Quickly he glanced at Ha Chin, then back, first at Eva's hands training the gun on him, then at her eyes, primed too like a weapon.

"You thought you had it all worked out, didn't you, Robie? Billionaire, scion of society—the only difference between you and the pushers on streetcorners is insulation. They're outcasts. You're an insider, so well protected. But it doesn't take much to shatter a life. You've done it so many times—indirectly, with your deadly little businesses, but directly too, with Sun Yi, almost with Cassie and me. It's so easy, isn't it, and you always thought you were immune, that your evil and cleverness protected you."

"So what are you, then, Eva? Cleverer? More evil?"

She marveled at his coolness, at the lucidity that stayed with him even now.

"No. I'm emotionally ruthless. I feel too much, I can't let things go. I wasn't just SIS. I'm doing this for myself. Perhaps I tip the balance just a bit."

As he rose to lunge at her, she raised the pistol, noticed with a fleeting respect that he remained silent, did not cry out to the guards as Ha Chin had tried to do. He kept his eyes on hers the whole time, the endless seconds it took—eyes full of horror and rage.

Eva pulled the trigger three times, saw the dark red

erupt from his heart. She saw him fall backward, his eyes on her, cursing her in death. A chair splintered as he crashed to the floor, and there was a distant cry. Eva stood frozen for a second, then wheeled around and ran out of the room into the corridor.

She didn't see the guard. All she saw was his forearm snatch around her neck, pulling her back against him. He increased the pressure, choking off her breath. She bent her right leg, lashed her foot back into his knee, scraped her heel down his shin. The pressure around her throat eased. She threw back her head, smashing it into the guard's nose. He let go. She wheeled around, drew back her right hand, and slammed the pistol into his windpipe, hard enough to immobilize him. He fell to the ground.

She glanced around. No one else was in sight. She ran into the bathroom, threw the window open wide, put her legs over the sill, and pushed herself through. She ran straight for the hole in the wire, the channel of light from Frazer's bedroom glinting off her bloodied skin as she ran. She heard more shouts, heard running footsteps. She threw herself to the ground by the wire and squeezed through. The shouts were nearer now, ringing with alarm. She pushed up and ran. There was a sickening blast of automatic fire, and the ground shuddered beside her. She ran on into the jungle, into the blackness. She kept on running, her eyes searching the blackness, discerning shapes, contours, her mind fearing a headlong crash into a tree, a fall, a smashed ankle. She ran until the sounds abated. It was a temporary lull. Frazer's men would regroup, get their jeeps and weapons, and come after her. She was only seconds ahead of them.

She ran in a straight line, angling into the jungle, away from the roadside, away from the direction they would expect her to take. There were no sounds of pursuit, but she didn't expect them this way. They would be at the roadside. After running for twenty minutes, she changed direction, heading back toward the jeep, to the roadside, where Frazer's men would concentrate their search. She moved slowly now, walking quietly, stilling her gasping breath. She checked her watch. After fifty minutes of walking, she knew she was getting near the road again. Her mind focused on her search for the jeep as she prowled through the jungle around her, listening for sounds, picking out shapes.

At one point she could hear distant shouts some way ahead of her. She moved forward more slowly. The voices moved farther ahead, evaporating into the night. Ten minutes after she started searching, her blood pounding wildly, she found the jeep. She looked around. Nothing moved, and there was no sound. She loaded another magazine into her pistol, then climbed into the jeep. She turned the key in the ignition. The roar of the catching engine sounded deafening. She strained to hear above it, fearing a hail of voices. She heard nothing beyond the motor.

She threw the jeep into gear and crashed out of the undergrowth onto the road. Driving without lights, she went as fast as she could go without risking overturning the jeep if she hit a rock. The juddering speedometer showed sixty miles per hour.

She had been driving for fifteen minutes and was approaching a bend when she thought she heard the sound of another engine in the near distance. She slammed on the brakes till she had cut her speed to twenty, then swerved off the road, down a steep bank into the jungle. The jeep crashed through the undergrowth. She felt the shudder and lurch as it hit a small tree, snapped it, and bounced over it. She wrenched the steering wheel around, just avoiding a solid trunk that would not have yielded. Branches slapped across her face, drawing blood. She switched off the engine as the jeep came to a halt about thirty feet inside the jungle, off the road.

The throaty sound of a jeep approaching rang in her ears. She could hear the gear change as it came around a bend, and the roar of acceleration as it straightened course. She almost felt the eyes of the men on board, imagined them seeing the breach in the jungle, stopping, coming to investigate. She made an easy target. The jeep came nearer; she could see its lights, felt certain of discovery. Then it passed by.

Unbelieving, she watched it go. She waited till it was out of earshot, then started up the engine and drove out of the jungle and onto the bank. For a second the wheels spun alarmingly on the loose soil. Then the traction caught, hauling the jeep upward and onto the road.

She drove on, imagining Frazer's men racing up and down the roads, making forays into the jungle. There would be other jeeps searching besides the one she had just avoided.

After twenty minutes she reached a junction. One road continued through the jungle, while the other led down toward the plains, toward Halong Bay. She turned off and counted one small victory. The men now had two roads to search.

With each mile she felt another pulse of freedom. She felt the beginnings of a wild euphoria, which she struggled to contain. She glanced at her watch. She had driven for an hour and a quarter now. Alongside her, the jungle thinned out, giving way to the plains. It was lighter here, and she could see farther. The road stretched out ahead, empty, drawing her on.

She was just beginning to feel hope when she saw,

glowing in the distance like an evil eye, a point of light. She felt her stomach clench as the light crystallized and grew. Now she could hear an engine. Dimly she could see a vehicle approaching. Its occupants would not have seen her yet. Her headlights were off; its lights were on. They wove out in front of it, bouncing as it covered the rough ground. She had about one minute before they saw her.

A minute to think. It was 2:30 A.M. A jeep out at that time, roaring through the countryside, would almost certainly be one of Frazer's. Eva realized his name still echoed, living in her brain. His power to kill had not died with him. She felt sure it was his men in the jeep. Either way, she would have to act as if it were. There would be no time to investigate, no second chance. She did not intend to kill; that was the only comfort she could give herself. There was nowhere to hide. The rice paddies on each side would swallow the jeep.

Leaving it on the road, the engine running, Eva climbed out and ran as fast as she could toward the approaching jeep. She had about thirty seconds before its occupants would see her. Just before its lights reached her, three hundred yards away, she slowed, pulled the pistol from her waistband, and jumped off the road into a paddy. She sank down, struggling for a sound footing. The water came to her thighs, trapping her in slow motion.

She waited, holding herself still, till the approaching jeep was within range. Then she struggled up out of the paddy onto the road, into the glare of its headlights. Now it was ten yards away, aiming straight for her. She took a second to focus and aim, then shot four bullets into the front right tire.

There was a scream as the vehicle veered wildly to

the right. Eva threw herself to the left. Silhouetted in the driver's seat was Le Mai, struggling frantically with the steering wheel. Eva saw him for a split second before the jeep careered away from her off the road and crashed into the paddy. It somersaulted twice, coming to rest upside down. Eva saw it sink slowly into the paddy, heard the nauseating burp as the water dragged it down. She turned away. No one would have survived that.

She ran back to her jeep and got in. For two minutes, just to be sure, she watched the paddy. Nothing moved. Her hand trembling, she released the handbrake and drove off.

FIFTY-THREE

Andrew Stormont sat in the quiet streets of Halong Bay and waited. It was three-thirty in the morning. There was no sound or movement, save that of the occasional slinking cat. Stray nocturnal wanderers had long gone home to search for sleep, and it would be a few hours before the fishermen took their boats out into the bay.

Stormont was stationed in a car his men had obtained for him, at the main road that led into and out of the area. On the men's earlier search, they had noted Tom's helicopter, which they knew from its usual schedules should have been back in Hanoi. They had found Tom drunk in the bar, looking queasy and defensive. Using their own brand of subtle questioning, they had elicited the information that he had transported Eva from Hanoi and that she had driven away hours earlier.

Stormont knew where she must have gone. He had missed her, probably for good. He saw, all too easily now, the inevitability of what she had chosen, and was stunned by his own inability to foresee it. He had thought he was the countervailing force. He felt sickened by his own arrogance and failure. Out of blindness, he had let her do the thing she most wished for.

He sat alone with his responsibility. Against logic, he waited. He had known the futility of pursuit. Going to Frazer's camp was out of the question. He lacked the resources for the inevitable confrontation, lacked the authority too. Direct action against Frazer was far beyond his mission. Eva had made her choice, and it was too late to stop her now. All he could do was wait and hope. He would wait until dawn. Then he would return to Hanoi.

He sat up suddenly as he heard the sound of a distant motor. He got out of his car and checked the pistol in the shoulder holster Courtney had provided him. Then he stood beside his car and waited. The throb of the engine grew louder.

It approached in darkness, the headlamps off. After a while, as it drew closer, he could make out the contours of a jeep traveling at high speed. It drove on, oblivious to his presence.

About thirty feet from him it stopped, and the driver got out. Disbelieving, Stormont saw Eva walking toward him. As she came closer, he almost recoiled. She looked as if she had bathed in blood. He saw her reach down to her waistband, saw the pistol, saw her aim it at him. He looked into her eyes. They were hard, glittering with cold logic.

"What's the pistol for, Eva?"

She continued to walk toward him. Looking at him, she felt the inevitability of his presence. As she drew near, her breath caught in her throat. She spoke with quiet rage.

"Someone destroyed my cover, revealed I was an addict, left the details lying around in my medical files, left me as good as dead. Only three people had that information—the chief, you, and Giles Aden."

Stormont spoke very quietly. "It wasn't me."

"You would say that. I hope you're right. Otherwise I'll have to kill you too."

So she had killed Frazer. Stormont's eyes traveled slowly, painfully, over her body. They came to rest on her face. They seemed to see and understand everything that she had left behind her.

Useless questions came to him. He wanted to say, "Do you think me capable of betrayal?" To which she would answer yes. She would know too that in the labyrinthine logic of the Firm he could have what would be called a good reason to do it. There were no words, no logic, he could use. He felt his hands limp by his sides.

"Hasn't there been enough death? Haven't you finished with all that, Eva?"

In his words was a gentleness that almost undid her. She looked at him, trying to read the truth in eyes schooled in deception. She wanted so much to believe him, but she was suspicious of her need, her yearning for a gleam of innocence, an absence of betrayal. She wanted more than anything to commit an act of faith, not to see him, of all people, destroyed in her mind, in her life. But her instincts were warped by betrayal and death, and she doubted whether she could trust even herself. She would rather be killed by an open enemy, by Frazer's men, than by Stormont's.

She looked at his eyes, eyes that seemed to wait for her. She thought, just for a second, of pulling the trigger, of watching him slip to the earth. In the impossibility of that was her answer. Very slowly, she lowered the pistol to her side and walked toward him. She stopped at arm's length from him.

Stormont kept his eyes on her, resisting the temptation to touch her, doing nothing to break the fragile truce. He opened the car door.

"We'll go back to Hanoi, then out of the country."

She climbed into the passenger seat. Stormont drove to his helicopter, radioing to the other men to meet them there. They moved quickly in the darkness, piling into the helicopter. Doors shut. Eva sat next to Stormont. The pilot started up the engine, which roared in the stillness of the night. They flew across the blackened landscape, back to Hanoi.

Stormont didn't try to speak to Eva. He knew the bare details of what had happened. He would debrief her later. Now he would leave her alone.

Eva looked down. The endless rice fields and the distant jungles looked unreal, harmless, like the pages of an atlas. The sudden absence of danger left her disoriented. She listened to the roar of the rotor blades spinning above, fragile as cobwebs. A bird could bring them down.

They landed in Hanoi just before dawn. Courtney drove Eva and Stormont to the embassy. Stormont took Eva's arm as she faltered up the steps; exhaustion, dehydration, and lack of food had finally weakened her. He led her through the silent corridors to a door set with a small window. A light glowed through the pane. Stormont turned the key in the lock. Sitting inside on a narrow bed, staring straight ahead, was Cassie.

Stormont opened the door. Cassie got up. She saw Eva standing before her, weary but upright. Her skin and clothes were covered in dried mud and blood. For a while they just stared at each other, then Cassie moved toward Eva and hugged her, felt Eva's arms close around her.

When they drew apart, Stormont said awkwardly, "I'll find you a shower, Eva, and some clothes. We'll have new passports made up here for both of you. It will be safer if you travel incognito." He turned to Cassie. "We'll send someone to the hotel later, after we're gone, to pick up your things."

While Eva was showering, Stormont returned to Cassie. "We'll fly out as soon as possible. First to Hong Kong. I'll arrange a military plane from there. We should arrive at RAF Brize Norton about six A.M. tomorrow. We'll have to do a lot of talking, I'm afraid, on the plane, and after you get back, over the next few days. But you might want someone there when you arrive. Is there any-one I could telephone? Someone to meet you back home?"

He spoke with a surprising tenderness. It was as if he could afford kindness now that Eva was back, alive.

Cassie smiled faintly, trying to cast her mind forward twenty-four hours, trying to imagine how she would feel then. After a while she said, "There is someone. Owen Quaid. I'd like him to be there. Here's his number."

Stormont wrote it down, then left her to make his arrangements. He sat in a quiet room, alone with a note-pad and a telephone. He called McKenzie in Hong Kong and asked him to arrange a military plane. Then he called Giles Aden.

It was 11 P.M. in London. Aden was at home. He answered the telephone after two rings in his brisk, self-satisfied voice.

"Giles, it's Andrew. Everything's fine. I'm flying back today, scheduled to arrive at six A.M. tomorrow, Tuesday, at Brize Norton. Meet me there, would you?"

Their plane left Hanoi for Hong Kong at seven-thirty. Stormont and Eva sat in one row, Cassie in front. As long as they were in Vietnam, Stormont still felt the contagion of danger.

The flight took one and a half hours. At the airport in Kowloon, a military aircraft awaited them. They flew west as morning broke across the skies before them. The engines roared around them. Again Cassie sat alone, in the row ahead of Eva and Stormont. Now, with the imminence of danger lifted, it was time to speak. Stormont turned to Eva.

"You killed Frazer, then?"

"And Ha Chin. They were together, in the same room. I had no choice. Earlier, Frazer tried to kill me twice. He was in the process of injecting me with a heroin overdose when Cassie burst in and knocked into him. The syringe fell out. I took only a tiny dose. Frazer said he would have to find another way to kill us both, to make it look like an accidental death. Heroin was a good death for me alone. 'Once a junkie, always a junkie,' he said."

Stormont watched her as she said the words, struggling for detachment, trying desperately to keep her voice level.

"So he decided to kill me and Cassie together. He pretended that he had done a deal with you, with the Firm, and that he was going to let us go. He gave us a jeep. As we drove off, I heard one of the guards joke about mines. I didn't get it then, but after we had gone about ten miles I realized he must have booby-trapped the jeep. We got out just in time. I left the engine running. Five minutes later, it blew up. We got a lift back to Hanoi with a farmer. I dropped Cassie off. You know that bit. She was supposed to lie to your men, or to you, if you were there." She paused, looking straight at him. "I had a feeling you might be."

"She played her part well. Stalled me until it was too late. I feared then what you would have gone and done."

"I'm surprised it took you so long. Would you have stopped me?"

"I was convinced you would be killed. Do you think I would have let that happen, even if it was what you wanted?"

"I didn't want to die. But remember, we made this trip over four years ago, you and I in the transport plane, when I was a junkie. What do you think got me out of that? It was what I lived for for four years, what I survived for. I couldn't let that die, make a lie of all my life to come. And when Frazer stuck that needle into me, all the pain came back in one lump. It would have crushed me. So I went back, and I got away, and here I am."

For a while they just looked at each other.

"I'll do what I can, Eva, to smooth things over," Stormont finally said.

She turned away from him, exhausted.

Stormont looked at her body slumped beside him. She had showered and changed into some clothes Courtney had provided for her at the embassy, but still he saw in his mind the woman in darkness approaching his jeep, covered in blood.

Silently he got up and went to sit next to Cassie. She was awake and staring into space. He took her hand, surprised at how easy it was to touch her. He so much wanted to touch Eva, but could not.

Cassie looked at him.

"What will you do now?" he asked. "After this is over?"

"I don't know. How can I return to a normal life after this? How can I go back to work at Case Reed, worry about deals, throw myself into that as if it really mattered?"

"What does matter?"

"You tell me. You live with this."

Involuntarily, he turned away.

"You see, you can't do it, you evade it. What really matters to you?"

He turned back to her. "My job, my work."

"Ah yes, your work. I heard Frazer talking about that as he was about to shoot heroin into Eva's arm. He said that you never wanted to remove people like him, you merely wanted to know what they were doing, with whom. He said that you were content to let them do it, because if they didn't, someone else would fill the vacuum of evil. That was what he called it." Her voice was hard now, filled with rage. "What are you going to do with Eva?"

He looked into her eyes and away again. "We'll clean things up at the camp. Frazer's men will disappear, go back to Hong Kong. I don't think there will be any comeback from them. Now it's not worth their while. As for what Eva did, few people need to know. With what she did, her role, there was always a chance of casualties. She won't pay for that, if that's what you mean."

"That really would be the ultimate betrayal, wouldn't it? But no, that's not what I mean. I never thought she would be held to task for it, but to say she won't pay . . . How will she live her life? That's what I mean. What will you do with her?"

He stared straight ahead, saying nothing.

FIFTY-FOUR

The plane landed on time at RAF Brize Norton and was met by the duty officer. The door opened and the steps were put into place. Stormont went out first, Cassie next, then Eva. Together they walked to the main airport building.

The duty officer took Stormont aside and introduced himself. "Mr. Aden is by himself in room two, sir, as instructed. Mr. Quaid is in room four. And I've set aside room one for your use."

"Thank you. We'll see Quaid shortly, then Aden. I'd like you to stick around too."

The man gave him a knowing look, foreseeing some kind of trouble. "Right you are, sir. This way."

Stormont stood with Eva and Cassie in room one.

"Are you ready to see Quaid?" he asked Cassie.

"Yes, I suppose so." He could see her holding herself in so tightly she could feel almost nothing.

Cassie moved toward the door. "See you, then, Eva."

"Yeah. See you, Cass." Another parting marked by casual words, as if they could not use any others.

Stormont opened the door. Cassie stepped through, then stopped involuntarily, turned abruptly, went back to Eva.

"I forgot to tell you. I've sold my stake in Genius to a character called Aubrey Goldstein, and I agreed to sell yours, if you want to sell. The rate I dealt at would get you about two million, seven hundred thousand pounds for your ten percent."

She turned to Stormont. "Goldstein is the man who came up to me in the bar in Hanoi. He was very keen to get his hands on Genius, so I made him pay." She paused for a second. "You'll telephone me, will you, Eva, so I can sort it out?"

"You negotiated all this when I was . . . away?"

"It helped."

Eva looked suddenly uncertain.

"The diamond shares are yours, Eva. Do what you want with them. The sooner, the better," said Stormont.

"I'll ring you," Eva said to Cassie. "And Cass, thanks."

They exchanged a last look, then Cassie turned and followed Stormont down the corridor, out of sight.

"I'll need to see you again in a few hours," said Stormont. "We'll have to go over everything. It might take a few days. We'll go somewhere quiet. Quaid won't be able to come with us, but you'll see him again soon enough. One thing I will ask, Cassie, is that you tell no one except us what happened to you and Eva. And you cannot say anything about me. You know why I ask, what's at stake."

"I know, and I won't."

"It's difficult to keep secrets, Cassie. If you ever want to talk about things, you'll always be able to talk to me."

"Thank you. I think I might."

Stormont let her into the room. Outside, out of

sight, he saw Quaid hug her. Then he walked back down the corridor to Eva.

He sat down opposite her and regarded her for a while in silence.

They spoke for two hours, Eva giving him all the operational details. Then Stormont relaxed. He appeared to Eva heavy with sadness.

"So what now?" he asked. "Where do you want to go when this is all cleared up?"

"Where is there to go except away? I've done what I set out to do."

"Now you can live, be free of Frazer."

"I'm not very good at just living, having a normal life. I can't be with people for any length of time. I feel panic if I have to spend a whole day with someone, with no escape route into my own mind, my own company. I don't trust myself. Perhaps I feel the bleakness will come out. I can't unlearn, I can't forget."

The flow of their words went back and forth, but never the right words, never the things she really wanted to say. She wondered if he too held back. How long would the futile silence last? Another thirty years? Till death? And yet there he was, sitting beside her. All she had to do was reach out and touch his arm, touch him anywhere. The act of deliberate touching could convey everything—just one touch, a look—and yet she could not do it.

She knew that if she were stranded on a desert island, she would choose him above all others, that he could fill the space of ten. Such a simple decision, so obvious. Yet still she could not reach out her hand to him. She was fearful of the acknowledgment, of the possible loss, if she did.

He spoke finally. "You don't have to live with strangers. You don't have to live a normal life."

She waited, watching him catch his breath.

"You could come and live with me." He reached out, across the space between them, and very gently touched her arm. He left his hand there. She looked from his hand to his face and waited again.

"First I want you to see someone, to answer something that may still be in your mind."

"Who?"

"Giles Aden."

"You think I would have come back here with you if I thought you had betrayed me?"

"You had no reason to believe me. Logically, there was a one in three chance that I'd betrayed you. I suppose I want to give you proof. And I want Aden to have to face you."

"Yes. I would like to see him, have him face me."

Whatever he said, she didn't need proof. She had decided to believe him because of her instincts, which she trusted more than an external proof, which could so easily be faked. She knew, even if he didn't yet, that if she looked into their wilderness of mirrors for someone else's proof, she would never stop searching among the fragmentary images. All she could rely on was her own belief. So she did not confront his understanding, just smiled at him.

He left the room. He watched Eva carefully as he returned with Aden. Rage passed across her face, but she was surprisingly controlled.

He turned to Aden. "I'd like you to tell Eva what you did with her medical records, what you did to her legend."

For a while Aden said nothing. He looked for as long

as he could into Stormont's eyes, until he saw the futility of the concealment that was his first impulse. When he knew there was no outlet besides the truth, his face took on a twisted petulance.

"You obviously know what I did, so why ask me?"

"I think Eva deserves an explanation, don't you?"

"She deserved to die. She wasn't fit to go back into duty. She could have compromised the whole operation against Frazer and Ha Chin."

"So you thought you'd compromise it for her. That's logical."

"Logic. That's all you see, isn't it?" He spat out his words, choking with bitterness.

"What else is there?"

Aden met Stormont's eyes again, then looked away, seeming to shrivel into himself.

"Can't you see?" Eva's voice made them both jump. "He worships you and he despises you. He's probably dreamed of being a field agent all of his life. You were the means, and I was the obstacle. You let him down, and I got in his way."

Stormont turned to look at her.

"You never saw the emotional logic, did you?" Her voice dropped, and she said gently, "You never do, until it's too late. Perhaps you will now."

Stormont kept his eyes on her. Looking at Eva, he felt a sense of surprise, and he realized that she would always surprise him, and how much he would love her for it. After a moment, he opened the door and spoke to the duty officer, who was waiting outside.

"Escort this man to one of your safe rooms, would you? One with a lock on the outside."

"What are you going to do with me?" asked Aden, all expression gone from his voice.

"Nothing much. You'll be 'let go.' " He used the euphemism derisively. "You'll lose your pension. You'll get off quite lightly, considering."

"Considering what?"

"What Eva could do to you, if she chose to."

Aden turned to Eva. He saw in her face not hatred, not anger, but, worse, pity.

"Go away, Aden. I won't touch you. You'll live with yourself, by yourself. Without Stormont, in oblivion. That will be enough."

Aden dropped his head, unable to look at her. The duty officer took his arm and led him away.

Stormont and Eva were left alone in the room. They sat opposite each other. For a while, both of them were silent. Then Stormont spoke.

"So will you come with me?"

Eva smiled, got to her feet, and walked to him. "What about all the rules, agents and their controllers— we'd be breaking them all. I don't want to have to act again, or to conceal, or to wait around here until a respectable time has elapsed, until it's all right—if it ever will be."

"Will it ever be right for you? Might you want it sometime?"

"I might."

"And in the meantime, what will you do?"

She smiled, and he saw the prospect of happiness in her eyes.

"I want to go somewhere hot with blue water and sun, where all I have to do is drink coconut juice all day. Somewhere quiet and forgiving, where nobody knows me."